MW01000600

Christmas Next Door

Print ISBN 978-1-64352-167-1

eBook Editions:
Adobe Digital Edition (.epub) 978-1-64352-169-5
Kindle and MobiPocket Edition (.prc) 978-1-64352-168-8

All scripture quotations are taken from the King James Version of the Bible.

This book is a work of fiction. Names, characters, places, and incidents are either products of the author's imagination or used fictitiously. Any similarity to actual people, organizations, and/or events is purely coincidental.

Cover photograph: Buffy Cooper / Trevillion Images
Interior line art illustrations by Jensine Eckwall

Published by Barbour Books, an imprint of Barbour Publishing, Inc., 1810 Barbour Drive, Uhrichsville, Ohio 44683, www.barbourbooks.com

Our mission is to inspire the world with the life-changing message of the Bible.

Printed in Canada.

Christmas Next Door

4 *Stories of Love Found Close to Home*

Susan Page Davis
Vickie McDonough

BARBOUR BOOKS
An Imprint of Barbour Publishing, Inc.

The Marshal Next Door

by Vickie McDonough

Chapter 1

Wiseman, Texas
November 1885

"Seriously, Marshal Yates, there's no call to point a rifle at us."

Though he doubted the Spencer brothers were dangerous, Justin Yates tightened his grip on his Winchester as he stared out his front door at the troublesome duo. On more than one occasion he had calmed irate townsfolk after the meddlesome brothers had egged a home, stolen a pie off someone's porch, or any number of things the problematic pair was known for. How they had the nerve to show up at *his* door and ask what they had, he'd never know.

"Yeah—I mean. . .yes, sir. All we want is to take Emma and Ella out for a walk." Barry Spencer, freshly shaven and armed with a flower bouquet instead of a slingshot, still looked more than a little dangerous. The sixteen-year-old stood an inch taller than his younger brother, Carl, but a good half a foot shorter than Justin.

Behind him, Justin heard a gasp then excited whispering. Evidently, his twin sisters were eavesdropping from the dining room. That was nothing new.

"Yeah, that's all." Carl cleared his warbling throat and jerked his head, flipping his shaggy blond hair out of his eyes. "Just walkin'. No. . .uh. . .hanky-panky." The boy's tanned cheeks turned the color of a ripe apple. His brother scowled and elbowed him.

More gasps from the twins.

Justin tucked his rifle in the crook of his arm, drawing the brothers' gaze back to him. Shifting from one foot to the other, Carl swallowed an audible gulp that made his Adam's apple bulge for a moment. Justin bit back a smile at the youth's discomfort and struggled to maintain a sober expression. But really, there was nothing humorous about their interest in his sisters. "Sorry, fellows, Ella and Emma are only fourteen. They're far too young to be courting."

"C-courting!" Carl shot a frantic glance at his brother. "You said a walk. I ain't interested in gettin' married." Without waiting for Barry, he spun and leaped off the porch, tossing the half-wilted bouquet of daisies in the yard.

"No," one of his sisters cried.

Justin lifted an eyebrow as he stared down Barry Spencer. "My sisters aren't about to be seen walking around town on a man's"—and he used the term generously—"arm, if said 'man' has anything on his mind other than marriage. And when the day comes that I do agree to let them, it will be with upstanding, God-fearing men."

Barry ducked his head, the flowers hanging from his limp hand. "Aw shucks."

"I suggest before you call on a young lady again, you straighten up your life. You two are a bit old for tomfoolery. No self-respecting father—or brother—is going to allow his daughter—or sister—to walk around with the town prankster. Get a job—and keep it—and maybe in a couple of years the men of this town will look at you differently." He closed the front door and shook his head. He couldn't believe the nerve those boys had. He braced himself for the chugging locomotive of emotion barreling toward him.

"Jus—tin!" His twin sisters screeched his name, making it sound like the high-pitched squealing brakes of an arriving train.

"I'm mortified." Emma covered her face then peeked through her fingers. "Why did you send them away?"

"Yeah." Ella, a perfect image of her sister, shoved her hands to her waist. "We *wanted* to go walking around town with them. They're the cutest boys in school."

Justin narrowed his eyes and prayed for patience. "Do you know how much trouble those two have caused in this town?"

Emma cast a glance at her sister. "But they're the *only* boys in school near our age."

"Barry is still in school?" Justin shook his head. "Isn't he sixteen?"

Ella had been staring at him as if she could burn holes through him, but her expression wilted. "He might've had to do a year over."

"Or two," her twin mumbled.

That's just dandy. "You need to set your sights substantially higher than those two. When you're old enough to step out with a man, I suspect God will provide each of you a good and decent one. You both need some patience—and a few more years—before you think about marriage."

Ella, older by four minutes, stamped her foot. "We *are* old enough. Mamie Sanford and Elizabeth Young both got married when they were fifteen, and we almost are."

"And Liza Mae Green was only sixteen." Emma's stern glare would have been comical if the topic wasn't so serious.

"Well, you're not stepping out, so get used to the idea." Justin sent them a glare that made grown men cower, but his sisters didn't even flinch. "And until you grow up, take more responsibility, and prove to me that you are maturing, you're not leaving this house."

"That's not fair!" they cried in unison.

"Does that mean we don't haveta. . .," Emma started.

". . .go to church tomorrow or back to school on Monday?" Ella finished for her.

"I don't believe I need to answer that." Didn't that question prove he was right? He stared at his sisters, identical twins with honey-blond hair and sky-blue eyes. Perfect little angels—if you didn't know them well. The only way to tell them apart was by the faint smattering of freckles on the bridges of their tanned noses. Emma had a few more than her sister. Justin blew out a sigh. "I need to get back to work. You're not to leave this house or open the door should those yahoos return. Do you hear me?"

"Yes, sir." Ella nodded.

"You're not our father." Emma crossed her arms over her chest and glared at him. "I still don't think it's fair we can't go for a walk with Barry and Carl. It's just walking."

"Your efforts would be put to better use starting supper and cleaning your rooms." He yanked his hat off the rack in the entryway, opened the door, then hurried out. He knew better than Emma that he wasn't their pa. He was only a big brother doing the best he could to provide for and raise his emotional adolescent sisters.

Difficult, stubborn, troublesome sisters—whom he loved dearly and needed to protect.

The idea of those hooligan boys wanting to step out with the twins curdled his gut. Those Spencer brothers had better stay away from his house. He'd been sixteen—only seven years ago—and *walking* with a girl certainly hadn't been foremost in *his* mind. Thank goodness his pa had been around to talk to him about how a man should protect a woman and her reputation. And he'd also taught him that certain things should be saved for the sanctity of marriage.

The twins needed their ma at this pivotal age. If only his parents hadn't been killed when a train derailed two years ago. What was he going to do with those girls? They certainly needed a woman's influence.

Justin nodded at Mr. Maynard, owner of the only shoe store in Wiseman, who swung his broom back and forth across the boardwalk. When the man didn't have a customer, he could be found rearranging or dusting the shoes and boots in his shop or sweeping the constant dust that clung to everything.

"Marshal!"

Justin spun around to see John Goodwin, the postmaster, striding toward him. "What's wrong?"

"I thought you'd want to know, there's a big ruckus at the mercantile."

Marta Buckley stood behind the fabric table of Lawson's Mercantile, watching the Begley cousins arguing over a dress they both wanted. Marta's hands fisted on the fabric she planned to buy, wishing her ears were covered. She'd never desired a dress so much in her whole life that she was willing to make such a racket, not to mention a public display.

"I told you yesterday that I had my eye on this dress." Phyllis Begley jerked on the hem of the dark blue day dress with mother-of-pearl buttons down the front.

"Well, Cousin, I'm the one who first laid hand on it today, so it's mine." Serinda hiked her chin and refused to let go.

Phyllis pursed her lips. "The only reason I wanted to come here was to buy this dress. You knew that."

"I knew no such thing."

Marta couldn't believe how the two fiftysomething women could make such a public spectacle. She tried to focus on the supplies she needed to make a new apron, but it was difficult with such a commotion nearby. And where was Pete? Her brother was supposed to meet her at the mercantile to pick out fabric for a shirt she wanted to make him.

Marshal Yates strode in the door, looking tall and in charge. His gaze scanned the store, landed on Marta for half a second, then moved on. "What's going on, Henry? I heard you had some trouble."

Henry Lawson, owner of the mercantile, swatted his hand at the Begley cousins. "Nothing serious, Marshal. Just those two cackling hens squabblin' over a dress."

"Well, I never." Phyllis Begley released her hold on the dress.

Serinda shoved the wrinkled garment back on the hook it hung from. "I'll not tolerate such rudeness. Shall we go, Cousin?"

"Most certainly." Phyllis stormed from the store with Serinda right behind her, giving the marshal and Henry Lawson a glare that could freeze boiling water.

Marta ducked her head, fighting a smile. Those ladies could be as nice as the preacher's daughter, but once crossed, they were a force to reckon with.

Henry chuckled. "Those ladies could scare a tornado into spinning backwards on a sunny day."

"Sorry if I caused you to lose a sale." Marshal Yates leaned his hip against the counter.

Marta's eyes drifted from the marshal's broad shoulders, past his shiny badge, to his trim waist. With his brown hair and blue eyes, Justin Yates was a mighty nice-looking man and wore authority like a tailor-made frock coat. Marta turned away, her cheeks burning at her thought and the fact she had been staring.

Shame on you, Marta Buckley. You know better than to ogle a man's physique—especially the lawman's. Marta's hand shook as she selected thread to go with the yellow calico she'd chosen for a new apron. Why did she always get the shakes whenever Justin Yates entered a room? Even though he was only a few years older than her, he'd earned the job as marshal, but that should hardly make her nervous, since she'd known him for several years. More than likely, it was because she'd been infatuated with him since her father first moved them to Wiseman three years ago and bought the house next door to the Yates family. Not that Justin had ever noticed.

He must have sensed her stare—oh dear, she was doing it again—because he looked at her and tipped his hat. Heat engulfed her face, but she returned his greeting with a smile. She dipped her head and checked the items in her hand, deciding that would do for today. If Pete didn't care enough about his own shirt to inform her what kind he wanted—for everyday or church—she'd simply not sew one for him.

As she approached the counter, Marshal Yates straightened. Her breath escaped in a gush. My, but he was tall.

"I reckon I'll mosey along since your crisis has been averted. Afternoon, Miss Buckley." He touched the brim of his hat again and ambled out the door.

"Is there anything else I can get for you, Miss Buckley?" A throat cleared, drawing her gaze to Henry.

She tugged her attention away from the marshal's fine form, shamed at her thoughts and ever so glad Henry had no idea what was on her mind. She smiled. "I believe that will be all for today."

He wrapped her fabric and supplies in paper and tied it with twine. She paid him then walked out the door. She stopped suddenly when she saw Marshal Yates standing in front of the store. He glanced at her, looking as if he had something on his mind, but she couldn't for the life of her imagine what it was.

He cleared his throat, his feet shuffling. He looked away.

She could hardly believe he was waiting for her, but he certainly seemed to be. "Was there something you needed, Marshal?"

"I. . .uh. . ." He yanked off his hat. "It's my sisters."

She gasped and touched his forearm. "Are they ill?"

"Uh. . .no. It's not that." He looked around, as if checking the town like she often noticed him doing. "Do you mind if we walk? Can I accompany you to wherever you're going next?"

Her heart fluttered. She dare not get her hopes up. Justin Yates had never shown the least interest in her. "You're welcome to walk with me. I'm headed home."

"Thanks." He ambled alongside her as they made their way across the town square. "I really could use some help—with Emma and Ella."

"What kind of help?"

He lifted his hat and forked his hand through his thick pecan-colored hair and sighed. "There are things they need to know that I can't teach them."

"Like what?"

"Cooking, sewing, how to deal with men. . .and"—his ears turned red as he swatted his hand in the air—"female stuff."

"Men?" Marta's cheeks heated. She stopped and turned toward him, glancing around to make sure no one had overheard him. What made him assume she knew much about men? Yes, she'd had a father, before he died last winter of influenza, and she had a brother, but she'd never had a beau—not with Pete scaring them all away.

The red crept down his neck, coloring his tanned skin an unnatural shade. "Yeah, you know. . .how to relate to men."

"It seems you would be able to teach that better than I."

He shoved his hands in his pockets then yanked them out, obviously as uncomfortable with the conversation as she. Was it because he was talking to her or because of the topic of their chat? "What exactly is it you're asking?"

His gaze lifted to the porch roof as if he were searching for a response. But then his expression hardened. "Never mind. It was a bad idea anyway."

Marta's mouth dropped open as he stalked away. The marshal had barely talked to her previously. Why had he picked her to chat about his sisters? Was he asking her for help in finding someone to work with his sisters, or was he wanting her to do the job? Had he found her lacking, not up to the cause?

If he did want her to work with the twins, he'd picked the wrong woman. Oh, she could show the girls how to cook and sew, but not how to deal with men. How could she teach anyone a thing about men when she found them utterly confusing?

Chapter 2

Marta sprinkled flour on her hands and bent over the blob of dough lying on the cupboard counter. A movement outside the back window snagged her attention. She leaned closer. Emma and Ella Yates dashed across her backyard, giggling and running like hoydens with their skirts bouncing up to their knees. Their behavior was far too childish for girls their age. They certainly needed mothering, but obviously Justin thought she wasn't the person for that task.

She pressed her forehead to the glass to see where they were. They'd already run past her yard and turned toward the next street. What were they up to?

The marshal sure had his hands full upholding the law in town and watching over his pretty sisters, although she suspected the twins were the more difficult task. It was a good thing there weren't all that many young men in the small town to chase after Emma and Ella. What would Justin do next summer when the girls finished their schooling? She almost felt sorry for him.

Marta blew out a heavy sigh, sending a cloud of flour dust into the air. She fanned her hand, turned away from her work, and coughed. As she returned to kneading the dough, she thought about the first time she'd seen Justin Yates when they moved to Wiseman. Just like when she saw him at the store earlier, her heart had sped up. He had been so comely at twenty, but in the years since then he'd muscled up more—his chest had expanded, and his shoulders were wide enough to carry the weight of the whole town's troubles on them. And yet his sisters burdened him.

What if there was a way she could help him? The twins more than likely could cook some, but perhaps she could teach them to prepare things they were unfamiliar with. Most girls their age were adept at stitching, having made a sampler or two in their younger years. They probably sewed their own clothing, although she remembered seeing Justin in the mercantile with them looking at ready-made dresses, so perhaps not.

She placed the dough in the pan then formed another loaf. What would Pete say to inviting Justin and his sisters to Sunday dinner? Surely the two men could take time off to enjoy a Sabbath meal. If Justin agreed, then she could casually chat with the girls and see what they knew and didn't. After that, she could come up with a plan—once she'd taken the matter to the Lord, of course. Prayer always helped, even when Pete was in one of his moods, which seemed to be more often these days. "Please keep my brother healthy and safe, Father."

She had hoped to be married by now, at twenty-one, with a

child or two in tow, but that hadn't been God's plan for her. Even though her heart ached for children of her own, she attempted to satisfy her longing by holding her friends' babies.

She stared out the window. "One day, Lord, in Your timing. Help me to be content until that day."

The front door banged open, causing her to jump. Pete stomped in. "When's supper?"

"Same time as always—five o'clock."

Her brother frowned and rubbed his belly. He yanked open her pantry door, making the dishes on the shelf rattle. "Got any more of that gingerbread?"

"Yes. There's some in the bread box."

He crossed the room, jerked open the door to the bread box, then pulled out several slices. He walked away, leaving the door open and dropping crumbs on her clean floor.

Marta sighed. "What's got your feathers so ruffled?"

"Those Begley biddies stopped me on the street, fussin' and squawkin' like angry hens. They were mad at Mr. Lawson and said they'd been treated rudely. Guess I know how that feels after listening to them for ten minutes."

Marta smiled, keeping her back to Pete. Her brother could stand up to a gang in a shootout or chase down a bank robber, but a couple of bickering women sure set him off. In his defense, she'd learned it was wise to steer clear of the Begley cousins when they were arguing.

"What's for supper?" He shoved the last of the gingerbread into his mouth.

Marta turned to face him. "One of the ranchers brought in a dozen chickens while I was at the mercantile, and I was fortunate to get one." She wouldn't mention again that if Pete would repair the chicken coop, she could have her own hens once more and save money. Perhaps she should try her hand at fixing it.

After placing the dough in bread pans, she mixed up another batch of dough, formed balls for dinner rolls, and set them in a pan. Then she cleaned up the mess she'd made. Tomorrow was Thursday and not usually too busy. Perhaps she'd tackle the chicken coop after going to the sewing circle. It would be wonderful to have fresh eggs again and not have to buy them, especially since Pete didn't make much money as a deputy. If only he didn't have a penchant for drinking, they wouldn't struggle so much to get by. At least he didn't gamble. *Thank You, Lord.*

With everything ready for her to start supper, she decided to run outside and survey the old coop. She threw on her shawl and headed to the backyard. She shook her head as she stared at the mess. A pack of feral dogs had tormented Wiseman for a time last spring and wreaked havoc on the town. She was thankful for the men who'd hunted down and shot the beasts, but the damage had been done.

She pulled on a piece of bent wire and poked her finger on a sharp edge. Hissing at the pain, she lifted her hand, pressing a finger against the spot to stop the bleeding.

She would need a pair of gloves, a hammer, and pliers, for starters. Cocking her head, she studied the coop. The wire was too bent for her to repair it, so she'd need to buy a new piece to fix the section with the huge hole. How hard could it be?

What a disastrous mistake. Marta stared at her poor dress. She should have had the sense to change into her old calico before tackling the henhouse repairs, although it probably wouldn't have fared any better against the sharp edges of the wire than the sateen dress she'd worn to the sewing circle this morning. And now she was stuck.

The wire had been on a roll at the store, and it had kept curling as she tried to attach it—and now it was curled around her, trapping her. If she moved, she'd only damage her dress more. She tossed down the hammer and grabbed one edge of the wire and pulled back. A ripping sound made her cringe.

She glanced around, for once wishing they didn't live so near the edge of town. Hours could pass before someone came her way. How was she going to get out of this mess?

If she could reach the shears, she could cut her way out, but that would ruin the fencing she'd just paid for with the money she'd budgeted for Pete's shirt. She couldn't bring herself to ruin the wire. She tugged harder, tearing her dress more. She wrestled the fencing away from her skirt several inches, but then it slipped from her grasp and snapped back. Pete's overly big gloves that protected her hands made it hard to grip the stubborn wire.

A part of her wished her brother was home, but then he would laugh his head off at her predicament. At least he would eventually help her out of it.

She tried clutching the wire again, but the same thing happened. Why did she have to be such a weakling? And why couldn't her lazy brother have tended to this task instead of forcing her to do it?

She lifted her face to the sky, relishing the warm November day. At least it wasn't chilly today. A strong southern breeze had brought with it much warmer temperatures than normal for this time of year. Fat, cottony clouds drifted past, reminding her of her old friend Florence and how they had lain in the grass and found shapes in the clouds when they were girls.

Behind her, someone cleared his throat.

Thank goodness! Help!

Marta looked over her shoulder. *Oh no. The marshal.*

Justin leaned on his saddle horn and looked to be fighting back a smile. "Looks like you got yourself in quite a predicament."

She would have liked to argue the fact, but the evidence was too great. "I misjudged how stubborn this wire could be."

He pushed his hat up on his forehead, grinning. "I see that." He dismounted and looped his horse's reins over the back fence. He entered through the gate and walked toward her.

Marta's heart beat faster with each long-legged step he took. Why did he have to be the one to find her? He already thought poorly of her. She ducked her head, surprised at the pain clenching her heart. Had Pete complained to Justin about her? Was that why he walked away from her the other day instead of finishing their talk?

He circled her, shaking his head. "I'm afraid that dress is a goner. That's a shame. The green color looks good with your auburn hair."

She turned her head so he wouldn't see how his compliment had surprised her. "Thank you. Do you think you can get me out of this before Pete comes home?"

"Shouldn't be a problem. But I don't want to hurt you."

His tenderness touched a parched spot in her heart. How long had it been since her own brother had cared for her welfare? Not that Pete was a bad brother. He just didn't want to be pestered, so he said.

Justin rubbed his jaw, creating a bristling sound she found intriguing. Odd, when her brother did that same action, it annoyed her. The marshal was usually clean shaven each morning. Something must have interrupted his morning's ablutions.

He blew out a loud sigh. "I can get you out of this, but I may have to move a bit closer than is proper." He glanced up, his eyes locking with hers and setting her insides to quivering. "You all right with that?"

"Yes, please get me out of here." Before Pete came home and she became the laughingstock of the whole town.

He dug through his saddlebags and pulled out a pair of gloves. "I'll unravel this edge in front, so stand still. I'll work my way around you, getting the wire free."

She nodded, hoping he didn't notice how mortified she was. Why did he have to see her like this? What must he think?

He slowly unwrapped her. Another piece of fabric ripped. "Sorry," he muttered.

"Don't worry about the gown. I can replace the skirt." Someday, when she had the funds.

"You can do that? Sew, I mean?"

"Yes. I usually make my own clothing and Pete's shirts." Did she sound like she was bragging? Oh dear.

"That's good. I've noticed the quality of Pete's shirts and wondered where he gets them. I have trouble finding ones with sleeves that are long enough."

Marta blinked, once again surprised by the marshal.

"All right, I think it's safe for you to step forward."

She did, then turned around to see him easily holding the now-behaved wire wide open. "I don't know how I can thank you."

"Not necessary. If you want to grab that hammer and some nails, I'll get this fixed for you."

"That would be wonderful." She spied the hammer where she'd tossed it and picked it up, then grabbed the bag of U-shaped staples. She'd have to bake him a pie as a thank-you, if only she knew what his favorite was. Perhaps she would ask the twins.

Justin made the repairs in quick order, and then he fixed the loose hinge on the coop gate. He stood back with a satisfied smile.

"Thank you, Marshal."

"Call me Justin. We're next-door neighbors after all."

Her heart fluttered. "If you will call me Marta."

He smiled. "That's a pretty name. I don't recall ever hearing of anyone else with that name."

"It belonged to one of my great-grandmothers."

"Well, it's nice." He handed her the hammer. "That should do it. I reckon you're going to get some chickens now."

"As soon as I'm able. I'm eager to have my own supply of fresh eggs again."

"If you end up with extras you can't use, bring them over, and I'll buy them."

"That's not necessary. I'm happy to share. I owe you for coming to my rescue."

He stared down at her. "You don't owe me. It was my pleasure."

Marta started to reach up to touch her cheek, which she was sure was bright red, but she lowered her hand.

He glanced at his horse then back to her. "Like I mentioned the other day, I could use help with my sisters."

"What kind of help?" If he mentioned teaching the girls about men again, she didn't know what she would do.

He shuffled his feet and scratched one ear. "It's what I tried to ask the other day before I chickened out. I need help with the twins—making them into ladies."

"Oh." The town had been shocked to learn nearly two years ago that both of Justin's parents had been killed in a train wreck. It was such a sad time. "It must be hard for a man to raise two girls on the verge of womanhood."

He removed his gloves and walked over to the picket fence that ringed her yard, front and back, protecting her flowers and vegetables from cattle, drunken cowboys, and others bent on ruining the bit of beauty she managed to eke out of this dry Texas land. She was especially proud of the bluebonnets that stood tall and beautiful each spring.

He stuck his gloves back in his saddlebag and blew out another loud breath, as if deciding how she could help was one of the hardest things he'd ever done. Why did he ask *her* when he could have approached any number of women in town? Perhaps it was because they were neighbors.

Justin cleared his throat. "They need to know how to cook better, sew their own clothes, and. . ." He looked away, rubbing the back of his neck, which had turned red, as well as the tips of his ears. "Like I mentioned before. . .how to relate to men."

Marta's own cheeks flamed again. "I can certainly help with the first items on your list, but I'm not so sure about the last one."

"You're a woman. You're talking just fine to me without getting all flirty like so many do. That's what I want my sisters to learn. To be ladies and not to go chasing after boys. They need to understand that males are dangerous and shouldn't be trifled with."

Marta couldn't help that her eyes widened. "Not all men are

like that. There are plenty of good men in Wiseman. Take you, for instance."

His gaze flicked to hers. "Me?"

"Look how kind you've been to me. You didn't have to help."

"Any decent man would have."

"And that's my point."

She glanced away when she noticed his ears had reddened again. "Why don't I start with sewing and cooking, and we'll see how it goes. Once the girls get more familiar with me, I'll be able to talk to them about more personal things, but it will take time."

"Could you teach them how to make that molasses pie you brought over after my folks died?"

"Of course." She smiled to herself, knowing just what she would make for him as a thank-you.

"Would you be willing for them to come over after school a couple of times a week? And maybe part of the day on Saturday? I'm willing to pay you for your efforts."

"I don't want to be paid to help a neighbor. It's the Christian thing to do."

He rubbed his jaw again. "It doesn't seem right not to pay you something. It will be a difficult job to teach my sisters."

Considering the sad state of her pantry, she wasn't sure how much cooking they'd be able to do. "What if the girls supplied the food for the things they want to cook? They could take most of it home, and if there is enough, perhaps Pete and I could keep a bit."

He nodded. "That's more than fair, although you should keep more than a bit. I can also buy fabric and whatever they need to make dresses and stuff. Pa left us some money, so that helps in raising a pair of sisters that seem to need something every other day."

Marta smiled. She could imagine his plucky sisters pestering him until they got what they wanted. After all, it was two against one, even if the one was the town marshal. "What if I work with them on Tuesday and Thursday after school and on Saturday morning? Is that schedule good for you?"

"Perfect. Sounds like we've got a deal." He held out his hand.

Marta stared at it then reached out, clasping his big palm. Tingles charged up her arm, leaving her stunned. She glanced up and saw him blinking fast. Had he felt the same bolt of lightning that she had?

Chapter 3

Two days after the chicken coop incident, Justin couldn't get Marta out of his mind. What was that he'd felt when their hands touched? It was unlike anything he'd experienced with a woman before. Was he simply happy because she had agreed to help?

He walked toward the town square, nodding at the men he knew and tipping his hat to a pair of ladies. The town was peaceful, as it generally was during the day.

His thoughts shifted back to Marta. He'd certainly noticed Pete's younger sister before, but he had mostly steered clear of her since he and her brother had to work together. Pete had fussed about her from time to time, but Justin hadn't given it much thought since his deputy was cranky most of the time. He'd actually felt sorry for Marta on occasion when Pete had been more upset than usual.

Justin sighed as he entered his office. The postmaster must have come by, because a new stack of wanted posters sat on his desk. He thumbed through them, but nobody stood out. Wiseman was mostly a sleepy little town like so many in Texas, except for on the weekends when the cowboys came to the saloon and some evenings when the locals got into fights.

The one thing hanging over him lately was that people had been reporting jewelry and other valuables missing. The odd thing was that the thief only took one or two pieces, leaving the rest of the valuables behind. What kind of thief did that? Did he hope that no one would notice the missing items?

He swatted at a fly and riffled through the posters again to see what crimes the outlaws pictured had committed. Most were bigger thefts like train or bank heists, and several men were wanted for murder. He tapped his fingers on his desk, wondering who the thief was.

Could it be the Spencer brothers? He doubted they would have had the nerve to show up at his door if they were stealing from the townsfolk.

His door opened suddenly, and Pete stormed in. "I was over at the saloon, talking to Sam. He said he overheard a couple of men talking about some cattle that were rustled at the Langston ranch. You want me to ride out there and talk to them?"

Justin shook his head. "I'd rather you get some sleep so you'll be alert tonight when you're on duty."

Pete dropped down in the chair across from Justin's desk. "You know I don't sleep good durin' the daytime."

"I'd think you'd be tired after working till midnight."

Pete shrugged and then grinned. "I'd sleep better if you took the evening shift."

Justin grunted, letting the issue drop. He couldn't remember how many times he and Pete had talked about swapping shifts. Justin didn't want to be away from his sisters at night. Plus, he was the marshal, and people expected to see him during the day.

Quick footsteps headed their way. Jacob Callen, a ten-year-old boy, skidded into the office. "The Youngs' pig got out, and it's eating the Begleys' flowers. One of them cousins went inside for a gun, and the other is whacking the pig with a broom. You'd better come quick, Marshal."

Justin stood and put on his hat. "I'll see to the pig then head out to the Langstons'."

Pete nodded and pushed away from the wall. "I'll keep an eye on the town."

Justin jogged across the town square and past the feedstore. He'd told Todd Young to fix his pigpen more than once. Maybe he'd need to issue the man a citation to get him to comply, but he hated to do so, because the family was often struggling to make ends meet. And there was the fact that Elizabeth Young was his sisters' good friend, and he'd never hear the end of it if he did.

"Shoo! Shoo! Oh no, not the chrysanthemums." Phyllis Begley pounded on the pig's back, but to no avail. The creature just grunted and kept munching.

"Here, let me have that." He grabbed the broom, receiving the stink eye from Miss Begley. "If you'll step aside, ma'am, I'll see to the pig."

"Well, it's about time. That foul creature has eaten half of our mums, and just look at our poor pansies. They're squashed."

"I've got the gun, Cousin." Serinda Begley raced out of the house, pausing to shut the door. "You'll have to shoot the beast though. You know I have a delicate constitution. Oh Marshal Yates, what a relief. You can shoot the varmint."

"You gonna kill the Youngs' pig? Todd won't like that," Jacob shouted from the next yard.

"Jacob, would you fetch Todd for me?" Justin saw the boy nod right before he raced off down the street. He looked at the women. "I don't think we'll need to shoot the pig."

"Well, you'd better do something about the beast, because if it gets into our flowers again"—Phyllis lifted a hand over her heart—"or dare I say our vegetable garden next spring, I'll shoot the critter myself."

"I'd appreciate if you would take your gun back inside."

Serinda held the weapon with her finger looped through the trigger guard. "Very well. At least I know where it is, should anyone try to steal our jewelry or other belongings."

Justin hoped no one was dumb enough to take on the Begley women. They might actually shoot the thief. "You'd best step back," he told Phyllis.

For once, the woman hurried toward the porch without back-talking.

Justin stepped inside the fence, leaving the gate open. He sidled up behind the big pig, bent down, and lifted. He grunted, and so did the pig. He hauled the critter back, but it started squealing and wiggling then slipped out of his arms.

He lunged for it before it could snag another flower. Gripping tighter this time, he hoisted the heavy beast up and waddled toward the gate. He managed to get it through the gate then let go. It was a race to get the gate closed before the pig got back in, but he was the victor.

Justin dusted off his hands then lifted up his shirt and sniffed. He smelled like a pigpen. He looked up into the smiling brown eyes of Marta Buckley.

"It seems we're both having issues with animals this week." Marta covered her mouth with her hand, but her eyes still twinkled.

"In truth, a chicken is a bird," Justin stupidly responded.

"I suppose that is true. Do you wrestle pigs and help ladies in distress often?"

Justin dusted his shirt. "More often than I chase down outlaws."

"I'm glad."

He looked down at her. "You are? Why?"

"Pete's told me how hard it is at times keeping the peace in town with so many rowdy cowboys here on the weekends. It sounds like that is risky enough without having shootouts with criminals, especially when you have your sisters to be concerned about."

"They're never far from my thoughts. Do you know when you want to start working with the twins?"

"I do. In fact, I was looking for you."

Justin's heart bucked at the thought of her seeking him out. Though most of Marta's pretty hair was covered with her bonnet, the part that hung out glistened in the sun like a new penny. "You were?"

She nodded. "I thought I'd invite the three of you over for Sunday dinner so the girls could get to know me better."

His stomach begged him to accept. How long had it been since he had a home-cooked meal made by someone other than his sisters, whose food was barely edible? "That would be very nice. Thank you for the invitation."

"My pleasure. Is there anything special you or your sisters would like to eat?"

He shook his head. "We'll eat whatever you fix."

"Well, that certainly makes it simple."

He smiled. Marta was sweet and kind, so unlike her cranky brother. Pete had told him that their mother had died trying to birth another baby. She'd already lost several babes in between Pete and Marta, which explained the seven-year gap between them. Pete had told him Marta was twenty-one. He couldn't help wondering why someone hadn't snagged her for a wife.

"Well, I need to pick up thread at the mercantile and head home."

"Why don't I buy the meat for the meal?"

"Oh, that's not necessary. This one is my treat."

"You sure?"

"Yes."

"Very well then. I'll be looking forward to it."

"Afternoon, Justin."

He watched her walk away, his heart tripping over itself at hearing his Christian name on her lips. He heard a snipping sound and turned to see Serinda with a pair of shears. She clipped off several broken stalks of flowers then rose.

"I have the water, Cousin." Phyllis exited the house, carrying a vase.

Serinda handed several stalks to Justin. "If you would take those to Phyllis, I'd be grateful."

He nodded then remembered the pig and scanned the street, but he didn't see it. Maybe Todd had arrived with his rope and taken it home. If not, he was sure to hear about it.

He walked up the porch steps and handed the flowers to Miss Begley.

"I hate to see such a big hole in our flowers out here, but at least we can enjoy the pretty blooms inside." She sniffed the gold and dark red flowers then looked up with a twinkle in her eye. "You and Miss Buckley sure seemed friendly."

Uh-oh. He knew matchmaking when he saw it. "I helped her out of a predicament the other day, and she was merely thanking me."

She lifted one brow. "She sure came a long ways just to do that."

He wasn't about to tell her that Marta had invited him to Sunday dinner. Word would be around town in only a few hours. "Well, since I was here, and she wanted to talk to me, she had no choice but to walk across town." It wasn't like it was all that far in such a tiny town.

"I've got to ride out and see about some rustled cattle. Good day, ladies." He tipped his hat to the women.

Serinda joined Phyllis on the porch. "If only I were thirty years younger."

Justin hurried away. The cousins were nice enough most days, but they tended to meddle in other people's business. And he sure didn't want them interfering in his.

Even though they lived on the edge of town, it wouldn't be long before everyone learned that Marta was helping him with the twins. Once people noticed the girls coming and going, there would be talk.

He led his horse out of the barn then mounted him. Wildfire's shiny roan coat reminded him of Marta's hair. It was odd that he was thinking about her so much lately. Was it merely because they were doing business and talking more frequently?

Surely that was the reason.

Justin nudged Wildfire into a lope as he headed to the Langston ranch. He'd best focus on business, not a pretty woman.

Chapter 4

"Why are we going to your deputy's house for dinner?" Emma asked as they walked away from the church on Sunday morning.

"I, for one, am glad we didn't have to cook today." Ella retied the strings of her bonnet.

Justin glanced around the town square. The girls had talked to one of their friends after the service, so they were late leaving, and few others were nearby. "I asked Miss Buckley to work with you girls to teach you things you don't know."

Both girls stopped and turned toward him.

"What?" Ella covered her mouth with one hand.

"You didn't." Emma scowled.

"I did." He looked around again to make sure no one was listening. "You need to learn to fix more than eggs, potatoes, and porridge."

"We can cook more than that." Emma hiked her chin.

"Yeah." Ella repeated the action.

"There's still much more you need to learn, like how to become ladies."

The twins gasped.

Justin held up his hand. "This isn't open for discussion. Miss Buckley is a very nice lady, and I expect you to treat her kindly."

The girls crossed their arms in unison.

"That's not. . ." Ella scowled.

". . .fair," Emma finished.

"Just give it a try, please. I'd really like for you to learn to bake a pie."

Ella lowered her arms and looked at her sister. "I'd like to learn that and how to make other treats."

Emma yanked off her bonnet. "Well, I wouldn't. And besides, why does it have to be your deputy's sister? He's mean."

Justin shook his head. "Pete isn't mean. He's cranky."

"It's the same thing." Emma's chin hiked higher.

"Well, we're going for dinner, and that's that. I expect you to be polite. Miss Buckley has gone to some trouble to fix us a good meal, and I intend to enjoy it." Justin started walking. "C'mon. We're late."

The girls followed behind him at a slower pace.

"Traitor," Emma said to her sister.

"I'm not a traitor simply because I want to learn how to cook pies. Just think how nice it would be to eat one whenever we wanted."

"Humph. It sounds like a lot of work to me."

Justin glanced at the sky, asking God for patience. He sure wished he knew why the good Lord thought he was capable of raising two adolescent girls.

As he drew near to the Buckley house, he caught a whiff of cooked beef. His stomach urged him to hurry. He trotted up the steps and knocked on the door. He glanced back, relieved to see his sisters entering the gate and that no one else on the street was watching them.

It wasn't usually a big deal for neighbors to dine with one another, except when both neighbors weren't married. At least they had Pete and the girls to make it all respectable for the biddies who worried about those kinds of things.

Marta appeared at the door, her cheeks red. "Welcome." She pushed the door open, and he stepped in.

Justin had never been in the Buckley house before. It was sparser than he'd expected. Even his house had nicer furniture and doodads.

"Thank you for inviting us. It was kind of you." Justin removed his hat and hung it on the rack by the front door, noticing that Pete's was missing. "Is your brother not here?"

Marta shook her head. "He said he had something to do. He wolfed down his meal then left about ten minutes ago."

Justin felt a bit odd being here without Pete, but he was here for the twins, and that was all. He turned to face his sisters. "You know the girls, Emma and Ella."

Marta smiled. "Yes. It's a pleasure to have you join us."

Both girls mumbled a thank-you.

Justin frowned at them.

"Well, the food is ready. Shall we eat?" Marta didn't wait for an answer but walked into the kitchen. "Feel free to choose whichever seat you'd like."

The girls sat across from one another, which meant he and

Marta would have to do the same. Justin walked over to where Marta stood. "Can I help carry anything?"

"Oh. . .um. . .I suppose so. I'm not used to having help."

Justin frowned. "Pete doesn't assist you at times? Is that why you were repairing the henhouse?"

Marta's cheeks reddened even more. "Pete is a busy man, so I don't expect him to help around the house."

He couldn't help wondering just what was keeping Pete so busy. His deputy didn't start working until four in the afternoon, so he had all morning and most of the afternoon to help his sister. It ate at him to think Marta didn't have a man she could depend on. Was he adding to her workload by having her teach his sisters?

"Excuse me."

He looked down to see Marta holding a platter of roast beef, sliced potatoes, and carrots. He reached out. "Allow me."

She frowned. "Are you sure?"

"It's a small thing, Marta."

She relinquished her hold on the platter. "Very well. Thank you."

She turned back to the cupboard then walked to the table holding a bowl of biscuits that looked so flaky his mouth watered. She placed it on the table and looked at him. "Would you like some coffee?"

"Water is fine." He reached for his glass and took a sip. Then he glanced at his sisters, who were unusually quiet. Their gazes flicked from him to Marta. He wished he knew what they were thinking.

Marta took her seat and stared at him. "Would you care to bless the food?"

"Sure." Justin bowed his head. "In a world where so many are hungry, may we eat this food with humble hearts. In a world where so many are lonely, may we share this friendship with joyful hearts. Amen."

Marta lifted her head, looking surprised. "That was very nice."

Justin shrugged one shoulder. "It's a prayer my grandma used to pray, and it seemed to fit this meal."

Marta lifted the platter and passed it to Justin. "So, girls, what types of things do you enjoy doing?"

Emma scowled, and Justin nudged her foot with his.

"I like being with my friends and reading, mostly." Emma reached for a biscuit.

"I enjoy that too, I suppose. And school." Ella passed the platter to Marta.

"What about cooking or sewing?" Marta asked.

Ella slathered butter on her biscuit. "Cooking is all right, but it's a lot of work."

"Anything worth doing takes effort." Justin ladled gravy on his meat and potatoes.

"That's easy for you to say, since you don't have to cook." Emma glared at him.

Justin pierced her with an icy stare. *Behave*, he mouthed.

"When you get older and start looking for a husband, you'll wish you knew how to cook well. That's one of the most important things to a man." Marta smiled. "And knowing how to sew can help if money is tight."

Justin wondered if she was speaking from experience. Was Pete stingy with his income? His deputy had mentioned their folks left them nothing when they died. And bill collectors had hounded him for payment, which was the reason they had moved from Missouri to Texas.

"Did you make the dress you're wearing?" Ella asked. "It's very pretty."

Justin had noticed the soft green dress with blue flowers. It wasn't nearly as fancy as some, but it looked good on her. He liked the simplicity of the calico. Marta didn't try to catch a man's eye by wearing fancy clothing, and he liked that.

"I did. My mother taught me to sew when I was young."

"So did ours, but I fear I've forgotten a lot of the things she taught us." Ella reached for her cup and sipped her water.

"It will come back. You simply need to practice. Did you ever make a sampler?" Marta took her empty plate and Justin's to the kitchen then returned for the girls'. When she came back, she was carrying a dark brown pie.

Justin's mouth watered, in spite of the fact that he was stuffed. He thought the pie was pecan until she brought it closer. His eyes widened. "Is that molasses pie?"

"Yes. You mentioned it was your favorite, so I thought I'd bake one as a thank-you for helping me with the henhouse."

"Well, thanks. This is a wonderful surprise."

She sliced the pie and served them each a piece. Justin waited until she sat, and then he forked a bite and stuffed it in his mouth. Sweet flavors exploded on his tongue. He closed his eyes, feeling as if he'd gone to heaven. When he reopened them, all three females were staring.

"You just moaned." Emma quirked her lips.

"That doesn't surprise me. This is the best molasses pie I've had since Ma's."

Marta's cheeks were pink again. "Thank you. That's quite a compliment."

"It's the truth." Justin slid in another bite. He had no idea that Marta was such a good cook. He sure hoped she could teach his sisters to cook like her.

On Tuesday afternoon, Marta opened the front door. "Ella, how nice to see you. Where's your sister?"

Ella shuffled her feet. "She. . .um. . .doesn't want to come."

Marta had gathered as much from Emma's remarks at Sunday's dinner. "Perhaps I'll run over and talk to her."

"It won't do any good. Emma has a stubborn streak."

"Well, it won't hurt to talk to her. If you'll have a seat, I'll be right back."

Ella looked a bit unsure. "Is your brother here?"

"No. He's out and about somewhere. There's a newspaper on the side table if you'd care to thumb through it."

"All right."

Marta smiled. "I won't be long."

She hurried out the door, through the gate, and walked across her neighbors' mostly dirt yard. Perhaps she could teach the girls some things about gardening. They really ought to know about growing vegetable and herbs, as well as flowers to make their yard look nicer.

She hurried up the steps and knocked on the door. A long minute passed before it opened. Emma appeared with a book in her hand. She rolled her eyes. "What do you want?"

Marta remembered what it was like to be around a fussy adolescent. Pete had tormented her during his early teen years. She willed herself to be patient and smiled. "I was hoping you'd join Ella and me today. I have some fun things planned."

"Cooking isn't fun."

"Perhaps not, but it is a delight to enjoy the fruits of your labors."

Emma must have agreed, because she didn't argue.

"Why don't you bring your book and come over to my house. Your brother is expecting you to be there, and we don't want to disappoint him." She omitted the fact that she felt responsible for the girls. "We're making sugar cookies."

Emma's eyes brightened a speck. "Fine. I can read over there just as well as here." She stepped out and shut the door.

"Have you made cookies before?"

"Once, after Mama died, but it was a disaster. We burned them and filled the whole house with smoke."

"Don't let that keep you from trying again. Every cook has a flop now and then."

"Have you?"

Marta pressed her hand against her bodice. "Oh heavens, yes. I once made some shortbread to go with sliced strawberries, but I burnt it when a comely boy I knew came calling. And not only that, I was so enamored with him that I added salt to the fruit instead of sugar. Mama was very disappointed because strawberries were her favorite fruit."

"Did you get in trouble?"

"No, but Mama did have a talk with me about paying attention when I'm cooking. She sure didn't want me to get burnt because I was careless." She opened the front door and let Emma precede her.

"I remember my mama saying the same thing."

"It's good advice. Many a woman has been injured when her clothing caught fire."

"Whose dress caught fire?" Ella rose from the settee.

Marta smiled. "Nobody's. We were talking about safety in the kitchen."

"Oh." Ella almost looked disappointed.

Marta tapped her fingertips together. "Since Christmas is less than a month away, I thought I'd teach you how to make decorated sugar cookies. Doesn't that sound like fun?"

Once again, Emma rolled her eyes.

Ella glanced at her sister then shrugged. "I suppose."

Marta drew in a steadying breath. She sure had her work cut out for her. She walked into the kitchen, and Ella followed. "First thing, before we work in the kitchen, we need to wash our hands."

While Ella cleaned her hands, Marta returned to the parlor. "Are you certain you don't want to help us?"

Emma nodded.

"My mother had a rule that if you don't work, you don't eat. If you'd like some cookies later, you'll need to work with us."

Emma hugged her book to her chest. "I don't need any cookies."

"Suit yourself." She returned to the kitchen, half suspecting the girl would change her tune once the first batch was baking and the delicious aroma filled the house.

Marta had prepared four tiny bowls of white ingredients. "While I wash, I wonder if you could tell me what you think is in these."

Ella bent down and studied the bowls. She picked the third one. "I think this is sugar."

"Very good. But that one's the easiest since it glistens. How about the others?"

"My guess is that they are flour, salt, and, um. . .I don't know."

Marta dried her hands then touched the first bowl. "This is salt.

Number four is baking powder, and the second one is cream of tartar."

"Oh. I thought for sure that was flour."

"Your first lesson is the importance of labeling your supplies. Using the wrong item in a recipe can have dreadful results, and it's wasteful. Later you can ask your sister about my cooking disaster. I told her on the way over."

Ella's pretty eyes widened.

Marta placed the recipe on the table. "First, we follow the recipe."

"Mama often didn't use one."

"Many women cook that way, but I don't trust myself to remember each ingredient correctly, so I prefer to follow a recipe."

Ella added the various items then stirred the mixture.

"You're doing very well."

Ella glanced toward the parlor then leaned closer. "Don't tell Emma, but I rather like cooking."

Marta smiled. "I do too. It's especially nice when you can watch someone enjoy the goods you've made." She couldn't help thinking of Justin's response to her pie on Sunday.

"Justin loves sweets. It will be nice to know how to make some for him. Mama tried to teach us to cook, but we weren't interested and didn't pay attention. I wish now that I had."

Marta wrapped her arm around the girl. "I know how you feel. I wish I'd listened more to my mother when she was still alive."

Not wanting to spend too much time on the sad topic of their deceased mothers, Marta showed Ella how to roll out the dough and then use the cookie cutters to make shapes.

"This is fun. I really like the star shape, except it's hard to keep from smooshing the points."

"I wish I had more than just three patterns, but we'll make do."

Ella bolted upright. "We have some at home, but I don't know where they are."

Marta placed the first batch in the oven. "Perhaps you could find them, and then we could use them to make some cookies for the baskets that we give to the less fortunate at Christmastime."

"I'd like that."

They rolled out more dough and made another batch of shapes. A fragrant aroma filled the air.

Ella lifted her face and sniffed. "Doesn't that smell wonderful?"

"It does." Marta peeked in the oven. "Looks like the first batch is done."

As she placed the cookie pan on the counter, Emma moseyed in. Marta bit back a smile. Fresh cookies were hard to resist, even for the most stubborn girl.

"We need to get these off the pan so they will cool. Would you like to help, Emma?"

The girl shrugged.

"Remember, if you want to eat some cookies, you need to help."

Emma frowned, spun around, and stomped back to the parlor.

Marta's hopes sank. The girl was going to be more of a challenge than she'd expected.

Chapter 5

"You made these?" Justin looked at Ella then took another bite of the delicious cookies.

Ella beamed. "I did. It was fun, especially baking with Miss Buckley. She's a lot nicer than I thought, considering how mean her brother is."

Justin couldn't figure out why the twins thought Pete was mean. Sure, he was cranky, but he thought it was because Pete had run for marshal against him and lost. He had hoped to mend fences by hiring him to be his deputy.

He looked at Emma. "Did you also help?"

She shook her head. "I think it's stupid that we have to be watched over like we're infants."

Justin leaned back. "That's not what's going on, and you know it. You girls need to learn stuff I can't teach you. Marta knows those things, and that's why I asked her to help."

Emma reached for a cookie, and Justin snagged the plate. "No cookies for you since you didn't help."

"Now you're the mean one."

Justin placed the cookies on the counter. "No one gets a free ride in life. There's just plain too much work to do. Once I finish my job, I come home and chop wood, do repairs, and even help you girls in the kitchen most days. I know you miss Mama, but fussing and fuming won't change the fact that she's gone."

Emma pushed up from the table. "You don't know nothin'." She rushed from the room.

Ella sighed. "She almost helped. I think if we give her time, she'll warm up to Miss Buckley. I really like her."

Justin reached over and squeezed his sister's hand. "I'm glad. I had to admit that I wondered if I was doing the right thing."

"I think you are. I didn't like the idea at first, but now I'm excited to learn new things. It's almost like having Mama back, but not quite."

"I miss her too."

Ella rose, her eyes shiny with unshed tears. "I should start on the dishes. I have some work I need to do for school."

"I'll help."

"No, that's all right. You go sit and read or something. You work hard to take care of us."

He stood and walked over to her, wrapping his arms around her. "I love you, El. And I'm proud of you for making such wonderful cookies. Not only do they taste good, but they're pretty to look at with that icing and colored sugar sprinkled on."

"Thank you." She squeezed him back. "I love you too. I'll work on Emma and get her to like Miss Buckley."

"I'd appreciate that." He released her, helped clear the table, then scooped out a basin of hot water for her from the stove's reservoir before going into the parlor.

He sat down on the settee and put his feet on the coffee table. If only Ella could win over her sister. Emma had always been the more stubborn and less cheerful twin. Surely, given some time, she'd come around. He would pray for that.

Justin reached for the newspaper, but a sharp knock on the door stopped him. He sighed. So much for relaxing.

He rose, crossed the room, and opened the door. "What do you need, Pete?"

"Reverend Ross stopped by the office. He said that there were several dollars in the poor box at church this morning. He meant to collect them but had to rush out when he learned that Herb Aster had died."

"So?"

Pete scratched his chest. "When he came back this evening, the money was gone. The reverend wants to talk to you."

Justin clenched his fist. He needed to find out who was stealing and stop them. This was getting out of hand. "Who would steal from the church?"

Pete shrugged. "Lots of folks. Strangers. Men down on their luck. Outlaws."

"Let me tell the girls where I'm going, and then I'll head over to the parsonage."

Pete nodded then ambled away.

"You're leaving?" Ella walked in, drying her hands on a towel.

"Yep. I shouldn't be gone long." He bent and kissed her head. "See you in a bit."

Justin looked around as he cut across one corner of the town square. Things seemed peaceful, but a thief was hiding somewhere, unless the man had left town. How could anyone stoop low enough to steal from a church? That was just plain wrong.

He knocked on the door to the parsonage, and Regina, the pastor's daughter, answered. "Come in, Marshal Yates. Papa is waiting."

"Thank you, Miss Ross." He watched the pretty blond walk away. Regina was a lovely woman, but she'd never sparked his interest. How long would it be before some other man set his cap for her? He guessed she was only a year or two younger than Marta. Perhaps the fact that her father was the town's minister had kept potential suitors away.

The parson walked into the parlor. "Thank you for coming so quickly, Marshal." He shook his head. "It saddens me that someone is willing to steal from the church. Doesn't he realize that God sees all?"

"It is disturbing. How much money do you reckon they got?"

Reverend Ross shrugged. His normally cheerful gray eyes looked troubled. "Somewhere between two and three dollars. Not a lot, but it would have helped buy food for one of the poor families in town."

"Are the ladies doing food baskets again this year?"

"As far as I know. Regina asked for names of less fortunate families last week, and I assumed that was for the baskets."

Justin rubbed the back of his neck. "I wonder if our secret benefactor will bring hens and geese again this year."

"I sure hope so. It's truly a blessing for the poor families to get meat with their baskets. I wish I knew who the donor was so I could thank him."

Justin curled the brim of his hat. "I reckon he doesn't want everybody knowing."

"A Good Samaritan." Reverend Ross smiled.

Nodding, Justin put on his hat. "I'll ask around town and see if anyone knows anything about the theft."

"Thank you, Justin. God knows who the thief is. I'll pray He convicts the man and inspires him to return the money."

Justin walked out the door.

"Oh, there were a couple of pesos included with the stolen money. That's a bit uncommon this far north."

"If you think of anything else, let me know."

Reverend Ross nodded then shut the door.

Justin walked toward the saloon. Maybe he'd get lucky and someone there would know something about the stolen money.

Marta pulled a fresh loaf of bread from the oven and set it on her worktable. Then she added two pieces of wood to the stove. By the time they burned down, she and the twins should have something ready to go in the oven, and the temperature would be just right.

The sound of giggling in her backyard drew her to the window. What were Justin and his sisters doing out there?

Marta removed her apron, smoothed her hair, then walked out onto the back porch. "What are you three up to?"

Justin backed away from the chicken coop, looking guilty. Then he smiled, sending Marta's stomach into a tizzy. He glanced at the girls. Ella wore a big smile, and even Emma looked on the cheerful side.

Justin cleared his throat and shuffled his feet. "We. . .uh. . . thought we'd do something special for you since you've been so helpful.

Just then a rooster crowed.

Marta's heart leaped. She hurried down the steps. "You got me a rooster?"

"And some hens." Ella gestured to her. "Come see. They're so precious."

"They're just chicks." Emma crossed her arms.

"But look how sweet and fuzzy they are." Ella stooped down for a better look.

Marta crossed to the coop and looked in. "It does my heart good to have chickens again. I've missed them."

"Don't they peck you?" Emma took a step closer.

"Usually, the rooster is the only one that pecks. I toss down a handful of feed to keep him and the hens busy while I grab the eggs. That generally does the trick."

"I'd like to gather the eggs sometime, if you wouldn't mind." Ella looked at her with hope in her pretty blue eyes.

"Of course you can, although it will be awhile before those chicks are big enough to lay eggs. Thank you, girls." She turned to face Justin. "I'm in your debt. Thank you, Justin."

His wide smile made him look so handsome. His blue eyes gleamed. "It seemed a small thing to do when you'll be spending so much of your time to help the girls."

"It's my pleasure. I enjoy having them over."

Emma eyed her as if she didn't quite believe her.

"What do you have planned for the twins today?" Justin asked.

Marta wondered if he was actually asking what they were cooking. There was little doubt he was pleased with their arrangement. The man definitely had a sweet tooth.

"It's a surprise."

His happy expression fell. "Oh. Well, I'm sure it will be delicious."

"I just pulled a loaf of bread from the oven. Would you like a slice?"

"I would, but I need to get back to work."

"How about one for the road?"

"That I would accept. I need to run home and grab the sack of feed for your birds though."

"Really, you didn't have to buy food for them."

Justin shrugged. "I didn't want you to have to make a trip to the feedstore when you already have plans."

"That was very kind of you. When the hens start laying, the first eggs will be yours."

"I'll look forward to that." Justin picked up the crate the chicks had been in. "Be right back. You girls should get washed up."

Marta admired her baby chicks for a few moments then turned to the girls. "Thank you for the wonderful surprise."

"You're welcome. What are we making today?" Ella tapped her fingertips together, as if eager to get started.

"How are your biscuit-making skills?"

"Passable," Emma muttered.

"Since biscuits are such a staple, I thought I'd teach you how to make flaky ones that almost melt in your mouth."

"Justin would like that. He says ours are hard enough to use as a weapon." Ella giggled.

"It's not funny." Emma crossed her arms. "We try our best."

Marta wrapped her arm around Emma's shoulders. "I'm sure you do, and that's why I'm here to help. Nobody is a natural-born cook. They have to learn from someone else or by closely following a recipe. I know a few tricks to help, and I'm happy to share them with you. You two go on inside and wash. I need to get the bin that I keep chicken feed in. I don't want to leave it in the bag, or some varmint will get into it."

Marta scrabbled through the pile of broken crates on the back porch that Pete was supposed to cut up into firewood. Beneath a pile of boards, she located the wooden bin with a hinged lid and dragged it across the porch to the other side of the door. She needed to find a piece of twine to secure it shut once the feed had been deposited.

"I would have moved that for you." Justin trotted up the steps with a ten-pound sack of feed on his shoulder. He dropped it into the bin then closed the lid and dusted off his shirt and hands. "That should keep them happy for a bit."

"I need to give them some water, and they'll be set." Marta wrung her hands, a bit nervous in the face of Justin's generosity. "How can I repay you for this?" She waved her hand toward the bin.

"You already are. That pie the girls brought home the other night was wonderful." He glanced around. "What do you want to put the chickens' water in?"

"There's a tin bowl in the coop that I use."

"I'll take care of that, and then I need to make my rounds."

"Thank you so much. I'll run in and get that slice of bread. Would you like jam on it?"

"Sure. I could get used to this." His smile sent her stomach into another tizzy.

Marta dashed inside before he could notice her blush. Given the chance, she could easily get used to taking care of him. She'd been infatuated with Justin Yates ever since her family first moved in next door to him, but he'd never paid her much attention. After his parents' deaths, life had been quite difficult for a long time, but it seemed as if things had finally settled back to a routine for him and the twins.

Though Justin only saw her as a friend who was helping his sisters, she would enjoy this short moment where she got to take care of him by teaching his sisters to be better cooks and housekeepers.

Chapter 6

Three days after delivering the chickens to Marta, Justin sat at his desk in the jailhouse, cleaning his pistol. He couldn't get Marta off his mind. Her smile of appreciation for the chicks had hit him in the gut as hard as a bullet.

How come he'd never noticed how pretty she was when she smiled? Why hadn't he paid more attention to his lovely neighbor? Perhaps it was because she was Pete's sister. Or had he merely been too busy with his sisters and his job?

He cleaned each chamber of the cylinder and then scrubbed the back of the barrel and several other parts with a small brush. Discovering how sweet and kindhearted Marta was had surprised him. Pete was usually crotchety. Justin figured that was just his nature and that his sister was the same.

In hindsight, hiring Pete as deputy probably wasn't the wisest decision. He had hoped to mend fences after beating Pete in the election for marshal, but his deputy still had a burr under his saddle.

The door flew open and Pete stomped in.

Justin put his revolver back together. "Afternoon."

Pete grunted and dropped a box of cartridges on the desk. He walked straight to the coffeepot, poured a cup, then swigged down the lukewarm sludge. He added several sticks of wood to the stove. "Lawson wants to talk to you."

Justin glanced up as he returned the cleaning supplies to the drawer. "Did he say why?"

"Nope. Just that he needed to talk to you."

Justin rose and stretched. "Guess I'll mosey over there and see what's up. That's Elliot Parker curled up on the cot in the cell. Go ahead and let him out if he's sober when he wakes up."

"And if he isn't?" Pete took the seat Justin vacated at the desk.

"Get him a plate of something over at the café." Justin pulled a couple of coins out of his pocket and tossed them onto the desk. "I'll head home after I talk to Henry. Come get me if anything happens."

"Always do." Pete pushed back and lifted his boots onto the desk then yawned.

Justin pulled on his jacket and headed outside. Winter had returned with a cold north wind. He ducked his head and hurried across the empty town square to Lawson's Mercantile. He quickly opened and shut the door, enjoying the warmth of the store and the fragrant smells of coffee, spices, and leather. "You know it's getting close to Christmas when it turns this cold."

Henry Lawson didn't smile or respond with a humorous quip as he often did.

Justin glanced around, glad to see the store was empty. "What's going on, Henry?"

The man exhaled a loud sigh. "I don't like to blame folks for things I didn't see with my own eyes, but as much as I hate to say it, I think one of your sisters or Barry Spencer might've stolen a knife from me."

Justin's heart lurched. Henry wasn't the kind of man to make a false accusation, so he must feel strongly. "What kind of knife?"

"A Mappin Brothers sterling silver fruit knife, with a mother-of-pearl handle." He picked one up from the display case and laid it on the counter. "Looks the same as this one, except it has a bird engraved on the side instead of a flower. The bird looks like it's flying."

Justin picked up the knife and studied it. The pretty thing was just the kind a lady would use for cutting up fruit.

"Abijah Tanner was looking at three knives as Christmas gifts for his sisters—or maybe his daughter—but he couldn't decide. I was measuring fabric for the Begley ladies. Your deputy came in and got a box of cartridges, laid his money on the counter, and left. Abijah followed Pete out. The only other ones left was the kids.

"After I measured the cloth, I went back to the counter and discovered there were only two knives. Your sisters and Barry Spencer were here walking around, looking at things and whispering. I didn't think nothin' about it since folks tend to do that this time of year, looking for Christmas gifts and what all. But your sisters and the boy left without buying anything, and the knife was gone."

Justin didn't believe for a second that the twins had taken the knife. If they needed something like that, they would tell him, and he'd buy it if he thought it was necessary. "You're sure the knife wasn't already missing before the girls and Barry left?"

Henry tapped his lips and glanced upward. "Pretty sure."

"What about when Abijah Tanner and Pete were here?"

Henry shrugged. "Things were busy."

Justin shouldn't be throwing suspicion on his own deputy, but he couldn't entertain the notion of one of his sisters being a thief. There had been nothing previously to indicate that. Abijah Tanner certainly had enough money to buy whatever he wanted, but that didn't let him off the hook either. Justin's bet was on the Spencer boy, but he needed proof.

"Was anyone else in the store?"

"Just the Begley ladies."

"Did you have a clear view of the counter the whole time?"

He glanced up again. "Well. . .no. The Begley cousins were blocking my view part of the time."

"Do you know if the Begley ladies went home after leaving here?"

"I might've heard them say they were going over to the Tanner house."

"All right. I'll go talk to them and see if they happened to have noticed anything. I'll do my best to find whoever stole your knife."

Henry nodded. "I appreciate that, Marshal. It pained me to have to tell you about your sisters."

"I'll certainly talk with them, but I have to tell you it would be very out of character for one of them to steal something. As far as I know, neither of them ever has."

"Losing loved ones in a tragedy like y'all did sometimes causes a person to change. I hope it turns out it wasn't the twins, but the evidence is leaning toward them or the boy."

Justin wasn't so sure. In his eyes, Pete and Abijah Tanner both had equal opportunity. He knew his sisters, and he didn't believe for a second that one of them had taken the knife.

As he passed the Griffiths' house, the fragrant aroma of something baking made his stomach growl. He continued down the street he lived on. The Tanners' big lot was the second one on the street, with their rental house next, and then his clapboard home. The Buckley cottage was the last on the street.

He hurried up the steps and knocked on the door. Rachel Jones answered and invited him in. Abijah's daughter was known to be married, but no one had seen her husband in many years. "What brings you here on such a chilly day?" she asked.

"I'm wondering if the Begley cousins are here."

"In here, Marshal," one of the cousins hollered.

"They're in the parlor." Rachel held out her hand to indicate the way.

Justin wasn't often intimidated, but walking in on the town's four spinster matrons gave him pause. They were a force to reckon with. "Afternoon, ladies."

"Marshal, to what do we owe the pleasure of your visit?" Priscilla Tanner, Abijah's sister, rose and walked over to him.

He glanced across the room to where the Begley cousins were sipping tea. A roaring fire kept the room comfortable. "I need to speak with the Begley ladies."

"Rachel, if you'll be so kind as to wheel my sister out, we'll leave the room to our guests," Priscilla said.

"Nonsense, we have nothing to hide. No sense moving that cumbersome wheelchair." Serinda Begley pinned him with a stare. "What is it you need to discuss with us, Marshal Yates?"

Justin wished now that he'd waited until they had returned home to question them, but he'd wanted his sisters cleared as quickly as possible. "There was an incident at the store a short while ago."

"Oh, you're referring to the stolen jewelry." Priscilla set down her cup. "Phyllis told us about it."

"And the church was robbed." Lois Tanner shook her head. "Such a dreadful thing to happen in our small town."

Phyllis mirrored Lois. "What's our town coming to? It's hardly safe to walk the streets anymore."

Justin shoved back a wave of annoyance. The streets were perfectly safe, except perhaps at night. But few ladies ventured out then, and rarely ever without an escort. "I'm doing my best to find out who is stealing."

"I'm sure you are." Serinda smiled. "We all voted for you, I hope you know."

"Thank you, ladies. I appreciate that."

"Would you care for some tea?" Rachel asked.

"No, but thank you." He'd never quite figured out how a curmudgeon like Abijah had ended up with such a sweet daughter. She must have taken after her mother, someone he'd never met.

He focused on the Begley cousins. "I need to know what you saw when you were at the store. Mr. Lawson claims a fruit knife was taken?"

"Well, we certainly didn't take it." Phyllis harrumphed.

"I should say not." Serinda frowned then looked at her cousin.

"Your sisters were there, Marshal, and one of those rascally Spencer boys. And—" Phyllis glanced at the Tanner sisters. "Um. . . well, your brother was also present, not that I'm accusing him of anything, mind you. He was just there."

Serinda tapped her cousin's arm. "And that deputy, Mr. Buckley."

"Yes. He was also there. I believe that's all." Phyllis set her hands in her lap.

"Did you happen to see anyone pick up a pearl-handled knife?"

Both ladies shook their heads.

"I can tell you that there were two or three knives on the counter when we left, but I'm not certain which," Phyllis said.

"I believe it was two." Serinda held up two fingers. "A black one and a yellow one."

"Are you sure it wasn't a black and a silver one?" Phyllis asked.

"No, I'm sure."

Justin resisted the urge to sigh. He hadn't expected to get much from the ladies. "If you happen to think of anything else, please let me know."

He turned to Priscilla Tanner. "Is your brother here? I need to talk with him too."

She shook her head. "No. I'm sorry, but he hasn't returned yet. He said he had some errands to run."

He needed to talk to Mr. Tanner, one of the wealthier men in town. Tanner had a reputation for being a wily businessman, but Justin wasn't likely to get much out of the tight-lipped man.

Rachel escorted him to the door. Justin bid her good day then trotted down the steps. He wasn't looking forward to his next conversation.

Marta supervised as both girls placed dough into pie plates. "That's good. Now you can either use a fork to press down the edge, or you can crimp it with your fingers."

"I'm using a fork." Emma reached for one.

"I'll try the finger method. How do you do it?" Ella looked at Marta.

She stepped closer and stuck out her index fingers. "You simply press one way with your right finger while pushing the other way with your left hand. Like that. Or you can try it with your index finger and thumb."

"Oh, that looks easy. I can do it." Ella made a rough zigzag pattern all around the edge of the piecrust then looked up with a big smile.

"You did a fine job. Emma too. Both pies will look lovely." She crossed to the cupboard and picked up the bowl of custard. "Now you just pour in the custard mixture. Would you like to go first, Emma?"

The girl nodded. "What if I spill it?"

"If you're concerned about that, you can use a mug to dip it out in small portions."

Emma smiled. "I'd rather do that. I don't want to waste any of the custard."

Marta took a mug from the shelf and handed it to her. She had been so delighted when Emma announced she wanted to help make the pies today. The girls would now be able to prepare their own dessert for Christmas, although Marta still harbored hope that Justin and the twins might join her and Pete. She hadn't yet broached the subject with her brother.

The girls filled their piecrusts with the sweet, pale yellow filling then placed them in the oven. They started on the cleanup without her even having to ask them. She'd been a bit nervous to assist the girls at first, but things were turning out better than she had hoped.

A hard knock at the door jolted her into action. She opened the door, happy to see Justin, even though she hadn't expected him. "Come on in out of the cold."

"Feels good in here. Smells good too."

"We've been baking."

"I can tell."

Something was definitely bothering Justin. He wasn't his normal congenial self. "I need to talk with my sisters."

"Of course. Why don't you have a seat in the parlor, and I'll send them in."

"I think it would be better if I took them home."

"Home!" Ella walked toward them. "But we haven't had our sewing lesson yet."

"And we have pies in the oven." Emma crossed her arms over her chest.

"What I need to talk to you about is best done in private."

The girls looked at one another then back at their brother.

Emma crossed her arms. "We haven't done anything. . ."

Ella mirrored her twin. ". . .wrong."

Justin sighed. "Please gather your cloaks and come on."

Though upset, the girls did as he asked. They quickly walked out, and Marta closed the door behind them.

What in the world could be wrong? The girls had been happy

and eager to learn lately. She couldn't imagine them doing anything so bad that Justin would be that upset.

She walked into the parlor and sat in her chair by the fireplace. As she stared out the window at the cold day, she prayed for Justin and the girls.

Chapter 7

The twins stomped up the steps and into the house. Justin entered after them and closed the door. Both girls turned to face him, arms crossed.

"What was so important that you made us leave Marta's before we were done?" Emma hiked her chin up.

"Let's go sit down." He motioned toward the parlor.

The girls flopped down on the horsehair settee. Justin took his chair by the fireplace and turned it toward them. Feeling exhausted, he dropped into it.

How should he go about confronting his sisters? They were surely going to be upset. There was no way other than jumping in with both feet.

He blew out a loud breath. "Henry Lawson said you girls and

Barry Spencer were in the store when a fruit knife was stolen."

Both girls' eyes widened.

Ella looked at her sister. "He thinks. . ."

". . .we stole it?" Emma scowled.

Judging by their shocked expressions, Justin felt certain they were innocent of the crime. His sisters weren't that good at feigning innocence. He could usually tell if they were telling a falsehood.

"He simply said that after you three left, the knife was gone."

"We weren't the only ones in the store." Emma crossed her arms.

"That's right. Mr. Tanner, the Begley cousins, and Mr. Buckley were all there." Ella's blue eyes begged him to believe her.

"Who was in the store when you left?"

The girls looked at one another. "Just the Begley cousins," they said in unison.

"Barry left when you did?"

The twins nodded.

"You didn't happen to see him take it, did you?"

"No!" they screeched.

"He's trying hard to be better." This time it was Emma's eyes begging him to believe her.

Justin rubbed the back of his neck where the muscles had tightened. "Henry is pretty certain that all three knives were on the counter after Pete and Abijah Tanner left. That's why he thinks one of you three took it."

As if scripted, they both fell against the back of the settee, arms crossed.

"Well, we didn't take it," Emma huffed.

"Why would we, when we already have a fruit knife?" Ella's question sounded perfectly reasonable.

"And besides, if we were of a mind to take something, which we never would do, we'd take something prettier than a knife." Emma scowled at him.

"Why were you at the store in the first place?"

Once again, the girls glanced at one another. Justin recognized the flash of guilt in their eyes. His stomach churned. Were they lying to him about the knife? Why else would they look guilty?

"Girls?"

Ella nibbled on her lower lip, but Emma stared him in the eye. "It's simply too close to Christmas to be asking a question like that."

They were shopping for a gift? For him? The smattering of guilt he'd experienced at questioning them now swamped him like a flash flood. He felt lower than a snake's belly.

"Can we go back to Miss Buckley's?" Ella asked.

"I think it's best if you stay home. It's almost time to start supper." Justin stood, ready to get away from their disappointed gazes. "I'll let Marta know not to expect you back today."

"Aw. . ." the girls said together.

"But what about our pies?" Ella asked.

"I'll see if they're done and bring them back if they are." He wanted to ask what kind they'd made but decided against it. He set a log on the fire then donned his coat again.

He walked back to Marta's and knocked on the door. She opened it and stepped aside so he could enter. The house smelled like freshly baked pies, teasing his senses, but Marta's worried expression gnawed at him.

"Is everything all right?" She twisted the towel she held.

"Could we go into the parlor for a minute?"

"Of course." Marta hurried in and took a seat near the fireplace.

Justin followed but remained standing. He glanced around the sparse room. Everything was neat and tidy, but there were very few decorations. Was money so tight they couldn't afford any? Was Marta dipping into her own food supplies to teach his sisters?

"First off, let me say how much I appreciate what you're doing for the twins. Even Emma seems happier these days."

Marta smiled. "I enjoy having them over. They're very sweet girls."

They could be, but they also had a stubborn streak. "Thank you, although the credit goes to my parents."

"Don't sell yourself short, Justin. You're a good brother. Not many men would ask a friend to help them like you have."

Her praise made him stand a bit taller. Reverend Ross had encouraged him that he was doing well raising the twins, but no one else had. It was something he desperately needed to hear. He dropped onto the edge of the couch. "I appreciate hearing that. Sometimes I really wonder."

"God knew you'd be up to the task."

He glanced at her. "You think so?"

"Yes. God never asks us to do something without giving us the abilities first. You're a good man, Justin, with a good heart. Your sisters are lucky to have you." She looked away, but he caught the flash of pain in her pretty eyes.

Was Pete mean to her? "Has Pete ever hurt you?"

Her gaze flicked back to his. "He has never hurt me physically, but he isn't the easiest person to live with."

"You want me to have a talk with him?"

Her eyes widened. "No! Please don't do that. It would only make things worse, I fear."

He reached out and laid his hand on hers. "All right. But if you ever need me, be sure to let me know."

Her cheeks pinked up in a pleasing blush. "Thank you."

Justin scooted back and cleared his throat. "The girls were in Lawson's Mercantile when a knife went missing. Henry seems to think one of them took it."

Marta gasped. "I don't believe for a moment that they would steal something. We've been talking about ways to help the poor this Christmas, and they're excited about sewing clothes for some of the needy children. They have good hearts, like you. Mr. Lawson must be wrong."

"I'm thinking you're right. But the only others who could have taken the knife were the Begleys, Abijah Tanner, Barry Spencer, or Pete."

Marta's mouth dropped open for a moment. "Pete? He's cranky, and things are sometimes tight around here, but I've never known him to stoop to stealing. What kind of example would that be to the town?"

"I know. I don't believe it either. But that leaves Mr. Tanner, and he has near enough money to buy the whole store, so I can't see him doing it either."

"There are no other possibilities?"

"Just the Spencer boy, but the girls feel certain he's not the guilty party. I haven't questioned him yet, but I will."

Marta folded the towel she still held. "I'll pray that you discover the truth. The girls are so young. I'd hate for them to get a bad reputation, especially one they don't deserve."

"Thanks. Talking with you reinforces my belief that the twins are innocent." Their shocked expressions when he'd questioned them had told him as much. He rose, and Marta did too.

She ducked her head. "I've never had anyone I could talk things out with before. Pete tends to be impatient, so we don't chat much."

"I can see that you'd get lonely. I can understand that. After my parents died and I became guardian of the twins, my life changed so much that I lost touch with most of my good friends. I just want you to know that I appreciate your time and encouragement."

Marta's wide smile sent his insides into a tizzy. "I'm glad I could be of help. Feel free to chat anytime you need to."

He smiled back. He was surprised how easy Marta was to talk to. The more he learned about her, the more he liked her.

"So the girls won't be back over today?"

He shook his head. "I told them to stay home and start supper."

"Their pies are ready. Would you like to take one of them home?"

"You sure don't have to ask twice. I'll take a pie any day of the week."

Marta's eyes twinkled. "Let me get it for you."

After a moment, she returned with a golden pie, which she handed to him. He lifted it up and sniffed. "Custard, yum. . . Another one of my favorites."

Marta chuckled. "Aren't all pies your favorite?"

He thought of all the pies he'd had. "No, as a matter of fact. I don't care much for lemon or mincemeat."

"Duly noted."

"I could get used to you spoiling me."

Marta's brown eyes widened, and her cheeks turned an even darker shade of pink. "The girls made the pies. I believe the one you have is Emma's."

"And she's humble too." Justin winked at her then stepped out the door before he did something completely crazy, like kiss her.

He juggled the pie, almost dropping it when he realized that he actually wanted to kiss her. How had he gone from barely knowing Marta to caring about her so quickly?

Two weeks before Christmas, Marta knocked on the door of the Tanners' house. Rachel answered the door. "Marta, welcome. Please come in."

"Thank you."

Rachel took Marta's cloak and hung it on one of the hooks on the ornate hall tree. "We're meeting in the parlor."

Marta followed her and discovered the elderly Tanner sisters, Mrs. Ross and Regina, and Alice Singer, a woman close to Marta's age who lived with her father. The number of ladies often varied from week to week, but it was mainly the same ones. "Will the Begley cousins be attending today?"

Rachel shook her head. "They sent their regrets. Serinda is ill, and Phyllis stayed home to care for her."

"We'll have to pray for her quick recovery." Mrs. Ross looked around the room. "There's no good time to be sick, but it's even worse at Christmastime."

"I agree," Lois Tanner said.

Marta took one of the remaining chairs and set her sewing basket on the floor. She took out the shirt she was making for Pete's Christmas gift.

"It's good to see you, Marta." Priscilla Tanner smiled at her. "I hear those Yates twins have been keeping you company."

All eyes turned toward her. Justin hadn't said anything about keeping it a secret, and besides, trying to was useless in such a small town. "Yes. Marshal Yates asked me if I could help them learn to cook more things and to make their own clothes."

"I would think they would already know how to sew at their age." Lois Tanner threaded her needle. "What are they—fifteen now?"

"Almost. Their birthday is this Sunday. They'll be turning fifteen." Marta glanced down to find her scissors. "They do know how to sew, although they haven't done any since their parents died. They are catching on quickly, as we've been making some things for the town's needy children."

"That's a wonderful way to teach them to sew," Mrs. Ross stated. She glanced at her daughter, a pretty blond with blue eyes. "That's how Regina honed her skills."

The young woman blushed. "Thank you, Mother." Regina glanced at Marta. "We'll be happy to distribute any clothing you wish to donate. Father always escorts us because he says we shouldn't venture into the poorer part of town alone."

Most of the ladies nodded in agreement.

"How many Christmas baskets are we doing this year?" Lois asked.

Mrs. Ross laid her sewing in her lap. "We did four last year, so we thought we'd add one this time. So five. The Griffiths have kindly offered to put one together, the Tanners and Begleys are each graciously doing a basket, and I thought Regina and I can do one with the items that are donated by our parishioners. If there are extra, we can add them to the other baskets."

"I'm happy to help with the baking for your basket, if you'd like," Alice said.

Mrs. Ross nodded. "Thank you. We would very much appreciate that."

Marta suspected that Reverend Ross and his family didn't have much extra to share. "What if I do the fifth basket? I'm sure the Yates would help. And perhaps the Lawsons would donate something as well."

"That would be wonderful, dear." Mrs. Ross beamed a smile at her. "If you could deliver it to us by the twenty-third, that will give us time to pass them out on Christmas Eve morning."

"What a blessing that will be to the families," Lois said.

Marta marveled that the wheelchair-bound woman was so happy. She couldn't imagine being confined like that. It was a blessing that she had her sister and niece to help her.

With the matter of the baskets settled, the conversation turned to the town thefts.

"Did you hear that the Griffiths were robbed two days ago?" Rachel asked.

Not another theft. Marta's heart clenched. Poor Justin. There were some stern people in town who'd surely talk about firing him if he didn't discover who the thief was. She needed to pray harder.

"Yes, that's why Anita isn't here. She was so upset about the family heirlooms that were stolen that she's taken to her bed."

"I'm sorry to hear that. I was so shocked to learn that the church poor box had been robbed." Alice snipped a thread on the red plaid shirt she was sewing.

Mrs. Ross nodded. "It is sad."

"People should find work instead of stealing from those who have so little." Priscilla Tanner pursed her lips.

"And there was that knife stolen from the store, right out from under Mr. Lawson's nose. Such a shame." Lois shook her head.

Several pairs of eyes turned to Marta, and her heart jolted.

"I heard the Yates twins were suspects." Priscilla looked at her with inquisitive eyes.

Marta's first response was to mention that Priscilla's brother was also a suspect, but she held her tongue. A week had passed, and Justin was no closer to discovering the thief, so he'd said. "I don't believe for a moment that those sweet girls would steal from someone. All I can tell you is that they were looking through the mercantile for an idea of something to buy or make their brother for Christmas. It was my suggestion, because I thought they could work on such a project at my house. I feel awful that they are now being looked at questionably."

"I do the same thing—shop the store for ideas to make." Alice smiled, as if reassuring Marta. "That way I get an idea of the newer styles of clothing. Sometimes I thumb through Mr. Lawson's catalogs. I don't feel bad doing that, since I buy my fabric and other supplies from him."

"That's a good idea," Regina said.

Marta wanted to move the conversation far away from the thefts. "What types of things do you put in your Christmas baskets? I donated a fruitcake and cookies last year, but I've never organized one before."

"We always try to put in a pound of flour and one of cornmeal, as well as some canned goods or jars of things we've canned ourselves. If the donations have been good, we add a half pound each of coffee and sugar. Everything else is baked goods."

"Last year we had an anonymous donation of dressed prairie hens and a couple of geese." Regina glanced at her mother.

"Wouldn't it be wonderful if that happened again this year?"

"Yes, it would," her mother replied. "Also, others in town who can't donate money or put together a whole basket will often donate items on the Sunday before Christmas."

"I remember that." Rachel rose. "Would anyone care for some tea? And we have some delicious pound cake that my aunts made."

The sewing was set aside as tea and cake were served. Next to Marta's time with the twins and the Sunday service, the sewing circle was the highlight of her week. Until the twins and Justin had started coming over, she hadn't realized how lonely she'd become.

What would she do when the girls no longer needed her help?

Chapter 8

On Friday morning, Marta walked into the marshal's office. She'd never been in the jailhouse, even though Pete had worked there for a year and a half. The place smelled of coffee and gun oil.

Justin looked up then shot to his feet with a big smile on his face. "Marta. What a pleasure to see you."

His eyes darted to the small basket she held then back up.

Her heart bucked. He was such a nice-looking man. She'd always been attracted to men with blue eyes. And his pecan-colored hair was so thick with a slight wave to it. "I. . .um. . .wondered if you'd have time to talk about something."

"Of course. As you can see, I'm sitting here twiddling my thumbs. Most of the time my job entails helping ladies with packages, strolling about town making sure everything is peaceful, jailing troublesome drunks—and the occasional pig wrestling." His eyes twinkled.

"Ah yes, the pig wrangler. Does that happen often?"

"More often than I'd like." He stepped around from his desk and gestured toward his chair. "Would you care to sit?"

"No, thank you." She reached into her basket and pulled out a red-checked napkin. "I made cookies this morning and thought you might like a few."

His eyes lit up. "I would love some."

"They're oatmeal raisin. I hope that's all right."

"Perfect." He took them from her, set the package on the desk, and unwrapped it. He snagged a cookie then took a big bite. His eyes closed. "Marta Buckley, you've got to be the best cook in town. These rival the bakery's cookies."

"Thank you." Warmth flooded through her. Pete devoured the treats she made, but he rarely complimented her efforts.

Justin reached for another cookie. "What did you want to talk to me about?"

She shifted the basket to her other hand. "As you know, Sunday is the twins' birthday."

His hand paused right in front of his mouth. His gaze shot to the calendar on the wall beside him. Marta could see that he had circled the girls' birthday, but it was obvious that he had forgotten.

Justin set down the cookie, sat on his desk, and moaned. "I hate to admit it, but I forgot all about it."

She wasn't overly surprised, considering how Pete never remembered hers. "It's not too late. I was wondering if you would like to come over to my house for Sunday dinner. I thought I could bake a cake to celebrate. I'd like to give the girls a gift, but I haven't got one yet."

He ran his hand through his hair. "I need to get them something." He looked at her with panicked eyes. "What should I do?"

"If you have time, we could walk over to the mercantile and look around."

He hopped up. "That's a great idea. Perhaps you could guide me to select something they would actually like. I got them things for the kitchen last year, and that didn't go over so well."

Marta chuckled. "I'm practical enough that I would have loved that, but I think the girls would like something more feminine. Since the twins are in school, this would be a good time to shop. Shall we go see what Mr. Lawson has? I would imagine his stock may be low, though, with Christmas coming."

"If he doesn't have anything, I could ride to Dallas tomorrow and find something."

"I hope you won't need to do that. How are things between you and Mr. Lawson since you haven't found the thief? Did he believe you when you told him your sisters didn't take the knife?"

"Not one hundred percent. I offered to pay for it, but he said no. The Spencer boy is never around when I go looking for him, so we haven't talked yet. Both Abijah Tanner and Pete got angry when I asked them about it."

Marta shook her head. "That's too bad. If they're innocent, they shouldn't get upset. That actually makes them look guilty. I wish I knew why Pete is grumpy so often, but then, he's always been that way as far back as I can remember."

"Me too. But let's not talk about them."

"Agreed."

He put his hat on then held open the door and closed it after she'd walked out.

Marta raked her mind, trying to think what the girls might like for a gift. Ella enjoyed sewing and cooking, but Emma was more of a bookworm. But Marta didn't know what books the girl had. Perhaps an inexpensive piece of jewelry or a new dress for both girls would work for a gift from their brother. Deciding was difficult, since she didn't know how much money Justin could afford to spend.

Marta was relieved when she walked into the store to find it empty except for Mr. Lawson.

The store owner glanced up and smiled. "Miss Buckley. Marshal. What brings you here today?"

"We're looking for something I can get the twins for Christmas." Justin glanced around the store as if it were the first time he'd been there.

"I got some ready-made dresses in this week. There's probably something in their size. I also have a nice stock of jewelry and kitchen accessories. Oh, and doesn't one of them like to read? I have quite a few books, although some are still in the back." He bent down and pulled out his cashbox. "Miss Buckley, I sold that lace you made and got a tidy profit. Here's your share."

"That's wonderful." Marta smiled at the unexpected income. Maybe now she could find something she could afford.

Mr. Lawson handed her a dollar. "Anytime you want to bring in more, I'd be interested."

"As soon as Christmas is past, I'll start making some."

She pocketed the money and returned to Justin's side.

"I didn't know you made lace. You're a woman of many talents."

Marta smiled a thank-you. They looked at the dresses and picked two calicos that Marta thought the twins would like, and then they walked over to look at the jewelry.

Justin bent and looked into the glass-covered case. "Those bracelets are quite pretty, but I think they cost more than I want to spend, especially since I'm getting the dresses."

"What about a necklace? They're less expensive, and I don't recall ever seeing either one of them wear one." She bent down beside him.

The door jingled, and the Begley cousins walked in. Both of them stopped and stared at Marta and the marshal. They suddenly turned and strolled back toward the clothing section, whispering and glancing toward Marta and Justin.

Marta's stomach clenched. What were they thinking? They didn't even bother with a greeting. She tried to focus on the necklaces but felt the need to distance herself from Justin. She walked over to the sewing section.

She wanted to get the twins something special for their birthday. For Christmas, she'd already decided to give Emma a novel she bought for Pete that he never bothered reading, and for Ella, a pattern book of doilies, table runners, and antimacassars.

The girls had their mother's sewing kit, but many items had gotten lost over the years. The store had a nice supply of different sizes of sewing boxes. She settled on two made of dark wood with mother-of-pearl inlaid patterns of flowers and leaves for their birthday gifts. She had enough money left to purchase a small pair of scissors and a needle with a needle holder for each girl. More than a little satisfied with her choice, she carried the items to the counter.

Justin decided on two heart-shaped lockets on chains for his sisters.

"Oh Marshal Yates, they will love those." Marta studied the pretty necklaces. Both had a flower on the front, but one was a rose and the other had a flower with ruffled petals.

Justin smiled. "You think so?"

"I know so. They will be delighted."

"They'll just be happy I remembered. I think I'll give them the necklaces for Christmas and the dresses for their birthday."

He was probably right about remembering the girls' birthday. They had hinted to Marta that their brother wasn't the best at recalling important dates.

After they paid for their purchases, Justin paused and turned back to Mr. Lawson. "Miss Buckley is teaching the twins to cook and sew. If she or they come in to buy the supplies they need, I want you to put it on my account."

Marta gasped. "That's not necessary." Although really it was an answer to prayer. She knew she couldn't keep baking things without buying supplies soon.

"I think it is. You've been so kind to work with them. I don't want you using up your own stock when we're eating more than half of the things you prepare."

Marta glanced back at the Begleys, who made no effort not to stare. What were they thinking? And worse, what would they tell the ladies of Wiseman about what they saw and overheard?

Sunday morning Justin waited for the church aisles to clear before following the twins outdoors. He nodded to the townsfolk who looked his way and chatted with a few. Mr. Griffith, lips pursed, walked up to him as the church was clearing.

"Good afternoon." Justin smiled.

Mr. Griffith shook his head. "It doesn't look like your deputy told you what happened at our house this week."

"What happened?"

"We were robbed while we were visiting at the Langstons' ranch. We left before noon and didn't return until around five."

Justin's gut clenched. Not another robbery. "I'm real sorry to hear that. What kinds of things were taken?"

"Jewelry, my wife's silver tea set, some gold coins I had in a box on my dresser. That's what we've discovered missing so far." The man stared Justin in the eye. They were neighbors, and Mr. Griffith had always been congenial, but not today. "I want to know what you're doing to stop this."

"I've questioned a lot of people, but so far, I have no evidence. Nobody has witnessed the robberies. I can't accuse someone without evidence."

"This has got to stop. It's one thing stealing from us, but what if they break into the Begleys' home? Those old ladies are alone with no one to protect them."

"So far no one has been hurt. I believe the thief is wanting to line his pockets, not harm someone."

"It's only a matter of time."

Justin hoped that wasn't true. He needed to catch the thief, but the culprit had hit at different times of the day. There was no pattern to the thefts. Several houses, the store, and the church poor box.

With a heavy sigh, Justin put on his coat and went outside. After shaking Reverend Ross's hand, he glanced around to see if the twins had waited. He found them chatting with four other young people, including the Spencer brothers.

Justin didn't like thinking badly of anyone without just cause, but something about the Spencer brothers didn't sit well with him. Perhaps it was merely because they had their eyes on his sisters. This was his chance to talk to Barry.

As he walked toward the group, Barry Spencer glanced up. He said something to his brother, and then they waved at the twins and set off down the road.

"Hey, Spencers, wait up." Justin jogged past his surprised sisters. He was relieved to see the boys stop and turn.

"Barry, I need to talk to you."

"I ain't done nothin'."

"Carl, you run along."

"I want him here." Barry hiked his chin.

"Suit yourself. Mr. Lawson says you were in his store with the twins when a knife went missing."

"Well, I didn't take it. I got me a knife. Besides, ask your sisters, since they were there too." Barry didn't have a look of guilt about him.

"I have talked to them."

"Didn't they tell you I didn't take it?" The boy glanced past Justin to where the twins waited.

"They did, but I still had to talk to you. I may have more questions later on."

"My answer will be the same." The boy straightened and looked Justin in the eye. "I'm tryin' to clean myself up like you told me to, Marshal."

Barry looked sincere. And that was the problem. Everyone he'd questioned had looked the same.

Justin nodded. “All right. We’re done here.”

The boys waved at the twins as they walked away.

The girls walked over to him.

“I don’t like you hanging around with those Spencer boys.” Justin frowned.

“We were only talking.” Emma scowled back.

“And they did attend church.” Ella hiked up her chin a tad, as if attending services made them acceptable. “Were you talking about the knife?”

He nodded.

“Barry didn’t take it, did he?” Emma gazed down the road at the boys.

“I can’t talk about my investigation, especially since you two are involved.”

Emma sighed. “Then will you tell us where we’re going to eat?”

Ella looked up at him. “Everything is closed today, so we must be going to someone’s house. But whose?”

He’d kept the party a secret to keep them guessing. Marta had slipped out as soon as the service was over, but he didn’t miss the excited gleam in her eyes as she passed him while hurrying down the aisle. Several ladies had watched him and whispered to each other, but he hadn’t figured out why. “Marta has invited us to dinner in honor of your birthday.”

The girls squealed and clapped their hands.

Justin smiled at their enthusiasm. They started across the town square. “I’m glad to see you approve. I need to stop by the house and grab your gifts.”

“We get a gift too?” Emma asked.

"Don't I always get you something?"

"Not that first year after Mama and Papa died." Emma ducked her head, as if the memory still pained her.

That was something he dearly regretted, but they'd still been in mourning, and the special date had slipped by without him noticing. He'd made sure that never happened again. Although it might well have this year if Marta hadn't asked him about the party when she had. He glanced heavenward. *Thanks for that reminder, Lord.*

The girls chatted about one of their friends while Justin scanned the town, looking for anything out of place. He needed several more pairs of eyes, but the town couldn't afford to hire more deputies. Perhaps he could recruit some volunteers.

At the house, Justin stopped. "Wait here for me while I run in and get your gifts."

"Can't we go on over to Marta's?"

"No. I'd like us to go together."

"Aw. . . I mean yes, sir." Emma kicked a rock.

"I don't see why it matters," Ella said to her sister as Justin went through the door.

He wanted to see their surprise when they discovered Marta had made a cake and also had gifts. He took the wrapped dresses down from the shelf in his wardrobe. Marta had suggested he buy each girl a ribbon to match her dress, which he did. She then tied a bow on each package with the ribbons. Lavender for Emma and blue for Ella.

As he walked outside again, the girls' eyes widened at the sight of the gifts. He wasn't sure what they expected, but it was probably something smaller than the ones he carried.

They quickly made their way next door, and both girls knocked.

Justin lifted his nose and sniffed. His stomach grumbled at the delicious aroma of fried chicken, if his guess was right.

Marta answered with a towel in her hands. "Surprise! I'm so glad you're here. Come in. Things are almost ready."

"It smells wonderful in here." Ella walked into the house.

"That's chicken cooking, correct?" Emma looked as excited as her sister. Both girls walked into the kitchen, obviously comfortable doing so.

"You're a good guesser." Marta turned to Justin. "They look excited. I wish we had thought to invite some of their friends to join us, but then, my house is too small for a group."

"Perhaps next year, when they turn sixteen. So Pete's not joining us?"

Marta shook her head. "I don't think so, not since he's working. He said he'd stop by later whenever he got hungry."

"You think he's not here because we are?" Justin rubbed a hand down his face.

She shrugged. "It's possible, but I'm used to him eating at odd times because of the job. Oh! The chicken." She spun and rushed through the small house.

Justin followed. The kitchen table had been set with a flowery tablecloth. Dishes with tiny blue daisies and blue napkins added to the loveliness. In the center was a lit candle. Marta sure had the knack for prettying up a place that most would find on the pitiful side.

"Good. The chicken is done. If you would all have a seat, I'll serve the meal."

"Can we help?" Ella asked.

"No, thank you. I want you girls to sit down and enjoy yourselves.

This is your special day."

They smiled and took their seats.

"It's not my special day. Can I help?" Justin walked toward her.

"Sure. Take this." She handed him the bowl of steaming mashed potatoes. And he didn't see a single lump in them. How did she manage that? He set them down and returned to where Marta was taking the chicken from the cast iron skillet and putting it on a platter. A big fat thigh called to him.

"That looks wonderful. It's been a long while since we had fried chicken. And it never looked that good."

She smiled over her shoulder then bent down and removed some puffy golden rolls from the oven.

Justin carried the platter to the table, enjoying how the girls leaned forward to sniff it.

Marta handed him a bowl of green beans then carried the rolls to the table and sat. She looked at him. "Would you bless our food?"

Justin nodded. He took hold of Emma's hand and Ella's then bowed his head. "Lord, we ask a special blessing on the girls today and the food and for Marta for preparing such a nice meal. Thank You for Your provision. Amen."

He dug into the wonderful meal. The chicken was some of the best he'd ever eaten. As he ate, he felt a sense of family. Marta and the girls chatted like magpies. With his belly near bursting, he sat back and enjoyed the scene. The twins seemed happier since spending time with Marta.

She hopped up and started clearing the table. He stood, gathered up the plates, and carried them to the counter. He returned for the chicken platter, which held only a wing and a drumstick.

"Would you mind carrying the cake?"

"Of course not."

The twins gasped when they saw the pretty cake.

"What kind is it?" Ella asked.

"Chocolate with boiled icing."

Marta sliced the cake and handed the pieces out then reclaimed her seat.

Justin bit into it and groaned. "This is so good. What did you season it with?"

"Cinnamon and nutmeg."

"It's wonderful." Ella closed her eyes as she savored the cake.

Emma cut another bite. "You'll have to teach us how to make it."

Their cake was soon gone and the table cleared again. "Shall we go into the parlor for the gifts?"

Justin nodded. "Good idea."

In the parlor, the twins sat on the couch. Justin handed each girl her package. "Go ahead and open them."

They squealed and quickly untied the ribbons and then unwrapped the gifts.

"How pretty!" Ella stood and held the dress against herself.

"That's a lovely shade of blue." Marta smiled. "And that lavender looks pretty on you, Emma."

"I love it." Emma smiled at Justin.

He was glad to see her happy again.

"I have a little something for you too." Marta walked over to the mantel and picked up two gifts wrapped in calico and tied with twine at the top. She handed one to each twin.

They quickly removed the twine and fabric, both oohing and aahing over the pretty boxes.

"Look inside." Marta clasped her hands, excitement lighting her eyes.

"Oh, it's a sewing box!" Ella pulled out the scissors.

"There's a needle too." Emma pressed the lid back on the needle holder.

They rose in unison and hurried over to hug Marta and then Justin.

He didn't want this happy moment to end, but it would. As he hugged his sisters, he glanced at Marta, and she smiled. His heart clenched. He was falling for Marta. This sweet scene could be one he came home to every day.

Dare he hope she felt something for him?

Chapter 9

Monday morning, Justin walked the streets of Wiseman, looking for anything abnormal. A week had passed with no robberies. He hoped the thief had moved on, even though he regretted not capturing the culprit.

He leaned against the livery's corral and stared at the horses. Dane McDermott, the owner, took good care of his livestock. Once the weather warmed, he'd have to think of taking the girls riding again. They both loved it.

"Can I help you?"

Justin turned to see the livery owner walking out of the barn with a toothpick in his mouth. The man stopped suddenly, looking surprised for a quick moment, then moved with a normal expression. Instantly on alert, Justin studied him. Why should McDermott be surprised that he'd stop by?

Dane was a quiet man who kept to himself for the most part. Other than at church services, Justin couldn't ever remember seeing him at any of the town's activities. But some men were shier than others, so he'd never thought anything about it—until now.

Justin smiled. "You sure have good-looking mounts."

McDermott tossed his toothpick away. "You in the market for one?"

"Not today. But once the weather warms, I'd like to take the twins riding again."

"Just let me know. I'll have my gentlest horses waiting."

Justin chuckled. "The twins would probably prefer faster mounts, but I don't think their riding skill is ready for that."

McDermott nodded. "That's usually the way of things."

Justin studied the man, who looked away from his stare. "I wonder if I could ask a favor of you."

The man's head snapped back. "Me?"

Justin nodded. "I noticed that you often ride around town, exercising your horses. Because I can't be everywhere at once, I'm having trouble stopping the robberies that've been happening. So I'm asking a few men to help."

McDermott straightened. "What do you need me to do?"

"Just exercise your horses as normal, but maybe take different routes and keep an eye out for anyone who looks suspicious."

The man actually cracked a brief smile. "I'd be happy to do that, Marshal."

Justin stuck out his palm. "I'm obliged."

Lips pursed, the livery owner shook his hand.

"I guess I'll mosey along then." Justin pushed his feet into motion. McDermott seemed nice, but there was something in his gaze that Justin couldn't shake. He sure hoped he hadn't just asked the thief to keep a watch out for himself.

Perhaps what he'd noticed was nothing. Lots of folks felt funny around lawmen, even prime citizens. Then again, maybe he needed to look at some of his older wanted posters.

He returned to his office to do just that. He'd barely got his coat off when Pete stormed in.

"What's the matter?" He hadn't seen his deputy since Friday.

Pete scowled. "I want to know what's going on with you and my sister."

"You know. She's teaching the twins—girly stuff."

"It looks to me like you and Marta are getting mighty friendly."

"So? I like her."

Pete poked his index finger in Justin's chest. "You leave her alone."

Justin grabbed the finger and pushed it back. "Why?"

Pete blinked. "Because."

"That's no reason. I like Marta. A lot."

Pete stomped over to the coffeepot and poured a mugful. He swigged a big drink. "Don't you think it'll make things awkward between us?"

"Not if you don't make it be that way."

The deputy slammed down the cup. "Well, I don't like it. Besides, you oughta be keeping watch on your own sisters, not mine. I've seen them all over town lately, even with those Spencer hooligans. I'm still not convinced one of them isn't the thief." He stormed through the small office and slammed the door, acting like a naughty child.

Justin sat down. The girls had been out with the Spencers?

More than that day at the store? He would definitely talk to them about that.

And why had Pete reacted so to his interest in Marta?

Elbow on his desk, he rested his cheek in his hand. What should he do now? He'd been tossing around the idea of asking to court Marta. Pete certainly wouldn't give his consent, but would that matter to her?

Justin walked into the mercantile. He glanced around, glad to find the place empty. Mr. Lawson walked in from his storage area, carrying a crate. He set it on the counter and looked at Justin.

"You have any luck catching the thief?" Henry pulled something covered in brown paper from the crate and began unwrapping it.

Justin resisted the urge to squirm. "Not yet, but I have several men helping to keep an eye out. I'm hoping the thief will get sloppy since he's gotten away with his bad deeds so far."

"He? So you've ruled out your sisters?" Henry set a clear candy jar on the counter and tossed the paper on the floor.

"I talked with them, but I honestly don't believe they stole the knife. I can tell when they are lying, and they were genuinely surprised when I confronted them about it."

"Maybe. But it could be that you're too close to the situation and aren't the right one to be conducting the inquiry." Henry shuffled his feet then stared at Justin again. "Did you. . .um. . .ever look through their stuff? You know, in case they were hiding something?"

Justin stiffened. He respected his sisters' privacy, and searching their dressers and wardrobes seemed a breach of trust. But it was his job to find the thief, even if it turned out to be one of his sisters. "No, but I will, just to give you peace of mind."

"I'd appreciate that. I honestly hope it turns out not to be them."

"Thank you."

Justin left and headed straight home. The girls had been excited this morning because they would be baking the goods for the Christmas basket at Marta's this afternoon. They had gone straight to her house after school, but they would be home soon. There was no better time than now. He mainly wanted to rule them out, because he was certain he wouldn't find a thing out of the ordinary.

As he walked into Ella's room, his conscience got the better of him. This wasn't right, but he'd pretty much promised Henry. Taking a steadying breath, he opened Ella's top drawer and rifled through her unmentionables. There was nothing out of the ordinary other than some dried flower petals.

He finished each drawer, leaving things as close to how they were when he found them as possible. The immense relief at finding nothing was nearly overwhelming. He checked her wardrobe and came up empty. As he walked out her door, he thanked the Lord.

Emma's room was messier than her sister's. He started with the jewelry box on top of the dresser. All he found were two necklaces that had belong to his mother and the cross on a chain Pa and Ma had given to each girl on their tenth birthday.

Next he looked through her drawers. Finally, he pulled out the bottom one. He lifted up a stack of Emma's summery shirtwaists and froze. He blinked, unable to believe what he saw. A fruit knife with a bird on the side, a gold necklace with an oval sapphire, and a gold bracelet.

Justin dropped to the floor and stared at the items. He couldn't believe it. Why would Emma steal? Wasn't she happy? Didn't she have all that she needed?

She'd been much less grumpy since she'd started working with Marta. He thought she was happy.

He ran a hand down the side of his face. Would he have to arrest his own sister? *No, Lord. Please.*

The front door rattled, and Justin jumped up. How long had he sat there in a stupor?

The girls entered, chatting about one of their school friends.

God, give me wisdom. Short of burying his parents, Justin had never done anything so difficult. He walked out of Emma's room.

The twins quieted and stared.

"Why were you in my bedroom?" Emma demanded.

"I decided I needed to know for sure if you were the thief, and I found out." He opened his hand, revealing the knife, necklace, and bracelet.

"Where did you get those? So you found the thief?" Emma looked happy. Not at all what he had expected.

"You know good and well where I found them."

Emma blinked and looked at Ella. She hugged her schoolbook to her chest. "What are you talking about? I've never seen those before."

"I found them in your bottom dresser drawer."

Emma took a step backward. "What? No. I was serious when I said I haven't seen those before."

"Really, Justin. Emma's no thief." Ella championed her twin. "We're always together, so when could she have taken those things? Not that she ever would."

Tears made Emma's eyes glisten. "I can't believe you think so badly of me to believe I would ever steal from our friends."

"I didn't, until I found these. If you didn't take them, how did they get in your drawer?"

"I don't know!" She dropped her book and fled to her room, slamming the door.

"You know she didn't do this." Ella eyed him like his mother had when he was young and had done something wrong. "I feel the same as Emma. How could you believe her capable of stealing?"

He sighed. "I don't know what to believe."

"Can I go be with her?"

"Go."

She picked up her sister's book and joined Emma in her room.

Justin dropped onto the couch, confused. He held the evidence in his hand, but his sister's eyes didn't lie. He'd seen the utter shock in them when he confronted her.

So what should he do now?

Justin stood on his front porch, his gut churning. He ached to believe Emma, but if she was innocent, how in the world did the stolen goods find their way to her room?

He needed to talk to someone. Get another perspective. He started for Reverend Ross's house, but when he reached the edge of the yard, he turned toward Marta's house. His head told him to go to the parsonage, but his heart needed Marta.

He knocked on her door and was rewarded with a big smile when she answered.

Marta's grin dipped. "What's wrong?"

"Is Pete home?"

"No. He's almost never here unless he's eating or sleeping."

"Good. I need to talk to you."

"Of course. Come in." She stepped back then closed the door once he was inside. "Would you care for some coffee and pie?"

"Not today."

"Let's sit in the parlor." She led the way and took a seat on one side of the settee.

Instead of settling in a chair, Justin lowered himself on the other side of the settee. He took off his hat and placed it on the scratched drum table on his right.

Marta waited patiently, although she clenched her apron in both hands.

He gazed at her. "You already know that Mr. Lawson thinks one of the twins took that knife. Today he asked if I'd discovered who the thief is. When I told him I hadn't, he asked if I'd searched the twins' rooms."

"No, Justin. He has no right to ask that."

Justin sighed, wishing he'd told the man as much. "I took up his challenge, thinking to prove once and for all that the girls were innocent. But I found this." He pulled the stolen items from his coat pocket and laid them on the seat between them.

Marta gasped then looked up with wide eyes.

"They were in Emma's bottom dresser drawer."

"I can't believe it. She's been doing so well lately. Both girls were excited today to bake cookies for our Christmas basket. We have it ready to go. Thank you for being so generous buying those canned goods. I don't suppose the girls remembered to ask if you would take the basket to the parsonage. It's a bit heavy for me to carry it that far."

"I don't mind, but I need to decide what to do about Emma. I have to treat her like any other criminal."

"Surely you're not thinking of putting her in jail."

His gut tightened. "I am. It's what I'd do with anyone else. I'm the marshal, Marta. How can I not consider it?"

"For one, Emma is a female. It's hardly proper to put her in jail. And two, you're not even positive that she's guilty."

"I can't overlook it completely."

Marta touched his sleeve. "What did you do when you caught Jacob Callen snitching apples from the store last summer?"

"That's different. It was an apple, not someone's jewelry. And he was only nine or ten."

"Emma is older, but she's still just barely fifteen."

He squeezed the back of his neck, trying to release some of the tension.

"What if the thief had been one of their friends? What would you have done then?"

"If it had been a girl, I'd probably leave her in her parents' custody and have her make some kind of amends."

Marta offered a weak smile. "See, I think you have your answer."

He jumped up and started pacing. "No, I don't. I'm the marshal, and I have to enforce the law."

She rose and came to him, reached out and took his hands. "Why don't we pray about what to do. God will show you."

"How do you know? He didn't spare my parents when the girls needed them so much. Why should He let Emma off?"

Marta squeezed his hands, becoming his lifeline. "You can't know how many times I've prayed for God to help me live with Pete. You of all people know how crochety he can be. I'm still here, and I haven't beaned him over the head with my skillet yet."

Justin's lips turned up at the image. "This is a bit more serious."

"I know. Let's pray about it, all right?"

He nodded and closed his eyes.

"Dear heavenly Father, Justin is in a difficult situation, and he needs Your help and wisdom. We ask that You show him clearly what to do about Emma. Also, please help him find the real thief, because I'm sure it's not that sweet girl. We trust and believe in You. Amen."

Justin cleared his throat. "Lord, I'm in a rough situation here. I need guidance and wisdom. You know my responsibility to this town and to my sister. If Emma is not the thief, I ask that You help me catch him—or her."

Justin gazed down at Marta, unshed tears stinging his eyes. She reached up and placed her hand on his cheek.

"It's going to be all right. We'll get through this, and one day it will be a distant memory."

He leaned into her touch. "I sure hope you're right."

Marta blushed as if suddenly realizing how bold she'd been. She lowered her hand, but he reached for it.

"Once all of this is over, you and me are having a talk." He bent down and placed a quick kiss on her lips, grabbed his hat, and walked out.

Chapter 10

Marta stood at the front window and watched Justin stride away. She touched her lips, amazed at how wonderful her first kiss had been. Although she had lost her heart to Justin years ago, she'd never truly believed that he could come to care for her.

Perhaps he'd kissed her because he was grateful for her prayer. She hoped that wasn't the only reason. But she'd learned long ago not to get her hopes up.

If it turned out that Emma was the thief, Justin's life would take another troublesome turn. As he reached the street, he stopped suddenly, spun around, and jogged back to the door.

Heart stampeding, she opened it. Had he come back for another kiss?

His lips quirked to one side. "I forgot the Christmas basket."

"Oh. Yes. The basket. It's in the kitchen." Disappointed, she hurried through the small house and reached for the crate.

"That's not a basket."

She smiled. "No, it isn't. We couldn't find one big enough to hold everything. Thus, the crate."

"There's an empty spot on the right. Should I stop by the mercantile and buy something to go there?"

"That's for the meat. We're hoping the person who anonymously donated the birds last year will do the same this Christmas."

Justin nodded. "That would be nice. If they don't, let me know. I could ride out to one of the ranches and see if they have any hens they could sell."

Marta laid a hand on Justin's upper arm, trying to ignore the bulge of his muscles as he picked up the crate. "That's very kind of you."

He smiled, but there was still a hint of sadness.

"Try not to worry about the situation with Emma. The truth always comes out."

"I sure hope so, and soon." He stared at her for a long moment, and then he glanced toward the front door. "I reckon I should get a move on."

She walked him to the door then grabbed her cloak at the last minute. "I think I'll walk over to the church with you. I want to see if anything else is needed for the baskets."

As Marta walked beside him through Wiseman, she was dying to know what he wanted to talk about. Dare she hope he wanted to come calling? Why hadn't he just asked her when they were alone?

Too soon, they reached the parsonage. Marta knocked, and Regina answered.

"Oh good! Come on in." She backed away. "Mother, another basket has arrived."

Mrs. Ross hurried out of a side room. "Wonderful. We only need one more, and we'll have all of them."

"Could you please place it on the kitchen table?" Regina indicated the way, even though it was obvious in the small house.

"I was wondering if you need anything else for the other baskets." Marta followed Justin and Regina.

"I don't believe so." Regina tapped her fingertips together, her eyes dancing. "This morning we found a bag on the porch that held two geese and three turkeys. There was a separate bag with our name on it that held another turkey. Wasn't that kind of our generous benefactor?"

"It was extremely benevolent." Mrs. Ross walked into the already full room. "I wish we knew who donated so we could thank him or her, but I know a reward is stored up in heaven for that person."

"I'm sure it will be." Justin nodded. "I should be going. It's time I did my rounds."

"We were hoping you might stay for coffee." Mrs. Ross smiled.

"Thank you, but I really should get going. Another time, perhaps?"

"Of course. Just stop by. I know Mr. Ross would love to chat with you."

Justin glanced at Marta then tipped his hat to the ladies. Regina saw him to the door.

"Would you care for some tea or coffee?" Mrs. Ross asked Marta.

"That would be lovely. Thank you." Marta was glad for a diversion from her confusing thoughts of Justin and disturbing ones of Emma's predicament.

Regina put the water on to boil. "The marshal didn't seem his normal friendly self today."

"He has a lot on his mind with all of the robberies." Marta followed Mrs. Ross into the parlor and sat.

Mrs. Ross glanced into the kitchen, where Regina was placing cookies on a plate. "There's talk about town that the two of you were looking at rings at Lawson's."

Marta sucked in a sharp breath. "Oh no! I was helping him find Christmas and birthday gifts for the twins. I'm sure everyone knows I've been helping the girls with their cooking and sewing skills."

The older woman nodded. "Such a kind thing to do. Just be careful to always be above reproach. You know how tongues wag in such a small town."

Marta well knew how quickly rumors traveled. She had never been so thankful that she lived at the end of the street. At least no one should have noticed Justin arriving and leaving on his own earlier, not to mention them kissing.

"I'm sure everything is fine, but I wanted you to be aware of the rumors so you'll be extra careful."

Marta ducked her head, embarrassed to think she and Justin were being discussed throughout the town. "Thank you. I will." Though she very much enjoyed talking to Justin alone, she'd have to make sure not to invite him in again if Pete or the girls weren't there.

On Thursday morning, the day before Christmas Eve, Justin rode his horse along the streets of Dallas. With the girls at school and then going to Marta's to bake afterward, he had just enough time to visit Logan Jennings, a marshal who was his friend. He stopped in front of the marshal's office and dismounted.

He walked into the office, and a man he didn't recognize looked up from the lone desk. The man's gaze shifted to Justin's badge.

"How can I help you, Marshal?"

"Is Logan around?"

"Back here," came a loud shout.

The man at the desk pointed to a side door. "He's in his office."

Justin walked to the door, and Logan rose with a grin on his rugged face. "Good to see you, kid. What brings you to my neck of the woods?"

Justin shook his friend's hand. "In case you haven't noticed, there's not much woods left in these parts."

"Don't I know it. The city just gets bigger and bigger. Have a seat and tell me what's been happening in Wiseman."

"It's not good. I need some advice."

"Happy to help." He held up a finger. "Richard, bring us two cups of coffee, will ya?"

Logan didn't wait for a response and waved at Justin. "Go on."

Justin told his friend about the thefts and how Mr. Lawson thought one of the twins stole the knife, and then he told him about finding some of the items in Emma's dresser.

The clerk brought the coffee in then left, and both men took a sip.

"That's quite a story. I can see why you'd be concerned. Do you honestly believe your sister stole those things?"

"That's just it. I don't. The look on her face when I confronted her was absolute shock. Neither of the twins can lie well and rarely bother anymore because I can usually tell. But if she didn't, then who did, and why would they plant the loot in my sister's room?"

"That's easy. They must have a vendetta against you. Can you think of anyone?"

"Not really. My deputy has had a burr under his saddle since I beat him out as marshal, but he isn't a thief. There are a couple of adolescent boys I've chased away from my sisters. I've wondered if they were the thieves, but my gut says they're just rowdy boys."

"Anyone else?"

"Not unless the boys' father is angry with me, but he hardly ever comes to town." Justin took another swig.

Logan scratched an ear. "It's a dilemma for sure."

"I think the main thing I need to ask you is if you think I should put my sister in jail."

Logan actually grinned, which caused Justin to frown. "What's so funny?"

"I can imagine the tongue-lashing you'd get from her and the other twin. There'd be no peace for you." He chuckled.

Justin failed to see the humor of the situation.

"How old is she now?"

"Just turned fifteen last weekend."

"Plenty old enough to know better but too young, I think, for jail. My suggestion would be to make sure she's supervised as much as possible. With her being a twin, I imagine the girls are generally together, right?"

He nodded.

"Are they still in school?"

"Yes, but today is the last day until after the new year."

"If you have someone who can stay with them when you're working, that would be the best thing. If not, ask the other sister to make sure they're always together. And keep her home as much as possible—house arrest." Logan scratched his jaw. "I also think I would keep this quiet, for the most part, until you know one way or another."

Justin clenched the arms of his chair. "And what if I never know for certain?"

Logan leaned back in his chair. "That's a tough one. I'm not sure I have an answer. You might confer with a judge."

He'd actually thought of doing that while in town, but it wasn't usually possible to see a judge without an appointment.

"You got time to eat some lunch?"

"A quick one. Thank you for your suggestions. I think I'll see if I can talk with a judge while I'm here, but with it being almost Christmas, I may not find one that's at his office."

"Try Bartholomew Evans. He's fair and honest. If you can't see him today, you might go ahead and set up an appointment for after Christmas."

"Good advice."

Logan rose, and Justin did also. Logan slapped him on the shoulder. "Don't worry too much. As a lawman, I'm sure you're a good judge of character. I'll keep all of this in my prayers and trust God to reveal the truth to you."

"Thanks. I appreciate that more than you know."

As they walked out onto the busy street, Justin felt better than he had in weeks. Knowing he didn't need to put Emma in jail was a huge weight off his shoulders.

On Christmas Eve after the service at church, Justin and the girls walked Marta home. She had invited them for dessert, and she wanted to give the girls their Christmas gifts.

Justin looked forward to the time with Marta and to the food. He prayed more than ever about the thief and asked God to reveal who it was. He was trying not to worry and to leave it in God's hands.

After the birthday party, Emma had returned to being reserved, but Ella chattered away about the young children who'd sung two songs during the Christmas Eve service.

They tromped inside Marta's house and removed their outerwear. Justin inhaled a sweet scent of something he was sure would be delicious.

In the corner of the parlor on the drum table sat a tiny Christmas tree decorated with a chain of popcorn and several ornaments made of felt. Guilt nibbled at him for not putting up a tree this year for the girls. "Pete's not here?"

Marta shook her head. "He's working, although I don't know who would cause mischief on Christmas Eve."

"You never know, but for the record, I told him to take the weekend off." Justin eyed her over the twins' heads.

"Well, come on into the kitchen. Everything is ready."

Justin watched Marta remove a towel from a platter of ham slices, cheese, and crackers. "Wow, we didn't expect such royal treatment."

Marta smiled. "It's just a little snack. It's been awhile since supper. I also have apple dumplings."

"I love those. Oh hey." Justin snapped his fingers. "I bought some apple cider for tonight, but I left it at home." He rose from the table. "Y'all go ahead and start. I'll run over there and get it."

"You don't have to," Marta said.

"I want to." Justin strode toward the door and didn't even bother with his jacket. He trotted next door but slowed his steps when he noticed the lantern light in Emma's room.

He had always instructed the girls to blow out their lanterns whenever they weren't in their rooms. He was certain they'd all been out when they left for church earlier.

The cold nibbled at him. He jumped over Marta's short fence and crept to the window. Peeking through an opening in the curtains, he saw someone's shadow moving on the wall, illuminated by the light.

He gritted his teeth, wishing he had his gun, but he never wore it to church. He crept to the back door because the front porch steps creaked. Slowly, he opened the door and quietly crossed the kitchen and dining room. Light from Emma's room illuminated the doorframe. His heart pounding, he moved across the parlor to the front door and pulled his gun from his holster where it hung on the coatrack.

Had the thief returned to plant more evidence?

He paused at Emma's door and peeked in. A tall, thin man wearing a bandanna over the lower half of his face squatted down in front of the dresser. He pulled a handful of jewelry from his pocket, dropped it in the drawer, and pushed it closed. Then he rose.

"Hold it right there."

Instead of complying, the man charged Justin, head down. Both hit the ground. They wrestled for control, but Justin had a good thirty pounds on the stranger. Justin rolled the man over and slammed his fist into his face. The man punched Justin in the ribs, and he sucked in a breath. Justin clenched his fist and clobbered the man two more times. Relief flooded him as the man relaxed.

Justin pulled the mask from the unconscious man's face, and Pete's image was revealed in the moonlight shining through the parlor window. He sat back, stunned. All the times Pete had accused the twins now made sense. He'd been setting them up, making them look bad and causing Justin to question what he knew to be true.

Poor Marta. This would devastate her.

Justin untied the bandanna and used it to tie Pete's hands. He lifted the man over his shoulder and carried him to the jail. With Pete locked up, he returned to Marta's.

She met him at the door. He tugged her outside, and she gazed up with a question in her eyes. "What took you so long?"

"I don't know how to tell you, but when I went home, I found Pete planting more jewelry in Emma's dresser."

Marta gasped and lifted a hand to her mouth. "Oh Justin, I'm so sorry."

"You're sorry?"

"Yes. Pete framed Emma to look like the thief. How could he do such a thing? I never would have thought it possible."

"Me either. I thought I'd wait and tell the girls after we get home. What do you want to do about our little party?"

"We need to finish it. And I think you should tell them now. Emma deserves to know as soon as possible."

"All right. She'll be so relieved."

Marta turned as if to go in, but Justin grabbed her arm. "I know this is going to make things hard for you. But I want you to know that I've fallen hard, and I'd like to court you if you're willing."

"You have?" Marta said, with wonder in her voice.

"So much that I'd like a short—very short—courtship."

"How short?" She reached up and laid her hand on his chest.

"Two months?"

She shook her head. "That's too long, if you're asking my opinion."

Justin grinned. "Two weeks?"

"How about one month? A girl needs time to plan a wedding."

"One month it is." He leaned down. "I love you, Marta. I don't want you to worry about a thing. Pa left me with some money, and I'm happy to buy whatever you need for your dress or whatever a gal needs for a wedding."

"That's mighty kind of you, Marshal."

He chuckled and pulled her close. Then he bent down and kissed her. She fit into his arms perfectly and returned his kiss with a vigor that made him wish she'd agreed to wait only two weeks.

The door suddenly opened, and they broke apart, both breathing heavily.

The twins stood in the doorway, staring. Then they looked at one another and started squealing and jumping up and down.

"I told you," Ella shouted.

"You were right." Emma smiled, but her sullenness quickly returned.

Justin felt sure his ears were red. "Let's go inside. Marta and I have something to tell you."

"You're getting married, right?" Ella smiled.

"Yes, but that's not the really good news."

The girls stared at him like he'd gone loco as they returned to their seats at the table.

"Emma, when I went home to get the cider, I found Pete planting more jewelry in your dresser."

Her eyes widened. "Pete was in my room?"

Ella jumped up from her chair and hugged her twin. "Don't you see—you're off the hook. That proves you aren't the thief."

A wide smile engulfed Emma's face. "What a wonderful Christmas present! I've been afraid you'd put me in jail."

Justin moved to her side. "I'm sorry I ever doubted you, sweetheart. I never truly believed you were capable of stealing, even when the evidence was there."

"Thank you." Emma rose and hugged him around the waist. "I love you."

"Love you too." He pulled Ella into his arms. "I love all three of you."

The girls pulled away, grinning, and rounded the table to hug Marta. Finally, they returned to their seats, and Marta served the apple dumplings.

After they finished dessert, Marta cleared the table. With tingles of excitement racing through her, she handed the girls the gifts she'd gotten them. She passed a gift wrapped in brown paper to Justin. "Go ahead. Open them."

The girls ripped open their presents.

"I love this." Ella caressed the pattern book.

"I haven't read this book. Thank you, Marta." Emma smiled at her.

"You're welcome. I'm glad you like them." She looked at Justin. "Your turn."

He grinned and slowly untied the twine.

"Hurry up," Emma squealed.

Enjoying seeing her happy again, he prolonged the torture, very slowly unwrapping the paper. He spied blue fabric. "A shirt. I really like the color." He shook it out and admired it. "How did you know my size?"

"I guessed. I used one of Pete's for a pattern and made it bigger with longer sleeves. The blue looks good with your eyes."

She'd noticed his eyes? "You're a thoughtful woman."

The girls giggled. Then Ella pushed a package toward Marta. "It's from Emma and me. We hope you like it."

Marta's eyes danced as she opened an embroidered picture of flowers with the Bible verse Jeremiah 29:11. "It's lovely, and that's one of my favorite verses. Thank you so much."

Justin relished seeing the females in his life so happy, but he had a prisoner to see to. "It's time for us to go. You girls head on home. I need to talk to Marta then run back to the jail and check on Pete."

"You need to 'talk'?" Ella's eyes twinkled.

"Oh sure." Emma pushed to her feet.

They both hugged Marta then hurried out the door.

"I hate to bring up something so unpleasant after our nice evening, but I need to check Pete's room and see if the rest of the stolen items are there."

Marta pursed her lips. "I understand. Would you mind bringing the lantern?"

He did and followed her to one of the two bedrooms. "Do you mind if I search through his things?"

She shook her head then stepped back.

Justin set the lamp on top of Pete's dresser and looked through each drawer. The man didn't have many clothes. The top drawer held several boxes of bullets and a spare gun, as well as several socks. He searched the whole dresser but didn't find the jewelry. He blew out a sigh and looked around the sparse room. Pete didn't have a wardrobe. His clothes hung from three hooks.

"Any idea where he might have stashed the stolen goods?"

She glanced down. "I'm not supposed to know, but he has a locked box beneath his bed."

Justin set the lantern on the floor and looked under the bed. Sure enough, there was a metal box. He pulled it out and shook it, hearing the clink of metal against metal. "What about the key?"

"I don't know. Can you break into it?"

"Do you have a hammer and a screwdriver?"

"Yes." She spun to the door and returned in a minute then handed Justin the tools.

He knelt on the floor, inserted the screwdriver in the crack below the lid, then pounded three times with the hammer. The lid popped open, and jewelry, gold and silver coins, and paper money fell out onto the floor.

Marta gasped. "Where did he get all of that money?"

"I imagine he either stole it or sold some of the jewelry. I don't think this is all that was stolen, but it's a good chunk." Justin picked up a peso and pursed his lips. "Reverend Ross said there were some pesos in the poor box when the money was taken."

"I can't believe Pete robbed the church and our neighbors and tried to blame Emma. My heart aches, and I'm so embarrassed."

Justin rose and came to her side. "Don't be. Pete made his own choices."

"I know, but it's still hard. I'm so thankful my parents aren't alive to see this."

Justin gathered up the stolen goods and put them back in the box. "I need to go check on your brother. Try not to worry. I'm sorry things turned out like this."

She nodded. But she dabbed her moist eyes.

He set the box down and took hold of her hands. "I love you and don't want you hurting. I wish I could take away your pain, because I certainly know what you're feeling." He let go of her hand and reached into his pocket. "I know this isn't the best time for gifts, but I have something for you too. I wanted to give it to you in private because I wasn't sure of your response before—although I am now."

Marta lifted a brow. "I'm curious."

He held out a small box. She took it, raised the lid, then wrinkled her forehead as she stared at the gold letters and chain. "MY?"

"It stands for Marta Yates."

She gazed up in surprise.

"I got it while I was in Dallas yesterday. I know it was a risk, but I really was hoping you felt like I do."

"It's perfect. I will cherish it forever." She leaned forward, and he caught her.

Justin bent down and kissed her, showing how much he'd grown to care for her. He loved holding her close and feeling her soft skin. He wanted to protect her from the pain she would surely endure in the coming days, thanks to her brother. But all he could do was encourage and comfort her. Before he was ready, he stepped back. "I'd really like to continue this, but I'd better not. For now."

Marta looked at him with an ornery gleam in her pretty brown eyes. "I've been thinking. . .how do you feel about getting married in two weeks?"

He grinned. "I think it would be perfect. And you won't have to wait as long to wear your necklace."

"You're a wise man, Justin Yates."

He leaned in for a final kiss. At the door, he turned to her. "Join us for Christmas tomorrow?"

"Only if you let me cook something."

"Nope. The girls already have something planned. Just come and enjoy."

"Very well. I'll look forward to it."

He squeezed her hand and trotted down the steps into the cold night. Two months ago, he'd never have guessed he'd be marrying his next-door neighbor. The past few years he'd been busy caring for his sisters and keeping watch over the town, never thinking much about marriage. But God had blessed him with a wonderful surprise—and she'd been right next door the whole time.

The Spinsters Next Door

by Susan Page Davis

Chapter 1

Wiseman, Texas
November, 1886

"I don't see why we can't furnish the place with things from the attic." Rachel Jones gazed about at the spotless but empty parlor.

Aunt Lois frowned. "The furniture in the attic over at the big house is too fine. If we're going to rent this place out, we can't expect the tenants to take as good care of it as we would."

"I don't see why not, if we rent to nice people," Rachel said.

Aunt Lois turned her wheelchair toward the parlor window. Her sister, Rachel's aunt Priscilla, was outside working her way steadily across the front porch, sweeping away dead leaves and dust. She looked like a raven in her black worsted dress.

"Ask Priscilla. If she thinks it's all right, then fine." Aunt Lois flicked her dustrag over the windowsill. She had helped Rachel and

Aunt Priscilla all day as they cleaned the little house that stood next to their large, gracious home. From her wheelchair, she was able to scrub woodwork and dust everything less than four feet off the floor.

"All right, I'll see what she thinks." Rachel usually deferred to her aunts, even though she was now legal owner of both houses. She stepped to the door and pulled it open. A tall, dark-haired man of about thirty was just climbing the porch steps.

"Good afternoon," he said with a glance from Rachel to Aunt Priscilla, who was now at the far end of the porch.

"Mr. Worth." Rachel felt a little breathless at the unexpected encounter. "May I help you?"

"I thought I'd stop in on my way home when school let out. I saw Miss Tanner out here sweeping, and Billy Griffith told me you were thinking of renting out this house. If that's so, I thought maybe I could put my name in as a possible tenant."

"Oh." Rachel smiled. Billy was the son of their neighbor on the other side of the big house, and he was a student at the local school where Mr. Worth was the schoolmaster.

"Unless you've already made arrangements with someone else," Mr. Worth added quickly.

"No, we—"

"We're not ready yet." Aunt Priscilla strode across the plank floor, frowning.

"Oh well. . ." He looked helplessly at Rachel.

"Maybe you could stop by in a day or two, when we've finished cleaning and furnishing the house," she said.

His face cleared. "I'll do that. But you know I'm interested."

"We'll keep you in mind," Rachel said.

"Thank you." With a perfunctory nod at Aunt Priscilla, Mr. Worth turned away.

Aunt Lois had wheeled over to the doorway and peered out at them. "Was that the schoolmaster?"

"Yes." Rachel stepped inside. "He seems like a nice man, and he's interested in renting from us. And we haven't even advertised yet."

Aunt Priscilla followed her in, carrying the broom. "I was hoping we could get a couple of nice ladies in here. We'd have some company then. Neighbors we could be friendly with."

"Why couldn't we be friends with Mr. Worth?" Rachel asked.

Aunt Lois waved a hand through the air as though dismissing her question. "You know how your father was about having men come around, dear."

Rachel's heart sank. Had her rash actions as a youngster doomed them all to a drab existence devoid of men?

"But he's respectable," she said. "And he would take care of the furniture."

Aunt Lois shook her head. "He's a penniless schoolmaster, Rachel. We don't want to rent to him."

"Why not?" Rachel asked. "It's true we don't know him well, but he seems nice enough. The Callens' house is too crowded for him to board there. I expect he has trouble finding a quiet spot to grade papers, since he often has to go over to the schoolhouse in the evening." She stopped. Had she said too much?

Rachel had met Mr. Worth on the street a fortnight past as she hurried home from the mercantile. When she greeted him, he had paused to speak for a moment, telling her he was just going back to the schoolhouse to catch up on some work. But that was before she and her aunts had decided to rent out the little house to supplement their meager funds. She hadn't told her aunts about the encounter, and if they learned about it now, they would set their minds even more against the teacher.

"Well, he does go to church every Sunday," Aunt Priscilla said.

Rachel turned to her, watching the old woman's wrinkled face for any sign of support. "You used to teach, Aunt Pris. You know how important it is to have quiet time to prepare lessons and read the students' papers."

"Yes, but this Mr. Worth is new in town. We don't know anything about him. Where is he from? Who are his parents? Is the school board pleased with his work?"

"It's too soon to tell that," Aunt Lois said. "He's only been here a couple of months. But we could ask him about his family. Maybe ask for references."

Rachel nodded. "Yes, and we could ask Mrs. Callen if he's been a good boarder."

"She might not like him moving out." Aunt Pris's eyes sparked. "The families get a stipend when they board the teacher now, you know. It's not like in the old days, when I had to move from house to house and it was considered the parents' contribution to good education in the township. I didn't stay in one home more than two weeks at a time."

"That must have been trying," Rachel said.

Aunt Pris smiled. "I admit it was sometimes a relief to know I only had to put up with the current situation for a fortnight. Then I'd be moving on."

"Abijah voted against Mr. Worth when he was on the school board," Aunt Lois said flatly.

"What?" Rachel stared at her. "Why?"

"I wasn't privy to his objections. Something in the schoolmaster's past, I expect."

"Now, Lois," Aunt Priscilla said, "our brother wasn't the easiest man to get along with. You know that. It's true he wasn't pleased when the majority of the board members voted to hire Mr. Worth, but he always voted against Mr. Frankle, out of spite. If the reason had been important, the board wouldn't have chosen him."

Aunt Lois clamped her lips together. She wheeled her chair around and surveyed the empty parlor. "We should settle what we're going to do about furnishings. Then we can discuss who will live here."

"There are two armchairs in Father's den, besides his desk chair," Rachel said.

"Oh, but those were Abijah's chairs. A matched set. We can't split them up." Aunt Lois looked at her sister.

"Well, the only seats over here are two straight chairs and a stool. The boarder must have something comfortable in his parlor," Aunt Priscilla conceded. "Perhaps Rachel and I can go up and look at the things in the attic tomorrow morning. I'm too tired to climb all those stairs now, and we need to start supper."

That settled the question for the moment, and Rachel prepared to help Aunt Lois get back to the main house. She brought the stool from the kitchen to the porch and helped the older woman out of the wheelchair to perch on the stool. Aunt Lois wasn't entirely helpless, but she hadn't been able to walk since a childhood illness. Aunt Priscilla waited with her until Rachel had moved the wheelchair down the porch steps, and then they both supported Lois down the steps and into the chair.

Aunt Priscilla was panting by the time they had Lois settled and had smoothed down the skirts of her mourning dress. Rachel pretended not to notice, but she knew the aunts were getting frailer. Priscilla was sixty-eight, and Lois had just passed her sixty-first birthday. Abijah had been the youngest sibling but had died two months earlier at fifty-eight.

Rachel knew it was up to her to continue supporting the aunts, as her father had done for many years. She had always assumed he would continue to do so for the rest of their lives, and apparently the aunts had too. *How swiftly things change*, Rachel thought as she pushed the wheelchair to the ramp her father had built on the big house from the sidewalk up to the spacious side porch.

Renting out the little house that had once been home to Abijah and his young family seemed like a logical next step since they had next to no money. Rachel had inquired around town about jobs but had found nothing suitable for a respectable woman. The school needed only one teacher.

She and the aunts had begun sewing shirts and aprons for the general store and private customers, but so far the income from that didn't even pay for their food. If it was supplemented with a fair rental fee for the small house, they might get by.

Rachel couldn't help thinking that renting to an intelligent, polite, handsome gentleman like Mr. Worth would make their poverty much more pleasant.

Stephen left the small house and ambled up the street. He was disappointed that he hadn't been offered a peek inside. From the outside, it looked like a perfect little home for him.

Rachel had seemed amicable, but the older woman had harbored some resentment. Did they think he wouldn't make a good tenant or that he wouldn't be able to pay the rent on time? Or was it something personal about him that bothered them?

He had met the aging Tanner sisters through church, as well as their niece, Rachel. He understood that the big Victorian-style house the three women occupied had belonged to Rachel's father. She must be widowed. He'd heard her referred to as Mrs. Jones but had seen no evidence of a Mr. Jones. She was the right age to have elementary school children, but none by the name of Jones were enrolled in the Wiseman school. He supposed she might have toddlers or a baby, but he hadn't seen those at church either.

He should stop thinking about her, though that was difficult after seeing her up close, her face flushed and wisps of her golden hair escaping her kerchief. She was a beautiful woman. And she seemed friendly, though not overly so. When he'd spoken to her on the street the other night, he'd sensed a reserve about her, but that just made her more attractive. The small Texas town had few eligible young women, and the ranchers and cowboys in the vicinity seemed to snap them up quickly. Stephen would have to keep his eyes and ears open to see if Rachel had a husband, because if she didn't, she would be worthy of pursuit.

He paused at the post office. He wouldn't have any mail, but checking in would postpone his return to the bulging Callen house. If John Goodwin, the postmaster, wasn't too busy, they could have a chat, always entertaining. John was his best friend so far since he'd come to Wiseman.

The post office was no bigger than a wardrobe. John had petitioned to move it out of the general store a year ago. He'd told Stephen that separating the mail from the merchandise gave the patrons more privacy and helped save John's sanity. Apparently the storekeeper had a tendency to hang about the post office counter far more than was comfortable for John.

"Howdy, Steve," John called out when he entered.

"Good afternoon." Stephen took off his hat, though he was sure John wouldn't mind if he kept it on. Mother's training was hard to break.

No one else was in the tiny room, and John was sorting a handful of letters. He set them aside and turned to check the pigeonholed shelves behind him. "Nothing for you today, I'm afraid."

"I didn't really expect anything." Stephen rarely received mail, unless it was from the state's superintendent of public instruction in Austin, advising him of some new regulations or explaining why he wouldn't be getting more state funding for the Wiseman school this year.

That was all right. Stephen was making do with what the previous schoolmaster had worked with last year. He was used to not rating top consideration, having grown up in the shadow of a much-loved older brother. When he decided to go into teaching rather than law enforcement, his whole family had demoted him to Least Appreciated. In school he always took third place in academic competitions, behind the Biddle twins—smart girls, it was true, but lacking in grace when it came to winning. True beauty lies within, Stephen had always been taught, but would it have hurt Bessie and Liz Biddle to have a little on the outside, since they were so self-absorbed inwardly?

"How's school?" John leaned on the counter and smiled. Stephen took that to mean he was ready to talk for a few minutes.

"Going well, for the most part. The pupils are enjoying our

readings about the Pilgrims from Bradford's history, *Of Plimouth Plantation*."

"Are you going to do something special for Thanksgiving?"

"You mean a program?"

John nodded.

"I wasn't going to. Is that customary?"

"No, just wondered."

"We'll save it for Christmas, I think," Stephen said. "I've spoken to Pastor Ross about what the children can do during the Christmas Eve service at the church, and we'll also present a short program at school on the last day before we close for the holidays."

"Sounds good."

"Thanks." Stephen eyed him keenly and ventured to ask, "Have you heard anything about the Tanners?"

"What do you mean?"

"One of my students said they might rent out the little house beside the big one."

"Oh, the old family place. I'm surprised they haven't sold it by now. Didn't want neighbors that close, I suppose." John shrugged. "I'll keep my ears open."

"I, uh, stopped by this afternoon. Mrs. Jones and her aunts were cleaning the place. But Miss Priscilla Tanner said they weren't ready to rent. I told them I'd be interested."

"That would be a good location for you," John said. "Now that Rachel's father has died, I'd think they'd benefit from having a man live nearby."

"Just the three ladies, then, living in the big house?"

"That's right. Abijah died a couple of months ago."

"So. . ." Stephen cleared his throat. "Rachel. . .she's not married then?"

"Funny you should ask," John said. "I know there *was* a Mr. Jones, but I think he's dead. Winthrop, if I remember correctly. No, Winfield—that's it. I asked one of the Begley ladies once, and she said he died shortly after they got married. Something tragic, I guess. People don't talk about it." John shook his head. "I would have been pretty young when she married him, and I don't remember the circumstances. It would have been ten or twelve years ago. I never dared ask any of the family about him."

"But she's been living there with her aunts for a while?"

"Yup, and her father. He was an odd bird. Pretty strict. Rachel's a nice lady though. I got the feeling that if any man wanted to spark her, he'd have to get through her daddy first. Or maybe she loved her husband so much she never got over her broken heart when he died."

"Hmm." The door opened, and Stephen looked up to see a genuine cowboy enter. The small post office seemed even tinier with the lanky man towering in the doorway, complete with broad-brimmed hat, high-heeled boots, and spurs.

"Hi, Fred," John said.

"Howdy, John. Anything for the Bar-G?"

"Yup, let me get it."

"I'd best get home," Stephen said. "I'll see you, John."

"Bye, Steve."

Stephen nodded to the cowboy and sidled past him to the door. When he opened it, a matronly woman in a claret wool dress was about to enter.

"Ma'am," Stephen said. He held the door for her then put on

his hat and set out toward the Callens' house. He would eat supper with the burgeoning Callen family and then go back to the schoolhouse to read through a sheaf of essays, but his mind was back at the little house down the street. If John was right, Rachel Jones's husband had been dead a decade or more. Her watchdog father was gone now. Would the merchants and cowhands line up at the door of the Tanner house once the strictest mourning period for her father was over?

If only he could gain the status of closest neighbor and tenant. Not only would he be much closer to the schoolhouse, but paying the rent each month would give him an excuse to go to the big house. Maybe he could strike up a friendship with Rachel.

He was dreaming. As he approached the Callens' whitewashed house on Pine Street, he frowned. An affluent, lovely woman like Rachel Jones would never choose him. Not only did she have the memory of her deceased husband to deal with, but Stephen would have to tell her about his past failures. Her father had been a forceful man too, from all he'd heard. If she ever married again, she would want a strong man. She would never settle for a man like him.

Chapter 2

Rachel bore most of the settee's weight as she and Aunt Priscilla half dragged, half carried it to the top of the attic stairs.

"Rest now," she called, and they lowered the bulky item's legs to the landing floor.

"Heavens, I don't know if we can get it down two flights without a mishap," Aunt Priscilla gasped, lifting her apron to mop her face.

"We might hire someone to help us for an hour," Rachel suggested.

Aunt Priscilla snorted. "You know our funds are dangerously low, dear. Even that would be a splurge."

"Well. . . You really shouldn't be doing this."

"Hogwash."

Rachel looked around the dim attic, frowning, then brightened as an idea surfaced. "If we told Mr. Worth he could rent from us, he might be willing to help move the larger pieces of furniture over to the little house."

"Well, I don't know."

"He might even get one or two of the bigger boys from school to help." Rachel swatted at a smear of dust on her black sleeve. "I hope I can clean this dress well enough to wear it to church tomorrow."

"You ought to have a change of mourning," Aunt Priscilla said.

"Yes, but as you mentioned, money is tight. I should have put on an old calico for today's cleaning bout."

"It wouldn't be proper, with your father dead only two months."

Rachel sighed. Though no one would see her wearing a scandalous non-black dress in the house, she might be viewed by anyone passing on the street when she and Aunt Priscilla scurried back and forth to the rental house.

She would be glad when they could lay aside their mourning attire, and not just for her own sake. Her aunts were so much prettier in their regular clothes—Lois in her pastels and Priscilla in bright cottons and silk blends. She was sure there were plenty of women in Texas who disregarded the old "rules" they'd known back east. Many of the ranchers' wives and daughters probably didn't own a black dress.

But Aunt Lois and Aunt Priscilla were old-fashioned, no matter how you looked at it. Rachel could only hope that they would let her start wearing grays and lavenders after six months had passed, but she feared she was in for a year of solid black. When her mother died, she and the aunts wore unrelieved black for twelve months.

But she was a child then. Rachel had never had the opportunity to mourn her husband, so she had no proper attire that fit her except this one dress she'd hastily made. If they stood by the tradition this time, Aunt Pris was right—she needed another dress or two.

"I suppose we'd best go down and discuss it with Lois," Aunt Priscilla said.

"All right." Maybe they would agree that having Mr. Worth as a tenant was not such a bad prospect. The aunts always had to hash over everything. One of them could not make a decision without the other's approval. If they didn't agree, nothing changed. Sometimes Rachel had to curb her frustration sharply when it came to her aunts. If only she dared to straighten her spine and say, "That house belongs to me, and as the landlord, I will decide to whom I will rent it."

But she couldn't do that. She had made one major decision on her own, and she had paid dearly for it. Aunt Pris and Aunt Lois were her elders, her wise counselors. Besides, she loved her aunts dearly. She wouldn't want to do anything that would hurt their feelings—Rachel was done with that.

Aunt Lois met them in the kitchen doorway, propelling her chair with her hands on the wheels.

"I thought I heard you coming down. The Begley cousins stopped in while you were upstairs. I asked them to have tea, but they said they had to get over to the doctor's office. They only stopped for a breather."

"That's quite a walk for the two of them," Aunt Priscilla said.

"Well, they sat down on the front porch for a few minutes to chat."

"To gossip, you mean."

Aunt Lois frowned at her sister. "Serinda has a medical concern, and they wanted to rest before continuing to the doctor's."

"She didn't tell you what's wrong?" Aunt Pris asked.

"No."

"That surprises me. Must be something embarrassing."

Rachel ignored the conversation and checked the icebox and the bread cupboard. "There's leftover pork loin and some squash and corn bread. Shall we make our dinner of that?"

"That's fine," Aunt Priscilla said, heading for the dish cupboard.

Aunt Lois turned her chair around. "I was going to say that I asked them about Mr. Worth."

Rachel and Aunt Pris turned to gaze at her.

"What did they say?" Rachel asked.

"They've heard he's doing a good job at the school. Phyllis said the school board all like him. Of course, Serinda had to mention Abijah's resistance to hiring the man." Aunt Lois's face pinched up. "She never can say anything good about him, even though he's passed on, God rest his soul."

"Miss Serinda and Father never got along," Rachel observed, taking the platter of pork out of the icebox. "But I do think we'd do well to let Mr. Worth move in next door. He's in need of lodging, and he has a steady income."

"I admit I was surprised the Callens took him in." Aunt Pris shook her head. "Nine children."

"I don't know where they put them," Aunt Lois agreed. "Probably stack them up like cordwood at night."

Rachel suppressed a smile. "If we took Mr. Worth in right away, it would be settled. But if we told him no, we'd have to advertise for another boarder. That would be awkward, don't you think? He'd wonder why he wasn't suitable—and now the Misses Begley would wonder too."

"It might take some time to find the right person," Aunt Pris said tentatively. They all knew the extra income was needed now. Rachel waited, not daring to speak.

"Oh, let's ask him," Aunt Lois said. "Rachel could take him a note."

"Nonsense." Aunt Pris scowled at her sister. "We'll ask him at church in the morning. There's no need to go fluttering about town as if we're desperate to get a man into our tenant house."

"I suppose you're right," Aunt Lois said.

"Of course I am. Come and fold the napkins, dear. I'll help Rachel get the rest of the food on."

Rachel exhaled and kept her expression serene. As she went to the icebox, she breathed a prayer of thanks.

Stephen could hardly believe it when Rachel Jones approached him in front of the church after the worship service let out.

"Good day, Mr. Worth." She smiled, and her face seemed alive and happy, as though she expected something good to happen today.

"Mrs. Jones. Wasn't that a wonderful sermon?"

"Heartfelt. I always find Pastor Ross's messages profound and yet practical."

Stephen nodded. "That's a good description of his preaching. Er—" He looked toward the church door. Mr. Griffith and the pastor were preparing to help Miss Lois Tanner down the steps to her waiting wicker wheelchair. "Are you ladies well?"

"Yes, we are," Rachel said. "In fact, we've come to a decision."

"Oh?" His heart fluttered. Was it possible they had considered his inquiry?

"If you are still interested in becoming our tenant, we would be happy to discuss the matter with you. In fact, if you have no plans for dinner today, we would welcome you at our home."

Stephen often had dinner invitations on the weekend, but today his only prospect was tough chicken shared among himself and the eleven Callens. There would be a potato for each person and perhaps some canned string beans or a spoonful of carrots from the root cellar, but there never seemed to be enough to fill up the nine growing children, let alone a spare schoolmaster. He was always reluctant to ask for seconds, knowing the serving dishes would be empty before they reached him a second time.

"That sounds delightful."

Rachel smiled, and he thought the impending good thing had made its appearance—for him, anyway, if not for her.

"Just give us a few minutes to get home and get Aunt Lois up the ramp. I see she's ready now. She doesn't like a fuss about her condition, so we'll go on ahead."

"Certainly. And thank you." He nodded, and she turned away. Stephen followed her progress to her aunts' sides and found that Miss Priscilla was eyeing him fretfully. He lifted his hat and gave a slight bow. She nodded in return.

Rachel, by this time, had grasped the handle of the invalid chair and was pushing Miss Lois toward the street. They made a striking picture, the three ladies in black. Rachel would have to push the chair the length of the town square and around the corner, but it wasn't really that far for a robust young woman. Still, he wished she had let him help. Maybe later, after Miss

Lois knew him better and was comfortable with his presence. He turned back toward the church. Two of his students' fathers were discussing the possibility of a cold snap. He strolled over to join them.

Not only had Rachel's aunts consented to taking Mr. Worth on as a renter, but they had served him an incomparable Sunday dinner, with Rachel's help. She had stretched the food budget to provide a pot roast, and everyone in Wiseman knew Aunt Priscilla's gravy could not be beaten. Add mashed potatoes, turnips, Rachel's graham bread, and succotash, followed by the best dried apple pie west of the Mississippi, and the schoolmaster was sated.

"My, my, that was a delicious dinner, ladies," he said, laying down his napkin at last on the damask tablecloth that had belonged to Grandmother Tanner. "I don't know if I'll have the energy to move furniture for some time."

"Oh, we won't move it today," Aunt Priscilla said primly.

"Not on Sunday," Aunt Lois added.

Mr. Worth dipped his head. "I beg your pardon. Shall I bring a couple of the older boys by after school tomorrow, to help transfer the pieces you mentioned?"

"That would be fine," Aunt Priscilla said.

Rachel smiled at him. "We've picked out a small settee that would go well in the parlor over there, and we'll send over a couple of side chairs. Also, there are several bedsteads in the attic. Perhaps when you and the boys arrive, you can pick out the one you like best."

"Or he could take the three-quarter bed from the spare room,"

Aunt Priscilla said. "We know there's a featherbed that fits that one."

"Whatever is most convenient for you ladies will be fine, I'm sure," Mr. Worth murmured.

Rachel wondered if he was embarrassed to be discussing with three women what he would sleep on. Surely he wasn't that bashful. She sneaked a glance at him, and he shot a half smile her way. Immediately he rose a notch in Rachel's estimation. He was only trying to accommodate the aunts, something she had spent years doing. Stephen Worth might turn out to be the perfect renter if he understood how delicate elderly ladies' sensibilities were.

"I don't know as I like the idea of boys poking through our attic." Aunt Priscilla's brow furrowed in distaste. "We've all manner of family relics up there."

"Perhaps Mr. Worth could tour the attic this afternoon," Aunt Lois said.

Rachel gazed at her in surprise. "Why, yes, Aunt Lois. That might save a good deal of time tomorrow."

"There." Aunt Lois nodded at her sister. "Rachel can take him up, and he can choose a bedstead and a chest of drawers. He can see if he likes the settee as well."

"I suppose so." Aunt Priscilla frowned, still a little doubtful.

"And when they come down, we'll have coffee ready in the front room." Aunt Lois seemed happy to be the one making the plans. Rachel reached over and pressed her hand.

"That's a lovely idea, Auntie. I'm sure it won't take us more than twenty minutes to seek out the right furniture for Mr. Worth. And I can have it all dusted by the time he comes to move it tomorrow."

"It sounds practical to me." Mr. Worth looked at Aunt Priscilla. Did he sense that she could squelch Miss Lois's idea with a withering look and a sour remark? Rachel thought he did.

But Aunt Priscilla nodded. "All right. Why don't you go on up there now? And, Rachel, take a lantern so he can see well. The sun doesn't reach all the corners from the end windows. Those things under the eaves might be hard to see without extra light."

Rachel pushed back her chair before anyone had a chance to change her mind.

"If you're ready, then, Mr. Worth, come with me."

He followed her up the two flights of stairs.

"Lovely house," he said midway across the upstairs hall.

"Thank you." Rachel opened the door to the attic stairs and reached for the lantern hanging inside. She felt just a bit giddy, as though she were setting off on an adventure. Showing the attic to a handsome gentleman was certainly a rare occurrence for her.

"Oh, let me get that." Mr. Worth took down the lantern and held it while Rachel lit it, and they ascended the steps in its warm glow. At the top she paused, waiting for him to gain the level floor and look about.

"Oh my. You *do* have an accumulation."

"Decades' worth. This is the settee we had in mind." Rachel touched the carved back of the upholstered piece they had left near the head of the stairs.

"That will do nicely."

"Of course, you haven't seen the house yet," Rachel said. "Perhaps I should have given you a tour first."

"After we're done here?" The lantern light reflected in his brown eyes gave him an eager air.

"Certainly. Now, the bedsteads are over here."

"Do you think they'd prefer that I take the one from the spare room?" he asked. "Please be honest."

"Hard to say. Whenever Cousin Elizabeth visits, she sleeps in there. It might be best to take one of these. Otherwise, the aunts and I would have to move down another and put it together for the guest bed."

"All right, let's see what you have here then."

"I think there are three," Rachel said. "One's rather ostentatious. But that mattress over there—under the muslin shroud—should fit any of them. And the first bedroom in the small house is quite roomy."

"There are two?" he asked, his eyes flickering as though she'd given him a prize.

"Yes, and the smaller room might make you a good study."

"Marvelous."

His pleasure was obvious as he surveyed the options, almost as if he were picking out furniture in a large store. He chose a plain maple headboard and the matching footboard. They made sure the side rails fit and carried them over near the settee. A dresser soon followed.

"Now, what else?" Rachel asked, brushing back a loose lock of her hair. Mr. Worth smiled, and she wondered if she'd just smeared dust on her cheek. "There's a small kitchen table and a couple of straight chairs over there. I thought perhaps you'd like an upholstered chair or two in the parlor, with the settee, but the only ones up here are horsehair and dreadfully uncomfortable. I'm sure you can use my father's chairs from his study, if I coax Aunt Priscilla a bit."

"Oh, don't ruffle any feathers on my account," Mr. Worth said. "You're already being more than generous."

"Nonsense. The house should come furnished. You'll want a nightstand, a small table in the parlor, and a lamp or two. Yes, lamps. Let's see. . . ." She turned toward the far end of the attic, near the south window. "I think there's one over here that's quite pretty. A brass base. Yes, here it is." She held it up in triumph. "The shade must be in that box."

Mr. Worth seemed quite taken with the lamp. She would make sure he got a couple of doilies from the linen cupboard to protect the tabletops.

When they had collected all the items he would let her press on him, they descended to the first floor. Aunt Lois was seated in her push chair in the parlor, with the cups set out before her, and Aunt Priscilla came through from the kitchen with the hot coffee on a tray.

"There, now, Lois, if you'll pour. . ." She set down the tray and took a seat on one end of the sofa. Rachel sat down beside her, and Mr. Worth took one of the stuffed chairs.

"Did you find some suitable things?" Aunt Priscilla asked.

"Yes, thank you," Mr. Worth said. "The furniture is quite lovely. The boys and I will move it all tomorrow."

"I thought I'd give him a quick look at the house after our refreshment," Rachel said.

"Of course. He must be eager to see it," Aunt Lois said.

"I am." Mr. Worth accepted the cup of coffee she handed him. "Thank you."

"Have you thought about perhaps letting him take Pa's leather-covered chairs from the study?" Rachel asked, looking as ingenuously as she could at Aunt Priscilla. "We didn't find any parlor chairs upstairs that weren't a bit moth-eaten." What she really wished was that she could offer the new tenant Father's desk. It was the only desk in the house, and Mr. Worth would love it. But she knew without mentioning it that her aunts would never consent to that.

"Well, I don't know." Aunt Priscilla frowned, but Aunt Lois shook her head.

"Now, Pris, there's no reason Mr. Worth shouldn't use those chairs. We never sit in them, and I'm sure he'll take good care of them."

"I assure you I would," he replied, passing Rachel her cup, "but if you'd rather—"

"Nonsense," Lois said. "They're just sitting there."

Aunt Priscilla took a sip of her coffee and eyed her sister over the rim. Rachel held her breath until she lowered the cup and said, "Very well. You see to it, Rachel."

"Thank you, Auntie. I will."

No more was said about the chairs until they had finished their coffee, and then Rachel helped clear the dishes away and snagged the key to the study off the rack by the dry sink. She returned to the parlor and spirited Mr. Worth away from the aunts' conversation about the morning worship service and took him down the hall to Father's study.

"We keep it locked," she explained, fitting the key into the keyhole. "Don't ask me why. I think it's rather silly, but the aunts seem to think it's proper now that my father is gone."

Mr. Worth said nothing. She straightened, swung open the door, and stepped back so he could enter first. He strode into the room and looked about. The light from the two tall casements revealed the domain of a wealthy man. Expansive mahogany desk, matching swivel chair, Turkish rug, lamps with handblown glass shades, velvet drapes the color of rich wine, and glass-fronted bookshelves filled with sets of leather-bound volumes. Paintings on two walls depicted a spirited sea battle and a Texas landscape inhabited by a herd of mustangs.

"What a wonderful room," Mr. Worth said. "Your father must have enjoyed his time in here."

"He did. Sometimes he'd disappear in here for hours." Rachel walked to one of the matching chairs that faced the desk. "When I was a girl, sometimes I would knock on the door, and if he said, 'Enter,' I would come in, and he'd let me sit in one of these chairs. They're the ones I spoke of, by the way. I always felt very grown-up sitting in one."

"They're very nice. I can see why your aunts are particular about them. If you think—"

Rachel waved a hand before he could imply that he wasn't worthy of the chairs. "It's fine. I, for one, will be pleased to know they're in use again."

"Well, thank you. And I'll try to make as little disturbance as possible when I bring the boys to move things."

She nodded. "Thank you. Maybe someday their grief will abate enough to open this room and make use of it." Her hand drifted to the surface of a small carved box that sat on a side table near the leather chairs.

"What's that?" Mr. Worth asked. "It's a pretty thing."

Rachel looked down at it. The dark cherry lid was inlaid with lighter-colored woods around the border, and in the center the head of a lion was carved.

"Just a box of my father's. He always had it in here, as long as I can remember. I used to pet the lion."

Mr. Worth smiled, looking quite young and ready to share a new adventure.

"What's in it?"

"I have no idea."

"What?" He eyed her closely. "You've lived here in the house with it all your life, and you don't know what's inside?"

"No. Perhaps some of Father's papers."

"But surely your aunts must have opened it after he died."

She shook her head. "They didn't want to. He'd kept it locked for years, and they felt it would be disrespectful."

They stood in silence for a moment. She watched his face. Did he think that was silly? Probably. She found it troublesome herself, but she loved her aunts dearly. If she didn't mention it, after a while they might be open to a suggestion of exploring the box. And if not, then she could wait.

"But surely," Mr. Worth said, "they would want to know. I mean, in the process of settling his estate—"

"You are mistaken." Rachel raised her chin. "I was my father's sole heir. This house and the one you will occupy both belong to me now. And so does this box. I choose not to open it."

Chapter 3

Within a few weeks, Stephen was comfortable in his new home, enjoying the fine old furniture, the freedom to relax, and the elbow room the little house gave him. He certainly slept better here than at the Callens' house, where he'd occupied a bottom bunk in a room with two boys.

He had also made progress, he felt, in winning over the spinsters next door. He had hardly been home from school twenty minutes one chilly afternoon when a brisk knock came at the door. He smiled as he walked across the parlor to open it. He could always tell Rachel's knock. It was livelier than Miss Priscilla's but not so pell-mell as the schoolboys'.

She stood on the front stoop wearing her dark green woolen coat accessorized by a knitted maroon hood and scarf. The only times he'd ever seen her in anything but black were when she wore her outerwear on cold days. She looked beautiful—but immediately Stephen felt vaguely guilty for having the thought.

Her hands, gloved in the same rich hue as her hood, held a bulky wooden frame with the back turned toward him. Snowflakes fluttered around her, landing on her shoulders and the top of her head, and she snuggled the frame closer to her, as though to protect it.

"It's spitting snow," she said. "I ought to have waited until tomorrow, but I couldn't stand it. I found the painting I told you about."

"Come in." He swung the door wide for her. "I hope you didn't spend a lot of time looking for it."

"It bothered me, once we'd talked about it. I couldn't sleep last night, wondering where Father had put it."

Stephen recalled the conversation vividly, over tea with Rachel and her aunts. He reached for the frame. "Let me take that. It must be heavy."

"It's not so bad as the big gilt frame Great-Grandfather Tanner is in." She surrendered her burden with a smile. Stephen carried it to the settee, placed it carefully upright on the seat, and stepped back to have a look. "Oh, I like it."

"I thought you would." She came to his side and stood admiring the picture with him. "Ever since you mentioned that you once had a beagle, and you spoke of him with such affection, I've wanted to find it."

"Yes, he looks very much like Mr. Spot." The painting showed a sweet-faced black, white, and tan dog curled up on a rug near a fireplace. The master could not be seen—only his boots were shown in the picture—but Stephen had the impression that this dog was only content when the man was near.

"Father wasn't much for dogs. I suppose that's why he took it down. It hung in his study when I was small. I missed it, and I wondered where it went, but then I forgot about it." Rachel smiled up at him. "Until you came. I found it up in Aunt Lois's closet, way up on a shelf she can't reach. Why it was there, I've no idea. I asked her, and she didn't remember it being there."

"But she didn't mind if you took it?"

"Not a bit," Rachel said. "In fact, she said that if you like it, you're welcome to it, and she hopes it makes this house feel like home."

"Thank you. I shall hang it over the fireplace. I'm sure it will remind me of Pennsylvania."

"Now I must go," she said briskly.

"Oh, can't you stay for a cup of tea?"

"Not without the aunts, I'm afraid." Her expression darkened, and she said in a conspiratorial whisper, "People would talk."

"Heavens, yes. Wouldn't that be something?" She answered his smile, but Stephen knew she was only half joking. Gossip about the schoolmaster was a sure ticket to dismissal, and he supposed that as a respectable young widow, Rachel couldn't afford to tarnish her reputation either.

"Besides," she said, "the sewing circle meets this afternoon and I'm expected there, and you probably have a lot of work to do. But come to our house after school tomorrow. We'll hold tea for you. Now, I really must get along."

"I'll look forward to tomorrow afternoon. And do extend my thanks to Miss Lois, and to Miss Priscilla too, if you think it appropriate."

Rachel's smile lit her whole face. "I will. Farewell, Mr. Worth."

She was out the door before he could say anything more, and he stood for a moment in the doorway, watching her wool-swathed figure recede into the swirling snow. What was it about Rachel that intrigued him so? It wasn't just her looks, though she was very pretty. Was it her graciousness? Everyone liked Rachel, and she always deferred to her aunts, though she was the one who owned their home and provided for them. Why hadn't some man snapped her up as his wife? It seemed illogical that a smart, kind, lovely woman like her would remain widowed for years. Was she still holding her deceased husband's memory so dear that she wouldn't even consider another man? And did every man in town know this? He supposed it could be an unspoken rule—nobody approaches Rachel Jones with romance in mind.

No, she hadn't given him that impression at all. In the weeks he'd lived next door to her, she hadn't been at all standoffish. In fact, she'd been friendly and helpful. She had treated him almost as a sister would, and yet with more respect. Stephen very much liked the way Rachel acted toward him.

But there was another layer to her personality, an air of mystery that seemed to follow her wherever she went. Maybe that was what kept the others away. Or maybe some had tried and been gently turned away.

He sighed and stepped back into the cozy little house. The puzzle that was Rachel stuck with him as he fixed his supper and settled down to prepare tomorrow's lessons.

Tea with Mr. Worth was an event to look forward to. The aunts had come around and admitted they enjoyed having an intelligent man to converse with on occasion. His knowledge of literature and history especially pleased them, and Aunt Priscilla was apt to lead him down a path of debate about some book they had both read and to recommend other volumes she was sure Mr. Worth would enjoy. Aunt Lois told Rachel she felt secure with an able man living so nearby. Apparently she wasn't taking Mr. Griffith, their neighbor on the other side, into account.

They had sipped their tea and munched Rachel's oatmeal cookies while they discussed the neighbors, the pastor's current sermon series, and Lew Wallace's novel *Ben-Hur*.

The teapot and cookie plate were empty, and the sunlight streaming through the parlor window drew lower.

"Aunt Lois, that sun is shining in your eyes," Rachel said. "Let me adjust the drapes."

She rose and pulled them together until Aunt Lois's face was bathed in kind shadow.

"Thank you, my dear."

"I'll take the dishes out," Rachel said, gathering their cups.

"Allow me to help." Mr. Worth rose and picked up the tray laden with teapot, cream pitcher, sugar bowl, tongs, and spoons.

"Oh, I hope you're not leaving yet, Mr. Worth," Aunt Lois said. "I was going to ask if you'd read Stevenson's *Travels with a Donkey*."

"Why, yes, I have, Miss Tanner. Perhaps we can discuss it when next we meet. I should get home and grade the pupils' mathematics exams." He followed Rachel down the hall and into the kitchen.

"Thank you," she said as she carefully set down her load of china. "Just set it there on the worktable, if you please."

"You are kind to your aunts," he said.

Rachel looked up from her task. "How do you mean?"

"I've noticed how solicitous you are of them, that's all. Today is not the first time."

"It is they who are kind to me." After all, Rachel thought, they were the only ones who knew her full story and still loved her. A change of subject was in order, she decided. She picked up a paring knife she had left on the counter earlier. "You know, when I was a child, I thought these were Perry knives—the name, you know, like Commodore Perry."

Mr. Worth smiled. "Why not? Like the Bowie knife."

"Exactly. I don't know how old I was when I figured out that it meant the knife was suitable for paring fruits and vegetables."

He laughed. "I have questions too, like you and the Perry knife—riddles to solve, when perhaps I've misinterpreted a situation."

"Oh?"

"Yes. May I ask you something?"

"I don't see why not," Rachel said.

"Well, I'm not sure the aunts would approve if they could hear me."

That tickled her. She often chose her words with care when the aunts were present. "Ask away, Mr. Worth."

"All right, if you will call me Stephen."

Her hands stilled, and she looked at him directly, trying to sort this out. "So your question is of a personal nature."

"Very. If you don't wish me to go on—"

"Oh, you may go on, but you should call me Rachel if we are going to speak on that level."

Something sparked in his eyes, and his shoulders straightened a bit. A dread fell over Rachel at once. Was she being too familiar with this man? She had actually sounded coy in her own ears. No, no, no. She mustn't encourage him. Could she take back what she had said? But he had already begun to speak.

"All right then. Here it is: I don't see why some man hasn't claimed you yet. I asked John Goodwin, at the post office, and he said he thought you'd been widowed many years. So I wondered. . ." He eyed her anxiously. "Forgive me if I've overstepped the bounds. Perhaps I shouldn't have spoken, but I hoped you would be agreeable to having me call upon you. Besides the teas with the aunts, I mean. Oh dear." He fell silent, and she knew her expression had given away her dismay.

Her heart was pounding. How very awkward. He was new in Wiseman. Of course he wouldn't know, although why would she think *of course*? It was a wonder John Goodwin or the town gossips or even his students hadn't told him of her state.

She drew in a careful breath and met his gaze. "I'm sorry, Mr. Worth. Perhaps I should have told you, but the truth is, I've enjoyed your company, and I didn't wish to put a damper on our pleasant conversations. I hope we can continue to be friends. But the postmaster is wrong. I am not a widow."

Chapter 4

Stephen couldn't help it. Whether he was writing arithmetic problems on the chalkboard or listening to his pupils read aloud or correcting the older children's essays, his mind drifted to Rachel.

How many ways could a married woman without a husband not be a widow? One moment, he supposed Mr. Jones was a sailor—a naval officer, perhaps—and only came home every couple of years. But surely the postmaster would know that. Another moment, he considered that maybe Jones was in the army. A Cavalry trooper might stay away for long periods of time and only make occasional visits home.

That probably wasn't it either. He didn't like to think it, but probably Rachel and her husband had decided to live separately, for whatever reasons. The thought saddened him. At least there didn't seem to be any fatherless children moping about. A worse thought struck him. Maybe *Mr.* Jones had the children with him, wherever he was. Maybe he and Rachel were even divorced, though that was a situation the town gossips would surely know about. There was no delicate way to inquire. As distasteful as he found the idea, he thought he could overcome his repulsion if he knew Rachel was not at fault.

"Mr. Worth?"

He jerked back to the present—his classroom.

"Yes, Billy?"

"I finished the reading selection, sir."

"Yes, of course." Stephen lifted the Third Reader and glanced at the next reading then at the clock on the wall shelf beside his desk. "That's all for today, class. We'll continue tomorrow."

It was nearly time to dismiss the children. He stood and began to give out assignments.

When he released the pupils, young Sarah Carr lingered behind.

"Teacher, my ma said to invite you to dinner tonight. She's making fried chicken."

"Why, thank you, Sarah." Stephen did a quick mental calculation of where the Carr home was and how long it would take him to walk there. A bonus was that he didn't think the Carrs had any eligible young women for whom they were trying to find husbands. When he ate in townsfolks' homes, he often found that the mother had ulterior motives in asking him. He smiled at Sarah. "Tell your mother I accept."

The little house next door sat in darkness until well after seven that evening. Rachel looked out the window several times, wondering where Stephen was having dinner tonight.

She chided herself for her curiosity. His social activities were none of her business. But still, she yearned to know him better. She ought to have explained to him the other day, when he asked about her husband. But his question was so unexpected that she wasn't prepared to answer it fully. Winfield was out there somewhere, and she couldn't let a hopeful young man think otherwise, could she?

For the first couple of years after her husband walked out of her life, Rachel had imagined the day he would return. What she would say, how she would act, even what dress she would be wearing. In some of her daydreams, he came to her humble and apologetic, longing to win her back. In others he was arrogant and demanding, and she sent him away. Sometimes she refused to see him and delegated Father to turn him away, and Father had been very good at such tasks. But that was in the painful time when she still felt something for Winfield. She had long ago given up hope that he would come back.

Stephen Worth seemed to be a steady, fine man—almost the opposite of the man she had married. The schoolteacher had spent a couple of evenings discussing education theory with Aunt Priscilla, a former teacher herself, and he had brought Aunt Lois some calico remnants from the mercantile to use in her quilting, one of the old woman's favorite pastimes. To Rachel, he was always courteous and friendly, with a glint in his eyes that told her he was eager for a closer relationship. If Father were here, he would no doubt run him off, but Rachel didn't want that.

"You keep looking over there. What are you thinking of?" Aunt Lois asked from near the fireplace, where her wheelchair was positioned to give her comforting warmth but not excessive heat.

"Nothing."

"One never thinks of nothing."

Rachel smiled in defeat and turned away from the window. Aunt Lois was working on a block for the intricate Feathered Stars quilt she had started last spring.

"May I help you, Auntie? Maybe I could cut out more pieces for you."

Aunt Lois shook her head without looking up from her stitching. "This is the last block, dear. You may help when I'm ready to sew them together."

"I surely will." Aunt Lois was always happy when a quilt was in the final stages, and Rachel caught some of her satisfaction.

She sat down opposite her aunt. She could hear faint sounds from the kitchen. Aunt Pris was probably starting some bread dough rising, to be baked tomorrow. Why wasn't this homey, pleasant life with the two older women enough? Rachel sighed.

"What is it?" Aunt Lois asked softly.

"I do think about Winfield sometimes, even now," Rachel admitted.

Aunt Lois glanced quickly toward the doorway, as though making sure her sister wasn't about to walk in on the conversation. She stopped stitching and gazed across at her niece with sympathy pouring from her wrinkled face.

"What is it that you think, child?"

Rachel looked down at her hands and smoothed her skirt across her lap. "It's not that I wish him dead." She glanced up at Aunt Lois, who was leaning forward slightly, her needle in one hand and the quilt square in the other. "It's just—not knowing is so hard."

Aunt Lois nodded slowly. "Sometimes not knowing is harder than knowing. And yet—"

"If I knew for certain that he doesn't want to be around me anymore. . ."

Her aunt was silent, her blue eyes turning broody and her pale brow wrinkling.

Rachel shook her head. "Sometimes I'm not even sure why I married him. He was handsome and charming, and yet even before we eloped I knew he had characteristics that weren't desirable in a husband. Still, I was drawn to him. And I suppose the fact that Father disliked him made Winfield even more attractive." Could Aunt Lois possibly understand how wretched it felt to have the only man you've given your heart to leave you forever? What had she done to make Winfield despise her that much? "I know you think Father drove him away—"

"Hsst!" Aunt Lois frowned and whipped her gaze toward the doorway. After a moment, she said in a low voice, "Pris is sure of that, but I do wonder."

Rachel's heart beat a little faster. "You think he may have gone away on his own then? I've always thought I wasn't. . .enough for him. I don't think he would run off and stay away this long merely because Father was angry with him."

"Perhaps Winfield had other motives."

Rachel frowned. She didn't like to think her father had paid Winfield to leave, but she'd caught a suspicion of that once in a comment from Aunt Priscilla.

"What if he didn't mean to stay away?" Her voice sounded pitiful and a bit whiny, even in her own ears. "I mean, what if he was planning to come back but something happened to him?"

"We would surely have heard."

"Perhaps not."

Aunt Lois stuck her needle through the calico. She took two stitches and then looked up. "Perhaps not."

The darkest thought, one that came only fleetingly to Rachel every now and then, flashed across her mind, and she shoved it away. She would not, could not, think that Father had actually done something to Winfield, something that would keep him from ever coming back into Rachel's life again. She shivered.

"But we don't know," Aunt Lois said.

"No. We don't." And Rachel would have to live with that, even if it meant avoiding entanglements that would otherwise be acceptable, even desirable. She wanted to go to the window again to see if Stephen had come home, but she made herself poke up the fire instead. "It's chilly in here, Auntie. Let me get you your heavy shawl."

As Christmas approached, Rachel wasn't feeling very joyful. Each time Stephen came to tea or she spoke to him at church, the longing in her heart grew stronger.

On Saturday morning, he knocked on the side door of the Tanner house, and Rachel went to admit him. Although the ground was bare and the mourning wreath still graced the door, she felt a bit of holiday anticipation. Stephen held an armful of pine branches, and his breath formed a cloud of mist in the air when he spoke.

"Good morning! It's only two weeks until the Christmas Eve program, and I'm going over to the church. I thought I'd take some greenery for the ladies who are decorating and check on how I'll position the children for their songs and recitations. Would you like to accompany me?"

"I'd love it." She'd been hoping for an excuse to get out of the house on this crisp, sunny day. "Just let me check with my aunts, to be sure they won't need me for an hour or so."

Stephen stepped into the hall, and she closed the door. She hurried to the back of the house, where her aunts were in the kitchen. Aunt Lois sat with her invalid chair pulled up to a low table, chopping carrots while Aunt Priscilla rolled out piecrusts.

"Mr. Worth has asked me to walk over to the church with him," Rachel said. "He's taking some branches for decorations, and he needs to plan the children's part in the Christmas Eve program."

"Well, if he needs your help," Aunt Lois began.

"Does he?" Aunt Pris continued rolling the dough. "Need you, I mean."

Rachel swallowed hard. "Perhaps *need* is a bit strong, but I can help him."

"Oh, why shouldn't she go?" Aunt Lois frowned at her sister.

"You know why. People in this town like nothing more than gossip." Aunt Pris's disapproval was evident in her sharp, short strokes with the rolling pin.

"There will be other ladies there," Rachel said quickly.

"No doubt ladies who will run their tongues after they see you gadding about with the schoolmaster."

Rachel took a slow breath. "I'd like to go if you don't need me here."

Before Aunt Priscilla could speak, Aunt Lois said, "Go along, dear. We're fine."

Rachel eyed Aunt Priscilla's rigid posture, but the elder sister said nothing.

"I'll be back before lunch." Rachel turned and scurried back to the front hall, and Stephen arched his eyebrows at her. "It's fine," she said. "Just let me grab my coat." She dashed up the stairs and returned in a moment wearing her warm woolen coat over her black dress. She liked her green coat, and her aunts didn't tell her it wasn't suited for mourning. They knew she couldn't afford to buy a black one—a small blessing, to her mind.

As they walked along the town square and over to the church, she kept up a running conversation about Stephen's pupils and the upcoming programs.

"Some of the songs and poems are the same as those they'll do on Thursday at the school program," he said, "but we've substituted a few more spiritual selections for the church service."

The minister's wife and the Begley cousins greeted them as they entered the chilly building.

"Oh good," Mrs. Ross said. "You brought some evergreen boughs."

They spent a pleasant hour during which Mr. Worth stepped out various positions on the platform and in the area in front of the pulpit while consulting his notes, and the ladies arranged branches, berry-laden boughs, and a few houseplants to give the sanctuary a festive air. They called on Stephen to climb a ladder and fix a few boughs above each window frame. While he was perched aloft, the front door opened, and Marshal Yates and his twin sisters entered, carrying boxes and sacks of food.

"These are for the Christmas baskets," the marshal called to Mrs. Ross.

"Wonderful." The minister's wife walked over to inspect their load.

"It's mostly staples," sixteen-year-old Emma Yates said.

"But we did get some peppermint sticks at the store too," Ella added.

Mrs. Ross smiled. "Wonderful. And I'm sure we'll get some baked goods as the day gets closer."

Rachel walked over and smiled at the twins. "Hello, girls."

Stephen climbed down from the ladder and eyed their offerings with approval. "This is for charity?"

"Yes," Mrs. Ross said. "We started a few years ago, making a few baskets for poor families in the community. Someone contributes meat—a few turkeys and prairie chickens and geese."

"Have you ever found out who it is?" Emma asked.

Mrs. Ross smiled. "We don't know. It's a mysterious benefactor who doesn't wish to be applauded. We hope he—or she—will do the same this year, but if not, the church will buy a few chickens for the baskets. I hope we can do at least five like last year."

"I'd like to help," Stephen said. "Can I make a contribution toward items you might buy to round out the things people bring?"

"That would be lovely, Mr. Worth," Mrs. Ross said. "You could pass whatever you feel led to give to my husband. We'll make up the baskets on Christmas Eve, so there is plenty of time."

Stephen nodded and looked at Rachel. "I'm about finished with my work here today, Mrs. Jones. Are you ready to go home?"

"I think so." Rachel looked around the church. "It looks lovely in here, if I do say so."

The marshal gazed around the sanctuary. "You ladies have done a great job."

"Is there going to be a Christmas tree?" Ella asked.

"In the church?" Serinda Begley frowned. "I wouldn't think that was suitable."

Mrs. Ross gave her a strained smile. "I'll ask my husband. He might think it's appropriate for the children's program."

"Oh, I hope so," Emma said, and both Begley cousins' mouths drooped.

"Put your things over there," Mrs. Ross said, pointing to an area to one side of the platform.

"Come on, girls, let's get home," the marshal said. "Marta will want your help fixing lunch."

"We should go too," Rachel said. She and Stephen followed the Yateses outside.

She was glad that Stephen walked slowly after cheerful goodbyes, allowing the marshal and the twins to move on ahead of them. The Yateses' house was on their street, just beyond the little rental where Stephen lived, and though she liked the Yates family, Rachel had hoped for a bit more time to converse privately with Stephen.

As they moved alongside the empty expanse of the town square, she shot a glance at Stephen. He seemed to sense her attention and smiled at her.

"This was a pleasant morning. Thank you for coming."

"Thank you for asking." If he were Winfield, Rachel would have slipped her gloved hand into the crook of his arm, but Stephen wasn't her husband, and she must be ever watchful. She kept her hands at her sides. Still, she knew Stephen wondered about Winfield, and she wanted to be open with him on that subject.

She cleared her throat. "I'm sorry I was curt the day you asked about my. . .husband."

"Oh." He caught a quick breath, glanced at her then away. "I'm sorry if I upset you. I shouldn't have asked."

"No, it's fine. I just. . ." She sighed. The air had warmed enough that she couldn't see her breath now. "My husband, Winfield. . . He left me about twelve years ago."

"Twelve years?" Stephen's brow furrowed. "You would have been only a girl."

"I was seventeen." She couldn't look at him, and she felt her cheeks warm. "We married very young, against my father's wishes. He stayed less than a year." She shrugged in apology. "I thought I knew better than Father. But he and Winfield argued many times. Violently. And it appears that my husband decided one day he'd had enough. I don't know, really. Perhaps I'll never know why he left. I've never heard from him since."

Stephen stopped walking, and Rachel paused too. "Never?"

"Not a word."

"I'm so sorry."

Tears filled Rachel's eyes, not so much for the sorrow she'd endured at Winfield's hand, but for the deep and genuine concern in Stephen's expression.

"Thank you. We don't speak of it. Especially when Father was around, we avoided the topic, and now. . .well, we've cultivated a habit over the years, and it's hard to break. Any mention of Winfield, and my aunts become agitated, so I rarely speak of him."

"That must have been—and still be—very hard for you."

Rachel bit her lip. How much should she say? Her recent talk with Aunt Lois marked progress. But she didn't feel she was ready to tell Stephen everything. About the sneering tone Winfield had begun using toward her after their wedding, or the way he made her feel like a child. Or worse, an unimportant possession. And she certainly couldn't tell him that she'd felt just the tiniest relief when Winfield left and she'd realized after a few days that he might not come back.

"Yes, it is hard," she said softly. She wanted to thank him for listening, for letting her talk about it. But their relationship was not at that level, was it? It shouldn't be. After all, she was still a married woman. Though the topic saddened her, still her heart felt lighter because she'd found someone she could confide in. Maybe someday she would be able to tell Stephen more. She found that the hope grew in intensity as she stood beside him.

A wagon came toward them down the street, and she began walking again. She mustn't be seen loitering with the schoolmaster. She dared to glance at him as he matched his stride to hers.

Stephen said, "If there's ever anything I can do. . ."

She gave a little laugh, which hurt her throat and brought more tears to pool in her eyes. "Thank you. Perhaps one day you can help me convince my aunts to let me open Father's box."

"I'd be happy to broach the subject. I think it's silly not to open it now that he's passed on."

"No, no." Her chest tightened at the thought that this new friendship could be endangered if he brought up a sensitive subject with her aunts. "I was joking. They're not ready for that."

"Will they ever be?"

"I'm not sure. But please wait on that."

"All right. Whatever you say, Mrs. Jones."

She glanced at him sharply. "Rachel. At least when we're alone."

He smiled. "Rachel."

Aunt Priscilla would heartily disapprove of that, and perhaps Aunt Lois too. And they would be right, she acknowledged with regret. She could keep this man as a friend, but she must be very careful not to repeat the past and let her feelings run away with her.

Chapter 5

Stephen walked to the mercantile after school let out on Monday to lay in a supply of Christmas candy for his students. As he approached the door, a man about his age came out. His hat was pulled low over his eyes, and he carried a box of shotgun shells in one hand and a sack of beans in the other.

"Afternoon," Stephen said, stepping to one side.

The man nodded and walked on. Stephen peered after him, curious. He couldn't remember ever seeing him in the small town before. Dressed in worn clothing, the man was lean and had a rugged build. A ranch hand, perhaps?

Mrs. Lawson was behind the counter today, and Stephen stepped up with a cheerful smile. When he had given his order of candy, he asked, "Who was the fellow who left just as I was coming in?"

She frowned for a moment. "Oh, that was Clint Wiseman."

"Wiseman? Like the name of the town?"

She nodded. "His family were the first white settlers here." She placed a paper bag of candy on the scale to weigh it. "Clint was captured when he was a boy. Stayed with the Indians a couple of years."

"Really?" Now Stephen was more curious than ever. "Did he go to school here?"

"I don't think the town had a school then." Mrs. Lawson handed him the bag. "There you go. Clint has had some trouble fitting in with folks since the soldiers brought him back. He's not violent or anything, just quiet. Keeps to himself. His folks are dead now, and he lives out in the hills. Their house stands empty, on the River Road. I don't think he likes sleeping indoors."

Stephen wondered about that. He wished he could get to know Clint Wiseman and ask him about his life among the Indians, but the man probably didn't like to be approached by strangers. Still, he apparently came into town now and then for supplies. Maybe he would run into him again.

He stepped briskly toward home to drop off the candy. Then he walked over to the Tanner house. His excuse for calling on the ladies was the order of the program for Friday night's event at the church. He would ask Miss Priscilla if she thought he had positioned the children's readings and carols to the best advantage. And, of course, he would seek Rachel's opinion too. He supposed they would all know that his real reason for the visit was to have contact with Rachel. The aunts didn't seem to mind so much now, but Priscilla was still a little prickly.

It was the elder aunt who opened the door to him, and Stephen put on his best smile.

"Miss Priscilla! How fortuitous. I wondered if you could give me some advice on the Christmas program, since you have experience in school presentations."

Miss Tanner shook her head, but a demure smile played at her lips. "It's been years and years since I taught school, Mr. Worth, but I'd be happy to give you any help I can."

"I do value your opinions." Stephen stepped inside.

"Come to the kitchen," she said. "We're all in there baking for the Christmas baskets."

Stephen gladly followed her, breathing deeply of the enticing scents of cinnamon and baking bread that wafted into the hall. Miss Lois sat in her wheelchair, taking a dish from the drainboard to dry it. Rachel presented a charming picture as she carefully poured batter from a yellowware mixing bowl into a cake pan. Her mouth was quirked to one side, as though the success of her task depended on holding just the right facial expression.

Both women glanced up at him and broke into smiles.

"Well there," Miss Lois said. "I suspected that might be you, Mr. Worth. Come for tea?"

"Oh, well, not unless I'm invited," he said with a quick glance at Miss Priscilla. "You are all so busy, I hate to interrupt you. I came for some advice on my plans for Friday evening's program. But I can come back another time."

"Nonsense," Miss Lois said.

He looked at Rachel, and she smiled as she scraped the last of the batter from her bowl.

"I'm sure you're welcome anytime, Mr. Worth," she said.

Her words and the warmth in her eyes reassured Stephen. Rachel set down her bowl and wooden spoon and pulled out a stool.

"Have a seat and tell us about your concerns," she said.

"Well, uh. . ." He sat and unfolded his list of presentations, which he had gone over a hundred times. It was fine, and he knew it, but it made a good pretext for coming. He couldn't think of another place he'd rather be than in the warm, fragrant kitchen with the three Tanner ladies. "I've put the youngest classes first, but I was thinking that perhaps I should save one of their songs for the end of the evening. They are so sweet and droll when they sing the 'Cradle Song.'"

Miss Priscilla cocked her head to one side for a moment. "No, I think your first instinct is right. The little ones get restless. If you put them early in the pageant, they can go and sit with their parents after that, and it will be up to the adults to keep them quiet."

"You're so right," Stephen said. "They can be a handful, especially when they are excited. What do you think, Mrs. Jones?" He almost slipped and called her Rachel but caught himself just in time.

"Oh, I agree." She took her cake pan over to the cookstove and slid it into the oven, quickly drawing out a pan of corn bread. She set the hot pan on a coiled fabric mat and smiled at him. "And I do hope you'll stay for tea. We've been working hard, but we're nearly finished now. Just a few more dishes to put through. Oh!" She frowned. "We don't have any coffee at the moment."

"Tea is fine, thank you." Stephen folded up the paper and slid it into his pocket. "I'll end as planned then, with Billy Griffith's recitation of a piece by Whittier—the Quaker poet—and the upper classes singing 'Silent Night.' That's always a favorite."

"And a good note to end on," Miss Priscilla said. She took the teakettle off the stove and poured hot water into a china teapot.

"Now, if you will be so kind, Mr. Worth, I'd have you carry the tray into the parlor." Already on the large parquet tray were cups, saucers, spoons, a sugar bowl, and a small pitcher of milk. She added an extra cup and a plate of raisin cookies and stood back so he could pick up the burden.

Stephen quickly stepped up to the task. "I'd be happy to."

Once they were all situated, Miss Lois poured their drinks. Over tea, Rachel told him about their baking spree.

"I told my aunts what we'd heard about the Christmas baskets, and we all agreed we'd like to take part."

"We are always happy to help the poor if we're able," Miss Priscilla said with downcast eyes.

"And what will you put in the baskets?" Stephen asked.

"We made small cakes for each one," Miss Lois replied. "Our mother's pound cake recipe—it keeps well."

Rachel flushed. "I made one for you too, Mr. Worth."

"I suppose single gentlemen with no family nearby could be counted with the poor," Miss Lois said slyly.

Stephen laughed. "Why, thank you very much. I'll accept it with proper gratitude, I hope."

They chatted and sipped their tea, until Rachel jumped up.

"Oh, that last cake. I'd better check on it. Shall I refill the teapot?"

"Thank you, dear. I'd like more," Miss Lois said.

Stephen stood. "Allow me." He picked up the teapot before anyone could object. Rachel hesitated and then led him to the kitchen.

"Thank you. Just set it there, please." She opened the oven and stooped to look at her cake. "Hmm. A couple more minutes, I think." She opened the tea caddy and measured out enough loose tea for another pot. Stephen leaned against the drainboard and watched her work.

"I'll ice your cake before you take it home," she said.

"That's most kind." She seemed in a complacent mood today, and he ventured, "Done any more thinking about that box?"

She paused with her hand on the handle of the teakettle. "Actually, I have." She glanced toward the doorway. "I think you're right. I should take a look. And I admit, I've been secretly longing to open it ever since Father died."

Pleased, Stephen straightened, ready to take action. "Is there time now? While the tea steeps?"

"Maybe. If we're quick." She gave him an almost conspiratorial smile. As soon as she had poured the hot water into the teapot, she set the kettle back on the stove and turned to him, putting a finger to her lips. "Come. But we must be quiet."

He felt a bit naughty as he followed her swiftly to the door of her father's study. Rachel unlocked the door and silently turned the knob, and they both crept in. She closed the door, leaving it just off the latch.

"If there's anything important in it, I'll tell my aunts." She looked anxious now, and he felt the need to reassure her.

"Of course. And if it's not important, there's no need to say a word."

Her brow cleared, and she stepped to the desk, opened a drawer, and retrieved a small key on a black cord.

"Here we go." She walked over to the small side table that held the carved box and reached for it. Just as she touched the cover, the door swung open.

"Rachel?" Miss Priscilla stood frowning in the doorway. "What on earth are you doing?"

Rachel jumped and whirled to face Priscilla.

Lois had drawn her wheelchair up behind her sister, and she peered in around Priscilla's skirt. "Rachel, what is going on?"

Seeing her frozen expression of remorse, Stephen longed to protect Rachel, but that was silly. They were only a pair of old women. Why did Rachel fear to stand up to them?

"It's my fault," he said genially, stepping toward the aunts.

"You put her up to this." Priscilla glared at him.

"No," Rachel said. "He didn't. I decided it was time for me to know what's in this box, and I asked Mr. Worth to be present."

"But why?" Aunt Lois's voice quavered. "Abijah was so adamant about that box. We were none of us to touch it."

"But he's dead." Rachel put her hand to the bridge of her nose, as though she had blundered and that knowledge had brought on a severe headache.

Priscilla moved aside, and Lois rolled into the room. Both women stared at the mysterious box.

Stephen stepped forward, hoping he could ease the tension in the air.

"Ladies, forgive me if I've encouraged Rachel to do something she shouldn't. But don't you see? If whatever is in that box wasn't important to your brother, he wouldn't have kept it and guarded it so zealously. Rachel, as his executrix, should know what it is."

"But he didn't want us to know." Priscilla set her jaw, and Stephen felt he was engaged in a losing battle.

"It would be disloyal to him to go against his express wishes,"

Miss Lois said doubtfully.

"If I may ask, was it mentioned in his will?" Stephen looked at the three of them.

"It was not," Miss Priscilla said. "It was simply included in his estate."

"Hmm." Stephen looked at the elder sister. "Did he want you to have access to his bank account while he was alive?" he asked.

"Of course not!" Priscilla's eyes narrowed.

Lois blinked at him. "What are you talking about?"

"I'm just saying that there are some things a man may keep to himself, such as his financial affairs. But now that he's gone, someone has to deal with those things."

"Rachel has the bank account now," Lois said, looking to her niece for confirmation.

"That's different." Priscilla wasn't going to budge.

Rachel stepped to her and laid a hand on her arm. "I'm sorry if I upset you, Auntie. I didn't think Father would want to leave any loose ends. You know he always kept his affairs in order. If whatever's in there was important, I was going to tell you about it. But we can leave it for now. It's probably nothing that will make a difference to our situation, or he would have told us about it long ago."

"I'm sure he would have," Lois said in soothing tones.

Stephen wasn't so sure.

"Shall we go and finish our tea?" The brightness in Rachel's voice seemed forced.

"I've had enough tea," Aunt Priscilla said. "We have more work to do."

Aunt Lois nodded. "Icing."

"Well, let me at least give you your cake, Mr. Worth." They all filed out into the hall, and Rachel closed the door behind them.

"Mr. Worth probably has work to do as well," Aunt Priscilla said stiffly.

"But I haven't iced his little cake." Spots of red adorned Rachel's cheeks as she shot him a glance.

"Oh, it's all right," he said. "I do have papers to grade."

"Run along then," Miss Priscilla told him as they approached the front door. "One of us can bring the cake over later, after the icing is done." She sent Rachel a disapproving glance and amended her verdict. "Or you can stop for it before you go to the schoolhouse in the morning."

Rachel didn't renew her protests, and Stephen realized he was dismissed. He took his hat from the rack by the door and tried to smile.

"Well, thank you, ladies. It was a delightful tea and. . ." He wanted to say that it was a pleasant afternoon, but the words choked him as the elder Miss Tanner continued to eye him malevolently.

"My cake!" Rachel spun toward the kitchen and dashed away.

Stephen drew in a deep breath and nodded to the aunts. "I'll stop by in the morning."

Chapter 6

Rachel worked in silence, but she could sense her aunts' displeasure—or at least Aunt Priscilla's. Aunt Lois threw her wary glances, as though she'd like to speak but didn't dare. After beating the icing extra hard for ten minutes, she felt better. She turned to face Aunt Priscilla.

"I'm sorry, Aunt Pris."

Her aunt didn't look up from the pan she was scrubbing. "We'll say no more about it."

Aunt Lois opened her mouth and then closed it.

"I've just been so fretful about that tax bill," Rachel said. "I've tried to trust the Lord, but I don't see where we'll get the money by the first of the year."

"We must pray harder," Aunt Lois said.

"I'm sure we're all praying fervently." Aunt Priscilla sounded almost angry, and her sister winced.

"I'm sorry," Rachel said again.

Aunt Priscilla plunked the pan down on the drainboard. "Stop saying you're sorry, Rachel. If God wants us in the poorhouse, we will be. That's all."

"But Father. . ." Rachel stopped. She'd gone over and over this in her head. Her father had always paid the bills. He never expressed concern that he might run out of money. But then, he wouldn't say anything if he was worried, would he? She pulled in a deep breath. "Father always said he'd made wise investments over the years. Why should we be in this situation?"

No one had an answer.

"Well," Aunt Lois said softly, "I think it's out of the question to buy Christmas gifts for one another."

Rachel gritted her teeth. She had put the extra groceries on the family account at the store so that they could continue to eat and make the cakes for the baskets. But at the end of the month, she would have to reconcile the account. What would Mr. Lawson say when she came in empty-handed?

"I know you've been working on something," Aunt Priscilla said.

"Well, yes." Aunt Lois's smile flickered briefly. "I had some scraps."

"And you work wonders with scraps," Rachel said. What would she do for her precious aunts? She would have to think of something she could give them that wouldn't cost anything.

Stephen hoped that by Wednesday afternoon Miss Priscilla had calmed down. Two days should be long enough to mellow the retired teacher—at least he hoped so. Knowing he'd caused friction between Rachel and her aunt troubled him. He didn't want any of the ladies next door to have reason to keep him away from their home. He hadn't seen Rachel the previous morning, when he'd collected the cake. Miss Lois had passed it to him through the doorway and spoken to him only briefly. He hoped today would go better.

He knocked and then braced himself in case he had to face down Miss Priscilla, but to his relief, Rachel opened the door. Her eyes widened, and then she smiled.

"Mr. Worth. Won't you come in?"

"Thank you." He stepped inside and took off his hat. "I wanted to express my thanks for the cake you gave me. It was delicious."

"Oh, you're welcome. We were doing so many for the baskets, one more was nothing, really."

"Well, I appreciated it. And I have a small offering for your aunts." He held out a bundle of cloth scraps and a diminutive paper sack, folded over. "The mother of one of my students sent over some remnants for Miss Lois, and she included some India tea. I thought perhaps Miss Priscilla would like that."

"But you like tea yourself," Rachel protested.

"Yes, but it's better if shared," Stephen said. "Besides, I'll admit I was trying to think of something I could bring your aunt that might help her look more kindly upon me. When I waved to her this morning, she pretended not to see me."

"Oh, that stubborn old woman." Rachel glanced over her shoulder and then leaned a little closer. "I love her dearly, but when Aunt Pris takes a notion into her head, it's hard to disabuse her of it."

Stephen smiled. "Well, I hope that over time I can prove to her I'm not determined to lead you astray."

Rachel laughed. "If you'd like to start now, come on in. They're sitting in the parlor, doing some mending."

"Perhaps not. I do have a lot to do this evening. But I also wanted to ask you if you'd walk over to the church program with me Friday evening."

"Oh, I don't know."

"Please," he said. "I promise not to urge you to open anything forbidden."

She eyed him soberly, and Stephen thought she understood that he wasn't only referring to the carved box, but to her past.

"Well, perhaps," she said at last.

"If your aunts want to go, I can help get them there."

"No, Aunt Lois doesn't venture out when it's cold. I'm sure they'll stay home."

"Rachel," came a voice from the front room. "Who was at the door?"

"Now you *must* come in," she whispered. She turned and called, "It's Mr. Worth."

"Tell him to come in." That voice was surely Miss Lois.

He looked at Rachel, and the longing she inspired in him swept over him. "Perhaps just for a moment."

"Yes, do give them your gifts yourself."

"It's not much."

"But it will please them." Rachel's blue eyes held an unmistakable invitation.

"All right then."

He kept his visit short and was gratified that both aunts seemed to like the items he'd brought them.

"So pretty," Miss Lois exclaimed over one of the fabric pieces.

"That looks like Mrs. Griffith's Easter dress," Miss Priscilla said.

"Well, it was Billy who brought me the scraps," Stephen admitted. "I hope you don't mind, Miss Lois, that I once mentioned the lovely quilts you make to his mother. She said she'd seen your work."

"Of course she has," Miss Priscilla said. "Lois donated a quilt to the missionary barrel last year. Everyone at church saw it."

Miss Lois's thin cheeks turned rosy. "It was one of my better efforts, if I do say so. Flying Geese, don't you know?"

"I'm sure it was beautiful," Stephen said. "And now I must go. I hope to see you again soon." He cast a meaningful glance at Rachel, and she stepped forward.

"I'll show you out."

At the door, she said softly, "I think I can persuade them that there's no harm in going with you on Friday. Especially if you need a hand getting the children in order."

"That would be wonderful," Stephen said. "Yes, I could certainly use an extra person. Shall I come for you at six?"

"That sounds good. That way we'll get there early and can do whatever needs to be done before the students perform."

Stephen walked to the little house feeling hopeful. Perhaps they could overcome Miss Priscilla's displeasure. It might mean never knowing what Mr. Tanner had kept in that box, but maybe it was worth it.

Rachel dressed with great care on Friday evening. Aunt Lois seemed pleased that the schoolteacher would walk to the church with Rachel, but Aunt Priscilla was definitely not happy. Of course, their recent discussions about their dwindling funds had contributed to the gloomy atmosphere in the house, but Aunt Priscilla's main concern seemed to be that certain people would gossip. To her way of thinking, doing anything that would make one the object of rumors wasn't proper.

"Your father would never allow it," she said.

Rachel didn't respond to that because she had a sinking feeling that Aunt Pris was right.

"There now," Aunt Lois said soothingly. "Our Rachel can't stay cooped up forever."

"But to walk out with a single man." Aunt Pris shook her head. "You know people will talk."

"Yes, but they'll talk about anything." Aunt Lois kept her attention on the stocking she was darning.

Rachel caught her own reflection in the mirror in the front hall. She looked. . .alive. Eager. Hopeful. Would she send Stephen a silent message that she wanted more of his company? Her heart sank and her smile faded. She wanted to know him better, but there was the gnawing fact of Winfield. She hadn't seen him for twelve years, but his presence haunted this house. They might never mention his name, but all of the women were conscious of the part he'd had in molding their lives.

On impulse, she walked to Aunt Priscilla's side and took her hand. "Please don't worry, dear Auntie. I promise I'll be on my best behavior."

Aunt Priscilla looked into her eyes and patted her hand. "There now. I'm sure you will. You're a good girl, Rachel."

Rachel wanted to say that she was no longer a girl. Nobody

called a twenty-nine-year-old woman a girl, but she supposed her aunts still thought of her that way. What a nightmare she had put them all through when she *was* a girl. When she married Winfield without consent, her father had been furious and her aunts brokenhearted. That knowledge alone was enough to keep her on the straight and narrow this evening. She had determined long ago never to disappoint them again.

A knock sounded on the door, and she hurried to greet Stephen. He stepped in to wish her aunts a pleasant evening, and then they headed for the church. As they walked along talking about the program and the students Stephen thought might need prompting, Rachel's spirits soared once more.

The pastor was already in the church, lighting the lamps. Stephen went to help him, and soon parents were dropping off their children.

Mrs. Ross came over from the parsonage, carrying a can of peaches to slip into one of the charity baskets.

"Hello, Rachel." Her eyes sparkled. "Would you like to help me make sure the baskets are fairly even as to their contents?"

Rachel went to help her.

"We don't have the meat yet," Mrs. Ross confided. "Last year it was brought over in the evening. I'm not sure what will happen tonight, since we're having the service right before delivering the baskets."

"What will you do if nobody brings meat?" Rachel asked.

"Mr. Lawson told us he butchered enough chickens today and has them hanging in his big icebox. He'll let my husband into the store after the service if we need them. We'll have to stretch the offering to pay for them, I guess."

Stephen rounded up the students to remind them of the order of their performances. Rachel helped the little girls straighten sashes and hair ribbons. To warm up their voices, Stephen led the children in quietly singing one verse of "Silent Night" as more parishioners filed in. Then he prayed with the students and made sure they all settled quietly in the front pews in the order in which they would stand when their classes were called.

Everything went beautifully, so far as Rachel could tell. Sarah Carr forgot a line and had to be prompted. Young Andrew Engels muffed his scripture recitation slightly, where the Gospel writer Matthew had written, "Behold, there came wise men from the east to Jerusalem." Andrew had practiced the passage faithfully—and perhaps a few too many times. When he reached that point, it came out, "Behold, there came Jerusalem from the east to Wiseman."

The boy didn't realize his mistake, and when the audience laughed, his eyes widened and he paused for a moment then went on, ". . .saying, where is he that is born King of the Jews? For we have seen his star in the east, and are come to worship him." He stepped back to enthusiastic applause, and the next pupil took up the recitation. When the program was over, Andrew received many comments on his good work.

Just before the closing hymn and prayer, Pastor Ross got up and reminded everyone that the Christmas baskets would be delivered that night, so any late donations must be made right away.

"They don't have the meat yet," Rachel whispered to Stephen. She wished she'd had some coins to put in the offering plate when it was passed earlier.

The church ladies had set up to serve cookies, lemonade, and coffee, and many people lingered after the service to talk. Several congratulated Stephen and his pupils on the fine performance. The Griffiths were the first family to leave. They stepped outside onto the steps, and Billy came running back inside.

"Pastor! There's a sack of chickens and stuff outside."

Sure enough, the anonymous donor had left off a burlap sack containing two ducks and three chickens, cleaned and plucked for the baskets.

Stephen smiled at Rachel. "Well, we know it's someone who wasn't inside at the program tonight."

"Not necessarily," she replied. "A latecomer could have dropped off the sack and then slipped in the door."

"I guess you're right. And anyway, it doesn't really matter, does it? The Lord knows who does it."

Finally, the crowd thinned out, and Pastor Ross, Stephen, and Rachel joined Marshal Justin Yates and his wife, Marta, to deliver the food baskets. Justin picked up one basket in his left hand and grasped Marta's hand with his right. Rachel smiled as she watched them go down the sidewalk toward the home where they would deliver the gift. The marshal and Marta seemed to have a very happy life together. Maybe someday Rachel could be as content as those two.

She and Stephen took one basket to a widow whose children were too young to attend school. She eked out a living by taking in laundry.

"Thank you so much," she told Rachel and Stephen. Tears flooded her eyes when she saw the overflowing basket they brought.

Rachel felt blessed as they turned toward her own house. Completing the errand with Stephen made it even more special.

"I'd better get you home," he said softly, and she wondered if he regretted the evening's end as much as she did. It was a bit late. Her aunts were probably anxious, as she rarely went out in the evening, and never with a man. And right now the dear ladies had so much to fret about. She had to find some way to make an income. Any small source of funds would be a help and would allay their worst fears.

"Your aunts were looking rather sad this evening," Stephen said as they walked down the dim street.

It was almost as though he'd read her thoughts, and Rachel hesitated. Stephen would keep her confidence, she was sure. Still, she didn't want to betray another family confidence or say something that would sound like a complaint to Stephen. "It's the money problem," she confessed. "I don't suppose I should tell you."

"Are you short? I could pay my rent early."

"No, please. You're fine. In fact, you're a wonderful tenant. It's just that, since Father died, things have been a bit worrisome."

"He was always the family provider," Stephen said.

"Yes, and we never guessed that when he was gone, we'd be wanting." Rachel's stomach roiled. She wished she hadn't said anything, although she regarded Stephen highly. Her intuition had been right—it was too private, and too painful. If she didn't settle the tax bill within a week, she feared they would lose their home, but she could *not* tell him that. She had to get a job, that was all. She hoped it would be enough, and soon enough.

"You're not. . .hungry, are you?" He peered at her anxiously, and she was glad for the shadows. The new moon fell on Christmas night, and this evening only starlight lit their way.

"No, no," she said. *Not yet anyway.*

"Rachel, if there's anything I can do—"

"I'm sure there's not."

"But I want to help. I care about you. Your aunts too, but my dear. . ." He stopped walking and grasped her arm lightly. "Rachel, I care deeply for you. I'd do anything to help you."

She drew a quick breath. "Please don't. You mustn't."

"I'm sorry." He sighed. "No, I'm not. Living beside you and getting to know you—though not as well as I'd like—I've come to care deeply, Rachel."

She couldn't hold back a sob.

Stephen looked up and down the street. A wagon approached from the town square, and two people walked along the opposite side of the street.

"I told you I was married, Stephen." She started walking again, but this time, as soon as the other pedestrians had passed, she took his arm. He crooked it and reached over with his other hand to pat her gloved fingers. It felt a bit scandalous, but she didn't pull away, though her cheeks felt as though they were on fire.

"You did tell me, and I'm sorry if I've upset you again. But I can't help feeling, there's got to be a way. . ."

She shook her head. "I must pay for my youthful indiscretion. I was only sixteen when I married him, but I knew better. I went directly against my father's instruction. He had told Winfield never to come back to the house or to try to see me outside it. He forbade me to have contact with Winfield. Alas, Father was right about him."

"He abandoned you."

"Yes." She looked up at him, her eyes swimming in tears. "I don't like to tell you this, but I feel that I must or you won't understand. Winfield had a temper, which I knew nothing about before our marriage. At least, if there were any warning signs, I willfully ignored them. I told myself it was only because he was so frustrated by my father's unreasonable attitude."

"Did he abuse you?" Stephen asked softly.

She drew in a shaky breath and nodded. "He did. And he began to argue with Father. A lot. Then he began arguing with me, mostly about Father."

"You lived in the family home after the wedding?"

"Yes. Father insisted. But that was probably a mistake." She shook her head. "It's impossible to tell now if things would have ended differently had we found our own lodgings. At the time, I was stubborn enough, and selfish enough, to think I'd taught Father a thing or two by marrying Winfield and living under his own roof as a married woman. And Winfield seemed not to mind saving the expense of living on our own. But he and Father did get into it." She sighed. "I see it now as Father's way to keep some control over me. But when they came to blows, that was the end. Father threw Winfield out. And he didn't take me."

"Surely he contacted you?"

"I waited, but no word came. I checked the boardinghouses in town and the friend he had lived with when I met him, but no one seemed to know where he was. Father was livid—Winfield had taken one of his carriage horses from the stable."

"Oh dear."

"Yes. Father lodged a complaint with the marshal, and so Winfield was labeled a horse thief."

"Marshal Yates took the complaint?" Stephen asked.

"Not him. The old marshal, before Justin Yates had the position." They were nearly to the house, and Rachel paused at the edge of the yard. "Anyway, Father may be gone, but Winfield is still out there somewhere. So you see why I told you, we cannot be more than friends."

Stephen nodded gravely. "I do. And as sad as it makes me, I promise to keep a proper distance. But I'm glad you are willing to remain friends."

"Of—"

A scream split the air, and a muffled thud came from the back door of the Tanner house. Aunt Priscilla's quavering voice was unmistakable.

"Thief! Thief!"

Chapter 7

Stephen ran up the path and mounted the front steps two at a time. He threw open the door. "Miss Priscilla! Miss Lois! Are you all right?"

"In here," came Miss Lois's shaky voice from down the hallway.

Stephen hurried toward her and found the sisters in the kitchen. The back door gaped wide, and Miss Priscilla stood staring out into the darkness, a rolling pin held high in her right hand.

"What happened?" Stephen asked.

Rachel hurried in behind him and stopped just short of plowing into him.

"Auntie, what's going on?" she cried.

"A thief," Miss Priscilla spat out.

"He robbed Abijah's study." Miss Lois's eyes were moist with tears. She wheeled her chair toward Rachel. "Oh sweetie, he took the box."

Aunt Priscilla nodded in misery.

"Fetch the marshal," Stephen said to Rachel. He ran out the back door and down the back porch steps. He stopped and let his eyes adjust, listening. At first all was quiet except for a dog barking in the Griffiths' backyard. Then he heard a rustling in the lilac bushes, and the dog's yapping increased.

Stephen ran toward the sound. The bushes shook and rattled, and a dark figure broke free and tore for the street. He sprinted after the fleeing person, with other dogs in the distance joining the racket the Griffiths' mutt was raising.

The man dashed across the street—Stephen was sure now that it was a man, as he could see the thief's outline and his gait in the light that poured from the Tanner ladies' parlor window. The felon was carrying a large, rectangular item. Stephen was certain it was Abijah Tanner's carved cherrywood box. He pulled in a breath and increased his pace, glad he'd joined his young students during their exercise periods.

When he reached the far side of the street, Stephen dove in an attempt to bring down the man before he could disappear into the hedge along the sidewalk. His quarry stumbled as he leaped from the street to the sidewalk, and the two of them crashed into the leafless bushes. Stephen wrestled the man for a moment but subdued him without much of a problem. For an instant, he had feared the thief was Clint Wiseman, but now he could tell this man was smaller and slighter of build than the returned captive. He was glad, because he liked Clint, though he'd only seen him once since that time at the mercantile.

The light of a lantern bobbed in the street, and Stephen turned toward it, his knee squarely on the thief's back. Miss Priscilla was running over from her house with the light, and now Stephen could see that the man he held was also older than Wiseman.

"Do you have anything I can tie him with?" Stephen asked.

"No. I'm sorry." Miss Priscilla leaned down and studied the man's face.

Stephen began working his belt off through his belt loops. "Who is it? Do you recognize him?"

"I don't believe I've ever seen him before," Miss Tanner said.

More footsteps drew their attention. Marshal Yates strode quickly across the street, with Rachel panting behind him as she jogged to keep up with Yates's long strides.

"What happened?" the marshal asked.

"This man broke into the Tanners' house and stole something," Stephen said. "I chased him over here and tackled him."

"Good job. Ease up now." Marshal Yates bent down and slid handcuffs onto the prisoner's wrists. "Who are you?"

The man moaned and sat up with the marshal's help.

"Name's Sutton," the man gasped. In the poor light, Stephen decided he was forty or fifty years old, and the scruff of beard on his face matched his pale hair.

"All right, Sutton, get up. You're under arrest." Yates sounded fierce, and Stephen was glad he wasn't the one the marshal was apprehending.

Rachel knelt on the cold earth and pulled the man's plunder to her.

"The top is cracked," she said, running a hand over the box's inlaid lid.

"Is that what he took?" Yates asked.

"That's it all right," Miss Priscilla said. "My brother's box."

The marshal turned to her, holding on to his prisoner's arms. "Anything else?"

"Not that I know of," Miss Priscilla replied.

"I'll search him."

"Thank you." Miss Priscilla shook her head. "It happened so fast. We heard a noise in the study, and I unlocked the door. Lois and I saw him with the box, and he pushed past us and ran into the kitchen and out the back door. He shoved me up against the woodwork. I'm sure I'll be all bruised tomorrow."

"I'm sorry, ma'am," Yates said. "Do you need to see the doctor?"

"No, I don't think so."

Yates nodded. "All right then. Is the box valuable?"

No one said anything for a moment.

"We don't know," Rachel said in a small voice. "Father kept it locked, and we've never opened it. May we take it back to the house?"

Yates frowned. "Sure. Maybe you ought to open it and see what's inside. I'll come by tomorrow and tell you anything else I learn. Meanwhile, look around and see if there's anything else missing."

"We will." Rachel held the box awkwardly.

"I'll carry that for you." Stephen bent and lifted it carefully, wondering if the box itself might be valuable. It was certainly pretty.

"I wonder if it just caught his eye, or if he knew it was there," Rachel said as they crossed the street to the big house.

That thought hadn't entered Stephen's mind. How many people even knew the box existed?

Miss Lois was waiting in her wheelchair just inside the front door.

"You've got it," she cried when she saw the box. "Oh Mr. Worth, God bless you! What happened to the burglar?"

"The marshal's got him," her sister said grimly. "Rachel, would you make some tea? I think we all need it."

Rachel hurried toward the kitchen.

"Where would you like me to put this?" Stephen asked.

Miss Priscilla came to him and ran her hand over the box's lid. "Oh dear. It's a large crack."

"Such a pity," Miss Lois murmured. "The carving and inlay is exquisite."

"It was wicked of that man to damage it like that," Miss Priscilla said.

Stephen opened his mouth to say that he might very well have caused the damage when he charged the man, but he restrained himself. Likely the box cracked when the fellow tripped and stumbled. No use sending himself further out of Miss Tanner's good graces.

The older sister led them into the parlor.

"Set it there, on that table." Priscilla nodded toward the low table where they usually set the tea tray, and Stephen complied. He examined the split in the lid.

"I think a good woodworker could glue this. The crack might still show, but at least it would be sturdy."

Priscilla sighed. "That would mean taking the lid off so he could work on it."

"Why not?" Lois asked. "After all this, don't you think perhaps we *should* open it? What if that man had gotten away? We would never know what we'd lost."

"The marshal said something along those lines," Stephen said gently.

Rachel appeared in the doorway, carrying a laden tray. The kettle must have already been hot, she'd returned so quickly. She'd added a plate of shortbread cookies. Seeing that the usual resting spot was occupied by the box, she took the tray to a side table. Stephen jumped up to move a few books and a candlestick that were on it, clearing the surface for her.

"Rachel," Miss Priscilla said, "your aunt Lois and Mr. Worth are of the opinion that we should open this box."

Rachel turned and stared at her.

"Apparently the marshal is too," Miss Lois added.

"Yes, he did say something to that effect." Slowly, Rachel walked over and gazed down at the box.

"Well?" Miss Priscilla asked.

"Why don't we have our tea first," Miss Lois said.

"No, it hasn't had time to steep." Miss Priscilla threw Stephen a challenging look. "I say we open first and have tea afterward."

Rachel looked up at him.

"Sounds sensible to me," Stephen said.

Rachel's lips quirked upward. "I'll get the key."

When she returned with the little silver key on the black cord, she held it out to her eldest aunt.

"No, my dear, it's your place," Priscilla said. "Your father left you in charge of the estate."

Stephen made no comment, though it seemed to him that things might have gone a lot differently if the aunts had recognized this when the will was read several months ago.

Carefully, Rachel inserted the key into the lock and turned it. She lifted the lid slowly. The crack did not extend all the way to the end of the top boards, so it rose in one piece. She laid it back on its hinges, and they all peered into the container. A small sack lay inside, along with a couple of envelopes.

"Is that money?" Miss Lois asked, her voice rising in excitement.

Rachel hefted the little sack, and it clinked.

"Here, Auntie." Rachel placed it in her eager hands. Miss Lois worked at the drawstring and opened the bag. She tipped it up and poured five gold pieces into her lap. They all stared at the coins.

"Double eagles," Rachel breathed. The twenty-dollar gold coins seemed to glow against Aunt Lois's black skirt.

"That makes a hundred dollars," Stephen said.

Aunt Priscilla's eyes glistened. "Not a huge fortune, but more than enough to pay the taxes. Rachel, you must take it to the bank on Monday and then pay our bills."

"Yes." Rachel smiled up at Stephen, but her eyes still held a fretful look. A hundred dollars might get them through this crisis and keep them for a while if they were frugal, but he realized that the three women could not live on that amount forever. A month or two at most, depending on how much went to their creditors. But maybe that would be enough time for Rachel to find a way to support the three of them.

"What are the envelopes?" practical Miss Priscilla asked.

Rachel picked up the first one and studied the front. She caught a sharp breath, and her face paled.

"What is it, dear?" Miss Lois asked.

Stephen could see that Rachel's name was written on the envelope, above the address of the house in which they stood. He could also see that it had been opened.

Rachel swayed a little, and Stephen reached out to grasp her arm and steady her.

She gulped. "It's—this letter is in Winfield's handwriting."

"Read it," Aunt Lois cried.

Rachel tried to take a deep breath, but she couldn't seem to get enough air into her lungs.

"Sit down," Stephen said softly in her ear.

She let him guide her to a chair and plopped into it. He took the letter from her hand and looked at the older women.

"Perhaps now is the time for tea. And plenty of sugar."

"Of course." Miss Lois took hold of her chair's wheels, and Miss Priscilla went into action to push her sister to the side table. There Miss Lois poured out a cupful of strong brew, and Miss Priscilla added two spoonfuls of sugar and stirred it, then carried the cup and saucer to Rachel.

"Here you go, dear. Drink up. This must be trying for you."

"It's a shock," Miss Lois said. She poured out more tea.

Rachel's hands shook as she raised the cup to her lips. The tea did seem to help, and her breathing steadied. Soon her aunts and Stephen were seated with their own cups, sipping away and throwing cautious glances her way.

Rachel took a good gulp and held out her cup to Stephen. "If you would. . ."

"Of course." He took it from her and set it aside. "Feel better?"

"Much. Now, where has that letter got to?"

He took it from the table and handed it to her.

"Would you like someone else to read it?" Aunt Priscilla asked.

"No, I think I'm ready." She took out the single page and

unfolded it. "It's dated November 1875."

"Less than a year after he left here," Miss Priscilla noted.

Rachel blinked and began to read.

"Dear Rachel, I long to write 'my dearest,' but I do not feel worthy of putting such sentiment to paper. I never should have left Wiseman, but I did, and now I am paying the consequences of my own rash actions."

She glanced up at her aunts, as though begging them to admit Winfield was not as wicked as they'd imagined. He admitted he'd been wrong.

"Go on, dear," Miss Priscilla said.

Rachel cleared her throat.

"As you know, I was very angry when I left. I was determined to prove myself a man to your father—and you. And now—"

She gasped.

"What is it, dear?" Aunt Lois asked gently.

"And now I am in prison, here in Kansas."

Rachel looked up, her eyes brimming with tears. She held the letter up in Stephen's direction. "Could you finish it, please?"

Stephen took it and looked into her stricken eyes. She nodded, and so he skimmed to where she had left off reading.

"It seems I took up with the wrong crowd. I wanted to make a quick return in triumph and sweep you away from your father's house. But alas, we were caught. I expect I'll be in here for a long while, and if I do get out in ten years or so, you probably won't want to see me. I'm no good, Rachel. You don't want to be married to a convicted bank robber. You should—"

Stephen glanced ahead at the next sentence and paused.

"Please go on," she whispered.

He drew in a deep breath.

"You should divorce me and be done with it. Please don't even think of coming here. I shan't write again. Winfield Jones."

Rachel's face had taken on a deep red hue, and she had her black-edged handkerchief out. Her aunts were also dabbing at their eyes. No one said anything for a long moment.

"Well," Rachel said at last. "At least our very worst fears weren't realized. Father didn't do away with him."

"We never thought that," Miss Lois said, looking scandalized.

Miss Priscilla shook her head sheepishly. "It crossed my mind. I'm glad it's not true. But still—married to a felon."

"Yes." Tears streamed down Rachel's face. "Father must have read this and then hidden it away."

"Dear girl." Miss Lois wheeled closer and patted Rachel's hand. "We all loved your father, but we all know he was a very controlling man."

Rachel bit her lip but said nothing.

"He had a fierce temper," Miss Priscilla said, wiping her eyes. "And strong opinions on everything. But even so, I'm surprised that he kept this from you."

Aunt Lois bowed her head. "Obviously, he preferred that you be left wondering over a family scandal."

"Well, a divorce in the family would be shameful," Miss Priscilla countered.

Rachel let out a little sob, and Lois stroked her hand. "There, there."

Stephen folded the letter and put it back in the envelope.

"There's one more in there." Rachel's voice croaked, and she didn't look at him.

Stephen stepped over to the box, placed Winfield's letter inside, and took out the other envelope. "This looks like a telegram."

"Do you mind reading it?" Rachel asked, staring at the carpet.

The top edge of the envelope had been slit, and Stephen drew out the form. He looked at the top portion. "It's addressed to you, dated five years ago."

"I've never received a telegram in my life," Rachel said flatly.

Stephen tried not to let his anger at Abijah Tanner show on his face. "It's from the prison warden in Kansas."

Rachel squeezed her eyes shut tight, and more tears spilled out. "Go on then."

Chapter 8

Inform you death of Winfield Jones April 5 *Stop*
Send instructions on arrangements *Stop*

"That's it," Stephen said.

Rachel sucked in a big breath. Five years ago!

"What should I do?" She looked to Stephen, not her aunts. Somehow, she thought he would have a better answer than they would.

He laid his hand lightly on her shoulder. "Your father must have sent a reply. There's nothing you can do now."

She breathed in and out several times, not trusting her voice.

"If you want to know where he's buried—" Aunt Lois began.

"No!" Aunt Priscilla's eyes flashed. "It's best to leave things be now. Abijah did what he thought best. Now you know your husband's gone, Rachel, and you can do as you please, but I think you should let him rest in whatever peace he achieved at the end."

Rachel stared at her, unable to come up with any words that would be profitable at the moment.

Stephen's comforting hand stirred, and he squeezed her shoulder gently. "If you want to, I'm sure you could send a wire to the warden. It might not even be the same man in charge now, but they'll have records. You ought to be able to find out something."

"I'll think about it," Rachel said. She knew she would mull over these revelations for many a long, sleepless night.

Five years. She'd been a widow for five years without knowing it. How would she have changed things if she'd known? How differently would she have lived? A bleak feeling blanketed her, until she looked up at Stephen. Something shone in his eyes. A sheen of tears perhaps. He was so sympathetic, she appreciated him more than she could say. But there was something else there. A gleam of hope?

She looked away. This meant she was free now. Free to marry. Did her thoughts mirror Stephen's?

"Of course you will," Aunt Lois was saying. "There's much to digest here."

"Father should not have kept this news from me," Rachel said. "Even if he didn't want me to know my husband was in prison, he ought to have told me when he died."

Aunt Priscilla nodded slowly. "He could have told us that Winfield had passed away, without the details."

"What details?" Rachel snapped. "We don't know how it happened or where his remains lie." She looked up at Stephen. "I think

I will want to write a letter to that warden. What I wish to say cannot be said in a telegram. But not now. Not until I've had time to think."

"All right," Stephen said. "If there's anything I can do. . ."

"Perhaps you could find out the address of this prison."

"I could ask the marshal," he said.

"Yes. Thank you. And now, if there's more hot water, I think I would like more tea."

"I'll get it." Aunt Priscilla rose.

"And I will help you." Aunt Lois rolled her chair forward, and Priscilla seized the handle and pushed her out of the room.

Stephen sat down in the chair next to Rachel's, still holding the telegram. "I'm so sorry. It shouldn't have come to you this way."

"No, it shouldn't have." The anger that still roiled inside her confused her. Hadn't Father loved her? He never said it, but she'd always assumed he did. Aunt Lois said he did, and before Rachel's mother died, she had said so too. Of course he loved her. He wanted to keep her safe and happy. She met Stephen's gaze. "My father always maintained that women should not have to worry about business and other troublesome affairs, but this? To not tell me my husband was dead? What kind of protection was that?"

"Misguided, perhaps." He took her hand and curled his warm, strong fingers about hers. "I think your aunts are correct. He most likely did it to save the family from becoming the object of scandal. I know there are gossips in this town, but I doubt they would shun you because your husband died in prison. I'd like to think the people here are better than that. That they'd gather you in and comfort you."

As Stephen was comforting her now. But if Aunt Pris entered

the room and saw them holding hands, she would hit the ceiling. Gently, Rachel disengaged her fingers.

"Thank you for that. I'd like to think so too. But I can't help the thought that Father didn't tell me because he didn't want anything to change. He wanted to remain the patriarch, and I don't think he wanted me to embark on a new life."

"To leave home, you mean?"

"Yes." She leaned back in her chair. "He insisted I live here, even after I married a man he detested. He could have thrown us both out in the street. But no. He wanted us here, where he could maintain some power over me, and to some extent, over Winfield. And finally, he got Winfield to leave of his own free will and not take me with him."

After a moment, Stephen said, "I don't like to think so ill of your father."

She gave a short little laugh that brought tears with it. "Is that worse than what Aunt Pris thought? That maybe Father killed Winfield and disposed of his body?"

"She never said that right out, did she?"

"The seeds were planted," Rachel said. "The possibility was there."

"When in reality, he merely wished for you to stay quietly and respectably under his roof."

Rachel bristled at that. "My father might have thought he would be humiliated if the community knew his ne'er-do-well son-in-law died in prison, but not knowing about it unfairly condemned me to a life of uncertainty."

"I know you've suffered much because of it."

Aunt Priscilla said sternly from the doorway, "Do not condemn your father, Rachel. Abijah saw this way as more honorable than casting you as the wife of a convict. He was trying to shield us all from social censure, as he did from financial concerns."

"Oh really?" Rachel's spine stiffened. "My father is gone now, Auntie, and we have to deal with all these things alone. How was that protecting us?"

"There now," Aunt Lois said, pushing her chair into the room. "Let's not fuss about that. Let's have our tea and be sensible."

"Perhaps that's best." Rachel felt that all emotion and energy had drained out of her.

Stephen got up and put the telegram back in the box. He hesitated and then came back to his chair holding something.

"This was in the bottom, beneath the envelopes."

Rachel frowned at the little booklet in his hand. "What is it?"

"It appears to be a bankbook, but not from the Wiseman bank."

"Where then?" She reached for it and read the words on the cover. "Austin Savings and Loan?" She looked at her aunts, who were refreshing their teacups.

"Your father made his fortune in that area," Aunt Lois said. "He probably banked his gains there."

Aunt Priscilla nodded. "Yes, he had a bank account in Austin when we lived there."

Rachel riffled the booklet and stopped on the last used page.

"There seems to be a healthy balance. That is—if he hasn't closed the account."

"Oh, he must have," said Aunt Lois.

"Surely he moved his funds here when he built this house." Aunt Pris cocked her head to one side. "Wouldn't he?"

Stephen took the bankbook and looked at each page. "It doesn't say 'canceled' or 'closed' anywhere. But it looks like he continued to withdraw money from that bank once a quarter until quite recently." He handed it back to Rachel and pointed to the handwritten figures on the last page. "See here?"

Rachel stared at the numbers. They appeared to be written in her father's hand. "I don't understand. Father didn't go to Austin that often. But the last withdrawal was made a month before Father died."

"Take that in to the Wiseman bank on Monday," Stephen said. "Show it to the banker there."

Rachel's lips trembled, and she pressed them together for a moment.

"It's a significant sum, dear aunts. If this is valid. . ."

"Praise God," Aunt Lois said, lifting her eyes heavenward.

"Oh my." Aunt Priscilla drew a shuddering breath. "Dare we hope?"

Aunt Lois asked eagerly, "Would that mean you wouldn't have to seek employment, Rachel? That you could stay home with us?"

At that moment, Rachel realized the thought of a job outside the home wasn't abhorrent to her. In fact, getting out of the house each day might be pleasant.

"We'll find out," she said.

Stephen smiled at her. "I'd be happy to escort you to the bank on Monday."

"But school," Rachel said.

"We're recessed until after the new year."

"That's right." If the news was bad and their hopes were dashed, Rachel didn't want to have Aunt Priscilla with her to absorb the blow in public. But Stephen's support could be comforting. She glanced at the aunts and came to a decision. "Thank you. I'd appreciate that. Ten o'clock then?"

"Oh, but you'll have dinner with us tomorrow, of course," Aunt Lois said.

He looked at Rachel. She wondered if he'd had a dozen invitations from pupils' families to share Christmas dinner with them.

Stephen smiled. "I'd be delighted."

On Christmas Day, Stephen took the small gifts he'd prepared to the Misses Tanner and Rachel. He'd wrapped them up a week ago and had wondered ever since if he would be invited to spend the holiday with them. He had a standing invitation from the Griffiths if he had nowhere to go, and it was true, two other families had taken pity on him, but he'd assured them his plans were made.

It wasn't until Miss Priscilla met him at the door with a smile on her often dour face that he felt truly welcome. He entered quickly and shut the door because the temperature outside had fallen during the night and was now near freezing. In fact, the house was a bit chilly, but he understood that the ladies were conserving their coal. He hoped the trip to the bank tomorrow would ease their worries.

"Merry Christmas, Miss Tanner," he said. "I brought some small tokens for you ladies."

She eyed the gifts he held and arched her eyebrows. "My, my. Won't you come into the parlor? The turkey is resting a few minutes before we attempt to carve it. Perhaps you'd like some mulled cider."

"I'd love it." Stephen hesitated. "If it's of any use to you, I have been known to carve a turkey or two before."

Miss Priscilla's smile broadened. "I should say it would be. This is our first Christmas without my brother here to wield the carving knife. We'd be ever so thankful if you took over that duty."

"I'd be glad to."

He followed her to the parlor, where Miss Lois was already sipping a cup of tea. Stephen walked over and placed a small package in her lap. "Happy Christmas, Miss Lois."

She looked up, flushing pink. "Oh, thank you, my boy."

Rachel entered, engulfed in an overall apron. "Hello, Stephen," she said. "Excuse my wardrobe. We're glad you could come." As she spoke, she untied her apron springs and lifted the neck strap over her head.

"I'm pleased to be here."

After she had set aside her apron, he handed her the present meant for her.

"Oh, how kind." Rachel's eyes danced. "We've got something for you too."

The fireplace mantel was decorated with pine boughs and red velvet bows. She walked over to it and brought down a small gift wrapped in butcher paper. "It's not much—"

"Thank you very much," he said quickly. "Anything from you ladies is a treasure."

Miss Lois had opened her package. "Oh lovely! Thank you so much, Mr. Worth." She held up the frothy lavender shawl he had purchased at the dressmaker's. "It's too much!"

"No, it's not," Stephen assured her.

"Auntie, it looks lovely against your dark dress and your silver hair," Rachel said.

"When we're out of full mourning," Miss Priscilla murmured.

Stephen had feared she might hold that opinion, so he'd

purchased a pair of black lacy gloves for the elder sister. Miss Priscilla slipped her hand into one and held it out to admire.

"Very nice. I shall wear them to church, Mr. Worth."

"You're most welcome," Stephen said, working to undo his own package. A book was revealed, *A Country Doctor*, by Sarah Orne Jewett.

"Oh wonderful," he said.

"You haven't read it?" Miss Priscilla asked.

"No, but I've wanted to."

"Well, Lois suggested *Great Expectations*, but Rachel was certain you'd read that," Priscilla said with a little nod.

"It's a favorite of mine," Stephen assured her.

"It brought me to tears," Miss Lois confessed. She stroked the frothy lavender shawl. "I believe I shall wear this to church as well."

"Now, Lois, you know we said we ought to mourn a full year, especially since we've got both Abijah and now Mr. Jones to remember."

Miss Lois frowned. "You said that, Priscilla. I certainly didn't. Mr. Jones has been gone five full years. It seems to me that a year of unrelieved mourning would be excessive." She looked at Stephen with wide, innocent eyes. "What do you think, Mr. Worth?"

"Oh, I. . ." Stephen felt as though he had stumbled into a trap. "Uh, whatever you ladies think, I'm sure. Of course, out here in the West, some traditions are less strictly observed."

"Yes, they are," Miss Lois said with a firm nod. "Thank you. I shall wear my shawl to church."

Rachel gave a little gasp. "Oh Stephen, it's beautiful." She held up a finely crafted silver pen. He'd spent more than he perhaps should have on it, but he knew she would appreciate it. He'd wanted to buy her a piece of jewelry or a bright new hat, but of course the aunts would never let her keep something so personal.

As it was, they all seemed pleased with the small gestures he had made. He hoped they hadn't spent too much of their meager funds to get him the book.

"Would you mind putting another log on the fire, Mr. Worth?" Miss Priscilla asked.

"Certainly."

"And when you're done, that turkey should be ready to carve," Rachel added. "We'll put you right to work today."

Stephen tended the fire, and as he headed for the kitchen afterward, he overheard Miss Lois's comment to her sister. "He can keep a fire going steadily and carve a turkey. Quite an accomplished gentleman."

The light mood was sustained throughout the meal. The ladies pressed him to eat second and even third helpings of turkey, dressing, potatoes, squash, beans, rolls, and pickles. Rachel and Miss Priscilla began to clear the table and refused his help, so Stephen sat and chatted with Miss Lois.

A loud knock came at the door. Rachel put down the turkey platter and hurried to the entry. A moment later, she returned with Justin Yates in tow.

He looked around at them and smiled. "Hello, folks. Merry Christmas."

"Merry Christmas," the aunts said together.

"Marshal, won't you sit down and have some pie with us?" Miss Lois asked.

"Oh, no thanks." Yates patted his belly. "I'm stuffed, ma'am. My wife and sisters just fed me the biggest dinner I ever saw in my life.

They sent you these." He put a small sack on the table. "Cookies," he said.

"Oh, be sure to thank them for us," Miss Priscilla said.

He nodded. "I'm sorry to interrupt you, but I wanted to tell you what I've learned from the prisoner."

"Please sit down," Rachel said. "I'll get you some coffee, if you've got room for that."

"Now, that's something I could use." The marshal took a chair next to Stephen.

"The program went well last night, Mr. Worth."

"Thank you," Stephen said. "I thought the children did exceptionally well, and they were on their best behavior."

Rachel set a cup of steaming coffee before Yates, and he took a sip.

"Thank you, ma'am. That's just perfect."

Rachel smiled and resumed her seat between Aunt Lois and Stephen, and Miss Priscilla sat down too, though dirty dishes and leftovers still littered the table.

"Did you find out who he is?" Rachel asked.

"Sure did." Yates set down his cup. "His name's Josh Sutton, and he's from up Kansas way."

Rachel's face blanched.

"Isn't that where Winfield Jones was incarcerated?" Aunt Priscilla asked. She looked at Rachel and then back to the marshal, her cheeks coloring.

"Yes, ma'am." Yates toyed with his spoon for a moment then looked over at Rachel and said carefully, "It seems Sutton was acquainted with your. . .your late husband."

Rachel eyed him for a moment and then said, "They met in the prison. It's all right, Mr. Yates. I've accepted the facts."

"I'm sorry." Yates paused, and Rachel nodded gravely to encourage him. He went on. "It seems this Sutton was a cellmate of your Mr. Jones. He said they talked a lot while they were in there. In fact, Jones told him about this family."

"How awful," Miss Priscilla said with a shudder.

"Mr. Jones gave him the impression that he had little use for Abijah Tanner."

"What else did he tell this man?" Rachel's voice had hardened. Stephen wanted to reach out to her, to comfort her and assure her that they were safe, but he sat still while the marshal continued.

"He mentioned a curious box his father-in-law kept. Said he'd seen it a number of times, but that his wife told him it was kept locked and nobody knew what was in it." Yates gave Rachel a deferential nod. "I'm sorry, ma'am, but I thought you'd want to know."

"Of course," Rachel said.

"He claims Jones speculated it held treasure."

They were all quiet for a moment, and at last Rachel asked, "Was he there when my husband died?"

Yates took a deep swallow of his coffee. "Yes, ma'am. He told me about that."

"We didn't know until last night," Aunt Lois blurted.

Yates focused on her. "Didn't know what, ma'am?"

"That Winfield was dead."

"We opened the box," Aunt Priscilla explained. "There was a letter inside from Mr. Jones, telling Rachel he was in prison."

Rachel's chin rose a quarter inch. "Apparently my father felt it was best to keep that news from me. He opened the letter and locked it away without telling us. But then there was a telegram from the warden saying Winfield had died. It didn't say how. I assume Father answered him, about the arrangements, but I don't know. He certainly didn't consult any of us."

Yates stared into his coffee cup. "I'm very sorry, ma'am."

"Did this Sutton say how Winfield. . .met his end?" Rachel's voice was much smaller now, and Stephen's heart ached.

The marshal drew in a big breath. "He was killed by another inmate during a brawl. They were let into an exercise yard together, and it seems a few of them had made weapons somehow. There were feuding factions. I'm not clear on the details, but your husband was stabbed in the riot, and several other prisoners were injured before the guards took control."

Rachel let out a long sigh.

Yates drained his coffee cup and set it down. "Anyway, when Sutton was released, he decided to come to Wiseman and see if the tale Jones told him a decade ago was true. He found that the box was still in the house, and he tried to steal it."

"He broke into this house while we were in here." Injury dripped from Miss Priscilla's words. "My sister and I were sitting in the parlor, waiting for Rachel to get home from the church program."

"We were a little late." Rachel threw a glance at Stephen. "As you know, we helped deliver the Christmas baskets."

"What will become of this man?" Stephen asked.

"I'll take him over to the county jail tomorrow. He'll be charged with theft and breaking and entering. Did he do any damage? You ladies could ask the court for recompense if he did." Yates looked at the aunts, his eyebrows arched.

"Nothing besides the box," Miss Lois said sadly. "He cracked the lid."

"He seems to have entered through a window in Abijah's study." Miss Priscilla sounded peeved with the thief. "We keep the room locked, but he apparently broke one window pane and undid the lock. When we entered the room, he pushed past us and ran out the back door."

Yates pushed his chair back. "Again, I'm sorry for the fright you ladies had. If you'd like, I can return this evening and fix that windowpane."

"No need," Miss Priscilla said. "Mr. Worth has already volunteered for that task."

Yates nodded at Stephen. "We've been neighbors for a while, but we haven't seen much of each other. I guess our jobs keep us both busy. Stop by the house or my office anytime, Worth."

"Thank you," Stephen said. "I might take you up on that, since I'm on holiday all week."

Yates nodded. "Merry Christmas, ladies."

Rachel rose. "Let me see you out."

"Oh, I can find the door by myself." Yates grinned. "Thanks again for the coffee."

Rachel looked around at her aunts and Stephen. "If you'll excuse me, I think I'd like a few moments alone."

"Of course." Stephen rose.

"My dear, if there's anything we can get you," Miss Priscilla began.

"She should go lie down," Aunt Lois said.

"I'll be fine." Rachel headed for the stairs. "I just need to think about all this. In private."

Stephen watched her go, his heart sore. He pulled in a breath and turned to face the ladies. "Well, I'm available to wash dishes."

Monday Morning, Rachel stepped up to the teller's window. "May I speak with Mr. Drummond?"

At her mention of the manager's name, the teller nodded. "Of course, Mrs. Jones. One moment."

He left his station, and Rachel glanced around. Half a dozen people had come to the bank to take care of post-holiday business. Stephen gave her a reassuring nod.

The teller reappeared at a door to their right. "This way, Mrs. Jones."

Stephen kept pace with her, and Rachel was glad she'd brought him along. She'd met the bank manager before, but she hadn't spoken to him since her father's death. She usually went to the bank and made her transactions as quickly as possible at the teller's window. The last time had been in early December, when she'd nearly emptied her father's account to pay the family's monthly accounts.

Mr. Drummond was well known to her father—she wouldn't say a friend. She didn't think her father had many friends, but he knew every businessman in town.

"Rachel, how good to see you again. And Mr. Worth, isn't it?" the white-haired banker said as they entered his office.

"Yes." Stephen shook hands with Drummond while Rachel seated herself in one of the chairs facing the desk. "I'm just here in support of Mrs. Jones."

Drummond turned his attention to Rachel. "How are you, Rachel? I haven't seen much of you since your father's funeral. And how are your aunts?"

"We're well, thank you." Rachel drew her father's two bankbooks from her handbag—the one for the local bank and the one from Austin. She laid them both on the desk and leaned forward. "Mr. Drummond, I came to seek your counsel on my father's financial situation."

"I trust everything is in order?"

"I was hoping you could tell me." She opened the Wiseman bankbook. "We seem to be scraping bottom here. Father never explained his income and financial affairs to me. Perhaps that was an oversight. We've tried to be frugal, but as you can see, we're nearly at the end of our resources."

Mr. Drummond took the small book in his hand and frowned over the figures. "Oh, but this isn't up to date."

"It isn't?"

"No, you had the usual wire transfer last week. If you'd come in to make a transaction, one of our tellers would have written it in your book."

"Would that be from this account?" She slid the second book toward him.

After examining it, Drummond nodded. "Yes, his old Austin account. I advised Abijah on a couple of occasions to transfer the balance here. But I suppose he thought our little bank and loan wasn't as secure as the Austin bank." His gaze snapped to hers. "Of course it is, I assure you. Our vault is top of the line."

"I'm sure it is," Rachel said. To her knowledge, the Wiseman bank had never been robbed.

"He had it set up to send him the same amount every quarter." As he spoke, the banker wrote something in her book from the Wiseman bank. He passed it back to her.

Rachel looked at the figures he'd written. She could hardly breathe.

"I trust that will take care of your immediate needs," Mr. Drummond said.

"Oh yes. Thank you." Rachel gazed at the older man. "My aunts and I appreciate this so much. And would it be too much trouble to transfer the Austin account's balance to your bank?"

"No trouble at all," the banker said. "I'd just need your signature."

Rachel sighed. "That would be such a relief." She caught Stephen's eye, and he smiled at her. He hadn't said a word throughout the conversation, but she knew he was relieved too, that she and her aunts would be secure.

Mr. Drummond took a form from his desk drawer. "I'm sorry this has been a worry for you. I assumed you knew about the second account."

"No, we only discovered it on Saturday."

"I'm so sorry. If I'd realized, I would have called on you and explained it to you. Now are you the sole heir, or are your aunts included?"

"Just me, but I will take care of them."

"Of course." He filled out the blanks on the form and set the paper and pen before Rachel.

"Just sign right here. I'll see to it right away. Then all your assets will be here in Wiseman."

"Thank you." Rachel signed her name, feeling a bit giddy. Her father had done well by her and his sisters after all. She and her aunts would never be in need again.

A few minutes later, they left the bank smiling.

"Your aunts will be so happy," Stephen said.

"Yes. I believe we should celebrate. Our Christmas was rather sparse. Of course, we must still live frugally, but if we do that and continue renting out the little house, we shouldn't have to ever leave our home."

An odd look came over Stephen, and for a moment she thought he would speak, but he didn't.

"Of course, I'm still shocked," Rachel said. "And sad, too, that Father hid so much from me."

"Your feeling is natural," Stephen said. "I wouldn't want to speak ill of your father, but it seems to me you all would have been a great deal happier if he hadn't kept his counsel so close."

He reached for Rachel's hand and tugged it inside the crook of his arm. She felt her face flush, but she walked along proudly beside him. She was a single woman, after all, and she had a right to keep company with a man if she wished.

Chapter 9

Two weeks later, Rachel was giving her hair a last brushing when a rapping on the front door sounded through the house. She smiled. Even Stephen's knock sounded more confident these days.

When she reached the bottom of the stairs, Aunt Priscilla had already let him in and ushered him to the parlor, where tea and oatmeal cake were laid out on a small table near the fireplace.

"He's in there, dear," Aunt Pris said.

Rachel leaned in to kiss her cheek. "Thank you, Auntie."

"Such a fine young man."

"Yes." Rachel's lungs seemed to swell. She glanced down the hall, where Aunt Lois was watching from her wheelchair in the kitchen doorway. Rachel blew her a kiss, and her aunt grinned and waved.

The firelight augmented the light from two lamps, casting the parlor in a soft glow. It was so nice not to have to scrimp on lamp oil or wood anymore. She had even become so daring as to wear a light gray woolen dress tonight, laying aside her black.

Stephen stood as she entered, and his eyes flared.

"Good evening."

"Glad you could come." Rachel walked forward and clasped his hand for a moment.

"You look lovely," he said.

"Thank you." She took her seat on the sofa. Stephen sat beside her, a decorous distance away. He was such a gentleman. He would drop the formality after a few minutes, but not the courtesy.

As they drank their tea and chatted, Rachel felt at ease with Stephen. She couldn't remember ever talking at length with someone so knowledgeable and yet so bighearted. He loved his students, that was clear, and was concerned about each family connected to his school.

"And how are you and your aunts getting along?" he asked. "I hope I'm not getting too personal, but I have wondered if everything smoothed out financially."

"Oh yes." Rachel waved a hand through the air. "Mr. Drummond has been wonderful, and I feel I can trust him."

"That's good," Stephen said. "I also got that impression the day we went to his office."

Rachel chuckled. "I should have gone to him months ago, as soon as Father died. But I had no idea he could help us."

"If you'd opened the box sooner, you would have," Stephen said. "I'm sorry, I don't mean to—"

"That's perfectly true," Rachel said. "Don't berate yourself. I should have told my aunts that I disagreed with them and gone ahead." She lowered her lashes but smiled at him. "This proves that sometimes being too nice is a detriment."

"Indeed. But I know you well enough now that I can say without a qualm that you would have managed. You and your aunts are intelligent, resourceful women, and if this bequest hadn't been discovered, I know you would be able to take care of yourselves. You would have found a way."

Rachel was silent for a moment then looked up at him. "To tell the truth, I was preparing to look for a job the next day. In fact, I had even thought of asking Mr. Drummond if there were any openings at the bank, though I suppose those are few. But I can sew and cook and clean houses. Yes, I think we could have found a way. The rent money helps, of course."

"Well, if there is anything I can do to help out, please let me know. Anytime."

"Thank you. We will." She smiled. "It was such a relief to pay off the tax bill."

"Of course." Stephen put down his cup and reached for her hand. "Rachel, I want to say something, and if I'm speaking too soon, please forgive me. I know it's not long since you learned that—well, what I mean is, I love you."

Her heart pounded and her cheeks warmed, but she held his gaze.

He went on, "If my saying so does not offend you, there is more I'd like to say."

"I. . ." She drew in a deep breath. Stephen wanted to hold a bigger part in her life. For a few days now, she'd wondered when this moment would come. Her own feelings for him had bloomed, but after years of guarding her heart, she wasn't sure whether it was right to feel this way or not. And now he had said it right out—he loved her too. "It makes me glad to hear you say it."

His eyes lit with joy. "Oh, dear Rachel. Dare I hope that you might consent to marry me? If you feel you should wait awhile, I don't mind. Well, I do, but it will be worth it. However long you think would be proper—that is, if you feel the same way I do."

Stephen held her hand in both of his and gazed deep into her eyes. Would she be able to go on breathing much longer?

"Yes," she said. "Yes, I do. I'm sure of it. And I'll try not to make you wait very long."

Was that too bold? He didn't seem to think so. She had never seen such happiness radiate from a man's face. Not Winfield's, and certainly not Father's.

"Darling," he whispered, "may I kiss you?"

Rachel was startled. Winfield had never asked permission the first time he caressed her. But then, she had known at the time that things were not quite as she'd wish them to be in Winfield's life and character. Still, she'd pushed those thoughts aside and allowed him liberties. Her face flushed hot at the memory.

"Yes," she whispered.

Stephen leaned closer, and his lips met hers in a sweet kiss full of promise and a hint of longing.

She reached up and touched his cheek. "Do you want to tell my aunts, or shall I?"

She could feel his laugh rumble deep in his chest. Stephen put his arms around her and gave her a warm hug. "Let's go and break the news together, shall we?"

They rose, and Stephen took her hand. They turned toward the doorway, but before they could take a step toward it, Aunt Lois rolled in with her sister close behind, pushing her wheelchair.

Lois's flushed face was wreathed in a smile. "My darlings, how wonderful! Isn't it, Pris?"

Aunt Priscilla's lips curved slightly upward. "Yes, Sister, it really is." She held out her arms to Rachel. "I am very pleased."

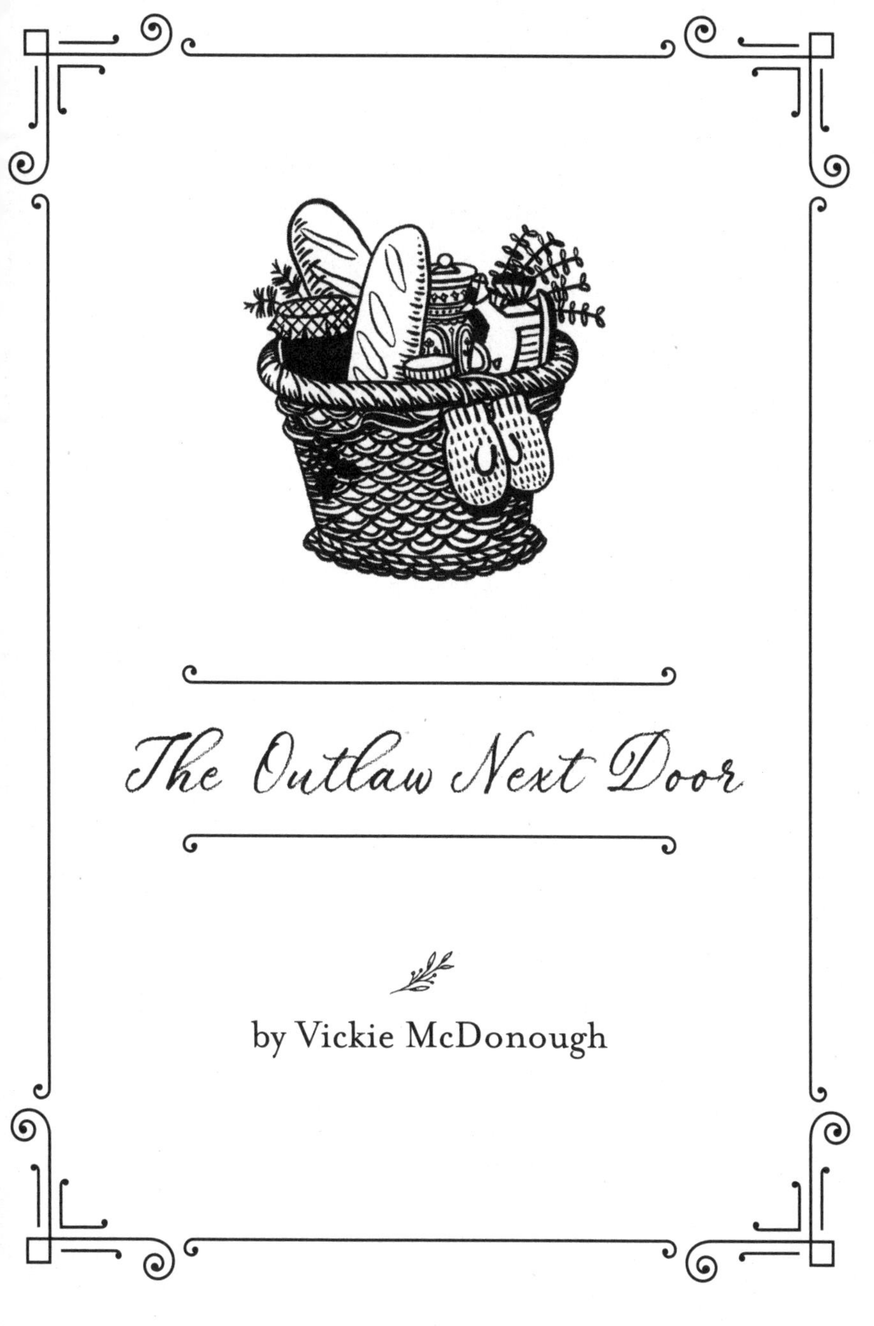

The Outlaw Next Door

by Vickie McDonough

Chapter 1

Wiseman, Texas
November 1887

The blast of gunfire filled the air, along with the pungent odor of gunpowder. Pa and Ned raced past him, toward the horses. Matt cried out then spun and fell to the ground, facedown. Will dropped to his knees, gutshot. Shaking, Dane knelt in the bloody dirt.

"Mr. McDermott?"

Dane blinked, jerked from the awful memory by a sweet voice. He shoved the dreadful thoughts away and forced a smile. Regina Ross stood a half dozen feet from him with a concerned look on her pretty face. He cleared his throat. "Afternoon, Miss Ross."

"Are you all right? I called to you several times."

He huffed a fake laugh. "I apologize. I was lost in some heavy thoughts."

"I sincerely hope they weren't too horrible. You were frowning."

They certainly were. He shrugged, needing to change the topic. "Thank you for your concern. What can I do for you today?"

"First off, Mama and I baked this morning, and we thought you might like a couple of muffins." She pulled something wrapped in a blue-and-white-checked cloth from her basket and handed it to him. "We wanted you to know how much we appreciate that you allow us to use your buggy for free."

Dane's stomach clenched at the thought of fresh muffins. His cooking was dismal, and most times he skipped breakfast. "Thank you. I look forward to eating these." He set the muffins on a shelf then turned back to face her. "You mentioned a buggy. Do you need one now?"

Miss Ross nodded. "Yes, please, if it's available."

"It is. I'll get it ready for you." He spun and headed into the livery for a horse. He'd anticipated that Miss Ross might take a drive, as she and her mother often did in the afternoons, to visit the sick or someone who lived a short way from town.

He led Ginger from her stall and gave her a quick grooming. As he rose up from brushing the mare's side, he glanced over her back to where Miss Ross stood just outside the livery. Though she wore a dainty hat, the sun glistened on her golden hair, which was curled into a bun at her nape.

Dane sighed. The little house he'd bought several years ago sat directly behind the parsonage. He'd seen Regina coming and going quite often. She'd captured his fancy a long time back, but there was nothing he could do about it. She was the preacher's daughter and deserved a man far better than him.

Dane put the harness and bridle on the horse then led her

outside to where the buggy sat between the livery and the corral. In quick order, he had the mare backed in, hitched, and ready to go. "If you'll hand me your basket, I'll secure it for you."

"Thank you, Mr. McDermott."

Dane settled the basket in the back of the buggy then helped Regina up to the seat. Her small, gloved hand fit into his perfectly. "So where are you off to this afternoon, if you don't mind me asking?"

"As I'm sure you've heard, Mamie Sanford had another baby. Mama wanted to send her some soup, so we made a batch, and I'm delivering it, as well as some muffins."

Since he mostly kept to himself, he hadn't heard about the new baby. Wasn't even sure who the Sanford woman was, but he reckoned she attended Sunday services, so he'd probably seen her before. "That's a kind thing to do. Have a nice ride."

He stepped back, wishing she'd invite him along, but that would hardly be proper, and Regina Ross was the perfect example of a genteel woman. She reminded him of his mother, who'd been the only light in his dark childhood.

"I will. The weather is perfect for a drive. Not too hot or too cold." Regina's pretty blue eyes twinkled. "I will see you again in an hour or so. I know you'll be wanting to get home to your supper."

Dane nodded, although all that awaited him was cold beans and hard corn bread. He wouldn't have minded a bowl of that soup she was taking to that woman. The scent of it made his belly growl. He stepped back as she released the brake.

Most females would be hesitant to drive a buggy alone, but Regina was an expert driver and rider. She once told him that she'd grown up on a ranch before her father felt the call of God. Dane couldn't help wondering what Regina had been like at the ranch. It was a bit hard to imagine since she was so refined, except for the rare occasion when she rode astride. Few women in Wiseman rode at all, much less without a sidesaddle.

Pulling his gaze away from the rear of the buggy, he plodded over to his horse. It was time he exercised the poor fellow. He tightened the cinch and unlooped the reins from the corral fence.

Another round of gunfire split the air, along with whoops and hollers. The cowboys had returned from the nearby ranches for their weekend of drinking and gambling. He searched for Regina's buggy, and his heart bucked. The mare had broken into a gallop and was racing out of town.

Dane vaulted onto his horse and slapped the reins against its flanks. "He-yah!"

They thundered down the road, chasing after the runaway horse and buggy. He had to get to Regina before she was hurt—or worse. The image of his bleeding and dying brothers rose up in front of him. "No!"

He couldn't let Regina be injured.

He hunkered down close to Rebel's mane and kicked the horse. "Ha! C'mon, boy."

The buggy grew closer as it bumped and wove on the road past the edge of town. It hit another bump, and the back wheels flew up then landed hard, bouncing the buggy even more.

Dane raced up beside Regina and glanced over, glad to see her concentrating on stopping the horse, pulling back hard on the reins, and not sobbing like most women would have been.

He drew alongside the speeding mare, stood up on his saddle, and dove onto her back. The jar of the landing sent him reeling sideways, and he fought to keep from falling off.

"Dane!"

Spurred by Regina's use of his Christian name and his desire to see her safe, he fought to right himself. He glanced up to see the bend in the road. If the horse didn't turn, they'd fall down the steep slope and land in the Brazos River.

With all his might, he hauled back on the reins. "Whoa, Ginger. You're all right." Relief washed through him when the roan mare slowed. She tried once again to pick up speed, but Dane held her back. "Whoa!"

Finally, the frightened mare pulled to a halt. Her sides heaved, and she danced in place.

Dane glanced over his shoulder. Regina's hat had blown off and her long golden hair hung down around her shoulders in beautiful waves, but at least she hadn't fallen off. He'd never seen a sight so pretty. He cleared his tight throat. "Are you all right?"

"Yes, thanks to you." She leaned back in her seat and blew out a loud breath. "I tried everything to get her to stop. I just knew we were going to end up in the river. I can swim, but it would have been difficult given the weight of my skirts and how shaky my arms are."

Dane slid off the mare, keeping a tight hold on her. She had relaxed and bent down to snag a piece of dried grass. He led the horse and buggy over to a tree, where he tied Ginger securely, and then he walked to the buggy. "Could I help you down?"

Regina rose and leaned over, putting her hands on his shoulders, and he lifted her to the ground. He'd never stood so close to her before and could see the different shades of blue in her lovely eyes. He held her gaze, knowing he shouldn't enjoy the closeness, but it had been so long since he'd felt a woman's touch. Reluctantly, he stepped back. "Are you certain you're not hurt?"

Regina surprised him by smiling. "To be honest, that's the most fun I've had in a long while. Trying to be the perfect preacher's daughter can be exhausting." She rubbed her upper arm. "I imagine I'll be sore tomorrow, but I'm alive and well, thanks to you. How can I ever repay you?"

A kiss would be nice. Dane's eyes widened at the impetuous thought. "You don't owe me anything. It's the least I could do, since it's my horse and buggy."

"Oh." The brightness of her eyes dimmed, making him wonder what she had wanted him to say. "I. . .um. . .should check the soup." She hurried to the back of the buggy and looked in. "Oh dear. The basket turned over, and most of the soup has spilled out. It's made a dreadful mess." She glanced his way but didn't look him in the eye as before.

Dane walked over and peered in. "Don't worry about it. I'll clean it up and bring the container back to your house. We should get you home."

Regina ducked her head. "Since I have no soup to deliver, I suppose I should return home. I'll make another batch and try again tomorrow."

Dane's heart bucked. At least he'd get to see her again soon.

"I'm ready to return home whenever you are." Regina stared at the dirt road. She'd been excited that Dane had gone to such efforts to rescue her, until he mentioned his horse and buggy. Of course, he was merely chasing after his property. Why should he care what happened to her?

"I should check the horse over and make sure the buggy wasn't damaged before we return to town."

Regina nodded. She needed to distance herself from her handsome champion. "I think I'll walk down to the river and wash the dust off my face."

"Watch out for snakes."

"I doubt they're active this late in the year, but I'll keep an eye open."

He pursed his lips, nodded, and then turned his back to her and ran his hands down the mare's leg.

Sighing loudly, Regina walked along the road until she found a place with easy access to the water. Slowly, she made her way downhill to the river's edge. The last thing she wanted was to trip and fall, landing in the water. Such a sight that would make.

She removed her gloves and knelt beside the slow-moving river. The setting was so peaceful after her frantic buggy ride. Why hadn't the mare slowed? She'd pulled on the reins with as much strength as she had, but the mare still ran. She'd never experienced a runaway horse before, not even when she lived on the ranch. It was both frightening and thrilling.

Mother would be shocked and would most likely forbid her to go driving again for a while. Perhaps she wouldn't tell her, so that she wouldn't worry next time Regina went visiting. Was that the same as lying? But then, how would she explain making soup again? She sighed. Of course she was better off telling her parents what had happened rather than trying to hide it.

Three geese flew down and landed in the water about fifty feet away. She watched the trio until they floated past her, and then her thoughts returned to Dane McDermott. She'd been curious about the quiet man ever since he moved into the house behind hers. He looked to be a bit older than her twenty-one years. If she had to guess, she'd say he was twenty-five or so. She had wrestled in the past with her attraction to his dark features—black hair with a bit of a curl, dark brown eyes, and tanned complexion.

Regina sighed. As the preacher's daughter, she wasn't supposed to gawk at men, but Dane drew her gaze whenever he was near. She was a woman who longed for a husband and children of her own, but most men seemed afraid to approach her—or perhaps none had ever been interested in her. Holding the church members' babies brought satisfaction for a brief moment, but she always had to return the child. One day she'd have a baby that would be hers. At least she prayed that was God's will for her.

And the image of Dane McDermott kept reappearing in her mind and dreams. Perhaps it was merely because she saw him so often when she went to pick up a buggy or a horse to ride. Yes, that must be the reason.

She pulled her handkerchief from her sleeve and dipped it in the cool water. Her eyes closed as she ran the refreshing cloth across her face. She rinsed the hanky and repeated the action then wetted it once more and squeezed as much water from it as she could.

"Are you ready to go?"

Regina yelped and scooted sideways.

"I'm sorry, Miss Ross. I didn't mean to frighten you."

Face warm with a fresh blush, Regina struggled to untangle her feet from her skirts.

Mr. McDermott bent down and lifted her to her feet. "There. That's better." He ducked his head then raised his mesmerizing eyes. "I'm truly sorry for sneaking up on you. It wasn't my intention.

I reckon I just walk quietly."

She forced a laugh. Making light of the situation helped her not to be so embarrassed. "It's like when I surprised you at the livery when you were lost in thought. That makes us even, so think nothing about it."

"Can I help you up the bank? It's a bit steep, especially with you in a dress." His ears reddened, and he looked away.

She probably should refuse, but in truth, she just might need his assistance. "Yes, thank you."

Regina picked up her gloves then looped one arm through his. "Were your horse and buggy all right?"

He nodded.

Regina sighed. It was difficult to make conversation with a man of few words. "I'm glad. I'd hate to see anything happen to that pretty mare. It's not her fault she was frightened by those reckless cowboys."

Dane glanced sideways as he helped her over a large tree root. "Most women would blame the horse."

She gazed up at him. Her heartbeat doubled as she looked into his dark brown eyes. "Not me. I know enough about horses to know it wasn't her fault."

"You're an interesting woman. Not like so many of the others in town."

"Um. . .thank you." She wondered how she was different, but she wouldn't ask.

They reached the top. Dane started to move away, but Regina stopped him. "I realize that you chased after us because you were concerned about your horse and buggy, but I want you to know how grateful I am. I could have been injured badly or killed. That would have devastated my parents, since I'm an only child."

"Not only your parents. Many folks in Wiseman admire you. And I didn't just chase after my property. You were my first concern."

Regina blinked, taken completely by surprise at his confession. "I. . .well. . .thank you."

A tiny grin tugged at Dane's lips, revealing dimples she'd never before seen. "Would you kindly stop saying that?"

The transformation that small smile made was amazing. If she thought she was attracted to Dane before, she was mistaken. Her heart threatened to pound out of her chest as he stood there staring at her.

Suddenly she remembered that they were alone. If anyone happened to ride by, it would look as if the two of them had planned a rendezvous. Then talk would be all over the small town. "I suppose we should get going."

He nodded and started toward the buggy, which he'd already turned around facing town. His saddle horse was tied behind the buggy.

Dane lifted her into the front seat then walked around the mare and climbed up beside Regina. He clucked his tongue, and the mare sedately started walking.

As they neared the edge of Wiseman, Regina turned to look at him. He had a nice profile with a straight nose and rounded chin. He glanced her way, reminding her of what she wanted to ask him. "I've been thinking about not telling Mama and Papa about the runaway horse. Do you think that would be lying? By not telling them so they won't worry?"

He shrugged. "You're asking the wrong person."

"What does that mean?" It sounded like he was a liar, but what did he have to tell falsehoods about? He lived a very quiet life. She saw him sitting in the back of the church on Sundays, but she never saw him at any other town events.

"It's just that you'd know much more what the Bible says about lying than me."

"Don't you read your Bible?"

He flicked a glance her way then refocused on the road. "Sure."

Regina resisted sighing. How did women talk to men who didn't like to chat?

As they rode back to town, she let her mind wander. Fighting the runaway horse and the fear of being hurt was almost worth it to spend a few extra minutes with Dane. If she closed her eyes, she could pretend for a moment that they were a couple.

"Regina?"

Her eyes popped open and her heart lurched at the sight of her father standing next to her. When had the buggy stopped?

Mr. McDermott stepped from the buggy and strode to the front, holding the mare.

"What's going on here?" Her father looked at her with kind but curious eyes.

She reached out, and he helped her down. She glanced at Dane and knew in that moment she needed to be truthful. "The gunfire I'm sure you heard earlier frightened the mare as I was driving her out of town, and she bolted. I couldn't get her to stop, but Mr. McDermott came to my rescue. He drove me back to make sure the mare was good and settled. That's all."

Her father's brows lifted. "That's more than enough, I'd say. You're not injured?"

She shook her head.

“Praise be to God. I’d say we’re in Mr. McDermott’s debt. You run along home while I express my appreciation.”

“Yes, Papa.” As she rounded the horse, she couldn’t resist thanking her champion once more. “I sincerely appreciate your help today, Mr. McDermott.”

Chapter 2

Regina's mother glanced around the crowded parlor at the Griffiths' house. Ten ladies had attended the sewing circle today, and all had stayed for the meeting about this year's Christmas baskets. As wife of the town parson, her mother organized the basket ministry each year. "So we're in agreement that we will provide nine Christmas baskets this year?"

Regina shared in her mother's joy as Mama's twinkling gaze scanned the room. She clapped her hands in delight. "Wonderful! So many families will be blessed this Christmas."

Emma Yates lifted a hand. "Do you suppose our secret benefactor will provide the meat again this year?"

Mama pursed her lips. "It's hard to say, since we don't know who the person is, but the Lord has always provided."

Mumbled agreements circled the room.

"Who is ready to commit to doing a basket? Regina, would you please write down the names?"

"Yes, ma'am." Regina opened her journal to a blank page.

Marta Yates's hand shot up. "The twins and I can do one again this year."

Mrs. Griffith cleared her throat. "Our family can do one."

Regina's mama smiled. "Wonderful. Thank you both for your generosity."

Rachel Worth's hand lifted. "My aunts and I can also do one."

In a matter of a few minutes, all but three of the baskets had been claimed. "I'll announce this Sunday that we're starting to collect canned goods. I'm sure others will volunteer. They always do." Mama took her seat, indicating she was finished talking.

Mrs. Griffith rose. "Who is hosting next week's sewing circle?"

The Begley cousins each lifted a hand.

"Very good. Our meeting is officially over, but feel free to stay and chat if you'd like."

The Yates twins rose and hurried toward Regina.

"Can you still go to the bakery with us?"

Regina nodded. "But I don't know that I'll be able to eat anything after that wonderful apple bread Mrs. Griffith served."

Ella smiled. "It was delicious. Marta is going to ask our hostess for the recipe."

Emma glanced affectionately at her brother's wife. "Perhaps we'll make it for Christmas. Wouldn't Justin love it?"

Ella's blue eyes gleamed. "It will be his new favorite dessert."

The blond-haired, blue-eyed twins giggled. Regina had learned that their brother, the town marshal, had a huge sweet tooth.

"Shall we go?" Emma asked.

"Let me tell Mama I'm leaving." At twenty-one, Regina hardly needed permission, but she respected her mama. She stopped at her mother's side and waited until Mama looked at her. "If you don't need me, I'm going to the bakery with Ella and Emma."

"That's fine, dear. Have a nice time."

She squeezed her mama's hand. "See you later."

Along with the twins, she left the Griffiths' stately house and walked northward.

Ella paused at the corner. "I want to stop in and see if Justin would like us to bring him something from the bakery."

Together they turned left, walking the short distance to the marshal's office.

"We'll wait out here while you go in," Emma said.

"All right." Ella reached for the door, but it opened before she touched it. She backed up, her eyes widening when two handsome men walked out.

The taller of the men stopped suddenly, staring at the three of them. A slow smile pulled at his lips, and he yanked off his western hat. "Is this the welcoming committee?"

Regina glanced at the twins. They were both mesmerized with the handsome strangers.

"We're new to town, but if this is a taste of the kind people of Wiseman, I'm sure we'll enjoy living here." The other man, obviously his brother since they looked so much alike, stepped forward. "My name is Logan Beaumont, and this is my brother, Mark."

The marshal had followed the men out, but Regina wasn't sure anyone but she had noticed.

Marshal Yates cleared his throat and frowned. "Two of these

ladies are my sisters, and the other one is the preacher's daughter."

Surprise engulfed the strangers' faces.

"We were merely introducing ourselves, Marshal." Mark Beaumont stuck his hat on his head.

"That's true. How else are we going to get to know folks now that we're bona fide residents?" Logan shuffled his boots.

Mark turned to face the marshal. "I can assure you, sir, that our parents raised us to be gentlemen."

"Good to know. Just don't forget it."

"Jus-tin." Emma drew out his name. "They were only being friendly."

"Yeah." Ella shoved her hands to her hips.

"Fine." Justin rolled his eyes. "I know when I'm outgunned." The marshal gestured at Regina and the girls. "The twins are my sisters, Ella and Emma, and this is Miss Ross. The Beaumont brothers bought the old Rutger store."

"Hasn't that been empty for years?" Ella asked.

"Isn't that the vacant building behind the bakery?" Regina looked across the square to where the bakery sat.

"Yep to both questions." The marshal nodded. "I was headed over to show them where it is."

"You bought it without seeing it?" Ella's brows lifted.

The brothers nodded then shared a concerned glance.

Mark frowned. "Is it in bad condition? The agent we purchased it through assured us it only needed cleaning."

Marshal Yates shrugged. "I have no idea—it's been closed up for years. Let's go have a look."

Together they crossed the town square.

Marshal Yates flicked a glance at Mark. "It will be nice to have a saddler in town. Most of us take our bridles and such to Dane McDermott at the livery for repair."

"We met him when we left our horses there. Nice man." Logan raised his face toward the sky. "Is it always so warm this late in November?"

Ella shook her head. "No. It depends on which way the wind blows. It gets quite chilly at times when the wind is out of the north."

"We even get snow on occasion," Emma piped up.

Regina glanced sideways. "When we first moved here, the weather was one thing I noticed too."

Logan smiled. "Well, I for one like it. No more snow a foot deep."

"Where are y'all from?" the marshal asked.

"Nebraska." Mark looked around the square. "Nice town you've got here."

"We like it." Ella looped her arm through her brother's and looked at Logan. "So, if your brother is a saddler, what do you do?"

"I'm opening a horse equipment and leather store. We'll sell all kinds of bridles, harness parts, belts, saddlebags—Mark's saddles. Pretty much anything made from leather, except shoes and boots."

The marshal slowed to let a wagon pass in front of them. He nodded at the driver. "The ranchers in these parts will be happy about that. Now they have to either ride to Dallas for most of those things or order them from the mercantile."

Mark scratched his ear. "We'll be glad to help them."

They reached the bakery, and Justin stopped. "You ladies go on in, and I'll see to the Beaumonts."

Regina could tell the twins were disappointed to leave the

company of the handsome men. Personally, she was relieved. As they walked into the bakery, she couldn't help wondering how the brothers' business would affect Dane's. Wiseman residents mostly rented a horse or buggy to visit people who lived out of town or to travel to Dallas. She couldn't imagine that Dane made much money. She hoped the Beaumonts' store didn't drive him out of business. She couldn't bear the thought of him leaving town.

The twins chatted with Mrs. Morgan, the older woman who ran the bakery, telling her about the newly arrived men who would be her neighbors.

"It's about time someone bought that ol' place. I just hope they'll be decent neighbors. Would you like anything, Miss Ross?"

"No, thank you. I filled up at the sewing circle."

The girls took a seat by the window. One twin had chosen an orange scone, while the other had a chocolate confection.

"Weren't those brothers dreamy?" Ella leaned her elbow on the table and rested her cheek in her hand.

"I do believe they are the answer to our prayers." Emma had the same enamored expression as her sister.

"Well, there's one for each of you." Regina smiled.

Emma sobered. "You don't have your eye on one of them, do you? I mean, they are closer to your age."

"Oh no." Regina placed her hand against her chest. "You're welcome to them."

The Beaumont brothers were comely men with light brown hair and blue eyes, but her taste ran darker. Dane's image appeared in her mind with his chocolate-colored hair and eyes.

Ella gasped. "Who were you thinking of just then?"

Emma reached out and squeezed Regina's arm. "You got all

swoony-eyed. Do tell. Who is it?"

Regina sobered. Had her thoughts truly been reflected on her face? Her cheeks warmed. "I'd rather not say. There really isn't anything between us." At least she didn't think Dane had feelings for her.

"Ooh! I'm so curious." Ella looked to her sister. "Who do you think it could be?"

"I'm curious too, but we should respect Regina's wishes and not pester her."

Regina slowly released a breath, proud of Emma. She'd made friends with the twins, even though she was closer to Marta's age, partly because she wanted to help the girls settle down. They'd become much more ladylike since their brother had married, but they could still be impulsive. "Did you actually pray for God to bring men to town?"

Mrs. Morgan set down a tray and placed a teacup and saucer in front of each of them. Then she set the pot on the table.

"But I didn't order tea." Regina glanced up at the gray-haired woman.

"You and your mother aren't the only people in town who can bless others." She hiked up her chin, but the twinkle in her eyes showed she wasn't upset.

"Thank you kindly." Regina smiled at the woman.

"Enjoy your treat, ladies."

Once Mrs. Morgan had returned to her work area, Ella looked at Regina. "We did pray. We'll be seventeen in a couple of weeks, and we'd like to be married."

Emma nodded. "Most all of our friends are."

Regina cradled her warm teacup, praying for wisdom. "You girls are still young. Enjoy life. Don't feel rushed to get married. I'm twenty-one and still single."

Ella sprinkled sugar in her tea. "But don't you desire to marry and have children?"

Regina glanced out the window as Mrs. Callen and several of her children walked by the bakery. One little boy pleaded with his mother to stop and buy a treat. "Sure, I'd like to marry, but God hasn't sent me a husband. I'm content to wait until the man God has for me comes along." Once again her thoughts shifted to Dane McDermott.

"But it's so hard to wait."

She looked at the girls. "Marriage is a lot of work. Look at us. We probably wouldn't be here now if we were married. We'd have a long list of chores waiting for us. That's why many of the town's women don't attend the sewing circle. They simply don't have time to go."

"I suppose, but I have a feeling I'll be dreaming of Logan Beaumont tonight." Ella sighed.

"I'm so glad you didn't say Mark. He's so tall and handsome." Emma's sigh mirrored her sister's.

Oh dear. Regina feared that Marta and the marshal might have their hands full keeping the Beaumont brothers and the twins apart.

Dane walked out of the feedstore with a fifty-pound bag of horse feed on his shoulder. As he headed down the street back to the livery, he noticed Regina and her mother leave the parsonage across the street and turn toward him. He slowed his steps, remembering

Pastor Ross's genuine expression of gratefulness for Dane's help with the runaway wagon incident.

Both women were about the same height, although Mrs. Ross carried more weight than her daughter. Regina wasn't as thin as the Yates twins and several other women in town, but he didn't mind. He preferred a woman who looked healthy. He huffed a laugh. Who was he kidding? No woman would look his way twice, except Regina, and as the daughter of the town preacher, she was only being kind.

Dane started forward but paused again when he heard his name called. He never should have dawdled. "Afternoon, ladies."

"Good day to you too." Mrs. Ross smiled.

"It's nice to see you again." Regina held up the basket she carried. "We're off to visit the Callens and to deliver cookies."

"You ladies are a true blessing to the families of this town."

Regina's cheeks pinked, and her mother's smile grew bigger.

"That looks like a mighty heavy load you've got." Regina gazed up at him with big blue eyes.

"Aw, it's not too bad."

They passed several small stores and then the mercantile. Dane's livery was down the next street to the left. He glanced ahead and spied two strangers standing out front of the saloon. His gut clenched. One man looked like he imagined his father might at this stage in life, although he was thinner than his pa had ever been. The stranger looked away.

There was no chance the man was Dane's father. He suspected that by now Pa was dead. If not, he was still in prison. He couldn't imagine him surviving nearly ten years in the Kansas State Penitentiary.

Shaking away thoughts of his pa, he glanced at the pair again. The ladies would have to walk right past those men and then turn down the next street to the poorer part of Wiseman. "If you ladies will allow me, I'll see you to the Callens' door."

Mrs. Ross glanced up, surprised. "That's quite kind of you, but that load looks cumbersome. We couldn't ask that of you."

"If you wouldn't mind turning here, I can drop this off at the livery then walk with you."

Mrs. Ross glanced down the street toward the strangers. "I thought we would be all right since the saloon isn't open, but perhaps you're right. We'd be happy to have you escort us."

"My pleasure."

Regina peeked up from under her bonnet and smiled. "Thank you."

Mrs. Ross shook her head. "Most days I wouldn't think twice about walking the town without Mr. Ross, but on Fridays and Saturdays there are so many strangers in town."

He nodded. "That's true."

Regina glanced up at him. "I hear you've met the Beaumont brothers."

Dane's dark eyes flicked toward Regina. "You did?"

"Yes. They were talking to the marshal when the Yates twins and I stopped by the jailhouse." Her cheeks burned at the thought. She'd never stopped there before. "The twins wondered if their brother wanted something from the bakery since we were headed there."

"We should invite them for Sunday dinner to welcome them to town." Mrs. Ross turned toward Dane and waved her index finger at him. "You should come too, young man, and this time I won't take no for an answer."

Tempted to back up a step, Dane stood his ground. "Uh. . .yes, ma'am. Thank you."

He gritted his teeth as he walked into the livery and set down the sack of feed. He avoided eating with folks because it gave them too much time to question him about his past. If not for the grace of God, he might be in a jail cell next to Pa.

He forced a smile as he walked outside where the ladies waited. Truth be told, it wasn't hard to smile when looking at Regina. Her blond hair peeked out from her bonnet and glistened in the sunlight. Peering into her pretty eyes was like looking at the sky on a cloudless day.

Mrs. Ross stared at her daughter then cocked her head as her gaze turned his way. "Shall we go, Mr. McDermott?"

"Uh. . .yes, ma'am." He pushed his feet into motion, hoping hard that she hadn't noticed his interest in her daughter. He was the last person in town they'd want Regina to be with if they knew the truth.

He escorted the ladies to the Callens' shanty and promised to return for them in thirty minutes. Returning to the livery, he hoisted up the heavy sack and filled the feedboxes in the stalls. Then he grabbed a rope and headed to the corral to bring in the horses. As he reached for the gate latch, his hand froze. The gate was open.

His head jerked up. Two of his horses were missing.

Chapter 3

Feeling hesitant, Dane slowed his pace as he approached the marshal's office. It was a lawman who'd changed his life. But Pa had drilled into him that lawmen were people to avoid at all costs. That was a long time ago, but old habits were hard to break.

Marshal Yates was well liked by the townsfolk and had a good reputation for upholding the law while being fair. He'd even had to arrest his own deputy once. Pete Buckley, brother of the marshal's wife, was still in prison for stealing from the good people of Wiseman.

Dane's gut churned. He started to turn back, but if someone was bold enough to take two horses in full daylight, they might return and steal from someone else. The marshal needed to know about the theft, but there'd been a few times when Marshal Yates had given him a hard stare, making Dane wonder what he'd been thinking. He sucked in a deep breath, shoved aside his reservations, opened the door, and stepped inside.

Marshal Yates walked out from the cell, holding a broom. For a split second, there was a speck of surprise in his gaze before he masked it. "Afternoon, McDermott. How can I help you?"

Dane rubbed the back of his neck, antsy even though he'd lectured himself not to be. "Got home from the feedstore a few minutes ago and went to get my horses to put 'em in the stalls for the night. Found the gate open. Someone stole two of 'em."

The marshal set the broom in a corner. "How do you know they didn't just wander off?"

"If they did, they bridled and saddled each other."

Marshal Yates's lips twitched as if fighting a grin. "Sorry, I realize this isn't a laughing matter, but the mental image of that gave me a chuckle. I'm guessing you'd left the livery open while you were gone?"

"Always do. Never had a problem before." Dane glanced around the small office, surprised not to see wanted posters hanging on the walls. "I did notice a couple of strangers waiting for the saloon to open, but I don't suppose they took my stock since they didn't seem in any hurry."

"Mind if I walk down to the livery with you and have a look around?"

"No, but I didn't see any evidence left behind."

"I'll just have a quick look, and then I want to question some folks near the livery before they all close up shop."

"All right. I gotta get over to the Callens'. I escorted Mrs. Ross and her daughter there because of the strangers. Told them

I'd come back for them."

Marshal Yates reached for his hat and placed it on his head. "Go ahead. That's a kind thing you did."

Dane shrugged, more than ready to leave. "Weren't nothin' much."

"I appreciate a man who watches out for the ladies of Wiseman. Not all do." He clapped Dane on the shoulder, sending Dane's heart stampeding. "I'll do what I can to find your horses."

Dane stepped outside. "I'd appreciate that. I think I'll go riding around before darkness sets in and see if I can find them."

"If you do, don't try to capture two men alone. Come get me first. I'll deputize you to make things legal."

They walked side by side until Dane swerved off toward the Callens'. Imagine that, him a deputy. Pa would have a conniption fit.

As he reached the Callens' sad little house, a herd of young'uns raced out the door in front of the Ross ladies. The kids whooped like Indians. He counted five, and the oldest couldn't be any more than eight or nine. The youngsters ran down the street and disappeared around the corner. Mrs. Callen, dressed in a tattered calico, followed the Rosses outside, holding a baby on her hip.

"Thank you kindly for stopping by. My young'uns loved your cookies. I'm glad I managed to save a couple for Jacob and Mr. Callen before they were eaten up by my little hooligans."

"It was our pleasure." Mrs. Ross laid a hand on Mrs. Callen's arm. "Please let us know if you need anything."

Mrs. Callen looked down. "That's mighty kind of ya, but Mr. Callen don't like others to know about stuff like that."

Mrs. Ross nodded. "I understand. Men have their pride. I just don't want you or the children going hungry."

Regina glanced at Dane and smiled. He nodded to her.

"Thank you kindly. I'd best get supper going." Mrs. Callen jiggled the baby on her hip.

Dane felt bad for the family. Jacob, who was only eleven or twelve, had already quit school and was working on a nearby ranch with his father. He wished there was something he could do for the family. Perhaps he could donate more cans of food for the food baskets the Rosses collected each Christmas. Or he could buy some and leave them in a box on their porch.

He was grateful that his mentor, Ellis Ferguson, had left him the livery when he died and also a surprisingly hefty bank account. Ellis had mentioned selling his ranch after his wife and only child died, but Dane had figured the older man had used that money to open his livery. Ellis said many times that God moved in mysterious ways. Dane had never dreamed he'd ever come by that much legally.

"We'll see you at church on Sunday." Mrs. Ross waved to Mrs. Callen then joined Regina. They walked his way. "That was a lovely visit."

Regina nodded. "It was. I wish there was more that we could do to help the poorer families of Wiseman."

Mrs. Ross pursed her lips. "I do too, dear, but you don't want to step on their pride. There's a fine line between helping and offending."

Dane understood that. On occasion, well-meaning folks had tried to help his family, but Mama had been afraid to accept their generous gifts for fear of angering Pa. But then, most things had angered Pa, especially when he'd been drinking. That was the reason Dane never touched liquor.

"Did you get a lot done while we were visiting?" Regina gazed up at him.

He hated to share his news, but word would be around town soon enough. "When I got back, I discovered someone had stolen two of my horses."

"Oh no!" Regina reached out as if to touch him but then lowered her hand. Her gaze flicked to her mother then back. "I'm so sorry."

Mrs. Ross clucked her tongue and shook her head. "Other than the Tanners' stolen carved box, there hasn't been a theft in Wiseman since Pete Buckley was arrested two years ago. I'm very sorry about your horses, but I do hope it's an isolated incident."

"Thank you. So do I." Dane walked them home, taking the longer route on the edge of town to avoid going past the saloon. He could already hear the ruckus, and the place had just opened.

He needed to get back to the livery. A good chunk of the money he made was from tending the horses of the cowpokes who came in for a night of carousing and didn't want to leave their mounts on the street. He'd have to keep a good watch to make sure none of those horses got stolen.

Mrs. Ross paused in front of her house. "Thank you so much for escorting us today. It was quite thoughtful of you."

"My pleasure." Dane nodded.

Regina smiled.

Too bad he couldn't have had some time alone with her. He'd gotten used to talking with her at the livery and missed it when she didn't come around. He tipped his hat. "You ladies have a good evening."

"Don't forget, we'll be expecting you for Sunday dinner this week," Mrs. Ross called out.

Dane looked over his shoulder. "I'm looking forward to it."

His gaze collided with Regina's for one last look, and then he headed toward the livery. He shouldn't have said he was looking forward to the meal. Yeah, the home-cooked food was something he was eager to enjoy, but he didn't like being questioned about his past, and that was sure to come up.

As soon as the Sunday service was over, Regina hurried home. She was so excited that Dane was coming to dinner that she barely managed to sit through the service. Mama had given her several questioning glances.

While her parents said farewell to the parishioners and wished them a good week, she had slipped away. She wanted everything to be perfect today.

Regina rushed into the house and hung up her cloak and bonnet. She added a couple of logs to the fireplace in the parlor then studied the dining table on her way to the kitchen. She'd already set it with an ivory damask tablecloth and matching napkins. A small vase in the center held a bouquet of lavender silk flowers. She'd be glad when they were able to enjoy fresh flowers again, but these would do for now.

In the kitchen, she donned her apron then pulled the roast from the oven. A quick poke with a fork confirmed that the meat and vegetables were done. Regina quickly stirred up some biscuit batter then rolled it and cut it into circles. She placed the biscuits on a baking sheet and put it in the oven.

Next she checked on the pot of green beans that she and Mama had canned last summer and the turnips that were sitting at the back of the stove. Both were steaming. All she needed was for her parents and the men to arrive.

She removed her apron and went back into the dining room, straightening a knife and two forks. Then she turned toward the mirror. Her cheeks were red from the heat of the stove, and several wisps of hair had escaped her combs. She pulled out the mother-of-pearl combs and pressed her hair back then pushed them in again. Turning, she glanced at her hair, which hung down her back in waves. Mama thought the style too young for her, but she much preferred it to a tight bun.

With nothing else to do, she sat on the settee and watched out the front window. What would Dane think of their house? It was a nice size for a parsonage and allowed them room to entertain guests. She tapped her fingers on the side table as she gazed out the window, watching the few people who lingered outside on the chilly day.

Dane had looked handsome in his fresh white shirt, string tie, black pants, and frock coat. With his ebony hair and dark eyes, he looked very comely in black. Why had he agreed to join them for dinner today when he'd turned down countless invitations in the past? Was it because they seemed to be growing closer since he'd rescued her? Or did it have something to do with the Beaumont brothers coming today?

She blew out a sigh. It wasn't like her to worry. The problem was that she wanted to impress Dane. She longed for him to like her as she did him. He was the only man ever to grab her attention. Leaning back in the seat, she closed her eyes and prayed. "Heavenly Father, if it be Your will for Dane and me to be together, I pray You'll make it happen. Forgive me for fretting. Help my parents to see Dane as an appropriate suitor, should he ever decide he wants to be one."

Footsteps sounded on the front porch, and Regina popped up, her stomach nearly leaping to her throat. She hurried to the door and opened it. Her mother entered with the Beaumonts following her. Dane and her father brought up the rear.

"Welcome!" Regina smiled at the two brothers. They looked almost enough alike to be twins, but she knew they weren't.

Her father held out his hand, indicating that Dane should enter next. Dane glanced at her, and a tiny smile cocked up one side of his mouth, giving her a glimpse of his dimple.

"Come in," Mama said. "You're letting the heat out."

Her father chuckled. "That's what I'm always telling her." He patted Dane on the shoulder, and they entered quickly. Regina closed the door. Her father slipped out of his coat and hung it on one of the pegs near the door, then walked over to where Mark and Logan Beaumont waited.

"May I take your duster?" she asked Dane. Other than the frock coat he wore to Sunday services, the long, black canvas coat was the only one she'd ever seen him wear.

"Uh, sure." He slipped it off then passed it to her. "Thank you."

She smiled up at him. "My pleasure." She leaned in closer and whispered, "I'm so glad you came."

Dane blinked several times then stepped back when her father approached.

"Here are our other guests' coats. You should come and greet them also."

"Yes, sir." Cheeks warming, Regina took their coats and hung them up.

Mrs. Ross clapped her hands. "Please, everybody, come and take a seat. Regina has everything ready. We're so happy you could all join us today."

Papa took his seat at the far end of the table, while the brothers sat at the two places on the right side. A thrill ran through Regina at the thought of sitting next to Dane.

She carried the bowls of food to the table while her mother removed the hot biscuits from the oven. Though her stomach grumbled, Regina wasn't sure she could eat a bite with so many men surrounding her.

Once her mother had taken her seat across from Papa, Regina sat next to Dane.

"Shall we pray?" Everyone ducked their heads as her father blessed the food.

Mama lifted the meat platter and handed it to Logan.

"The food looks wonderful. That's one of the things I'll miss about not being in Nebraska." Logan passed the platter to his brother.

"Me too. Mama is a wonderful cook." Mark took a slice of roast beef then speared several potato wedges and scooped up a small pile of carrots.

Papa glanced at the brothers. "What made you decide to come to our part of the country? Wiseman is such a small spot on the map." He handed the meat platter to Dane.

"It's partly my fault." Mark sliced his beef. "I fell off a spooked horse when I was eleven and severely injured my knee. The cold Nebraska weather makes it ache for months on end, so I thought I'd try moving to a warmer climate."

"Texas can be plenty warm. This cold never lasts long." Mama smiled at the men.

"I decided to tag along with Mark. It was a good chance to set up shop for ourselves. Our pa runs a similar store back in Brownville."

"I've never heard of that town. Texas has a Brownsville down south." Papa reached for his glass, took a swig, then turned his gaze on Dane. "And how about you, Mr. McDermott? Where do you hail from?"

Chapter 4

Dane nearly dropped his fork when he glanced up and found everyone looking at him. He cleared his throat. "I'm from a small town in Missouri, not far from. . .uh. . .Springfield."

"We lived in Missouri for a few years when I was small." Regina turned her head so that Dane could see her pretty eyes. They were similar to her mother's but darker.

"What does your father do for a living?" Reverend Ross asked.

Dane's heart clenched. "He was a farmer for a time." *But he much preferred stealing from other hardworking people rather than laboring himself.*

"So what does he do now?" Mrs. Ross dropped a spoonful of turnips onto her plate.

Dane's mind raced. The last thing he wanted was to lie to these kind people. "The truth is, I don't know. I haven't seen or heard from him since I left Missouri."

"How long ago was that? Right before you came here?" Regina asked.

Dane resisted shifting in his chair. The questions were getting far too uncomfortable.

"Let's allow the man to eat, dear." Regina's father smiled, but the look he sent Dane made him think they would be talking in the future. He should be relieved that the questioning had stopped for now, but all he wanted was to finish this delicious meal and to check on his horses.

They ate in silence for a short while, then Logan Beaumont cleared his throat. "The marshal told us that you repair bridles and harnesses. That right?"

Dane nodded. "And you'll be selling them."

"Yes. But I don't plan to get into the repair business, so I wanted you to be aware of that. If we have anyone come to the shop who needs something fixed, we'll send them your way."

"I'd appreciate that." Dane had thought that Logan's store would mean an end to his repair business, but he was glad to hear it wouldn't. Repairs kept him busy when the horse business was slow. Still, some men would prefer to buy new equipment instead of paying to have older pieces repaired.

When the plates were empty, Regina rose. "I have custard pie for anyone who'd like a slice."

Dane noticed the Beaumont brothers' eyes light up, so he guessed their vote was yes. He was stuffed from the delicious meal, but he'd manage to find room for pie.

A knock sounded at the door.

Mrs. Ross rose. "I'll see to it."

While Regina removed the plates, Dane couldn't help listening to the man at the door. Mrs. Ross hurried into the dining room, but her husband was already on his feet. "I suppose you heard there's been an accident on the McAllen ranch? The injured man isn't expected to survive, and he is asking for you."

"Duty calls, gentlemen. I'm sorry to have to leave, but we're glad you could dine with us." He kissed his wife's forehead and, with a twinkle in his eyes, said, "Thank you for another wonderful meal, dearest. Save me a piece of pie."

"I always do." Mrs. Ross patted her husband's sleeve.

Dane enjoyed the small glimpse of what normal family life looked like with a husband who cherished his wife. The pastor set a good example of how a man should treat a woman. If Dane ever married, that was the example he wanted to follow, not the despicable one his pa had set. Most all of the pain he'd suffered in his life could be blamed on Pa. Yes, he was responsible for his part, but God had set him on a better path, and for that, he'd always be thankful.

"Dane?"

He glanced up to see Regina holding out a slice of pie on a saucer. "Um. . .sorry. Lost in thought."

She smiled, driving away the dark memories of his past. "Good thoughts, I hope."

He smiled back. "This pie sure looks delicious."

Regina pursed her lips. He hadn't fooled her, but he wasn't ready to talk about his past, especially not with a group of people listening. If he had his druthers, it would stay buried forever, just like his ma was.

Two weeks before Christmas, Regina sat in the parlor, putting the final touches on a small quilt for the Callens' baby. "Have you talked with the other ladies who are stitching clothing for the poor? I wonder if most of them will be finished by December twenty-second."

"Everyone has promised to have their projects to me on time." Her mother carried a stack of children's clothing she'd ironed into the parlor and set it on the coffee table. "I wonder if you might check with the Beaumont brothers and see if they have any crates they could give us for the Christmas baskets. We probably should have started collecting those weeks ago."

"That's a wonderful idea. With all the supplies they've been getting for their store, I imagine they would have some they could part with. I'll walk over as soon as I finish this."

Her mother stopped beside Regina and fingered the quilt she was finishing. "You've done a lovely job on this project. The use of greens and blues is quite different from most quilts I've seen."

Regina smiled. "Thank you. Getting that large pile of fabric from the Begley cousins was a blessing. Some of the patterns were a bit flashy for us to wear, but they look pretty in a quilt—in small amounts."

"So true." Mama sat in her chair near the fireplace. The bright light from the sunny day made it easy to see their stitching. "How did you think our dinner went with the gentlemen last week?"

Regina glanced up. "They obviously liked the food. There wasn't much left."

"I'm glad. Unmarried men don't often get a good meal unless they can cook or can afford to buy something at the café regularly."

Regina's thoughts veered to Dane. What did he eat? Could he cook? Given the chance, she'd happily fix him meals. She blinked at the thought. How had her feelings for the man deepened so much that she could see them married?

Other than on Sunday, she'd only seen him twice since he'd joined them for dinner a week and a half ago, but each one had been a special moment.

"I noticed Mr. McDermott doesn't seem to like to talk about his past much."

"Not everyone has had a happy childhood."

Mama looked up from her stitching. "He didn't?"

Regina shrugged. "I don't think so, but he's never talked to me about it."

"It's so sad for children to grow up in harsh circumstances. Just look at that tiny cottage the Callens live in with all those children. I wish we could do more for them."

"I do too. But at least their children are happy. It's sad, though, that Jacob had to leave school at such a young age to go to work."

"That's not uncommon for boys his age. Many must help on their family's ranch or farm."

Regina tied a knot in her thread then clipped it with the scissors. She shook out the five-foot-by-five-foot log cabin quilt and held it up, happy with her work.

Mama set her sewing in her lap. "Mrs. Callen will be so happy to receive that lovely quilt. The one she had on her baby the last time we visited was in tatters."

"I imagine she's used it for most of her other children." Regina folded the quilt and set it on the table next to the clothing. She put her sewing supplies in the box and set it back on the shelf. "I'll go over to the Beaumonts' store now and ask about the crates."

Mama picked up her sewing. "After I finish this, I'll start on lunch. Oh, could you run by the post office and see if we have any mail?"

Regina wrapped her cloak around her shoulders. "I'd be happy to."

"Once you're done with your errands, could you please stop by the church and let your father know it's time for lunch?"

"Yes, Mama." She tied her hood, put on her gloves, then stepped out into the chilly morning air. She loved the crispness of winter but didn't especially care for the colder temperatures, especially on windy days. But today the sun shone in all its glory in a cloudless light blue sky, sharing its warmth with all those brave enough to venture outside.

Excitement skittered through her. The post office was across the street from Dane's livery, giving her the perfect opportunity to drop in for a quick moment. But first she headed over to the Beaumonts' store. Delicious aromas from the bakery tempted her as she walked past the little shop, but she kept her feet in motion. How could the Beaumonts work right next door and not stop in constantly? It would prove to be too tempting for her.

She paused in front of the door to the shop, uncertain whether to knock or simply go in. A movement through the spotless glass snagged her attention. One of the brothers was gesturing for her to enter. She stepped inside and was hit by the instant warmth of the potbelly stove in the corner.

"Good morning, Miss Ross. I didn't expect to ever see you in our store."

"I've come to ask a favor." She glanced around the small room.

The brothers had raised a wall with a door, which divided what was once a large area. Various types of bridles and halters hung from pegs on the far wall. Stacks of colorful saddle pads and blankets filled a table in the center of the room. The place smelled of leather and saddle soap.

"What do you think?" Logan asked.

"You've gotten a lot done. Are you open for business?"

"Yes, ma'am, we are."

On the back wall were several rows of coiled rope. "I imagine the local ranchers and horse owners will be glad to have your store in Wiseman. Traveling to Dallas and back takes most of a day, and ordering from the mercantile can take a month or longer."

Through the open door of the divider wall, Regina heard the low rumble of male voices coming from Mark's saddle shop.

Logan stepped around the counter, wiping his hands on a rag. "So, what can I help you with? Is your pa needing something for his horse?"

"He doesn't own one. We borrow horses from Mr. McDermott when the need arises."

A shadow moved across the open doorway, and then Dane stepped into the Beaumont shop. His gaze lit up when it landed on her. "Did I hear my name?"

Regina's heart flip-flopped. "I was merely explaining how we don't need to purchase any equipment since we always borrow horses from you."

"That's true." She could see the same question in his eyes that Logan had asked concerning her reason for being here.

She turned back to Logan. "Every year at Christmastime, the town assembles food baskets for the poor. Mama was wondering if you might have some crates you could spare since you recently set up shop. We use crates instead of actual baskets, since they hold so much more."

Logan glanced toward the rear of the store. "We have a stack of them out back. How many were you needing?"

"Nine altogether, but you're the first person I've asked. I can usually get some from the mercantile also."

"Let's go see if the ones I have are the size you're wanting."

"Mind if I tag along?" Dane glanced from Logan to Regina. "You might need help toting the crates."

"Sure." Logan motioned for Dane to join them. "Did Mark get you fixed up?"

"He will. There's a partially made saddle that he's going to rework for me."

Regina followed the men out the back door. Logan and Dane trotted down the steps, but Dane reached up to help her descend. "Thank you."

His warm brown eyes made her think he'd enjoyed assisting her.

Along the back of the building sat a stack of nearly a dozen crates, mostly on the large size. Logan lifted one, and a rabbit darted out from under the pile. He jumped backward and yelped, dropping the crate.

Dane and Regina shared a smile.

"I thought for sure a rattlesnake had me." Logan patted his chest. Then he reached down and lifted up the crate again. "How about this? Big enough?"

"That would work nicely. And they don't need to be the same size, since we give the families with more children a larger amount of food."

"That's a nice thing you folks do."

"Oh, it's not only my family. Most of the townsfolk contribute in one way or another. Some families even prepare a whole basket on their own. And there's a mysterious benefactor who has donated dressed hens, turkeys, and geese for each basket the past few years."

Logan straightened. "Really? I love a good mystery. I wonder who that person could be." He rubbed his chin as if narrowing down the list of suspected donors. "How can Mark and I help?"

"You're helping quite a lot by donating the crates, but if you want to do more, Mama will be making the announcement at church this Sunday about what items are still needed."

Mark stuck his head out the back door. "Hey, Logan, you've got a customer in here asking questions I don't know how to answer."

Logan started up the steps. "Help yourself to the crates. I can carry them over to your house when I'm done inside."

Dane pulled the wooden boxes down from the stack and placed them in a line. "Why don't you pick the ones you want, and I'll set them aside. Logan and I can deliver them later."

Regina sent him a warm smile. "Why, thank you."

"My pleasure. I'm happy to see you again."

"You are?"

Dane glanced around. "Sure."

If she was hoping for something more romantic, she was disappointed. She refocused on the crates. "Those three will do nicely, as well as the two bigger ones."

"That makes five." He reached for one that had been on the bottom of the pile. "This could work, but it has a couple of loose boards. I could fix it easily enough."

"That would be wonderful. So that gives us six." She pointed to two smaller ones. "Let's take those, and if we need to, we can use both for one family. That's seven. Just two more, but I don't think the rest are big enough. I'll check with Mr. Lawson. With all the shipments arriving at the mercantile, he usually can provide several."

Dane put the final crates with the others and restacked the ones they couldn't use along the back of the shop. He dusted off his hands and looked at Regina. "Are you headed home now?"

Was he as reluctant to say goodbye as she? "Actually, I need to stop in the post office and see if we have any mail. Mama is always so anxious for letters that she rarely wants to wait on Mr. Goodwin to deliver them."

"Mind if I walk with you? I need to get my hammer and a handful of nails to repair the broken crate."

"Of course I don't mind." She peeked sideways as they started walking. "I was actually glad when Mama asked me to check on the mail. I planned to stop in at the livery for a moment."

His gaze shot to hers. "You did?"

She nodded.

That tiny smile she adored lifted a corner of his mouth, and she got a brief glimpse of his dimple before it disappeared. What would it take to make him smile more often?

"I sure enjoyed that dinner you and your ma made. Best I've eaten in years."

Feeling playful, she gently nudged his arm. "You could have enjoyed it several times over if you'd accept our invitation more often. Why don't you?"

He shrugged. "I just don't like talking about my past."

Regina was curious, but she searched for a new topic. "Have you had any luck finding the person who stole your horses?"

"Not yet. I ordered a new saddle from Mark to replace one of the ones that was stolen."

Regina's heart went out to him. "I'm so sorry that happened to you. I know saddles and horses are expensive."

He shrugged again then paused as they reached the mercantile. "You want to stop in now or later?"

"Let's go ahead and get the mail before Mr. Goodwin leaves on his deliveries. I can run into the mercantile on the way back."

He nodded and turned left once they reached the next street. "I can get my tools while you stop in the post office, and then I'll walk you back. You might need me to carry the crates you get at the mercantile."

Regina nodded and reached for the handle of the post office door. Before she could turn it, the door opened, and Alice Singer stepped out, her cheeks pink.

"Good morning, Alice. How are you?" Although they were about the same age, she and Alice had never been very close.

Alice's brown eyes flicked back toward the post office door, making Regina wonder about her nervousness. "I'm doing well."

"How is your father? Is he home or traveling?" For as long as she'd known Alice, she'd lived alone with her father. Her mother must have died when Alice was young.

"He's away on one of his trips, but I expect him home tomorrow."

"Does it bother you to be alone?" That was something Regina had rarely experienced.

"A little, especially at night, but I'm mostly used to it."

"It was nice to see you again. Feel free to stop by and visit Mama and me whenever you'd like."

Alice's cheeks were still red. "That's kind of you. I'm almost finished with the baby gowns I've been sewing. I'll bring them over later this week."

"Wonderful." Regina loved this time of year when so many people worked together to bless others. "I hope you'll be able to stay for tea when you do."

"Thank you." Alice's gaze darted toward the livery. "I should be going. It was good to see you." She scurried off just as Dane stopped beside Regina.

"I'm sorry, but I got to talking. I'll be right back." She hurried into the post office without waiting for Dane's response.

"Good day, Miss Ross." Mr. Goodwin smiled then turned around and pulled an envelope from their box. "Just one letter today."

"Thank you. Have a nice day." Regina bustled out again then glanced at the letter and stopped abruptly.

"Bad news?"

"It's from my aunt Helen." How could she explain the tornado of trouble her aunt always stirred up whenever she visited? Regina sincerely hoped this was a newsy letter and not an announcement of a Christmas visit.

Chapter 5

Regina walked alongside her father as he carried an empty crate to the Tanners' house for their Christmas basket. He glanced down at her. "You're rather quiet, sweetheart. What's on your mind?"

"I'm sure you know, Papa."

"Ah, yes. It's Helen's visit that has you fretting." He patted her back. "I know my sister's visits are a test of your patience."

"I don't mean to speak unkindly of her, but her constant badgering to get me to go live with her wears me down." She tossed her hand in the air. "Why can't she see that I want to be here in Wiseman with you and Mama?"

"Though her methods are questionable, Helen has a good heart. However, she values her status in life far more than I ever did. I'm happy to be content with what God sees fit to send my way. My sister married into a wealthy family, and their values have become hers, I'm afraid."

Regina shifted the crate she carried so that it wasn't pinching her arm. "I can't imagine being happy in such a big city as Chicago. I'd feel lost and alone even with so many people around."

"Many people love living there, and I'm sure you'd discover plenty of things you'd like, but it's a different way of life than small-town living."

"I would enjoy visiting some of the sites, like their big lake, but I can't see myself staying there."

He glanced down and winked at her. "I don't mind saying that I hope you will live close to us once you marry. It would be a difficult thing to have our only child move away. Your mother's heart would be broken. Mine too, I'm afraid."

Regina thought of Dane. What would Papa say if he knew her interests rested in the man who lived next door?

They arrived at the Tanners' house, and Papa knocked. Regina set her crate down to rest her arms. Rachel Worth, niece of the two Tanner spinsters, answered the door. "Good morning, Reverend Ross. Regina. Come in." She stepped back and held the door open.

Regina's father motioned for her to go first then followed her inside. She couldn't help glancing sideways at Rachel Worth's large stomach. Her baby was due next month. "How have you been feeling?"

"Wonderful, although I do tire much more quickly these days."

"Mama and I are excited to learn what the baby is."

"Oh, us too. Stephen is wearing me out with all the silly names he's suggested, like Mephibosheth and Jehoshaphat." She leaned forward as if sharing a secret. "He even had the gall to suggest we name our sweet babe after Papa if it is a boy." She shook her head. "One Abijah in the family was plenty."

Papa chuckled. "Those are mighty fancy names to tack on a tiny infant, although some folks do."

Priscilla Tanner walked out of the kitchen. She smiled as she drew near. "What a nice surprise. Would you two care to stay for tea?"

"Thank you for your kind offer, but we have to deliver all of the crates for the Christmas giveaway this morning, and yours is our first stop. Is this one too big?" He held up the crate.

Priscilla studied the wooden box. "That should do nicely. What do you think, Rachel?"

"It's a little larger than last year's, but I do believe we have more things to put in it. I agree it should work well for our needs."

Papa smiled. "If you'll show me where you want it, I can put it there."

"Very well. If you'll kindly follow me, I'll show you where it goes." Rachel waddled away, keeping one hand on her back.

Regina stayed in the foyer with Priscilla while her father left with Rachel. "How is your sister faring?" she asked.

"Her sister is fine," Lois Tanner called from the parlor. "Come and visit with an old woman."

A soft smile graced Priscilla's lips. She gestured for Regina to go on in. "As you can hear, the lady speaks for herself."

Lois Tanner sat in her wheelchair near the fireplace. She held up a small pair of boy's pants. "I'm nearly done with these. I have one more pair to stitch, and then we'll be done with our contribution to the Callen family's clothing."

Rachel studied the tiny britches. "Those are darling. I especially like how you trimmed the denim in plaid flannel. I've never thought to do that."

"Actually, I lined them in flannel so the youngster would keep warm during the winter. As active as those children are, I suspect these will be worn out by summer, but by then it will be too hot to wear them."

"I suspect you're right, Sister." Priscilla wiggled a finger to catch Regina's eye.

"I've finished with the shirts, and Rachel is almost done with the dresses for the Callen girls. We're quite anxious to get back to sewing for our baby. Infants go through a lot of clothing."

"I love to make baby clothes." Regina couldn't help wondering if she'd ever sew for her own children. For now she'd be content sewing for others. She and Mama should make something for the Worth baby once Christmas was over.

Papa and Rachel entered the parlor. Rachel took a seat on the settee.

Papa walked over to where Lois Tanner sat. "How are you doing, Miss Tanner?"

"Quite well, thank you. My only complaint is when the weather turns cold and my bones ache more than normal. But I suppose that's the way of things for someone my age."

"Pshaw." Phyllis swatted her hand in the air. "If you're old, what does that make me, since I'm seven years your senior?"

A twinkle danced in Lois's eyes. "You're downright ancient, Sister."

"Humph."

Pastor Ross chuckled softly at the ladies' antics.

Regina wondered what it would be like to have a sister to tease.

For so many years when she was young, she had longed for a sibling, especially a sister. She'd even pestered her parents about it until she got old enough to see that her request pained them. Sadly, God had not chosen to bless her parents with another child.

Papa moved to Regina's side. "It's good to see you ladies are doing so well. We have quite a few more deliveries to make, so we'd best be going."

Priscilla walked them to the door. "Thank you for delivering the crate. I'll have Stephen drop it off at your house once we get our baking done next week."

"That would be wonderful." Regina smiled. "Thank you, all, for the nice clothing you're making and for putting together a whole basket. I know it will be a blessing to the family that gets it."

Priscilla nodded. "The blessing is ours. Have a good day."

Papa lifted up the crate Regina had left on the porch. "That was a kind thing you told her."

She raised her skirt as she walked down the porch steps. "I meant it. I wish more people could see how the poor folks' eyes light up each year when they receive their gift baskets."

"It is a wonderful thing to see."

They walked past the Tanners' rental house and knocked on the Yateses' door. A few moments later, Marta Yates opened it and smiled. "Pastor. Regina. Please come in."

They stepped inside. One of the twins was seated in the parlor, holding Justin and Marta's new baby. "Come see," she shouted.

Regina hurried over. As she drew near the twin, she decided it was Ella. The baby slept soundly, wrapped in a blue knitted blanket. "What did you name him?"

Marta walked over to stand beside Regina. "Justin Luke, but

we're calling him by his middle name."

"He's a stout boy," Regina's father said as he peered over her shoulder. "Thanks be to God for a healthy baby."

"Amen! Luke definitely takes after Justin in size." Marta smiled.

"But he's not as cranky as my brother." Ella's eyes twinkled.

"Yes, well, you're not the one who has to get up to change and feed him at night." Marta brushed her hand across her son's head. "But I don't mind. It's a privilege."

"Babies are a blessing. I remember when Regina was born—such a tiny thing."

"Papa, please." Regina looked over her shoulder. She sure didn't want him to get started telling stories of her childhood. They would never get the crates delivered.

Regina backed away from the baby and focused on Marta. "Is the crate we brought the right size for you?"

Marta nodded. "It will do nicely. Thank you for dropping it off."

"It was our pleasure." Papa gently ruffled the baby's dark hair. Regina saw his lips moving and knew he was praying a blessing over the child. After a minute, he straightened. "I suppose we should get on with our deliveries."

As they walked away from the house, a pretty cardinal in the tree overhead sang a cheerful tune, but it didn't lift Regina's spirits. She blew out a wistful sigh. How many years would pass before she would become a mother?

Friday afternoon, Dane looked up from the hackamore he was repairing to see Regina walking his way. She carried a box that looked a bit on the heavy side. He set down the headpiece and walked out to greet her. "Afternoon. Could I take that for you?"

"Yes, thank you. It seemed to grow heavier the farther I walked." Her cheeks were flushed, and wisps of golden hair curled around her face. "If you'd be so kind as to set it down, we can quickly lighten the load."

A belly-tingling aroma drifted up, teasing Dane's senses. "Is that chicken I smell?"

She nodded. "It's soup. We heard that Mrs. Langston is ill, so Mama asked me to run this out to her. That smaller crock is for you."

"Me?" His gaze jerked her direction and collided with hers. His heart took off like a horse in a race.

A sweet smile graced her lips. "You're so kind to loan us a vehicle whenever we have need that we wanted to do something for you."

"That's mighty kind of you."

She shrugged. "It's nice of you not to charge us when we need a horse and buggy so often."

"I'm happy to help you out."

Regina reached into the box, pulled out the smaller crock, and handed it to him.

"I will look forward to my supper tonight." He carried the crock over to a shelf and set it down. "I even have a box of crackers to go with it, if they aren't stale."

"If it turns out they are, run over to our house, and I'll give you some fresh ones."

"You're a kindhearted person, Miss Ross."

"Thank you, but I think most people are. And I do wish you'd call me Regina when we're alone."

Dane couldn't help frowning. He thought of his pa and his

cronies, and the man who stole his horses. "Not all people are kind-hearted. My own pa sure wasn't."

Regina walked up to him, reached out, and touched his arm. "I'm sorry you had such a rough childhood, but it made you the man you are today. You're kind, giving, and dependable. Who's to say you might have been much different if you'd had an easier upbringing?"

Her comment was meant to encourage him, but it didn't have that effect. If it had just been him who had suffered, things might have been different. But seeing pain in his mother's eyes and hearing her cry out when Pa squeezed her arm too tight or hit her had made him want to do things that weren't very Christian.

"I can see that it still pains you. Give your pain to God, Dane. Let go of it. God is the only One who can heal your aching heart and memories of the past."

He pushed his feet into motion. "I know that's true, but it's easier said than done. I've tried. I'll be right back." He strode out of the barn toward the corral. If only he could lay all of the pain of his past on God's altar and leave it there. Many times he'd asked that very thing from God, but the memories were still as alive today as when he was ten. Perhaps that was his penance.

He whistled, and four horses trotted over to him. He patted each one then grabbed the halter of a dun gelding that was harness broke and led him out of the gate. Nugget wasn't as calm pulling a buggy as the mare that had been stolen, but he was getting better with more use. Still, Dane hated for Regina to take the gelding out of town on her own. What if he broke free? She sure didn't need another fright like that.

He tied the horse to the corral rail. "I need to ride out to the Langston ranch and see if they have any horses for sale. How would you feel if I rode along with you?"

Regina's eyes brightened. "That would be wonderful. I have to admit that since that other horse ran away with me, I've been a wee bit nervous about driving again."

"Do you think your pa would mind?"

"Probably not, but we should stop by the church and ask him. He is there working on his sermon."

"Let's do that then."

In a few minutes, Dane had the horse hitched. "I need to close up shop before we leave."

Regina nodded.

Dane jogged back to the corral and opened the gate. It was a bit early to put the horses in their stalls, but he wasn't taking any chances on leaving them out while he was gone. With the horses safe inside, he closed the doors and locked them.

The dun looked back and whinnied.

Regina laughed. "He thinks you forgot him."

Dane was mesmerized by her laugh. It was like hearing a bird trill on a summer's day. A longing to hear her laugh for the rest of his days gripped him.

Regina sobered. "Is everything all right?"

"Yeah." Dane double-checked the lock on the livery door, shaking off his wistful thought. He would need to remain cautious and not get too loose-lipped on his ride with Regina. He searched for a safe topic to talk about. "I've been thinking about getting a dog. A man might think twice about breaking in if a dog was barking."

"That's a fabulous idea. I agree that it could be a deterrent to thieves. Would you get a puppy or a bigger dog?"

He shrugged. "I reckon it would depend on whatever the dog I find is. I haven't heard of anyone with pups they wanted to get rid of in a while. Maybe come spring there'll be some." After securing the box with the crock of soup, he handed Regina into the buggy then walked around, patting the horse on his withers. As he climbed into the buggy, he couldn't help wondering what he'd do if Reverend Ross refused to allow him to escort his daughter.

They drove past the town square, turned the corner, and stopped in front of the church. Dane glanced at Regina. "Should I go in on my own?"

She shook her head and rose. "No, let's go together. I don't want him interrogating you."

Dane hopped down and tied the buggy to the hitching post then helped Regina down. "You think he'd do that?"

She shrugged one shoulder. "I'm not sure. I've never asked to take a ride with a man alone before."

Dane was taken aback by her comment. The men of Wiseman were stupid. Just because Regina was the preacher's daughter was no reason not to take an interest in her. But for him things were different. He had to fight his attraction because he simply wasn't worthy of a good woman like her. One thing for certain, his ma would have loved the preacher's daughter.

Dane opened the door, allowing Regina to enter the church first. "Papa?"

As Dane removed his hat, he was assaulted by the scent of beeswax. Some of the town's ladies must have been here recently, polishing the pews and pulpit. Colorful lights filtered through the stained-glass windows on the south side of the church, making the sanctuary look like the inside of a rainbow.

Footsteps sounded, and Reverend Ross ambled out of a room

that sat at the very front of the church, behind the small stage. "Regina? Is everything all right?"

Today the pastor looked more like a farmer than a preacher, dressed in a red flannel shirt and black pants. His brown beard had started turning gray, and his eyes flicked from Dane to Regina.

"Nothing is wrong. I simply need to ask you something."

As they met in the middle of the church, Reverend Ross held out his hand, and Dane shook it.

"Mama has sent me on an errand of mercy to deliver soup to the Langston family. Mr. McDermott needs to talk to Mr. Langston about buying some horses to replace the stolen ones, so he offered to drive me, with your permission, of course."

The pastor cocked one eyebrow as he stared at Dane. "Is that so?"

"Yes, sir. That's most of the truth. The other factor is that the gelding pulling the buggy isn't quite as well trained as my mare that was stolen. I'd feel better seeing Miss Ross to the Langstons' and back, if you don't object."

Regina's father eyed him, but Dane held his gaze without squirming. "I promise to be a perfect gentleman. I respect you and your daughter too much not to be."

After a long moment, the reverend nodded. "I've never known you to be anything but respectful and kind. However, it will be sunset in a few hours. I trust you'll have Regina home well before that?"

"Yes, sir. I will."

"Very well. Have a nice drive. At least you got a warm day for it."

Regina's eyes danced as she glanced at Dane. Then she stepped forward and kissed her father's cheek. "Thank you, Papa."

Dane could feel the man's eyes on his back as he followed Regina to the door. Dane opened the door, allowed her to go out first, then looked up.

Reverend Ross stared at him. "She's my only child."

"I will guard her with my life, sir."

The reverend nodded. Dane touched the end of his hat and stepped out the door, closing it behind him.

Regina giggled, but it sounded different from the laugh at the livery. "I wasn't sure he was going to agree."

Neither was Dane. In fact, he was surprised the man had.

If he knew the truth about Dane, the results would have been far different.

Chapter 6

Excitement bubbled through Regina. This was her first ever drive in a buggy with a man, not counting the short trip back to town the day Ginger ran away with her. No, it wasn't a courting ride, but she would enjoy every moment she had alone with Dane. Perhaps they'd get to know one another better.

He guided the buggy out of town, down the road that led to the Langston ranch. Two cowboys on horseback rode toward town. Dane nodded at them as they passed, and the cowboys did the same. Regina was glad they weren't men she knew, because she wasn't ready for people to start talking about them as a couple.

Regina had held her breath while Papa and Dane had talked, not at all knowing what to expect. She'd never had a suitor. It thrilled her that Papa trusted Dane enough to allow them to be alone for over an hour. Perhaps Papa wouldn't object if Dane were to come calling.

She blew out a breath at her girlish thoughts. Dane had always been kind, but he'd never shown an overt interest in her. Although he did tell her he was happy to see her the day they picked out the crates.

Dane glanced at her. "Everything all right?"

"Yes. I was merely thinking about some things."

"It's sure a nice day for early December."

"You're right." She lifted her face, relishing the most pleasant temperatures they'd had in weeks. "This warmer weather in winter is one of the things I like most about living in Texas."

"Me too, although I can't say I love the heat of summer."

A large hawk floated across the sky then suddenly swooped down and back up, carrying something small in its talons. "Do you know what kind of hawk that is?"

Dane cocked his head and looked up. "It's a red-tailed."

"They're so colorful. I don't often see them in town. God sure made some pretty creatures." With the hawk gone, she studied the brown landscape, longing for the colorful flowers of spring. The only break in the mundane yellowish brown was an occasional patch of green weeds, a smattering of pine trees, and the sky.

He nudged his chin at the sky. "I figured you'd be upset for the critter that got eaten."

"I do feel bad for it, but that's life. The hawk needs to eat. Just so it doesn't snag one of my hens."

Dane leaned back, his hand holding the reins resting on his leg. "We had chickens when I was a kid. I had to take care of them since I was the youngest. Didn't like it much, but my ma loved those birds, so I did it for her."

They hit a rut in the road, and Regina's shoulder bumped against his. "I certainly understand that motivation. Most of what I do is to help Mama. She has her hand in so many pots. I don't know what she'll do if I ever marry."

His gaze flicked her way then back to the road. "You plannin' on getting married?"

"Well, no. Not anytime soon, but a girl has dreams. Don't you want to marry and be a father?"

He scowled. "I don't know as I'd make a good pa."

She turned in her seat to face him better. "Why would you say such a thing? Look how gentle you are with your animals. You're a good person, Dane, whether you believe it or not."

He shook his head. "My pa was mean. Real mean. I'm afraid to take a chance that I might turn out like him."

Regina longed to reach out and comfort him, but she clenched her hands in her lap instead. "What do you think made him that way?"

"The war, for one. I was born less than a year after the War between the States started. Ma told me that Pa was a kind man before they married and in the early years before he went off to fight. But the things he did and saw during the war changed him."

They rode on in silence for several minutes. Regina was searching for a question to ask that wasn't too personal.

"Ma said Pa never drank before the war, but afterwards he always kept a bottle or two in the house. When they first married, they moved to Missouri and bought the farm. Oddly enough, there were battles fought all around our farm in different directions, but never on our land. Soldiers did come through and steal from us at times, although my two brothers were old enough by then to wield rifles and usually scared them off. Still, Ma said times were hard during those years that Pa was gone."

Regina couldn't resist reaching out and touching his arm. "I'm sorry, Dane. I can't imagine how hard it must have been for your mother, living on a farm, raising crops and three boys without the aid of your father."

She placed her hands back in her lap. "I was born not long after the war ended. Pa sold our first ranch when there were rumors of war and moved Ma to Independence. For a time, he worked on a big ranch near town. He would also minister on Sundays at a church that had lost its pastor to the war. Mama told me how some people looked down on him for not fighting, but he felt God had told him that he was to minister to those left behind."

Dane scratched his shoulder. "So your pa must have bought another ranch at some point, since you mentioned you were raised on one."

She nodded. "Yes. Once the war was over, Papa bought another small ranch that had been abandoned in southern Missouri. We lived there until I was thirteen. Papa felt God calling him back into the ministry, so he sold it, and we moved here." Her gaze drifted to a herd of longhorns grazing on the dry grass. Those creatures had always frightened her, with their huge horns. She turned back to Dane. "It sounds like you've lived about half your life in Wiseman."

He shrugged. "Pretty close to it, I reckon. I came here when I was sixteen."

"Do you ever miss Missouri?"

He turned her way for a quick moment then faced forward. "No, but I miss my ma. She was a good woman. She didn't deserve the life she had."

Regina thought it odd that he didn't miss his brothers. He'd said very little about them. Were they still alive? If she'd ever had a sibling and lost him or her, she thought for certain she'd miss them the rest of her life.

A short while later, they drove into the Langstons' yard. Regina marveled at the large two-story ranch house. Stone chimneys rose up on each end like giant soldiers guarding the place. Inviting porches ran the whole length of the house, both downstairs and up. The house was white except for the dark roof.

A black-and-white dog stood at the bottom of the porch steps, barking up a ruckus that sounded more like a warning than a greeting.

"Hush, Jeb," a man said as he walked out the front door. He slapped on his cowboy hat, stopped at the top of the stairs, and gazed down. The dog trotted up the steps and sat next to his owner. "That you, Miss Ross?"

"Yes, Mr. Langston. We heard that Mrs. Langston is ill, so Mama sent me with a crock of soup for her."

The long-legged man ambled down the steps and helped her out of the buggy while Dane tied it to the hitching post.

Regina had always liked the older man with a bushy mustache and eyebrows. She thought it odd that he had so much hair on his face and yet his head was half bald.

Dane joined them, and Mr. Langston reached out his hand. "McDermott, isn't it?"

Dane shook hands with him. "Yes, sir."

"Are you simply enjoying a nice ride with a pretty lady, or did something else bring you here today?"

Regina ducked her head at the compliment. Did Dane think she was pretty?

"I did enjoy the drive, but I'm here mostly on business. Don't know if you heard or not, but someone stole two of my horses. I need to replace them and thought I'd come out to see if you had any for sale. I need a saddle horse or two and one broke to a buggy and buckboard."

Mr. Langston rubbed his chin. "I've got a few that are ready. Let me take Miss Ross inside, and then I'll walk you out to the barn."

"Thank you. I'll wait here then." His gaze shifted to Regina.

She smiled at Dane. "I'll make my visit short, since Mrs. Langston is feeling poorly, but feel free to take your time. I don't mind sitting on the porch and enjoying this nice weather."

Dane nodded. Regina followed Mr. Langston inside. She sincerely hoped the ride home would be as enjoyable as the one out to the ranch.

Two days after her trip to the Langston ranch, Regina straightened the sheet in the spare bedroom then spread out the blanket. She topped it off with a pretty Flying Geese quilt she and Mama had made about five years ago. The pink, lavender, and soft green colors that dominated the quilt looked pretty with the lacy white curtains and braided rug.

The sunny afternoon had been warm enough that she had

opened the windows earlier to air out the room. But she closed them now, removed her dustrag from her apron pocket, and wiped down the furniture.

She moved to the doorway and stared at the room. It was a tad smaller than her own bedroom, but it was still nice. Aunt Helen, though, would disagree and complain about its lack of features and old furniture.

Regina sat in the rocker and closed her eyes. She needed to change her attitude toward her aunt. This very morning she'd read in 2 Corinthians that believers were to bring into captivity every thought to the obedience of Christ. "Please, Father, help me not to think bad thoughts toward my aunt. Help me to be gracious and welcoming. And patient."

She leaned her head back. Why was it that Aunt Helen was the only person she struggled to like? Probably because of her aunt's haughty attitude and how she was always pressuring Regina to move to Chicago to live with her.

The thought of never seeing Dane again made her stomach churn. What was she going to do with her attraction to him? She'd prayed many times that the Lord would remove her fondness toward Dane if he wasn't the one God wanted her to marry. And yet it remained. That gave her hope.

She thought of their ride home from the Langston ranch two days ago. Dane had been less talkative on the return trip, but then, he'd been driving home a horse that he'd just bought, and he had three horses hooked to the back of the buggy. How had he had enough money to purchase three horses as well as the saddle he bought from Mark Beaumont?

Surely he didn't make enough money at the livery to cover all of that. She swatted her hand in the air, as if forcing the unwanted thoughts away. How deep Dane's pocket went was none of her business.

She had told him a little about her aunt and how she was visiting for a week during Christmastime. He'd nodded but hadn't said anything except that some relatives were much harder to live with than others. She had wondered if he was referring to his father or the brothers he hadn't talked about. Dane had surprised her when he dropped her off at the door and told her he'd be praying for her.

Regina blew out a sigh. Enough thoughts about Dane. She pushed her feet into action. Papa should be back from Dallas with Aunt Helen anytime. It was too bad her aunt was so finicky that she wouldn't ride the stage to Wiseman and save Papa the long drive.

Regina clenched her fist. There she went again. *Think good thoughts.*

She walked through the parlor, swiping any place where a speck of dust dared to reside. The aroma of cooked chicken drew her back to the kitchen where her mama was slicing noodles. "The bedroom is clean, and I dusted the parlor again. What else do you need help with?"

"You could debone and cut up the chicken."

"Yes, ma'am. I just need to wash my hands."

They worked in silence for several minutes. Then her mother stopped and looked at her. Regina paused in her work, knowing something was on Mama's mind.

"I know it's hard for you when Helen visits. It's trying for me as well, but we must do our best to be gracious to your father's sister.

She's his only family other than us."

"I agree. I've been praying almost constantly about that very thing, ever since you received her letter."

Mama sent her a sweet smile. "You'll do fine. You always do. Just excuse yourself and go to your room if things get too difficult."

"Thank you. I will."

Regina finished deboning and cutting up the chicken and put it in a bowl. She dropped the bones in the slop bucket, a thought circulating in her mind. Dare she ask it?

As she wiped down the counter where she'd been working, she talked herself into it. "Mama, what would you think of inviting Dane McDermott to Christmas dinner?"

Mama stopped her slicing and turned to face her, mouth open and eyes wide. She quickly regained her composure. "Why him? He only recently ate Sunday dinner with us."

She shrugged. "He's all alone, and he's been so kind to us."

"Is that all there is to it?" Mama looked intently at her.

"No. I. . .um. . .like him." She swallowed the lump in her throat. In for a penny, in for a pound. "A whole lot."

Mama's blue eyes widened again. "Oh. Oh!"

Regina ducked her head, hoping she hadn't made a mistake. But she needed someone to talk to about her infatuation with Dane.

"I noticed food disappearing lately. Have you been taking him things?"

"Only a few times. He doesn't have anyone to cook for him."

A smile danced on Mama's lips. "Neither do the Beaumont brothers, but you haven't taken things over to them, have you?"

Regina shook her head. "I really like Dane, Mama, but I don't know if he returns the feelings."

Mama dusted off her hands then took hold of Regina's. Wisps of grayish-brown hair curled around her pretty face, and her cheeks were red from the heat of the room. "I can't tell you how much I appreciate that you told me this. I noticed the day Mr. McDermott ate with us that you were exchanging far more glances and smiles with him than those Beaumont boys."

Regina felt her own eyes widen. "Truly? And here I thought I was doing well to hide my feelings."

"You did. I wasn't certain until now. I will talk to your Papa about inviting Mr. McDermott, but I suspect he will also want to ask the Beaumonts again so there won't be any talk, especially with your aunt here. You wouldn't want her to go on the attack and tell your Dane all the reasons he's not good enough for you, would you?"

"No, ma'am." She hadn't even considered that.

"I can tell you that your father was impressed that Mr. McDermott was concerned about you driving that buggy alone with the horse you weren't used to. It wouldn't surprise me if Mr. McDermott cares for you more than you suspect."

Regina's heart leaped at the thought. "You think so?"

"Talking about feelings comes hard to some men. And Mr. McDermott had a rough childhood, so it may be more difficult for him than others. And then there's the issue that you are the preacher's daughter. That alone intimidates most men." She cupped Regina's cheek. "You deserve a good man. I've been praying your whole life for him to come along when the time is right."

"You have?"

"Yes, dear. Of course."

"And you don't mind that the man I'm attracted to merely owns a livery?"

"I'm not your aunt, and forgive me for saying that, Lord." Mama glanced upward. "I'll be happy so long as you get a godly man who treats you well."

The front door jiggled. Regina locked eyes with her mother. The tornado named Aunt Helen had arrived.

Chapter 7

Regina followed her mother to the door to greet Aunt Helen. She took a deep breath, fortifying herself. She quoted the fruit of the Spirit: love, joy, peace, longsuffering, gentleness, goodness, faith, meekness, and temperance. *Please, Lord, help me to be an example of each of these to my aunt, and most of all, give me patience and help me not to become angry with her.*

She stood back while Mama greeted Aunt Helen. Regina felt a shaft of remorse. All she'd thought about was how she would act toward Aunt Helen, but it was equally as challenging for Mama. They owed it to Papa to be as kind as they could be.

"Welcome." Mama helped Aunt Helen out of her fancy coat and hung it on a peg, and then she hugged her sister-in-law. "I hope your trip was pleasant. At least the weather is warm for this time of year."

Aunt Helen lifted the back of her hand to her forehead, her eyes rolled upward, and she looked as if she'd swoon, but Regina knew better. "Oh! It was dreadful. All that shaking on the uncomfortable train and then the jostling wagon. I declare, my teeth are sure to fall out at any moment."

Mama glanced at Regina, her mouth quirking as she fought back a smile at Helen's antics. Mama had told her to try not to take her aunt so seriously, as the woman tended toward dramatics to get her point across. Mama thought it came from being the baby of the family.

"Speaking of the buggy, I need to return it. The horse is ready for his supper. I'll be back shortly." Papa hurried out the door but returned a moment later with her aunt's trunk. The marshal followed, carrying two large satchels. "Marshal, you remember my sister, Helen Grigsby."

Marshal Yates touched the brim of his hat. "A pleasure to have you visit our town again, ma'am. Welcome to Wiseman."

"Yes, well. Thank you." Aunt Helen lifted her hand to her nose.

"I appreciate your assistance, Marshal." Papa slapped him on the shoulder. "And for your willingness to return the buggy for me." Papa closed the door after the marshal left.

Regina studied her aunt's dress. Even her clothing shouted, "Look at me," with the bold purple, pink, and lavender striped taffeta skirt and the fancy purple bodice with pearly beads. Three-inch-wide lace around the neck and cuffs, and several rows along the bottom of her dress gave it a frilly look more fitting for a girl than a woman of fifty years. Regina could only stare at the exaggerated bustle.

Aunt Helen turned toward Regina, and she braced herself. It

had been two years since she'd last seen her, and Aunt Helen's hair had started turning gray like Papa's. "It's a pleasure to have you visit us again. You're looking quite well."

Her aunt stalked toward her, clucking her tongue and shaking her head. "My dear, you're so lovely. Why do you clothe yourself in that drab brown?"

"Now, Helen, Regina is old enough to choose what she likes to wear. And besides, I think those little yellow flowers go well with her hair." Papa walked to his sister's side.

Helen clucked again. "What woman in her right mind would wear calico when there are so many prettier fabrics to choose from?" For a split second, Aunt Helen's face paled. She turned to her brother. "That's not from a box of clothing donated to the poor, is it?"

Regina gasped. Mama hurried to her side and locked arms with her. "I should say not. Regina made this pretty dress herself. She's wearing a work dress rather than one of her nicer ones because we've been cleaning and baking all day. My daughter is very practical."

Regina appreciated how her parents stood up for her. Brown was a perfectly good color for winter. She'd chosen to wear the calico in part because the day had been quite warm, and she knew she would get hot with all that needed to be done. Five minutes into Aunt Helen's visit, and she was already wishing she could flee to her room.

Aunt Helen reached out and lifted Regina's hand. "I see you still don't have a ring. Well, I have some plans for that." Her brown eyes glimmered. "I have met several of the most handsome, eligible bachelors in recent months, and any one of them would be perfect for you, my dear."

"Thank you, but I'm quite content with my life here. It's very fulfilling."

"Pshaw! What in the world is there to do in a town so small? Why, you don't even have a theater. And only one puny restaurant, if you can even call it that. There is so much to do in Chicago. You could attend a different performance each night or go to a meeting like the poetry or botanical garden club. And the food there is scrumptious." She fanned her face. "Why is it so warm in here?"

"We've been cooking, and as we said before, we've been enjoying a stretch of warmer weather." Mama touched Papa on the arm. "Gideon, perhaps you could open the front door? I need to check on the food."

He nodded and moved toward the door.

"I'll see to the food, Mama." Regina spun around without giving her mother a chance to respond. She was a coward, that was for certain. She felt bad, but Mama had twice the patience she did.

After donning her apron, she stirred the chicken and noodles. The carrots and peas were almost done. Just another ten minutes. A quick touch of the teakettle on the back of the stove revealed it to be hot. She pulled down a couple of teacups and filled them with water and leaves. While those steeped, she fixed a cup of coffee for Papa. She placed everything on a tray and carried it to the parlor, where her elders had all taken a seat.

Aunt Helen shook her head. "I can't tell that this town has grown a speck since I was last here."

Regina handed their guest her cup and saucer first.

Her aunt lifted it up, sniffed, and made a face. "It must be so difficult to get good English tea this far south." She tipped two spoonfuls of sugar into her cup and stirred.

"A couple of brothers opened a new store just two weeks ago." Papa sipped his coffee.

Aunt Helen swatted her hand toward the dining room. "I see that you're littering your home with all those donations to the poor again. You'd think those people would get jobs like everyone else and support their families. I do hope those rough boxes won't snag my dresses."

Papa's lips pursed. He had more patience than any man Regina had seen, but even he had his limits. "Most of those baskets will go to widows with small children. Not everyone can be as well off financially as you were when Clinton died."

"Why don't they remarry if they can't feed their children?"

Mama set her cup down on the table next to her chair, albeit a tad bit hard. "I imagine they would if a good man asked one of them, but it's hard to meet anyone when you're scraping and working constantly to simply get by."

Aunt Helen shifted her gaze to Regina, and she struggled not to squirm. "And what about you? Have you finally found a man with whom to settle down?"

She didn't dare mention Dane. Regina well knew her aunt would turn up her nose at the livery owner, no matter how good-hearted and polite he was. "God hasn't yet sent me a man willing to propose."

"And that's exactly why you need to come to Chicago. There are hundreds, if not thousands, of men there who would take an interest in a pretty woman like you."

Regina didn't want a man who was attracted to her simply because of the way she looked. She wanted a husband who had a heart for God and who was kind and cared about helping others.

Dane was like that.

"Thank you for your concern, Aunt Helen, but I don't care to live in Chicago. I love the small-town life, where I can walk down the street and most everyone I see is someone I know—someone who attends church with us on Sundays. A small community allows you to get to know your neighbors and to help one another when you have problems."

"Humph. You may well become a spinster in this town."

Regina's heart clenched. She prayed it wasn't so. "If it be God's will for me, then I will accept it."

Aunt Helen's lips pinched, like fabric sewn too tightly. Her gaze shifted to Papa. "See what you've done to your daughter with all this religious nonsense? I don't know why you ever sold your ranch, not that I cared much for it. Don't you want Regina to marry? To improve her standard of living?"

Regina rose before she spouted out something in her father's defense. "If you'll excuse me, I need to get supper on the table." She hurried to the kitchen, wondering how she was going to be able to endure her aunt's tongue for a week. "Help me, Lord."

She sliced and buttered half a loaf of the bread she'd baked that morning, then stuck it in the oven to heat. She walked back to the parlor and waited for her mother to finish talking. When everyone looked her way, she announced, "Supper is ready."

Papa rose and offered a hand to help his sister up. "I, for one, am famished. Something about that drive to Dallas always makes me hungry."

"Now don't start, Gideon." Aunt Helen narrowed her eyes. "You know how I abhor riding in a stagecoach. All that bumping and bouncing makes me come close to retching."

Mama rose. "Yes, well, let's not talk about that at suppertime. Shall we?" She held out her hand, indicating her guest should go first.

Mama helped get the food on the table, and soon they were seated. "Gideon, will you bless the meal?"

He smiled. "Always, sweetheart."

Aunt Helen's gaze roved the bowls of steaming food, and her lip curled. Regina hoped she didn't make a stink about the meal. Mama had worked hard to make the noodles, and they were always delicious.

After a quick prayer for the food and thanks to the Lord for Aunt Helen's safe arrival, they started eating. Her aunt took tiny portions of the chicken and noodles, carrots, and peas. She completely ignored the delicious bread that was passed.

Regina kept her head down, enjoying the meal, while Papa asked his sister about all she'd been doing. Determined to finish before her aunt could spoil the meal, she ate faster than normal. When she glanced up for a drink, her aunt was staring at her.

"Good heavens, if you eat like that all the time, it's no wonder you haven't found a man to marry. A woman eats daintily, especially in public. You must take much smaller portions if you desire to lose that girlish chubbiness."

Chubbiness? Did her aunt just call her fat?

Regina glanced at her mother, whose eyes begged her to hold her tongue. She refocused on her aunt. "If a man doesn't care for the way I eat or how wide my waist is, he's not the man for me."

Aunt Helen sat back as if she'd been slapped. "Well, I never. Gideon, do you allow her to talk that way to all your guests?"

"Excuse me." Regina rose without waiting for permission.

Grabbing the nearest bowl, she took it to the kitchen and refilled it even though hardly any was gone. She set it on the table then took another bowl to the kitchen.

Aunt Helen continued to lambaste her parents. Regina closed her eyes. *How will I ever make it all week if my aunt is as cranky as this?*

Finally, Aunt Helen changed topics and was now admonishing Regina's parents on the many reasons that Regina should return with her to Chicago. They'd heard them all before. Her aunt simply repeated the same thing she had the last three times she'd visited.

Regina glanced around the kitchen, frantic for an excuse to escape. The last of the chicken and noodles sat in the pot. She took a bowl off a shelf, filled it, then wrapped the remaining half loaf of bread in a clean towel. Regina quietly opened the back door and stepped outside.

The sun hadn't fully set, so the night had not yet turned cold. Crickets serenaded her as she carefully made her way through the backyard and over to Dane's house. She took a moment to study the brilliant vermillion color of the sunset. Drifting smoke from the town's many houses filled the air, making it resemble a morning fog.

It suddenly dawned on her that the smoke seemed overly thick. She glanced back toward her stovepipe but saw nothing. She heard a crackle and spun toward Dane's house. Flames were licking at the back wall and racing toward the roof.

Dane led the last of the horses the preacher had borrowed into the stall and closed the gate. The new stock was settling in well, and he was happy with his purchases. He'd exercised both the saddle horses and had been pleased with how well trained they were. And they were all younger than the animals that had been stolen.

A sense of satisfaction washed over him. He liked caring for the creatures that God had entrusted to him. He'd always been fond of horses. Now chickens—they were only good for laying eggs and eating. His stomach growled at the thought of hot fried chicken.

A shadow darkened the barn door. Dane pushed away from the stall. It was late for a customer, but sometimes a need arose in the evening where someone wanted a horse. "Can I help you?"

"I sure hope so."

Dane stopped suddenly, instantly recognizing the gravelly voice of a man he could never forget. Ned Pickett had run with his father's gang of outlaws before his pa had been captured. "What are you doing here, Ned? Thought you were dead."

Ned leaned against the barn door as if ready for a casual chat, even though it had been nearly fourteen years since Dane had seen him. He wanted to ask if his pa was still alive, but he held his tongue. "I never thought to set eyes on you again, kid. You yellow-bellied weasel." He spat in the dirt. "You growed up."

"It's more than my brothers had the chance to do. I should have turned you all in sooner, and maybe Matt and Will would still be alive."

Ned stiffened, but he didn't take the bait.

"I asked you what you wanted."

Ned rubbed a hand through his shaggy gray beard. "Just want to know what you did with all that bank money your pa stole."

Dane clenched his fists. "You seriously believe my pa told me where he hid it? You didn't know him well if you think that."

"I think you know more than you're saying."

"You're wrong." Dane straightened, glad for how much he'd grown in the past fourteen years. He was no longer a kid who could be bullied. "My ma died because we didn't have the money to go to the doctor. You think if I'd known where that money was that I'd've let her die a horrible, painful death? She was the only good thing in my life."

He walked toward Ned. The man lifted his hand and rested it on his gun. "Where you think you're going?"

"Home. I'm hungry."

Something flashed in Ned's dark eyes, and he smirked. "I'll be back, and when I am, I'll expect you to tell me where that loot is." Ned spun away. Dane trotted to the door in time to see the man hop on his horse and race away.

He forked his fingers through his hair. How in the world had Ned found him? He thought he'd left no trail between here and Missouri. It had to have been by chance. His thoughts charged back to the men he'd seen outside the saloon, and his blood ran cold. He remembered thinking that one of them had looked like his pa. It had startled him so much at the time, he hadn't gotten a good look at the other man. Could it have been Ned? And if so, did that mean Dane's father was alive and staying somewhere near Wiseman?

Please, God, no.

What would Pa do to him if he ever found him?

Dane's mind raced as he locked the barn and headed toward home, his stomach grumbling. He wished he had a hot meal to look forward to, but he'd probably just slice a strip off the smoked ham he'd been working on for a time and eat some stale corn bread.

If not for Regina and the friends he'd made over the years, he might pack up and move on. But he'd lost his heart to Regina. She was so sweet and kind, but he was not the man she deserved. Especially now. What would Ned do if he knew Dane cared for the preacher's daughter?

A blanket of smoke hanging over the town thanks to the lack of wind drew his attention. He looked around, thinking it odd for there to be so much smoke on a warm evening. Still, folks had to eat.

He turned the corner, walking past the mercantile, and he heard someone scream his name. At the same moment, he saw a plume of dark smoke.

Chapter 8

Dane broke into a run. People poured from their homes. A building near the church was on fire. Fast steps brought him to his little house. Flames blistered the back of the structure and were creeping across the roof. On the ground was a cracked bowl with noodles spilled out and a partial loaf of bread. His heart lurched as he noticed the open door. Screams rang out from inside. He broke into a run. "Regina!"

"Fire!" someone behind him yelled.

Footsteps sounded from all directions. "Get your buckets," someone yelled.

Dane raced into the house. "Regina! Where are you?"

A shadowy figure stumbled out his bedroom door. He rushed toward it, coughing from the thick smoke engulfing the house. He reached Regina, bent down, and tossed her over his shoulder. On the way out the door, he grabbed the Bible a dear friend had given him from the table.

He carried Regina to her house and kicked open the door. A woman he didn't recognize screamed. Regina's parents rushed forward.

"My house is on fire. Regina must have thought I was inside."

Mrs. Ross gasped, covering her mouth. Her worried gaze followed him as she hurried toward her daughter.

He set down his precious burden on the settee, along with his Bible, and looked at Reverend Ross. "I've got to see to my house. I don't want the flames to get to yours—or the church."

He spun and rushed toward the door, wishing more than anything he could stay by Regina's side. *Please, God, let her be all right.*

"I'll go with you. My wife and sister will see to Regina." Reverend Ross shed his Sunday frock coat and dropped it on a chair, probably knowing it would be ruined if he wore it. "I'll go out the back and grab some buckets."

Dane raced to his house. A dozen folks had already started a bucket brigade from the horse trough across the street at the feedstore to the back of his house. His mind raced. Most everything he owned was inside, even though it wasn't all that much. For a moment, he thought about running inside to see what he could salvage. He then charged toward the door, reached inside for his gun belt and duster, and hurried out again. The smoke was thicker. He tossed the items he'd salvaged in the Rosses' backyard, glad that his Bible was safe with Regina.

Someone handed him a wet blanket. Dane jogged around the back of the house. Flames roared like a starving beast, determined to devour his home. The heat from the fire was almost unbearable. He slapped at the flames chewing the dry grass. He couldn't let them get to the Rosses' house.

Shouts surrounded him, and water hissed as it hit the flames. Dane yelled to his neighbors, "Don't worry about the house. Just keep the fire from spreading any further."

They worked as a team, and once the trough was empty, the line shifted to start at the church's water pump. Darkness settled as Dane and several other men beat the flames. Exhausted women passed buckets back and forth.

The fire-ravished wood creaked and groaned as if in pain. Dane heard a loud crack. "Get back! The house is going."

People scattered. Loud crackles echoed all around them, and then the house collapsed. A loud whoosh immediately followed as the fire spit embers in all directions, refusing to die.

Everyone returned to their work, and several hours later, Dane and a handful of men stood around the smelly, wet debris that had been the only house he'd ever owned.

Light seeped through several cracks in the barn, urging Dane to wake up. He rolled over and moaned. His shoulder ached from slapping that soggy blanket on the fire over and over. He reeked of smoke. A bath was in order, as well as a visit to the mercantile to buy some new clothes.

A part of him wanted to linger there in the hayloft of his barn rather than see his burned house again, but he longed to know how Regina was doing. He pushed up from his bed of hay and ruffled his hair to rid it of debris.

Below, horses stamped their hooves and kicked their stalls, impatient to be turned out to the corral. Dane stood, waded through the hay to the ladder, and climbed down. With all that he had to do, he was hesitant to turn out the horses. He made a quick decision to feed them and leave them locked in the barn until he'd finished all his tasks.

First was to check on Regina.

With the horses fed and watered, he locked the barn. He quickly walked the two blocks to the Rosses' house. It was a bit early to come calling, but he couldn't wait another minute to see how Regina had fared through the night. He'd prayed for her until he finally fell asleep, sometime after midnight.

As he neared his house, he glanced at the charred mess that had been his home. It hadn't been fancy, but he would miss it. He wanted to search the debris to see if anything survived the flames, but that could wait until he talked to Regina.

Dane also needed to tell the marshal about Ned's visit. He stumbled as a sudden thought hit him. Did Ned set fire to his house? That was the only thing that made sense, because he never left a fire burning. Where was Ned now?

He glanced around then trotted up the steps to the Ross house and knocked. His gut twisted as he wondered how badly Regina had been hurt. He should have checked on her last night, but he'd stayed after everyone else had left to make sure the fire didn't flare up again, and by the time he was done, the lights had all been extinguished at the Ross house.

The door opened, and Regina's aunt lifted her hand to cover her mouth, her eyes wide. "What in the world do you want?"

"I'm Dane McDermott, a friend of Regina's. I brought her home last night, remember? Could you please tell me how she's doing?"

"I most certainly will not. You're the reason my niece is near death. No one in this house ever wants to see you again." She slammed the door in his face.

Dane stood there numb, his heart shattered. Regina was dying? He ran a shaky hand through his hair and dropped down onto the step. His eyes stung with tears. He swiped at them and noticed his fingertips were stained with soot. Was his whole face blackened? No wonder Regina's aunt had been so shocked.

His gut clenched as he thought of Regina lying on her bed, struggling to breathe. Dane fought back the urge to cry. He learned long ago that it accomplished nothing, but the thought of losing her was more than he could fathom. He loved her. When had he fallen in love?

"Please, God. Save her."

The door to the Rosses' house opened. "Dane? What are you doing?"

He bolted up at the sound of Reverend Ross's voice. He swiped his eyes. "I came to check on Regina. Your sister told me she was. . ." He couldn't voice the words and just shook his head.

The reverend's face turned red. "What did my sister tell you?"

"That Regina was close to death."

The pastor stomped down the steps and took him by the shoulders. "Look at me, son."

Dane lifted his eyes and was surprised at the intense expression on the man's face. He'd never seen him angry before. And Dane deserved every bit of that outrage. He braced himself.

"My sister has a wicked tongue and a penchant for hurting people. Regina is doing well. She's nowhere near death, although her throat is sore and her voice a bit froggy. She's been asking about you and begged me to check on you."

Dane's relief was so strong his knees nearly buckled. "Regina is going to be all right?"

"Yes. Thanks to you. She told us how you rescued her." The pastor squeezed his shoulder. "I don't know how I'll ever be able to repay you."

"There's no need. I'd save her a hundred times over, given the opportunity. I care for her."

A gentle smile curved Reverend Ross's lips. "I believe the feeling is mutual."

Dane shook his head. "It doesn't matter. I'll never be good enough for a woman like Regina."

"No matter what you've done in the past, God will forgive you, but it's often harder for us to forgive ourselves."

Remorse gripped Dane's heart like a vise. "Once you hear my story, you may feel differently."

"I won't, son. But I would like to hear what you have to say. It will help me to know how better to pray for you and how to advise you."

"Could you walk to the marshal's office with me?"

"Don't you want to get cleaned up first? I'd loan you a set of my clothes, except I don't think you could fit into them."

"It's all right. I can pick some up at the mercantile later. First, I need to talk to Marshal Yates. There's something he needs to know."

"All right. Let's go talk to him."

As they walked toward the town square, Marshal Yates came around the corner and strode toward his office. He paused when he saw them and waited.

"Good morning, Marshal." Reverend Ross stuck out his hand.

"How's your daughter doing today?" Marshal Yates shook hands with the pastor and then Dane.

"She's much better, thanks to Dane, here. He saved her life."

Dane ducked his head, uncomfortable with the praise. He only wished he'd arrived sooner, and then maybe she'd never have gone into the burning house.

"Dane needs to talk to you, Marshal."

"That right?"

Dane lifted his head and locked eyes with the lawman. "Yes, sir."

"Then let's go inside. It's still a bit nippy out here. I'll start the fire and put on a pot of coffee."

Once the marshal got the fire going with the coffee heating, he took his seat behind his desk. Dane and Reverend Ross sat in the two chairs across from him.

"All right, Dane. What have you got to say?"

Regina stared out the window of her bedroom, looking at the charred rubble that had once been Dane's house. Her heart ached for him. What would he do now?

When she'd first seen the fire, she'd feared Dane was inside, and in that moment, she knew she'd fallen in love. "Thank You, Father, that we didn't perish last night."

She'd come so close to dying when she was searching Dane's house. How dreadful it would have been for her parents to lose her two days before Christmas. She'd called and called for Dane, but by the time she realized he wasn't in his house, she'd been so overcome by smoke that she could hardly breathe. Though the house was small, she doubted she would have made it back to the front door. She'd cried out to God, and then Dane had stormed in and rescued her.

She reached for the tea that had been her constant companion all night and this morning and took a sip. Its warmth and the combination of herbs, as well as the lemon and honey, were helping her throat to heal. Still, the doctor had recommended that she not try to talk for several days. She had welcomed his orders to rest, as it gave her a reprieve from her aunt's constant badgering. Her near-death ordeal had given Aunt Helen more fuel for her argument about her leaving Wiseman.

Regina glanced up at the sky. "Forgive me, Lord. Please give me more patience where my aunt is concerned. Help me to be a reflection of You to her. And please help her to understand that I'm happy here and have no plans to leave Wiseman."

Her gaze shifted back to the blackened rubble. Her room still held the scent of smoke. They probably would need to wash her curtains and bedding to get rid of it. Guilt riddled her. Papa said that Dane had told those fighting the fire not to worry about his house but to keep the fire from spreading. His thoughts had been for her house and the church. Everyone else but himself. Had he been able to salvage anything besides his Bible? She ached to know how he was doing. To see him.

Regina glanced at her door. Dare she?

Her normal strength hadn't yet returned, but taking the short two-block walk to the livery shouldn't be too taxing on her. And knowing that Dane was all right and hadn't been injured would help her to relax.

Her decision made, she drained her teacup and placed it on the saucer. Now was as good a time as any, since Mama and Papa had gone somewhere and wouldn't notice her leaving.

She opened her door and peeked out. Where was Aunt Helen? Regina tiptoed to the parlor and found her aunt sitting with her stitching in her lap and her head hung over, asleep. Perfect.

Smiling, she tiptoed through the kitchen to the back door. She slowly opened it and slipped out. The stench of burned wood assaulted her. She covered her nose and hurried past the debris, coughing from the pungent aroma. Pain radiated down her throat, but she continued on.

As she rounded her house and walked down the street, the fresher air helped her catch her breath. She took in the festive Christmas decorations adorning the shops she passed. Tonight her family would decorate the little tree Papa had brought home yesterday. Perhaps they'd allow Dane to join them. Just as she reached the mercantile, the door opened and the Yates twins walked out.

"Regina!" they squealed in unison.

"How are you?" Ella touched Regina's arm.

"We heard you nearly died." Emma frowned with concern.

"All right," Regina whispered as she touched her throat. "Can't talk much yet."

"Should you even be up?" Ella hugged her package.

Regina shrugged and offered an apologetic smile.

"Well, it's good to know you'll recover." Emma shook her head. "I can't imagine what a fright it must have been to be in that burning house."

She nodded and pressed her hand to her heart.

A twinkle drove away the worry in Emma's pretty blue eyes.

"Well, one thing's for certain, we know who it is that's captured your fancy."

Ella joined her sister in a giggle.

Regina couldn't hold back a guilty grin.

Ella patted her arm again. "Don't worry, your secret is safe with us. Have a nice Christmas."

Regina nearly laughed out loud. There were no secrets in a town this small, and the twins had just proved that. She smiled and waved as Ella and Emma walked away. She longed to ask them how things were going with the Beaumont brothers. The foursome had been seen walking about town and at the bakery and café. She hoped they wouldn't rush into marriage, if that was where things were headed, since the twins had barely turned seventeen. Many girls married younger than that though.

As she rounded the corner, the livery came into view. Her heart sank at seeing the doors closed. Was Dane inside? It would only take a minute to find out. She needed to hurry, as her strength was already waning.

She waved at John Goodwin as she walked past the post office, and then she crossed the empty street. The repetitive clanging of a hammer hitting an anvil at the blacksmith's shop on the far side of the livery echoed down the street. The headache she'd had all night threatened to return.

The front door was locked, but she knocked on it anyway. She wished she could call out to Dane. When there was no answer, she knocked harder. After a few minutes, she blew out a frustrated sigh. On a whim, she walked around the livery to the corral and nearly bumped into someone coming the other way. "Dane?" she cried in a froggy voice.

Rough hands tightened around her upper arms. "Well, what have we here?"

She looked up into the hairy face of a man older than her father. But there was something vaguely familiar about him, even though she knew she'd never met him before. She twisted, trying to get free.

"Stop struggling. Do what I say, and no harm will come to you." He looked past her then dragged her behind the livery and into a side door she'd never noticed before.

The horses fidgeted in their stalls, and one kicked the side wall. Regina blinked in the dim lighting. Her heart pounded in her ears. What did this man have planned for her?

"Who you got there?" someone called out from the room Dane used as an office and for storage.

"Got us some leverage to get my boy to do what we want."

Regina stiffened. She searched for a way of escape, but with the front doors locked, the side entrance was her only chance. But her strength was going fast. Her knees felt ready to buckle. *Help me, Lord.*

The man shoved her down in a corner near the office door. He rifled around and found a length of rope and tied her hands together in front of her. "Don't try to get away. I have no qualms about shooting a woman. And keep quiet, or I'll gag you."

He walked over and dropped down on a bale of hay. Regina laid her head on her knees. What could these thugs want with Dane? Suddenly she stiffened. The man who tied her had referred to Dane as "my boy." She peeked at him. Was that why he'd looked familiar? Could he actually be Dane's father? Why had she thought he was dead?

She knew Dane had a dark past, but perhaps it was worse than anything she'd imagined. Still, she felt certain Dane would do whatever he had to in order to protect her. *Please don't let him get hurt or do something that will get him in trouble with the law.*

She laid her head down again. Had she survived the fire only to die at the hands of these men?

Chapter 9

Dane glanced at the coffeepot, wishing he had a scalding cup of brew to steady him as he told the story he'd only shared with two other people, Marshal Frank Peterson and Ellis Ferguson. He cleared his throat and glanced at the two men.

"Reverend Ross already knows I had a rough childhood, but what he doesn't know is that my pa and brothers were outlaws. I was the youngest and expected to follow in the family business, but my ma had other plans. She taught me to read using the Bible, and the things we read settled deep inside of me to the point that I didn't want any part of outlawing."

He ducked his head, ashamed that these good men would think less of him when he was done. "I was only eight when Pa took me along on my first robbery. I held the horses while Pa, Ned—a man who'd been a friend of Pa's in the war—and my two brothers, Matt and Will, went into a small bank and robbed it."

Dane shook his head. "I'd never been so scared in my life." He left out the part about wetting his britches. "We'd lay low for a month or two then ride out for several days to a week until Pa found someone else to rob." He glanced up, relieved to see only interest on their faces.

The marshal rose, poured the coffee, and handed them each a cup. He fixed himself a mug then sat down again. "Go on."

"The first robbery when he made me go inside the bank scared me so bad that I upchucked on Pa afterward. He got real mad at Ma when we got home and told her she had made me into a sissy. The next time we went out, I held the horses again." He forked a hand through his hair then took a swig of the hot coffee.

Reverend Ross patted him on the shoulder. "You're doing fine, Dane. Go ahead and finish your story. You'll feel better once you do."

Bolstered, he plodded on, even though this next part was the hardest. "Things continued that way for several years—stealing then lying low. Right after I turned eleven, we rode to a little town named Munger. That robbery went bad. Pa got shot, but he and Ned got away. Both Matt and Will got shot. I was so scared they'd die that I ran to Matt's side, not even thinking I should try to get away." He cleared his throat, blinking his stinging eyes. "Both of them were already dead. Matt was only fourteen, and Will was sixteen.

"The town marshal caught me." Dane paused to sip his coffee, the warmth traveling down to his belly. "I thought then it was the worst day of my life, but I was wrong. Marshal Elijah Peterson saved my life. He talked me into telling him where I thought Pa would go. I did it to save my ma from his beatings and because I hated him for causing my brothers to get killed. Still, I felt awful turning on Pa, but now I know it was the right thing to do. Pa was a vile man."

"Was?" the marshal asked.

Dane shrugged. "Last I knew he was in prison in the Kansas State Penitentiary. That's a hard place to last this long."

"What happened after that?" The pastor's warm gaze encouraged him to finish his story.

"Marshal Peterson and his posse found Pa and Ned and captured them. I'll never forget the look on Pa's face that day the marshal let me out of jail and locked Pa up. I stayed with the marshal at his house until after the trial. He assured me over and over that I was doing the right thing. Then he let me go home. I was just a kid, but I had to tell Ma that her husband wasn't coming back and that her other sons were dead." He blew out a loud sigh at the gut-wrenching memory. "Ma and I struggled to get by for the next two years, but she took sick. We had no money to pay for a doctor, so she died. I buried her then left home and never went back."

"That's it?" The marshal gazed at him over his cup.

"No. Yesterday Ned confronted me at the livery. He thinks I know where Pa buried part of the stolen money."

Marshal Yates set his cup down a bit hard and leaned forward. "Do you?"

Dane shook his head. "Pa never told me a thing. He despised me because I wanted no part in the robberies. He'd never have trusted me with that information."

"Makes sense." The marshal sat back. "I reckon if you'd known where the money was, you would've used it to get a doctor for your mother."

"That's true." Reverend Ross squeezed Dane's shoulder. "You did the right thing turning in your father. He needed to be stopped."

"I just wish I'd done it sooner. Then maybe my brothers wouldn't have died."

Reverend Ross shook his head. "You can't dwell on the what-ifs, Dane. That's the voice of the enemy trying to wear you down. God had His hand on you from a young age. You did what was right, so let the past go. You have a lot to live for, especially one certain young lady, if my guess is correct."

Dane's gaze shot to the pastor's, and he stood, unable to sit still any longer. "You wouldn't object to me courting Regina? Not after all I told you? I was an outlaw."

"No, you weren't. You were a kid who was forced to do something awful by a man I suspect you loved, at least some."

Dane sat down again.

Reverend Ross smiled. "In Isaiah, God's Word says, 'Though your sins be as scarlet, they shall be as white as snow.' I know you believe in God. Listen to Him and trust His Word. He never lies to us."

Dane nodded. "You're right. I need to let it all go. But what about Ned?" He looked at the marshal. "I'm sure he's the one that torched my house. He's trying to get me to help him, but I want no part of it."

The marshal rubbed his chin. "What does he look like?"

Dane described the man, and the marshal leaned forward again.

"I saw a man who looked like that walking around the bank two days ago. There was a gray-haired man with a long beard with him."

"One of 'em was probably Ned," Dane said. "Ned and Pa used to study a bank for a time before they'd rob it. I wouldn't be surprised if he and his friend were planning on robbing the Wiseman bank."

Marshal Yates shot to his feet. He pulled open a desk drawer, reached inside, and dropped a badge on top of the desk. "I need a deputy, and you're it."

Dane stood and shook his head. "No thanks."

The marshal splayed his hands on the desk and stared at Dane. "That man is in this town because of you, and you're going to help me catch him."

"You don't know that." Dane narrowed his gaze. "I came to Texas over ten years ago, and I didn't tell a soul that I came to Wiseman. I think it was just bad luck he ended up here. I've been free of Pa and Ned for fourteen years. I don't think Ned knew I was here."

Marshal Yates put on his hat. "I'm sending a telegram to the penitentiary to see if your pa is still there. And then I'm going to draft a few more deputies."

Dane held out his hands. "What should I do?"

"Get cleaned up, for one. I can loan you a set of clothes if you need them."

"Thanks, but I'll pick up some at the mercantile."

"Go back to your livery after you wash, but keep your eyes open." Marshal Yates picked up the badge and held it out. "I'll set up a stakeout to watch the livery and the bank. I don't think it will be long before those two make their move."

Dane took the badge and recited the oath the marshal quoted. He shoved the silver star in his pocket. "Guess I'd better get going."

The marshal stepped in front of the door, making Dane's heart skip a beat. "It takes a brave man to do what you did and to share a story like that. Thank you. And call me Justin." The marshal held out his hand.

Dane managed a brief smile and a nod then shook Justin's hand.

Outside, Dane watched Justin's long-legged gait as he went straight to the telegraph office.

Reverend Ross stopped beside him. "So, how do you feel?"

"It's a big relief to have you know my history."

"How much have you told Regina?"

Dane hung his head. "Not enough. She knows things were hard and that Pa was mean. I've tried to tell her, but I'm afraid of the look of horror I'll see on her face once she learns the truth."

"Don't judge her too harshly. Regina is a loving woman, and if my guess is right, she cares a lot for you. She risked her own life because she thought you were in that burning house."

"She would have done that for anyone."

"No, I don't think so. She burnt her hand once when she was young, and she's always been real cautious of fire since then. Best you go get cleaned up and have a talk with her so you can quit wallowing in misery."

Dane smiled. "I'm good at that, aren't I?"

Reverend Ross slapped him on the shoulder. "I have a feeling that is about to change."

After a soaking bath in the chilly creek, Dane felt reinvigorated even with the little sleep he'd gotten the night before. He donned his stiff new clothes, fresh from the mercantile. Since there was no chance of getting his old clothes clean, not to mention all the tiny holes in them from the embers that had landed on him, he'd used them as kindling for the fire he'd started to stay warm. He kicked dirt over the dying flames.

Glancing around the wintery landscape, he wished for some

wildflowers to take to Regina, but there were none to be had.

He pushed his feet into motion and started walking back to town. He'd decided to walk to the creek, rather than getting soot all over his saddle and then on his new clothes. He jogged for a bit then slowed as he reached the edge of Wiseman. He needed to check on his horses, but the desire to see Regina and to know for himself that she was all right was far stronger. He'd make it a short visit, but he *had* to see her.

His gut tingled with strange sensations as he knocked on Regina's front door. He sure hoped that grumpy aunt didn't answer again. Mrs. Ross opened it, a worried expression on her face. She glanced behind him, as if looking for someone.

"Is something wrong?" Had Regina taken a turn for the worse? It was so unusual for her mother not to have a cheery expression.

"Regina is missing. She was supposed to be resting and recovering from her ordeal, but she must have stepped out while I was gone. Gideon is searching for her, but he seemed to think she might be with you."

"I haven't seen her since I brought her home last night. You have no idea where she might be?"

Mrs. Ross shook her head. "I do hope she didn't overexert herself. Perhaps she's merely resting in someone's home. But I don't understand why she left in the first place."

"I'll go look for her. Which way did the reverend go?"

"He went to the Yateses' house, since Regina is close to the twins. If she's not there, he is going to check the rest of that block—the Tanners' and Griffiths' houses."

Dane nodded, worry eating at him. Where could she be? "I'll check all of the stores to see if anyone has seen her."

"Thank you. I'll let Gideon know, should he stop back by."

Dane spun away. *Where are you, sweetheart?*

He started at the bakery, café, yard goods store, and mercantile. No one had seen Regina today. Next he stopped at the shoe store, dress shop, and milliners and heard the same thing from each store owner. No Regina.

He retraced his steps and headed for the marshal's office, his heart aching for the woman he loved. Why hadn't he told her sooner how he felt?

Gazing around the town square, he spied the marshal heading his way. Dane jogged toward him.

Justin pushed his hat up on his forehead. "What's up?"

"Regina is missing."

"Are you sure she's not out visiting or shopping?"

Dane shook his head and told him how he'd been to most of the shops Regina would go to. "Reverend Ross is checking with her friends to see if she might have gone visiting, but the thing is, she was supposed to be resting after nearly dying last night. I don't guess you've seen her?"

"No. I was sending that telegram and asking folks if they'd noticed that Ned fellow. Seems quite a few recollect having seen someone of his description, and most said he was near the bank."

Dane's heart leaped. "What if Ned is in the bank and took Regina hostage?"

Justin shook his head. "I was just there, and things are fine at the moment. Have you checked the livery?"

"No. It's locked, so if she did go there, she wouldn't have stayed long." Dane rubbed the back of his neck. "Where could she be? I've got to find her."

Justin rested a hand on Dane's shoulder. "She's here somewhere." He motioned with his chin. "Here comes John Goodwin. Perhaps he's seen something."

John trotted toward them, his expression serious. "Dane, I was looking out the post office window and saw Regina knocking on the livery door. After a few minutes, she walked around the side, but she never returned." He rubbed his jaw. "Got concerned, especially after what happened last night, so I walked over there and noticed the side door was open slightly."

Thank You, Lord. Dane allowed himself to relax. "You think she's waiting in the livery for me?"

John's lips tightened, and he gave a brief shake of his head. "I heard men's voices. Someone told her to shut up."

Dane's gut tightened again, and his gaze shot to the marshal. "It's got to be Ned. I'm going there." He took a step, but Justin grabbed his arm. Dane scowled at him.

"Hold on and let me think. You have a front and back entrance, as well as the side door by the corral. That it?"

"Yeah. There's a pair of double doors up in the hayloft, but I haven't opened them in years."

Marshal Yates looked at the postmaster. "John, it's a bit early for you to head out on deliveries, but could you go get your mailbag, like you're going out on delivery, and then go down the street to the butcher shop? Tell Mike to slip out the back and wait at the mercantile and not to let anyone go down the street the livery is on. Also let Bruce at the blacksmith know. He's a good shot. Ask him to guard the back side of the livery."

John straightened. "Will do. I'm a decent shot too. I can stand guard with Bruce."

Justin gave a quick nod. "Just make sure you act casual when you go down the street, and don't stare at the livery. We don't know if they're watching or not."

Dane couldn't imagine what Regina must be going through. Ned most likely was holding her hostage to get him to do whatever it was Ned wanted. He ached to hold her. To save her. *Lord, protect Regina. Keep her safe.* "Can I go now?"

"What are you going to do? You said you don't have the stolen money."

Dane shrugged and rubbed his neck again. "I don't know. I have some savings in the bank. If I have to, I'll swap every penny to save Regina."

"I don't think it will come to that. Follow me. I'll loan you a gun."

Dane trailed him into the jail. "I'd just as soon have a knife. Got one in my boot, but I could use another. I don't much care for guns, although I do have one—at the livery."

Justin bent and opened the bottom drawer and pulled out a six-inch blade in a sheath. He slid it across the desk. "I'd like that back. It was my pa's."

Dane nodded. "So what's the plan?"

"We need to know how many men are in there. Can you think of a way to signal me?"

"If I get the chance, I could kick the side of the barn real quick."

"All right. Good enough. Before we go, I'd like to pray."

Dane longed to run for the door and get to Regina to put an end to her captivity, but he knew the value of prayer. "Go ahead."

"Lord, we ask You to help us rescue Miss Ross. Grant us favor and wisdom to know exactly what to do. Help us not to get shot and to capture the men holding Miss Ross captive. Amen."

Dane headed for the door.

"See if you can unlock the front of the livery without the men inside hearing." Justin followed. "Make sure you walk like normal. Don't do anything to draw suspicion in case they're watching."

"What are you going to do?"

"I'll head to the mercantile and make sure the Lawsons know what's going on. Then I'll go to the saloon and make my way back to your place." He clapped Dane on the shoulder. "We'll save her."

Dane hoped he was right, because if he lost Regina, he wasn't sure he could go on.

Chapter 10

Regina shivered in the cold, dark corner. She longed to wrap her cloak around herself, but she couldn't since her hands were tied. Oh, if only she'd stayed in bed. She longed for it now—to be under the warm covers, safe from harm.

And where was Dane? It had to be close to noon by now. It was far past time for him to turn out the horses. They'd become even more restless, whickering and kicking the stalls, and one had even started gnawing on the stall gate.

"I don't like this sittin' around. Where's that stupid kid of yours?"

"Watch it, Ned. He's still my kin."

Ned hopped up and paced in front of the stalls. "How can you still claim him as your own after he turned you in? If not for that lucky prison break, we'd still be rotting away in that rat hole."

"Yeah, well, we ain't, so shut yer trap." The old man ruffled his beard. "I have a score to settle with Dane. I should have taken care of the whiney pup years ago."

"Dane's a good man," Regina croaked. "You should be proud of him." She coughed several times then hiked her chin, but just as fast, she regretted her outburst. Dane's father eyed her like he wanted to strangle her.

"Yeah, well, if he's so good, why's he running a stinkin' livery?"

"Goodness comes from your heart, not your job. Dane is a man of good character." Though her throat ached, she was glad she'd stood up for the man she loved.

Dane's pa rose. "You sound like the boy's ma. She's the one that ruined him."

Regina wanted to say that Dane's mother had saved him and made him into the man he was today, but she feared angering them. She ducked her head and prayed again. Her stomach reminded her that it was near lunchtime. Her family would know she was missing by now. Pa, and probably others, would be searching for her. *Please, Lord, don't let anyone get hurt because of my foolish choices. Keep Dane safe.*

She lifted her head, and her heart jolted. Through several cracks between boards on the barn wall, she saw a shadow moving toward the door on the outside of the building. She cleared her throat and forced out more words. "You two should leave while you can. People will be out looking for me."

Ned's anxious glance shifted toward Dane's pa. "Maybe we oughta go. There are other banks. And I don't think the kid knows where your gold is."

"Then who stole it if he didn't? It was good and buried when we went to prison. I didn't tell nobody where I'd hid it."

"Things was hard in prison. Maybe you ain't recollectin' right where it was." Ned scratched his chest. As he passed by the horse that was chewing on his stall, the animal reached out and nipped his shoulder. "Ow. Hey! Stupid critter." He pulled his gun.

"No!" Dane's pa started for Ned. "You use that gun, and I'll use mine on you."

Ned glared back and muttered a string of foul words. "That dumb beast bit me."

"Shhh! You want folks to know where we are?"

Ned sighed and lowered his gun. "I reckon not."

"We can get good money for that horse."

Regina shivered at the harshness in the man's voice. Her father was so kind and gentle. She'd never heard him use such a severe tone. She lowered her head and glanced back at the side door. Her heartbeat stampeded when she saw Dane peek in.

Dane quickly took in the situation. Both Ned and another man were in the alley in front of the stalls. He searched for Regina but didn't see her. Where was she? Was she all right?

Gunfire sounded outside at the front of the barn. His heart bucked as the two men turned toward it, firing. Dane slipped inside. "Stop shooting. And put your hands up."

Both men spun toward him. Regina squealed as Dane dove behind the nearest stall divider. His heart pounded hard. The man with Ned had resembled Pa. Could it actually be him? "Pa, it's me. Dane. Stop shooting."

More gunfire erupted. The wood above Dane's head splintered.

He was pinned down. He shifted his gaze toward the office, and his heart lurched as he caught a glimpse of Regina sitting just outside the office. He swatted his hand toward the door. "Get in the office."

Suddenly the right front door swung open. No one was there, but Dane knew the marshal was nearby. Pa fired in that direction. Dane rose and peeked over the half wall of the empty stall. "Drop your gun, Pa. We've got you surrounded."

"I ain't goin' back to prison." His pa ducked behind the water barrel, leaving his back exposed to Dane. Though the man had been so cruel, it would pain him to watch him die.

"Why did you come here?"

"Just stumbled on you by accident when we was scoping out the bank. Saw you riding in one day. Couldn't believe my eyes. You're all grown up."

The man sounded like he actually cared, but Dane knew better. He was merely trying to play on Dane's emotions so he'd drop his guard. He peered through a crack in the wood—saw his buckboard roll in front of the open door. A pair of legs showed through the spokes on the wheel.

"I'm Marshal Yates. Drop your guns and come out."

Ned ran toward the front of the barn. Justin fired, and Ned spun around then fell. Pa rose up and his gun blasted. Horses squealed and pranced nervously in their stalls. Dane rose and threw the knife hard, into Pa's right shoulder. He cried out as the gun fell from his hand. Dane charged the man he'd hated so much as a boy and knocked him off his feet.

Pa bucked like a wild mustang, but with Dane lying across him, he couldn't get free. But it didn't stop him from trying.

"Stay down, Pa."

The loud click of a rifle being cocked echoed through the barn. Dane glanced up, relieved to see Justin.

Pa froze. "Just shoot me."

"Not happening. Go ahead and get off him, Dane. I've got him covered."

Dane pushed up, but as soon as his weight was off, his pa rolled.

"Gun!" Dane yelled.

A loud blast reverberated through the livery. Pa jerked then collapsed as blood seeped from a hole in his chest and spread out across his filthy shirt. The heavy odor of gunpowder filled the livery. Dane's horses squealed in fright. Pa's glassy gaze slid to Dane's. "Sorry I weren't a better pa."

Dane crawled to his side. "Call on Jesus, Pa. It's not too late."

"He don't want a lousy coot like me."

Dane took hold of Pa's clammy hand. "He does. Just cry out to Him and ask forgiveness, and you'll spend eternity in heaven. With Ma."

He shook his head. "She's better off without me. You too." His eyes closed, and he heaved a final breath.

Dane stared at him for a moment, grieving his father's wasted life. Then he thought of Regina. He bolted up and hurried to his office. "Regina, are you all right? They didn't hurt you, did they?"

She shook her head.

Dane's heart clenched at seeing her tied up. He reached for the knife the marshal had loaned him but realized it was still in Pa's shoulder. He pulled out his boot knife and carefully slit the rope that bound her hands.

She rubbed her wrists then gazed up at him. "You're not hurt? I was so afraid, but I prayed and God helped me." Her hoarse voice made his gut twist.

"I'm fine, but we need to get you home. Your parents are frantic."

Dane helped her to her feet. "Can you stand?"

"Yes. Haven't been here long." She held her hand at her throat as she gazed up at him. "Was that awful man truly your father?"

Dane clenched his jaw. Would she hate him now? He nodded. Regina frowned. "He was an outlaw?"

"Yeah. I tried to tell you several times, but I couldn't find the words." He gazed up at the ceiling. "I was afraid you would despise me."

She reached up, took hold of his chin, and gently pulled his face down. "Nothing could be further from the truth," she whispered. "But I would like to hear the whole story one day."

He blinked, unable to fathom the grace she offered. "You don't hate me?"

She smiled so sweetly his heart could hardly take it. "No, Dane. The woman isn't supposed to be the first to say it, but I love you." She stared at him for a long moment, and then her cheeks pinked and she ducked her head. "Um. . .perhaps you don't feel the same."

This time Dane lifted her head. "But I do. I thought my life would end if something happened to you today. I love you so much, Regina, but I don't think I'll ever be good enough."

"Stop!" She placed her soft fingertips across his lips. "I don't ever want to hear those words come out of your mouth again. You're a good man. Kindhearted, honest, faithful, hardworking. Shall I go on?"

He shook his head, but his lips quirked up. He pulled her into his arms and held her tight. "I'm so grateful to God that you're safe."

She clung to him. He closed his eyes, enjoying the closeness.

He gently pressed her head against his chest. "I've already spoken to your pa, and he's given me permission to court you."

She jerked back, eyes bright. "You did? He did?"

Dane smiled. "Yes and yes."

Regina smiled back, her eyes dancing. "It's about time," she squeaked.

Dane laughed. Then he sobered as his gaze landed on her pink lips. He leaned forward, and Regina rose up on her toes, meeting him in a sweet kiss he would never forget.

Outside the door, Dane heard Justin clear his throat. He stepped back reluctantly but knowing it was the wise thing. "We need to get you home."

Regina nodded, but her eyes told him she wished she didn't have to go. "Mama and Papa will be worrying."

As they stepped out of the office, Justin chuckled. "Guess she told you, huh?"

Dane made a face at him and walked on Regina's right side so that she wouldn't see his pa's body, but Justin had already covered it with a horse blanket. Dane nodded his thanks.

As they stepped out into the bright sunshine, Dane knew his life had changed forever. His pa and his past had lost their power over him, and his future looked quite promising.

Exactly one month after the fire, Dane stood at the front of the sanctuary, waiting for his bride to appear. He glanced at Justin, his best man, all gussied up in his Sunday suit. Dane pressed his hands down the black suit Regina had helped him pick out in Dallas.

He thought back to Christmas and how special it had been as

he'd spent it with Regina's family. On Christmas Eve, he'd helped Reverend and Mrs. Ross hand out the Christmas baskets, and the mysterious donor had come through once again with the meat donation.

Christmas had been wonderful, especially with Regina at his side. He hadn't enjoyed one quite like it with delicious food, the reading of the Christmas story, and gifts. He hoped it was the first of many. His life was so different now. He had experienced what it was like to be part of a loving, God-fearing family. Gideon had even tutored him in the Bible and was helping him to become a stronger Christian.

The music started, and Dane's gaze jerked to the back of the church again. One of Justin's sisters walked down the aisle. Her twin stood at the back, waiting for her turn. He'd never understand how Regina could tell those two apart.

The church was filled with people he called friends and others he only knew from seeing on Sunday mornings or around town. He felt blessed that so many had come today.

Dane's gut churned with excitement. Any second he'd see the love of his life, and in a half hour or so, they'd be officially wed. He never thought this day would come. He didn't deserve a woman like Regina, but God had forgiven him and washed him white as snow. Now God was blessing him with the greatest gift he'd ever received, except for salvation.

Excitement boiled through him. He was looking forward to living with Regina in the little house he'd rented from the Tanner sisters. It would do until next month when the town was hosting a house-raising for them on the land he'd purchased just outside of town.

The music changed. Dane froze as Regina stepped into view. She looked like an angel in that beautiful pale blue gown. Her gaze latched onto his, and her lips turned up in a lovely smile. She took hold of her father's arm, and they started down the aisle.

Dane gave a little shake of his head. Who'd have ever thought that the preacher's daughter would marry an outlaw's son? God sure did work in mysterious ways.

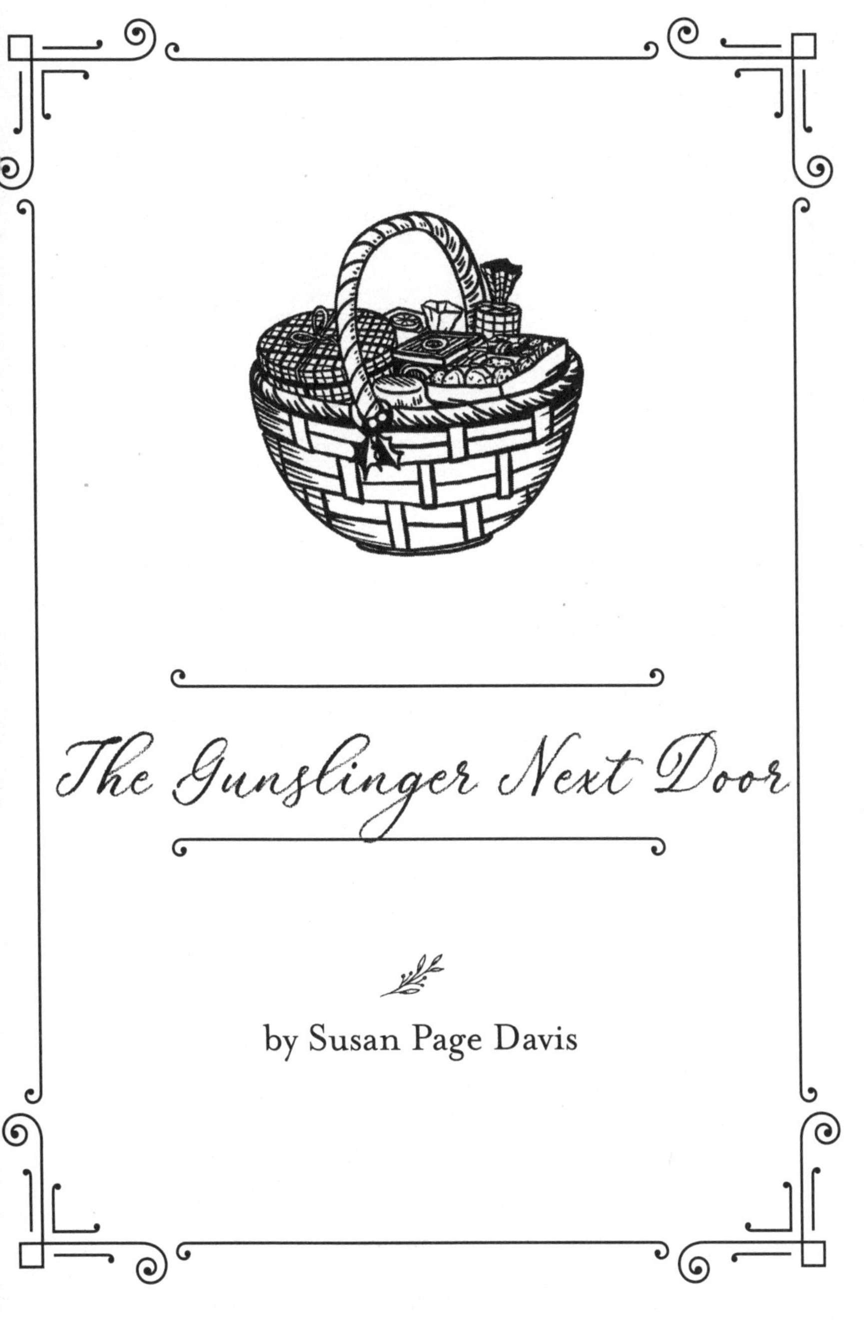

The Gunslinger Next Door

by Susan Page Davis

Chapter 1

Wiseman, Texas
November, 1888

Alice Singer kneaded the next day's bread at her worktable while her father sipped a cup of coffee and read to her from the Dallas newspaper.

"The statue of the Goddess of Liberty was lifted into place on top of the dome. This completes the construction of the new capitol building in Austin, for which ground was broken more than six years ago. The new building was dedicated in May, and the state's legislature now meets in its new halls, which replaces the structure that burned in 1881."

"That must have been quite a sight to see." Alice shaped a loaf and plopped it into a greased bread pan.

"I'm sure." Her father reached for his ironstone coffee cup.

Movement outside the window above the table caught Alice's eye. "There's a wagon pulling up next door."

"Must be our new neighbor." Her father pushed back his chair and walked to her side. They stood together, watching through the window. "That's the old man," her father said.

Alice frowned as she watched a younger fellow jump down from the wagon seat and reach to give the elderly passenger a hand.

"Do you think he's really a killer?" she asked.

"No, Alice, you mustn't heed all the gossip you hear."

She turned to her father, still uncertain. "Well, I certainly won't repeat it, but Phyllis Begley says she heard it from—"

Her father snorted. "Oh, those Begley women. I'm telling you, they're a couple of old busybodies with noses as long as a heron's beak. Even if that codger does have a past, he's got to be eighty years old now. Look how slow he's moving. Must be all stiff with rheumatism."

"I suppose he's harmless." Alice watched the old man move slowly up the steps to the small house next door, with the younger man supporting him. It almost hurt to watch him. "That fellow with him looks sinister though." She shivered. The man's crooked nose and the jagged scar on his chin were enough to make her glad she wasn't closer.

"Well, he's probably not staying," Pa said.

The door to the wood-frame house closed behind the men, and Alice forced herself to turn her attention back to her bread. She shaped one lump of dough into rolls. Once the scary-looking man was gone, she would take the new tenant a plate of hot rolls for his lunch. Maybe meeting the old man face-to-face would allay some of her fears.

A few minutes later, the younger man came out, retrieved a suitcase and two boxes from the wagon, and carried them into the house next door. After that, he left the house and climbed aboard the wagon. As he drove off toward the center of town, Alice let out a pent-up breath.

"Well, I've got to get over to the stockyards," Pa said. He put on his hat and grabbed a pad of paper he nearly always carried with him to and from his business.

"Will you be home at noon?" Alice asked.

"I expect so."

She smiled at him. "All right, I'll see you later."

The door clicked shut, and she washed her hands. Drying them on a clean towel, she gazed out at the rental house. Phyllis Begley had been certain about the tale she'd heard. Their new neighbor was an old gunslinger, come here to retire. Was he safe to live near? Alice's family had lived here more than ten years, and Alice had never felt unsafe. Maybe Phyllis was wrong. And maybe Alice was imagining things.

John Goodwin, the postmaster, looked up from sorting the mail. The door had opened, letting in a gust of cold air, and with it came Miss Alice Singer, the daughter of the stockyard owner.

"Good morning, Alice," he called out with a smile.

She returned his greeting and approached the counter. Her cheeks were rosy, but it was probably just from the cold snap.

"Your father was in this morning and picked up his mail," John said.

"Oh good. I just stopped in to buy a few postcards. I need to send some notes to our family back east."

"How many would you like?"

"Half a dozen should do it."

John opened the drawer where he kept printed postal cards. He wished he could keep Alice here a few minutes longer since there were no other customers in the post office at the moment. He counted out her cards, trying to think of a brilliant line of conversation, but came up short. "Here you go. Everything well at your house?"

"Yes, thank you. And you?"

"I'm fine." John smiled sheepishly. "Guess I won't have to stop at the Singer house when I make deliveries this afternoon."

"Well. . ." Unless he was mistaken, Alice had a twinkle in her lovely brown eyes. "I might have some postcards to send by then."

"Right," John said heartily. "I'll stop by and see. I know I'll be taking some mail to your new neighbor, so I'll be going right past your house anyway."

"Oh. How nice." Alice's expression darkened, despite her words.

John raised his eyebrows and waited.

"Sorry," she said. "Just. . .our neighbor. Not to be nosy, but have you met him?"

John chuckled. "I surely did. When he moved in a couple of days ago, a young man brought him by here to see if anything had arrived for him by general delivery. I think the old man's harmless."

Alice's eyebrows drew together. "I've been telling myself the same thing. Although I've heard. . .rumors. About his past."

John shrugged. "Well, he's quite elderly, and as I understand it, he's getting a bit feebleminded."

"Feebleminded?"

"Yes. The fellow who was with him told me on the sly that if Mr. Willard ever came in asking for any mail addressed to Benjamin Franklin, I should go ahead and give him his own mail—mail addressed to Dirk Willard, that is."

"That certainly *is* odd," Alice said. "Benjamin Franklin?"

John glanced toward the door. Still no other customers. He leaned on the counter and lowered his voice. "I don't spill everything I hear, but since you're his closest neighbor and you seem a little concerned, I'll tell you what his friend said. It seems that a few years ago—maybe quite a few—Mr. Willard had a bullet crease his temple in a shootout."

Alice drew back with a quick intake of breath. "That's horrid!"

"Yes. Well, ever since then, the young fellow says, he's suffered some forgetfulness and senility. Some days he thinks he's Ben Franklin."

"You mean the statesman."

"That's right. Said he talks about the Continental Congress and his time in France when he was the ambassador."

"Goodness."

John nodded. "I don't think he's dangerous though. Not now."

"But if he suffers delusions. . . I mean, he was a gunfighter, as you say."

"Long in the past, according to his chum."

The door flew open, and Mr. Maynard, the shoe store owner, came in and pushed it shut against the wind.

"Nippy out there," he said, and nodded at Alice. "Morning, Miss Singer."

"Hello, Mr. Maynard." She picked up her postal cards and looked at John. "I'll look for you later to pick up my mail."

"Right," John said. He watched her go, the wind whipping her hair and her woolen scarf as she turned to pull the door shut. Mr. Maynard stepped over to help push on it until it latched.

"A poor day to be out," the store owner said. "Could you put my mail in a sack, John, so I don't lose anything?"

"Of course." John turned to collect mail for the Maynard family and the business. As he handed it to Maynard, the door flew open and Clint Wiseman came in.

"Clint," Mr. Maynard said, touching his hat brim. He hurried out, and Clint wrestled with the door.

"Just one item for you," John said, taking Clint's piece of mail from a pigeonhole. "I'm afraid it's a bill."

"That's all right. Thanks." Clint took the envelope and tucked it into his jacket.

John walked out from behind the counter. Clint had been captured by Comanches when he was a boy, and he'd always had trouble fitting in with society since his return. After his folks died, he'd lived up in the hills for several years, rarely coming into town. But this summer he'd quietly moved back into town, occupying his parents' house. It was good to see lights on in the place at night after it had been vacant so long. John was forming a friendship with Clint, but it was slow going.

"How's everything?" he asked with a smile.

" 'Bout the same," Clint said.

"Stop by my place some evening if you want to play checkers," John said.

"I might."

That was progress. John shoved the door securely shut against the wind when the young man had gone out, but his thoughts had already turned back to Alice. Surely she need not be afraid of that frail old man who'd moved in next to her. Although she may have a point about his delusions. John smiled to himself. It could have been worse. The old gunslinger might have settled on Blackbeard or some other cutthroat, rather than the peaceful and well-respected Benjamin Franklin.

"Thank you so much," Alice said to Mrs. Ross, the minister's wife.

"It's no problem, my dear. And my husband says you may borrow books anytime you wish."

"That's very nice of him." Alice tucked the large volume under her arm. She had asked Reverend Ross at prayer meeting the evening before if he happened to have a copy of *The Autobiography of Benjamin Franklin* in his large personal library. He'd assured her he did, and that he would get it to her. Mrs. Ross had brought it along to the sewing circle meeting for her.

"How is Regina doing?" Alice asked. The Rosses' daughter, Regina, had married Dane McDermott, owner of the livery stable, less than a year ago.

"Oh, just wonderfully," Mrs. Ross replied with a smile. "Dane treats her like a princess. They're going to spend Christmas with us, and I'm quite excited about it. The house has been too quiet since she got married."

"At least she's not far away," Alice said. She left Mrs. Ross and her other friends outside the church and headed for home. It wasn't far down the street, toward the end of the next block, but in December darkness fell early, and the night chill had set in. She shivered and hurried her steps.

Seeing a light shine out from the parlor window cheered her. Pa was home from the stockyard. Some evenings he stayed late to settle up his accounts. The two of them had lived alone together since Alice's mother had died six years ago. She didn't like to come home to a dark house and find the fire had burned down in the stove and the air was uncomfortably cold. No chance of that tonight.

As she stepped onto the path leading to the front door, a form moved out from the shadows in the next yard, and she jumped.

"Evening, miss."

Alice's heart pounded and she gulped in a breath. "Oh Mr. Willard. You startled me."

"So sorry." He was holding something bulky under one arm, and he held it up in explanation. "I was just out trying to fly my kite by moonlight."

Alice squinted and realized the object he held was indeed a kite, such as schoolboys would play with. Hadn't she learned something long ago about Benjamin Franklin flying a kite with a key tied to the string?

"Oh, uh. . .a scientific experiment?" she ventured. Suddenly conscious of the book she had borrowed, she snugged it close against her side and hoped he wouldn't ask what she was reading.

The old man beamed at her. "Why, yes. Sometimes a spark will jump down the kite string, but I've concluded that's only when there's lightning in the air. It's windy tonight, but alas, no lightning."

"Pity," Alice said.

"Yes. But I did have a good flight with it. Got a nice gust of wind up in the town square." He peered at her in the dim light of the quarter moon. "Do you know what electricity is?"

"I've heard about it," Alice said. "They're using it for lights and things back east."

"Yes, and lots of other things," Willard said eagerly. "Streetcars, even."

She frowned. "How does that work?"

"The cars are powered by electricity instead of horses."

She shook her head. "I can't picture it."

"Someday you'll see them here in Wiseman."

She laughed. "Wouldn't that be something?"

"Thank you again for the delicious rolls you brought me the other day."

"You're welcome. Well, good night, Mr. Willard."

He tipped his hat. "Early to bed, early to rise, miss. It will make you healthy, wealthy, and wise."

"So I've heard," she said drily. She walked up the steps to the front porch and hurried inside.

"That you?" her father called from the parlor. He came to the doorway.

"Yes, it's me," Alice said. "I met our neighbor outside, and guess what? He's carrying a kite around and spouting Ben Franklin at me."

Her father laughed. "I've heard he's quite a character."

"Well, if he's struck by lightning in the next thundershower, don't say I didn't warn you." She laid the autobiography on the kitchen table and hung up her coat.

"It wouldn't hurt to stay on his good side, I'm guessing." Her father rubbed his chin thoughtfully.

"I'll take him some jam tomorrow," Alice said. "That way we'll be sure he hasn't accidentally shocked himself to death."

"What's this?" Pa lifted the cover of the big leather-bound volume.

"It's Franklin's autobiography. I'm borrowing it from Pastor Ross."

"So you can learn more about our neighbor?"

"Maybe," Alice said. "Or maybe so I can tell when he's speaking the truth and when he's fabricating."

The next day dawned sunny and cold. After her father left for the stockyard, Alice did her housework while planning her next visit to Mr. Willard. If he showed any signs of unfriendliness or discourtesy, she would of course leave immediately. And what if he showed hints of madness? She shuddered. Perhaps she should enlist a friend to make the call with her.

She went through a mental list of women who might agree to go with her, but those who lived close by had young children to watch or work to do. By lunchtime she hadn't come to a decision. Maybe Pa would walk over with her when he came home to eat. She sighed. Pa had told her he would be eating lunch in town today with a cattle buyer. She made herself a plate of leftovers and ate alone.

A knock at the door while she gathered up her dishes startled her. She walked over and called cautiously, "Who is it?"

"John Goodwin."

Of course—the postman. She opened the door with a smile. This was one person she was always glad to see.

"John."

"Good day, Alice." He held out an envelope. "Something for your father. I didn't see him this morning, so I thought I'd stop in on my rounds this afternoon."

"Thank you very much. You're early today, aren't you?"

John sighed. "I decided to walk down here first because your new neighbor has a package. I thought I'd deliver it and not have to lug it all around town that way."

She noticed then that the canvas bag in which John carried the mail bulged.

"Oh, so you're going to Mr. Willard next?"

"I am."

"Would I impose too much if I asked to go with you? I wanted to take him a jar of jam and—well, you know—just check on him. I saw him last night, and he was, er. . .in the Franklin mode, if you take my meaning."

As she talked, John's expression changed from a broad smile to a slight frown of concern.

"His delusions were on him?"

"I'm afraid so. He'd been out flying a kite in the evening."

"Flying a kite? Oh, I see."

"Do you mind if I accompany you?"

"Of course not. You'll want your coat though."

"Would you like to step in while I fetch it and the jam?"

"Thank you." John came into the kitchen and stood by the stove while she scurried to put on her warm coat, hat, and gloves, and took a jar of last summer's strawberry jam from the cupboard.

"There, I'm ready."

John was gazing at her with a dreamy look in his eyes, and Alice felt her cheeks flush.

"Shall we?" He walked to the door and opened it for her.

They walked across the yards together without going out to the street. The ground was hard beneath their feet.

"Do you think it will stay cold?" she asked.

"Can't for very long, can it?" John asked.

"I suppose not. At least not this cold."

They reached Mr. Willard's front door, and John knocked boldly. "Postmaster, Mr. Willard. You have some mail."

A few seconds later, the door opened and the old man stood blinking at them. He had on a striped shirt, a vest, and worn black trousers, and his feet were clad in gray wool stockings.

"Oh, good afternoon," he said. "Miss. . . Hello again, miss."

"Alice Singer," she supplied. "My father and I live over there." She pointed to the house.

"Yes. Won't you come in?"

"I have a package for you," John said. "Would you like me to bring it inside?"

"Oh, thank you." Mr. Willard stood back, and they entered the little house. The large front room served as both kitchen and parlor, and his cookstove's top held a steaming coffeepot. A quick look around told Alice that the man had few personal possessions and kept his living space fairly neat. No dirty dishes in sight or rumpled clothing lying about. The only disorder was in one corner, where it appeared he'd been busy with a woodworking project.

"I brought you a jar of jam." She held it out while John set down his pack and rummaged in it for Mr. Willard's parcel.

"What? Oh, thank you. That's most kind of you." Mr. Willard took the pint jar and held it up toward the window. The sun glinted through the glass and the red jam.

"It's strawberry," Alice said. "I hope you like it."

"Above all things," Mr. Willard replied with a smack of his lips. Alice wondered if he cooked for himself. Perhaps she should have made him some biscuits.

"Here you go." John set a box on the table with a thump.

"*Merci beaucoup.* Do I owe anything?"

Alice wondered if the French thank-you meant he was acting as Franklin again.

"No, we give free delivery," John said.

"Oh. Well, much obliged." Mr. Willard nodded.

Alice's curiosity was piqued by the tools and wood shavings on the floor in the corner, and she took a step closer. "What are you working on, Mr. Willard?"

"Just a little project of mine. It's going to be a chair."

"A chair?" John said. "That's ambitious of you."

Mr. Willard laughed. "More than you'd think. I intend for it to be my loafing chair. I'm going to rig it up so I can rock it."

"A rocking chair?" John asked. "That will be nice."

"Yes, it will," Alice said. "You must be very clever."

"Well, I like to fiddle with things." The old man smiled and cocked his head to one side.

John nodded. "It's good to work with your hands."

Mr. Willard smiled at him. "I always say, 'Work as if you were to live a hundred years, and pray as if you were to die tomorrow.'"

"That's good advice." Alice couldn't help it—she was beginning to like the old man. Would a gunfighter really talk about hard work and prayer that way?

"Well, I must get on with my route," John said. "Good day, Mr. Willard."

Alice smiled and held out her hand. "Goodbye. I'll bring my father around to meet you one of these days."

"I shall look forward to it," Mr. Willard said. *"Au revoir!"*

Outside, she and John walked back toward the Singer house. "Well, he answered to his proper name," she said.

"Yes, and the box was addressed to Dirk Willard." John's forehead wrinkled. "Do you think he really supposes he's Ben Franklin?"

"I don't know, but. . .didn't Mr. Franklin invent the rocking chair?"

"Hmm. I'll have to do some reading. But I'm sure that bit he said at the end was a quote from Franklin. 'Work as if you were to live a hundred years.' The almanac, you know."

"Yes. He said something to me last night that I thought was Franklin too. You know that old saw, 'Early to bed, early to rise. . .' But everyone knows that."

"Right." John smiled. "Well, I must get moving. Just keep your eyes and ears open. But really, I don't think you need to fear him."

"Nor do I." Alice watched him go and waved when John paused and looked back before turning the corner. She went back into her home feeling much more at ease than she had earlier. After all, what would Mr. Willard do to her—ask her to sign the Declaration of Independence?

Chapter 2

Alice didn't see her neighbor for several days, but the smoke continued to plume from his chimney, and she smiled when she thought about his projects. He reminded her of her grandpa Singer, who had died a few years back. When she and her parents visited him, Grandpa had often been at work tooling leather. The skill had become his passion in his old age, and he decorated saddles for several wealthy cattlemen. Mr. Willard was like that with his inventions, and if he took his inspiration from Benjamin Franklin, what harm was done?

She was hanging out laundry Monday afternoon when he came around the corner of his house, carrying an armload of firewood.

"Good afternoon," Alice called.

He turned toward her and smiled. "Good day, Miss Singer. Forgive me for not tipping my hat, but my hands are occupied."

She laughed. "I take no offense. It's nice to have warmer weather, isn't it?"

"It is indeed. I thought I'd take advantage of it to fill my woodbox, in preparation for the next cold spell."

"And I thought it was a perfect day to do the wash." She wondered if Mr. Willard did his own laundry. She hadn't seen him hang clothes on the clothesline behind his house, but she hadn't seen anyone bringing and taking away anything that looked like bundles of laundry either.

"What have you been doing these past few days?" she asked.

"A little puttering, a little writing, and much reading. I like to keep busy. Lost time is never found, you know."

She smiled at him. "Sounds like a recipe for a pleasant day. And what are you writing?"

"I'm thinking of resuming my almanac."

"Your—you mean *Poor Richard's Almanac*?"

She wished she hadn't voiced the thought. She didn't want to encourage his delusions. But the look of pleasure on his craggy face told her she'd said the right thing.

"Oh, you've heard of it?" he asked.

"Of course. Everyone has."

"Well, it's been a long time since I put out an issue, but I'm thinking of starting it up again. I've ordered some books and extra paper."

"Those must be in the packages Mr. Goodwin brings you."

"Yes, that's some of it." He looked down at his load of wood. "Well, I must get this burden inside and get to work."

"Don't tire yourself out," she called as he nudged open his door.

At the supper table, Alice's father told her, "I met your aging gunfighter this afternoon."

She looked up at him in surprise. "You did? Where?"

"He was at the mercantile, buying a bottle of ink."

"Well, he did tell me he was doing some writing."

Her father speared a baked potato with his fork. "He says he's converting his main room into a workshop for his inventions. Do you know, he thinks he invented the parlor stove?"

Alice smiled and shook her head. "Do you think he really supposes he's Benjamin Franklin?"

"Hard to say." Pa forked open the potato and slathered it liberally with butter. "He was answering to 'Mr. Willard,' but he was entertaining some of the town's regular loafers with tales of his time abroad."

Alice arched her eyebrows in question.

"When he was the ambassador to France." Pa laughed. "I couldn't say whether he believes it or not, but he spins a good yarn."

"Yes." Alice recalled the "au revoir" Mr. Willard had flung at her. She felt a little relieved now that her father had met him. Pa was a good judge of character.

"Do you want a Christmas tree this year?" Pa asked doubtfully.

"It might be nice." They hadn't bothered since Alice's mother had died. She saw the sadness creep over her father and said hastily, "Maybe just a few green boughs."

He sighed. "I miss your mother."

"I know, Pa. I do too. She loved Christmas." That made the season more poignant. The memories of her mother's joyful preparations for the holiday brought tears to Alice's eyes, but she wouldn't let that stop her from celebrating. "She wouldn't want us to ignore the day," she said quietly.

For the last few years she hadn't decorated for the Advent season, but she had still prepared a special dinner on Christmas Day and taken part in the holiday services at church. And she and Pa had continued to exchange small gifts.

Pa nodded. "I'll see if I can get you some greenery then."

"Thanks." Alice knew what she was going to give her father as a Christmas gift. Her mother had always given Pa a new shirt at Christmas, along with a new ledger for his business records. Alice had continued that tradition. But she wanted to give him something that was entirely her idea too, and she'd been saving up for a new pair of boots. The pair he wore to the stockyards every day was comfortable and worn. At the moment the leather was still whole, but she doubted they'd last through the winter, and so she'd set aside a little bit from the housekeeping money he gave her every week. Mr. Maynard at the shoe store was holding a pair for her, and she intended to go in and pay for them later this week.

As she refilled his coffee mug, he said, "And what are you wanting for Christmas this year, Alice?"

"Nothing, Pa. I'm just glad I've got you."

He chuckled, and she knew he'd get something. The year Ma died, he hadn't bought her anything, but every year since, he'd found some little trinket for her.

"Maybe I can get Mr. Willard to make you a rocking chair," he said.

Alice scowled at him. "Don't you dare suggest it."

John knocked on the Singers' door and set his heavy mail sack down on the porch. He rubbed his aching shoulder. Next time something this heavy arrived, he would get a wagon from Dane McDermott at the livery.

When Alice opened the door a moment later, he had no more thoughts of his aching muscles. She wore a pretty green calico dress, and her large brown eyes almost sparkled. He didn't think she'd ever looked so beautiful—but then, every time he'd seen her lately, he thought she looked lovelier than the last time.

"Hi," he almost stammered. "Your mail." He held out two envelopes, feeling a bit stupid.

"Oh, a letter from Aunt Mabel. Thank you. And one for Pa from the Cattlemen's Association." She glanced at the full bag he was hefting. "More packages?"

"Yes. For your neighbor. I can't think what he's ordering this time."

"Is it heavy?"

"As an elephant."

Alice laughed, and John caught his breath at the musical sound.

"He tells me he wants to revive *Poor Richard's Almanac*," she said. "I expect he needs a lot of paper for that."

"Well, one of these boxes may be paper, but the other one rattles like hardware. Oh!" John stopped and looked at her with a flush of guilt. "Sorry. I'm not supposed to discuss people's mail with other folks."

Her smile didn't shrink one bit. "I won't tell anyone what you said."

"Thank you. Mr. Willard did tell me yesterday that a lot of his orders are supplies for his inventions." He eyed her again, trying to fix this picture of her in his mind. He stole moments with her when he delivered the mail and cherished each memory until the next time. On days when the Singers didn't receive any letters or bills, he languished about his rounds. Today was a good day, and he shouldn't be complaining. "Well, I'd better move on if I want to get all the deliveries made on time."

"I'll see you tomorrow," Alice said.

If you get any mail, he thought. Or maybe she would stop in at the post office to check. "Well, goodbye."

He lugged the sack over to Dirk Willard's front door and set it down. He knocked then pulled out Willard's boxes and an envelope that looked like a bill. The door swung open.

"Hello, young man," Willard said. "Brought my wrenches, have you?"

"Well, I might have." John handed him the noisy box. "There's another one here. It's bigger and heavier. Paper maybe?"

"Oh, that's probably it," Willard said, "though I did order several books from a publisher in Boston."

"Would you like me to set this inside?" John asked.

"Thank you, yes."

John carried his sack inside and was glad to unload another heavy burden.

"How are things going in the post office?" Willard asked.

"Fine, sir. Pretty quiet most days."

"Ah." The old man eyed him keenly. "I used to be postmaster, you know. Postmaster General, actually."

John smiled. "Yes, sir. I'd heard that. Boston, was it?"

"Philadelphia. Back in '75, that was."

John tried to hold his tongue, but it was too tempting. "You mean 1775, is that right?"

"Of course." Willard looked as if only an idiot would think he meant any year within a century of the present.

"Of course."

"You'll probably need to hire some men to do deliveries for you."

"Well, we do, for the ranches and farms outside of town limits. But if the town grows much larger, I might need another helper," John conceded. "Or we could require folks who live within a mile or two to pick up their mail at the post office."

"That would be difficult for some." Willard frowned.

"It would put a hardship on older folks, I'm sure," John said. "For now I'll go on keeping the post office open in the morning and delivering in the afternoon. But I'll keep your suggestion in mind." He smiled and shouldered his lighter sack. "Have a pleasant day, sir."

Alice woke on Sunday still brooding over her thoughts from the night before. She'd seen two men drive up to Mr. Willard's house the previous day and carry several bundles inside. They stayed about two hours and then left. Her curiosity burned inside her.

"Oh, be glad the old fellow has a few friends," her father said when she'd expressed her concern over the supper table. "Perhaps they brought him some supplies so he won't have to carry his groceries home from the store."

"But they were strangers. Nobody from Wiseman, I'm sure."

"They probably weren't strangers to him." Her father smiled and stirred his coffee. "You fret too much, Alice."

Did she? As she dressed for church, she wondered. Should she just keep her nose out of her neighbor's business?

After church, she and her father ate dinner, and then Pa put on his hat.

"I'm going over to the stockyard. We've got a lot of cattle we're holding over until the auction tomorrow."

"Surely you've got someone on duty," Alice said, knowing he wouldn't leave the place unattended when animals were penned up there.

"Rufus is over there, but I just want to check in and make sure everything's all right. I won't be long."

Alice was used to this. Pa was a conscientious man when it came to keeping the stock entrusted to him safe. After he'd gone, she looked over at Dirk Willard's house. No strange horses or wagons were tied up in front. His chimney let out a thin plume of smoke. She took a small plate from the cupboard and arranged two slices of pound cake on it and removed her apron. Before she could change her mind, she put on her coat and gloves and hurried across to Mr. Willard's door.

"Hello," she said when he opened the door. "I've brought you some cake."

"How delightful," Mr. Willard said, taking the plate eagerly. "That's most neighborly of you."

"Oh well, we had plenty, and I wanted to be sure you were all right. I haven't seen you at church."

Mr. Willard raised an eyebrow. "Oh well, I don't. . ."

"I didn't mean to chide," Alice said quickly. "It's just that there are certain friends we have, that if they don't show up at services, we go to check on them."

"That's a nice way to keep track of your friends," he said.

She nodded, wondering if he considered her a friend—or if she thought of him that way. Somehow, the classification didn't seem quite right. Perhaps she should get to know him better, and then she wouldn't be so suspicious of his activities.

"Would you come in for a moment and join me?" he asked. "I see you've brought two slices."

"Oh, those are both for you." She peered beyond him. "If you have water hot, I might take a cup of tea though."

"Yes, I enjoy tea myself. Not coffee. That should be thrown in the harbor." He cackled and Alice gave a little chuckle.

"Why, yes, I see your jest. My father wouldn't find it the least bit humorous, I'm afraid."

"Big coffee drinker?"

"That's about *all* he drinks."

As they spoke, she entered and walked with Mr. Willard to his table. The room was warm, and she unbuttoned her coat.

"Have a seat," he said.

"Mayn't I help you?"

"Yes, the teapot's over there." He waved vaguely toward a shelf, and Alice walked over to it.

She spotted the plain blue china teapot and reached for it. As she lifted it down, she noticed that on the sideboard beneath it lay a revolver. She caught her breath and threw him a glance. The old man was opening a canister of tea leaves. She decided to say nothing, but she wondered what he needed a gun for in his kitchen. Her father kept one in a drawer in his little office at the stockyard, but they didn't have one in their house. The rumors of Dirk Willard's past resurfaced.

She forced a smile and carried the teapot to the table.

"You had visitors yesterday," she said.

"Yes." He looked over at her and smiled. "A couple of Frenchmen."

Alice blinked. "French?"

"Diplomats," he said, as if that should explain everything.

"Oh. You, uh. . ."

"Spent time in Paris, yes. I thoroughly enjoyed it. Met some fascinating people there, and I gave that general invitation we issue so often—if you're ever my way, drop in. You know how it is. They show up at the most unexpected times."

"Oh yes." She knew how annoying it was when Phyllis and Serinda Begley showed up unannounced and expected refreshments, or when Pa brought home a cattle buyer for lunch without notice. But French diplomats? Out here in Texas?

Maybe when he believed he was Benjamin Franklin he thought he was still in Philadelphia, she reasoned. But still, those men who came here yesterday were not figments of anyone's imagination. And they hadn't looked French to her. But then, would she know what a Frenchman looked like? Exotic, she thought. With luxuriant mustaches and finely tailored clothing. The two men she'd seen looked much more rough-and-ready—like a couple of thugs. Scruffy beards and trail-worn clothing.

Mr. Willard brought the steaming teakettle from the stove and poured hot water into the teapot. Perhaps it would be best to launch a different subject that would carry them through the next ten or fifteen minutes.

"So, tell me about your writing," Alice said cheerfully. "You said you're planning a new edition of *Poor Richard's.*"

His face brightened. "Yes, I'm seriously thinking about it. I did think of starting a newspaper, since your fair town doesn't have one of its own, but that would mean hiring staff and drumming up subscribers."

"And the almanac won't?"

"I thought I could interest a publisher in New York. Or perhaps there's someone in Dallas. That might be more practical to start with."

"Now that's clever," she said. "Would they print it for you?"

"Maybe. Or if I printed it myself, I might find someone to distribute it."

"It sounds like a complicated business."

"Well, it is. Now, when I had my own press back in Philadelphia. . ."

He poured her a cup of tea. Alice sipped and nodded while he alternately nibbled at the pound cake and rambled on about the old days in the Quaker city. He seemed to know a lot about Philadelphia and pre-Revolutionary times.

"Do you know that for a while I wrote under the name Silence Dogood?" he asked.

Alice tried not to let her surprise show. She'd been reading the autobiography last night, and she'd come across that very name. Franklin had written newspaper articles when he was young, using Silence Dogood as a pen name. If she could get him to talk about that, maybe she'd be able to tell if he was just relating anecdotes from the book.

"Tell me about that," she said and settled in with her cup of tea.

Chapter 3

"Sorry, nothing today," John told Alice the next morning. "If anything comes in, I'll bring it by this afternoon."

"Thank you." Alice looked around and leaned closer, and John could smell her fresh scent. "Have you learned any more about Mr. Willard?" she whispered.

"No," John said. "Has something happened?"

She told him about the so-called French diplomats and Mr. Willard's discourse the previous day. "He really seems to believe that we're living in the last century, and that he's done all these things." She shook her head. "He must have read a lot about Mr. Franklin, that's all I can say. But he did not make up those men."

John thought about that for a moment. He didn't like the idea of strangers frequenting a house so close to Alice, especially when she was at home alone.

"I could ask Marshal Yates about him," he said. When she nodded, his heart soared. Reporting to her on whatever he learned would give him an excuse to visit Alice outside his postal duties. "I'll see if I can have a word with him this afternoon, and maybe come by your place this evening?"

"I'd appreciate it so much," Alice said. She held his gaze for a long moment, and he wondered if she could hear his thumping heart. She looked away, blinking. "Well, I must get on my way."

John hurried through his sorting duties between patrons and laid his plans. At first he considered going straight to the marshal's office, but people got upset if he didn't stick to his usual route. He would hurry along on his rounds and get down to Maple Street as quickly as he could. He'd allow himself a few extra minutes to chew things over with Justin Yates, or to track him down if he wasn't in his office at the jail.

Fortune was with him. Yates was sitting behind his desk writing on a piece of paper when John walked in.

"Hello, John," he said. "Coffee?"

"Thanks." John dropped a handful of mail on Justin's desk and went to the stove. Justin kept a few extra cups for prisoners and visitors on a shelf, and John soon settled in a chair near the desk with a cup of hot brew. He and Justin had been friends since John came to Wiseman as a ranch hand, before he was postmaster or Justin was marshal.

"I was wondering if you'd heard anything about Dirk Willard," John said.

Justin set down his pen and shrugged. "I've been keeping an eye on him, but from a distance. I've gathered some information since he moved to Wiseman, just to keep myself informed."

"Like what, if I may ask?"

"You may. Nothing secret about it." Justin picked up his mug of cooling coffee and took a swallow. "Seems Willard started out forty years or so ago as a guard for treasure convoys from the goldfields in California. Somehow he survived that dangerous job and became a stagecoach 'shotgun messenger.' His stages were held up at least three times, but he lived through those and several other attempts, where he got some shots off fast enough and accurately enough to make the outlaws change their minds and not rob the stage after all."

"Huh." John sipped his coffee. "So he started out on the right side of the law."

"That's my impression," Justin said.

"So how did he come to be a gunslinger?"

Justin frowned and tipped his chair back. "It's a short journey from hired guard to hired gun. I was told Willard served a stint as a sharpshooter during the War between the States. After that, he signed on as a mercenary during a range war. When it wound up in favor of the side he was working for, several angry men from the other side targeted him and called him out for gunfights."

"All of which Willard survived," John mused.

"Yep. Well, I hear he was wounded a few times. It always seemed like self-defense in those shootouts where he shot someone though. Willard never started anything, and so he was never arrested. But I heard he killed at least three men in gunfights, maybe as many as ten."

John whistled softly. "That's a lot."

"Seems like it to me," Justin said. "But he's gettin' pretty old now. I can't see him out in the street gunning people down at this point."

"But you're keeping a sharp eye out."

"That I am."

"Well, Miss Singer, being his closest neighbor, is concerned about some visitors he's had recently."

"That so?" Justin lowered the front of his chair to the floor, interest sparking in his eyes.

"Strangers."

"Go on."

"Willard told her they were diplomats from France—being as he was acting like Ben Franklin that day. You know about his Franklin mirage, or delusion, or whatever you call it?"

"I've heard tales. Did you see these strangers?"

"No, just heard about 'em. But Miss Singer's trustworthy, I'm sure." John told the marshal everything he could remember and then stood. "Well, I'd best get on my rounds or people will fuss about the mail being late."

"I appreciate the information," Justin said. "I'll do a little asking around about these odd visitors."

Alice took her hands from the dishwater and dried them on her apron. Through the kitchen window, she watched John pull up in front of Mr. Willard's house in a wagon. A few days had passed since John had shared with her what the marshal had told him about her neighbor. It was hard to reconcile the violent gunman of the past with the frail old man who lived so close to her now.

John climbed down from the wagon, hitched the horse, and

walked up to the door. When Mr. Willard opened it a few seconds later, John spoke to him and gestured toward the wagon. Alice couldn't hear a word he said, but Mr. Willard swung the door wide and John walked to the back of the wagon, where he removed a wooden crate. The box was obviously heavy, and John moved slowly up the steps and into the house. A moment later, he emerged and took a second crate from the wagon and carried it inside.

Alice went to the door, and when John came outside again and headed for the wagon, he looked her way. She waved, and he nodded. He mounted the wagon and walked the horse over to stand before the Singer house. Instead of making him climb down again, Alice dashed out to meet him at the edge of the street.

"I don't have anything for you today," John said.

"That's all right. But I see Mr. Willard—or should I say Mr. Franklin—is receiving more boxes."

"Yes. Heavy ones. He says it's all paper, but I don't know. It had a return address from a company in Pittsburgh. If it *is* paper—well, what a fellow his age would want with it all, I couldn't say. Maybe he's going to write his memoirs."

Alice smiled. "Remember I told you that he said he might resurrect *Poor Richard's Almanac*?"

"But surely he wouldn't print it himself." John cast a disapproving glance back at the rental house. "Wouldn't the publisher be the one to lay in tons of paper? And wouldn't you think that if he was really doing that, he'd have all the supplies delivered to Benjamin Franklin?"

"That is puzzling," Alice admitted. "May I offer you a cup of coffee?"

"No time." John picked up the reins. "It's good to see you. Maybe next time we can talk about more pleasant things."

She nodded, and he clucked to the horse. As the wagon moved down the street, she watched, wondering what sort of things John wanted to talk about. Whatever he had in mind, the idea warmed her. John Goodwin was a very nice young man, and she wouldn't mind spending an hour in conversation with him, whatever the topic.

When he was out of sight, she turned toward her kitchen. As she prepared a roast of beef for supper with her father, she mulled over everything she knew about Dirk Willard. How much was fact, and how much was rumor? Surely the things Justin Yates had told John were true. That meant Mr. Willard had indeed made his living as a hired gun. But killing people? After the range war business, she supposed misguided young men had challenged him. She'd heard such stories. It was all so pointless.

The old man she knew was creative and industrious. He offered wisdom to those around him. Though most of his axioms were borrowed from one of the founding fathers, he seemed to know when to throw out an appropriate bit of advice or a pithy observation. That in itself took some wit. No, Dirk Willard wasn't stupid. But was he sane?

She basted the roast and put potatoes in the oven to cook with it. She had promised to meet the schoolmaster, Stephen Worth, and his wife, Rachel, for an hour this afternoon. The students were beginning to practice for their Christmas program. Since Alice played the piano, she had offered to help with the music. She would meet them at the church at three o'clock.

That left her time to pay a short call on Dirk Willard. *Just to see how he's doing*, she told herself. Perhaps she could learn more about the almanac. Would he write new material or reuse items from Franklin's original publications?

"Hello, Mr. Willard," Alice said when her neighbor greeted her at the door. "I hope I'm not disturbing you."

"Come in, come in," he said cheerfully. "Any man who isn't glad of a visit from a charming young lady has lost his wits."

"Oh, thank you." She held out today's offering—a small dish of roasted peanuts. "I wondered if you care for these."

"Lovely." He took the dish and set it on his sideboard. He always washed the dishes she took him and returned them on her next visit.

His kitchen table was anything but neat today, with papers spread out in piles all over it.

"What are you working on?" Alice asked, walking over next to the table.

"This is all for my almanac. Notes, you see. I'm getting quite excited about it."

"You're writing up new articles for it?"

"Yes, indeed." He plucked a sheet of paper from the top of one pile. "See here? Signs that we're going to have a hard winter."

Alice took it from his hand. "Thick hair on the nape of a cow's neck?"

"Rancher Gillespie told me his cattle have prodigiously thick neck hair this year."

"Oh." Gillespie had a ranch south of town, but she didn't suppose Mr. Willard had ventured that far from his hearth. "Have you been out to the Bar-G?"

"No, I met the rancher at the mercantile yesterday. Oh, and this one." He pointed to an item farther down the list. "Did you notice the ring around the moon the other night?"

"No."

"That's a good predictor of snow."

Alice shivered. "Are we going to have a snowstorm?"

"Perhaps. And I'm told the ducks and geese went south earlier than usual this year."

"I hadn't thought about it." She perused the list, frowning at the subtle omens she had entirely missed. "Thicker than normal corn husks." She looked up at him expectantly.

"Mrs. Carr told me that at the post office."

"I see. Well, it seems you've been out and about, gathering a lot of information. Are you intending to publish the almanac soon?"

"I thought perhaps in February. I should be ready by then. But I may submit an article to the Dallas newspaper this month, to whet people's appetites and to warn them of the impending winter."

"We don't usually get a lot of snow here," Alice said.

"Prepare for more than usual this year." He set down the paper and walked slowly to the stove. "Would you like tea?"

"Oh, I have to get over to the church. I've promised to help the schoolmaster and his wife with the children's rehearsal for their Christmas pageant."

"Ah," Willard said. "You must come again when you have more time."

"Thank you." Alice gazed at the opened crate on the floor. Rectangular parcels were stacked inside—reams of paper, she supposed. The stacks on his table were of thick, good-quality stuff. Why would he use expensive paper for his notes? She would think a writer would use cheap copybooks, like the children used for school.

She smiled and pulled on her gloves. "I'll leave you to your work."

"Have an enjoyable time with the youngsters," he called after her.

Alice turned her steps toward the church. Was he right? Would they have a cold and snowy winter? A couple of years ago, the winter had been brutal. She hoped that didn't happen again. As she walked, she pondered how the old man could pay for all the things he had delivered to him. Perhaps he had saved all his ill-gotten wages. But still, it had been several years since that range war. The marshal hadn't mentioned any paying jobs since then.

She felt a chill go through her. Had the former sharpshooter and mercenary taken on other commissions no one knew about?

"What are you doing?" Pa asked, walking into the dark kitchen. "Don't you want a light?"

"No!" Alice jumped back from the window.

"Are you looking at something?" Her father joined her and peered outside. "Horses."

"Yes," Alice said. "I heard them ride up fifteen minutes or so ago. By the time I got to the window, the riders were inside."

"So?"

"So who has horsemen riding up to their door quietly in the middle of the night?"

"Would you rather they arrived noisily?"

Alice sighed. "It's not normal, Pa. Not in town anyway. Clandestine, that's what it is."

"People can have visitors anytime they want them. There's no law against it."

"True, but. . ."

"But what?"

"What if it's the ambassadors?"

"The what?" He laughed. "Oh, I get it. The French diplomats again. Do you think so?"

"It could be."

"And it could be George Washington and John Hancock. Really, Alice, I think you should go to bed."

"No, wait."

The door of Mr. Willard's house opened and light spilled out onto the path. Alice jumped back from the window. "They're coming out. Two in the morning, and they're coming out."

Her father pulled her back a little more into the shadows. "Are they the same men you saw before?"

"The one with the beard, yes," Alice said. "The other one looks like the fellow who helped him move in, but I can't be sure in this light. Can you see any scars on him?"

"No, we're too far away," Pa said.

Through the glass, she heard one man call faintly, "See ya!"

Mr. Willard stood watching the two men until they had mounted their horses and headed off northward, and then he looked over at the Singer house.

"Don't move," Pa said softly.

Alice stood stock-still, hardly daring to breathe. Finally, Mr. Willard went inside and closed his door.

"Do you think he saw us?" Alice asked, glad she hadn't listened to Pa and lit a lantern.

"No, I don't. He was just being cautious."

"But why would he need to be cautious if those men were

upright, law-abiding citizens?"

"Maybe he just wanted to be sure they hadn't awakened his neighbors."

Alice shook her head. "Well, why would a Frenchman say, 'See ya,' instead of 'Au revoir'? And he certainly didn't have a French accent."

"Oh, what can you tell from two words?" Her father chuckled. "Maybe 'see ya' is French for something else."

Alice bristled at that. "Make fun of me if you want to, but I tell you, something odd is going on over there."

Chapter 4

Justin Yates leaned on the post office counter, thumbing through the new batch of wanted posters. "You don't recognize any of these hombres?"

"Afraid not," John said. "But the only one of Willard's cohorts I've seen is the one who helped him move in, and I only met him that once."

"Well, he's not in this bunch." Justin sighed and slid the stack back into its envelope.

The door opened, and Alice came in.

"Hello, Marshal. Hello, John."

"Good morning." John couldn't help smiling. His day was always brighter when he saw Alice. "The marshal and I were just discussing those men you said visited your neighbor a few nights ago."

"I've got some new posters," Justin said, pulling them out again. "Maybe you'd take a look at them."

"Gladly." Alice removed her gloves and laid them on the counter. She browsed slowly through the half dozen sheets and paused on the fourth one. "Hmm."

"Recognize him?" Justin asked.

"I'm not sure. If it's him, he has a beard now. It was dark, and I was twenty yards away from him." She shook her head and glanced at the last two posters. "I'm sorry, Marshal. I'd have to have a better look at him. The one I'd recognize for certain—the man with the scar—is definitely not in here."

John nodded. "That's what I said. I'd know the man who brought Willard in that first day anywhere."

"And he's the one that tipped you off about Willard thinking he's Ben Franklin?" Justin asked.

"Yes," John said.

Justin rubbed his jaw, frowning. "I wonder if the old coot sees a doctor regularly. I think I'll ask Doc Melvin if he's consulted with him."

Alice nodded with approval. "A doctor could tell if he was really losing his mind or not."

"Maybe." Justin stacked the posters and put them in the envelope.

"What can I get you, Alice?" John asked. "Your pa picked up his mail earlier."

"Thanks. I'll take half a dozen penny stamps."

John opened his drawer. "Your father said he's going to Fort Worth on business."

"Yes." Alice's mouth drooped. "I wish he wasn't going right now."

"Because of the activity next door?" John asked.

She smiled apologetically. “I suppose I shouldn’t let an eighty-year-old man scare me. But it’s his friends.”

“I understand. The one I’ve seen was a tough-looking customer.” John handed her the stamps.

Justin said, “Well, Miss Singer, if it would help you feel safer, I could ask my wife if you could stay at our place while your father’s out of town.”

“Oh, thank you, but that won’t be necessary.”

John figured she was thinking about Justin and Marta’s little one. Alice wouldn’t want to make extra work for Marta or put one of Justin’s sisters out of her bed to make room for her.

“All right,” Justin said. “I’ll stroll by your place several times in the evening while he’s away.”

“Thank you,” Alice said. “I’d appreciate that.”

Justin nodded. “Well, I’ll mosey on. Have a nice day, folks.”

After the marshal left, Alice smiled at John. “I suppose it’s silly of me. I’ve stayed alone dozens of times while Pa was out of town. And when the Lewises lived next door, I could always look out and see their lamp shining or smoke coming out of their chimney, and I knew someone friendly was close by.”

“It seems different since they moved away, doesn’t it?”

She nodded. “Mr. Willard is nice enough to talk to, but he’s so odd. I’m never quite sure whether or not to believe what he says.” She frowned as if that wasn’t quite what she’d meant. “Of course, when he talks about his almanac and the Continental Congress, I don’t believe that. But you know, he seems so sincere at other times.”

“You feel as though he’s a bit unhinged,” John said slowly.

“That’s a good way to put it. All these rumors. And according to what the marshal told you, some of them are more than rumors."

"I'll stop by after supper." John straightened.

"Thank you." Her smile came out again, and she looked so pretty it was hard for John to keep his calm. "I'll be baking."

"Baking? For Christmas?"

"Yes, actually. Did you know the church is giving ten food baskets this year?"

"That's more than last year."

"It is." Her forehead puckered. "Seems we have a lot of folks who find it hard to pay their accounts at the general store. So I'll be baking some cookies to contribute."

"Sounds like fun. Can I help?"

"If you like."

John's anticipation surprised him. He'd never been excited before about baking. "Can I bring anything?"

"Hmm, maybe some raisins? If it's not too much trouble."

"Sure. I'll pick some up when I go into the store on my rounds this afternoon. How many? A pound? Two?"

"One pound should be plenty." Alice slid the strap of her handbag over her arm. "Well, I should be going."

"I'll see you later."

Her smile shone from her eyes.

John showed up at six thirty, and Alice let him in with a little flutter in her stomach. Belatedly, she wondered if she'd been indiscreet to invite a man over while her father wasn't home. But John was such a gentleman, and he wouldn't stay late—she wouldn't let him.

And their nearest neighbor was Dirk Willard. He wouldn't start any stories.

"Thank you for bringing the raisins," she said as John hung up his coat near the kitchen door. She opened the package and took one out to taste it. "Oh, they're so fresh and soft. Mr. Lawson must have gotten a new shipment."

"I believe he did," John said. "He and Carl Shaw were still unloading crates when I was there, and Mrs. Lawson waited on me. When I told her they were going into cookies for the baskets, she opened a fresh box of raisins and weighed them out from there."

"The Lawsons are such good people. I was just about to put the first sheet of gingerbread men in the oven." Alice slid the pan in and then took a clean apron from a drawer. "Do you want to cover your clothes? We might get a bit floury. I'm planning oatmeal cookies and sugar cookies too."

John laughed and accepted the apron. "What do you want me to do?"

"How about if I bring you the ingredients for the oatmeal-raisin ones, and you mix up the dough?"

"Sure." He pulled the apron strings behind him to tie them. "I haven't worn one of these since the last time I was home at Christmas and my mother talked me into helping her do the dishes."

"How long ago was that?" Alice asked.

"Three years." A faraway look settled in John's eyes. "I haven't been able to make the trip since."

"Where is your family?"

He let out a short breath. "Near St. Louis. I really should take a train up there soon. The folks were disappointed I couldn't come this year—they are every year. But the post office is so busy in December."

"You could go after the holidays," Alice suggested. "January, maybe?"

He nodded thoughtfully. "I'm sure I could get Mrs. Lawson to fill in for me at the post office for a week or two, or even Mrs. Yates."

"Or Rachel Worth," Alice said.

"Yes, she'd be good at it, and her husband would be at school all day. Maybe I could get someone else to make the deliveries and she could mind the office in the mornings."

"Maybe you could just tell everyone they'll have to pick up their mail at the post office that week or wait until you come home."

He laughed. "I'm not sure how that would go over. We have to take an oath, you know, to get the mail through no matter what."

"Shhh," Alice said. "If Mr. Willard hears us, he'll want to be your substitute mail carrier."

"No," John said, choking on a laugh, "he'd want to run the office. He was Postmaster General at one time, you know."

"One time a hundred years ago. So I've been told."

They both laughed aloud, as though that was the funniest thing anyone had ever said. As Alice got control of her mirth and wiped her eyes with the corner of her apron, a knock sounded on the door. She jumped and looked guiltily at John.

"You don't suppose he really heard us?" she whispered.

"No, but I'll go to the door if you like."

"Would you?" The uneasiness that had fled for a few minutes swept over her once more.

John strode to the door and flung it open. "Oh Justin. Hey."

Relieved, Alice stepped forward. "Evening, Marshal. Won't you come in?"

"Tell me I smell fresh gingerbread."

She laughed. "You do. In fact, the first batch of cookies is probably just about ready."

She hurried to the stove and grabbed a pot holder. When she turned around with the pan in her hands, Justin breathed in a big whiff of the spicy odor.

"Mmm."

"Well, we're making three kinds of cookies, and I planned to have more than we'll need for the Christmas baskets," Alice said. "You two can have some of these if you want."

"Are you sure?" John asked.

"Of course. And there's coffee on the stove, or milk out in the entry keeping cool."

While the two men sat at the table and demolished half a dozen gingerbread men, she shaped another dozen and put them in the oven and then started on the oatmeal-raisin dough.

"Oops," John said, eyeing her over the rim of his coffee cup. "I think that was supposed to be my job."

"Don't worry. There'll be plenty of work left for you. Someone's going to have to clean up when the baking's done, and I hear you have practice washing dishes."

He laughed. "You got me there."

Justin stood. "Well, I should get on. I'll walk through the neighborhood again later, but it seems pretty peaceful here now, and Willard's house looked as though he was buttoned in for the night."

"Thank you, Marshal," Alice said. "Would you like to take a few cookies?"

"No, I'd better quit eating them so you'll have enough for the baskets." Justin buttoned his wool coat and clapped his hat on his head. "Good night, folks."

" 'Night," John said as they walked to the door.

"Thank you," Alice called.

"Seems like I got the best end of the deal. Thank *you*." Justin grinned and went out.

Alice and John worked hard for the next hour and a half, but it was pleasant labor. Alice felt slightly on edge the whole time but happy as she worked beside him.

"That's the last batch," she said as she closed the oven door on the final sheet of sugar cookies.

"Should I add more wood?"

"No, I think it's fine. And this room is so warm, I hate to have you build the fire up any more." She dabbed at her brow with a dish towel.

"The pastor said to take the food for the baskets over to the church tomorrow," John noted. "I'm just going to give some bags of coffee."

"People will appreciate that so much," Alice assured him. "It's probably a luxury some of them have had to give up."

John leaned against the worktable. "I wonder who the person is who started all this basket tradition. The one who provides the poultry, I mean."

"I have no idea. He's generous, whoever he is, and thoughtful."

"Yes."

Alice looked up at him. Something in his eyes made her pulse flutter.

"I've had a really nice time," he said with that easy smile she was coming to love. "I hate to leave."

"I've enjoyed it too, but it is getting late."

He looked at the clock. The hands were approaching nine o'clock.

"Yes, I'd better get going, or we'll set tongues wagging for sure."

She felt her cheeks flush, and not from the heat of the cookstove.

"Shall I wait to wash the last of the pans for you?" He stepped closer to her, and Alice's heart raced faster.

"I'll get them," she said. He was very close now, and she dared to look up at him.

"Alice."

"Yes?" It was barely a whisper.

"I. . ." He cleared his throat. "I wondered. . .maybe when your father gets back. . ."

"Yes?"

"Could I call on you again?"

"I wish you would." She wished Pa was coming back before Christmas Eve.

John reached out for her, hesitating only a moment. When she leaned toward him, he seemed to gain confidence and swept her into his embrace. He kissed her, and Alice knew this was what she had wanted, the hope that had kept her a bit nervous all evening. She'd never been kissed before, but it seemed the most wonderful thing—especially since it was John who bestowed the honor.

He drew back, gazing down at her in question.

Alice smiled. "Please do call again."

"I'll be sure to." His easy grin was back, and he walked to the door and pulled his hat off the rack beside it. "Good night, Alice."

"Good night." She shut the door firmly behind him and then

went to the window. As she watched him walk down the path toward the street, she noticed that a lamp was still burning in Mr. Willard's front room. Perhaps he was sitting at the table, working on his almanac. At any rate, no horses were tied to the hitching post out front.

She turned away and checked the cookies in the oven. Almost done. While she waited, she washed the wooden spoon and measuring cup that sat on the worktable. She was tired, and her uneasiness had left her. Between the time she'd spent with John and the marshal's promise to keep an eye on the house, she felt safer than she had in days.

Chapter 5

A freight wagon pulled up outside the post office, and John sighed. He handed the Ross family's mail to the reverend and reached for his gloves.

"What's the matter, John?" Pastor Ross asked.

"Another heavy delivery. Washington needs to figure out how to differentiate between mail and freight. But until they do, I guess I'll have to rent a wagon again this afternoon."

"Can't you ask the person it's addressed to if they'll pick it up here?"

"I can try, but we're bound by oath to deliver what comes through. I think they're working on some standardization for how to handle parcels, but it's hit or miss right now."

The pastor walked outside onto the boardwalk with him. The

freighter had the wagon's tailboard down and was shoving a large crate toward the back of the wagon bed.

John waved to the pastor and walked over to look at the address.

"Whoa, don't take that off," he said.

The driver arched his bushy black eyebrows. "I have to."

"No, this guy lives just a few blocks away. Can't you drop it at his house?"

"Well. . ." The driver frowned at the crate.

John made a quick decision. "I'll pay you the dollar I'd spend renting a horse and wagon to deliver it myself, and I won't have to load and unload it later."

The driver's expression cleared. "Will the recipient be able to help unload it?"

"Doubt it. He's an old fellow."

"Then can you come help me unload it?"

John turned and looked at the door to the post office. Mr. Maynard was just going in.

"All right, but give me a second to get this man his mail. You can turn around while I'm at it." He pointed toward the town square. "We're going that way."

"Reckon I can." The big man climbed back up to the wagon seat.

John hurried inside. Mr. Maynard stood before the counter and looked at him expectantly.

"Sorry about that," John said. "I think you have a couple of items this morning." He quickly located the shoe store owner's mail and placed it in his hand. "There you go."

"Thanks, John."

As he headed for the door, Mrs. Griffith came in.

"Sorry, ma'am," John said. I have to go out for a short time and make a delivery. Can you come back later?"

"Oh, I just wanted to drop these off." She laid two stamped letters on the counter.

"That's all right then." John dropped them in the outgoing bin and grabbed his Back in Ten Minutes sign, though he doubted he would actually make it back that quickly. It would probably take them ten minutes to drive the big wagon over to Church Street and down to Willard's house, and then he'd probably have to walk back. But it was the best he could do on short notice, and he hurried to hang the sign on the door before another customer came along.

He guided the driver through the streets of Wiseman, waving to people they passed. When they arrived at Willard's house, he hopped down. Alice was in her backyard hanging out clothes. John could just see her as he approached Willard's front door, but she hadn't noticed him. He knocked on the door.

"Well, well. It's the postman." Willard smiled and swung the door wide. "What do you have for me today, young man?"

"It's a rather heavy package, sir," John replied. "Would you like me and the freighter to bring it in?"

"Yes, thank you."

The driver already had the back of the wagon open. Moving the crate was quite a struggle. By the time they'd gotten it to Willard's stoop, Alice had abandoned her clothes basket and stood near the low fence that surrounded her vegetable garden, watching them from her yard.

John puffed and strained as they hefted the heavy box up the steps and inside. They set it down just within the main room.

"Whew," the driver said. "Barely missed my toes. What's in there?"

"It's a small printing press, what you might call a job press." Willard's eyes glittered.

"You going into the newspaper business or something?" the driver asked.

"No, it's for my almanac. I intend to start publishing it soon."

"Almanac? That's like a calendar, isn't it?"

"It's much more than that," Willard said with a chuckle.

John could foresee this becoming a drawn-out conversation engendering confusion if Benjamin Franklin was mentioned.

"Uh, didn't you say you need to get going?" he asked the driver.

"I sure do. Have fun with your newspaper, mister."

John shrugged at Willard and followed the driver outside. "Here's your dollar. Thanks again."

The man pocketed the coin. "All in a day's work. Funny old bird, ain't he?"

"Uh, yes." John flicked a glance toward the house, but Willard had closed the door behind them.

"You want a ride back up to Main Street?"

"No thanks. I'll walk." John's declaration surprised even him. He really ought to get right back to the post office, but Alice looked so charmingly festive in her green coat and red mittens, he couldn't drive away without talking to her. He'd just have to walk quickly after they'd exchanged greetings.

The freighter drove away, and he sauntered over to Alice's yard, where she waited for him, a bright smile on her face.

"I see you've made another delivery," she said.

"Yes. He says it's a printing press. He's going to print the almanac himself."

"Really? That's quite a job. I thought he would have a professional printer do it."

"Saving money, I expect, although that thing must have cost him a pretty penny." John stretched his arms. "It must be made of cast iron. I thought we'd break our backs carrying it inside."

"Oh dear, I hope you didn't strain any muscles." She looked worried, and her cheeks flushed, but John couldn't tell if it was because of the chilly weather or the subject of muscles.

"I wonder how he'll get buyers," John said. "Maybe he'll advertise in the newspaper."

"Who knows." Alice looked past him, frowning at Willard's house. "I find it suspicious. I mean, how can he possibly make money on this venture? He'd have to get subscribers or some such thing."

"Maybe the post office will get more business if he mails them out," John said.

"I think I'll go and visit him." A slight frown wrinkled Alice's forehead. "I can take him a couple of the gingerbread men we made night before last."

"I'm sure he'd appreciate that." John wished he didn't have to end the conversation, but he had long outstayed his ten minutes away from the post office. "Well, I really have to get back."

"Goodbye."

Did she regret the parting as much as he did? John headed up the sidewalk, hoping he hadn't inconvenienced too many people by making the delivery.

Alice retrieved her clothes basket and took it inside. As she went about her cleaning, she thought about Mr. Willard. He was an odd man, but she didn't really consider him dangerous. It was those friends of his who looked sinister, and today they were nowhere about.

She put clean sheets on her father's bed and went to the kitchen, determined to learn more about her neighbor's activities. She had cookies to spare from her and John's evening of baking. She wrapped a few gingerbread men in a scrap of paper and tied a peppermint stick into the string she bound it with. Donning her green coat and red mittens, she decided that after completing that mission she would run a few errands on Main Street, so she picked up her market basket. She would pick up Pa's new boots today and get them wrapped up before he got home. She closed the door behind her and strode across to the house next door.

"Merry Christmas, Mr. Willard," she said brightly when he opened the door.

"Oh! Uh, come in." He looked a bit disheveled, with his hair on end and a smear of ink across his cheek.

"I'm disturbing you," Alice said. "I'll just give you these treats, and you can enjoy them when you're not busy." She peered past him and spotted a black machine set up on his kitchen table. "Is that the press?"

"Yes. Would you like to see it?"

She was surprised how much she did want to see it. She hadn't been around machinery much, and the idea of producing a book, or even a small pamphlet, intrigued her.

He walked over to the table and quickly moved some papers to the seat of a chair. It may have been accidental, but he dropped a rag on top of them.

"This is where the type goes. I have to set the type for each line, and then for each entire page. The paper goes in here. . . ."

He demonstrated by inserting a sheet of the high-quality paper she had seen before.

"And then I ink the typeface, and the top comes down and presses on it—hence the name press—and leaves an impression on the paper. I don't have anything set to print yet, or I'd show you."

"That's all right," she assured him. "It's a fascinating process. Is this how newspapers do it?"

"Yes, but most of them have larger presses nowadays. And mechanical ones. Why, big companies even have steam-driven presses. But in my day, we used small job presses like this." His hand lingered on the top of the machine. "I put out thousands of copies of *Poor Richard's* with the help of an apprentice. That was a long time ago."

"In New York?" She tried to sound innocent.

"No, Philadelphia is where I learned, my girl."

"Of course," Alice said. She couldn't trip him up that easily. "But you weren't born in Philadelphia, were you?"

"Boston."

"Aha." That sounded right, but she would have to look back at the first few chapters of the autobiography to be sure of Benjamin Franklin's birthplace. "Are you happy here in Wiseman?"

He gave her a knowing smile. "Happiness depends more on the inward disposition of mind than on outward circumstances."

"Oh. Yes, of course." She frowned. Was that a Franklin quote? "Well, I must go. My clean laundry is probably dry. And later I must get my baking over to the church. It's for the poor baskets. Have you heard about that?"

"Yes, Mrs. Lawson enlightened me. But I find that the best way to help the poor is not to let them feel too easy in poverty, but to lead them or drive them out of it."

She blinked, not sure what to say to that. "But. . .Christ told us to care for the poor."

"Yes, He did. But we'd all be better off if some of the poor learned to work their way out of it, don't you think?"

"I. . .suppose so." She couldn't help thinking of the widowed mother who would receive one of the baskets. How could a woman in her situation remove herself from poverty? "Well, I'll be going. I hope you'll come to the Christmas Eve service."

"I will think about it. Thank you for your kindness. I'm sure anything you baked will be delicious."

"You're very welcome." She frowned as her gaze lingered on his printing supplies. "Is that green ink?"

"What?"

She nodded at the bottle of deep green liquid on the table.

"Oh yes. I was just practicing with a trial run. That was left from another project, and I need to conserve my supply of black for the actual almanac."

"I see." Leaving his house, she walked toward the stores. She didn't need much—with Pa away for several more days, she had plenty of food at home, but she would like to pick up a spool of green thread and some soap. Her main errand now was to pay off the account for the boots.

Her shopping was finished by eleven o'clock. The wonderful boots were wrapped up in her basket. Pa would be so pleased!

She couldn't resist stopping at the post office. Several people were waiting to do business with John, and she got in line. Miss

Priscilla Tanner stood just ahead of her, and she soon turned around and began a lively conversation with Alice.

"It's such a joy to have a child in the house again," she said. "Little Stevie isn't quite a year old, but we're using him as an excuse to go quite wild for the season. Rachel had her husband bring us a Christmas tree. Can you imagine? When my brother Abijah was alive, he would never have one in the house. Are you decorating for the holidays?"

"I put up some greenery," Alice said. "Pa is away on business, and there would be no one else to enjoy it if I did more."

"Oh, such a pity," Miss Tanner said. She and her sister lived in their family's old house with their niece, Rachel, and her husband, who was the schoolmaster.

"We don't do much since my mother passed away," Alice confided.

"Of course. I do understand. We're having such fun at our house. It hasn't been so merry since Rachel was a child and her mother was living."

Alice smiled. "It must be wonderful to have a baby to fuss over."

"It truly is. I'd forgotten how precious a time it is to have a young child about. Do you know, my sister Lois takes him in her lap in her wheelchair and reads him stories. Stevie loves it!"

"Does he listen well?"

"Listen? He coos and squeals and points to the pictures. I wouldn't be surprised if he was the one reading to Lois by next Christmas."

Alice laughed. "You'll have to give him some new picture books for Christmas." The butcher had turned away from the counter. "Oh, I believe you're next, Miss Tanner."

"Oh yes. Well, come over and visit anytime, Alice. In fact, you're welcome to take Christmas dinner with us."

"Thank you, but my father will be back by then. But I might drop in someday to visit you ladies and the baby."

"Please do. We'd all love it." Miss Tanner quickly concluded her purchase of stamps and left off a couple of letters to be sent. She turned toward the door. "Goodbye, Alice. It was a treat to see you."

"The same to you," Alice said. She was relieved that no one else had come into the post office.

"Hello again," John said with a broad smile. "Getting your errands done?" He nodded toward her basket, which held both the boots and her other small parcels.

"Yes, and I thought I'd drop in for a moment. I don't want to keep you from your work though."

"I can spare a minute." He leaned affably on the counter.

"Well." Alice set down her basket. "I went to see Mr. Willard, and I have to tell you, I think his dementia is getting worse."

"Oh?" John frowned.

She nodded. "He seems to stay inside the Ben Franklin character more and more as time passes."

"Hmm. That's a good way to put it," John said. "He's created a character like an author would for a book, only this character happens to be a real, historical person."

"I've heard of such things before," Alice confided. "Last year the paper ran an article about a man in Boston who fancied he was Napoleon."

"I saw that story. It's an illness."

"Yes. So sad."

"I'm not sure there's anything we can do to help him." John

picked up a stack of papers.

Alice felt that she could tell John anything. He wasn't a large man, but he had an inner strength that made her feel safe in his presence. He cared about the same things she cared about, and he understood her tumult over Dirk Willard. He never made fun of her concerns, but she could tell he wanted what was best for the old man.

She pulled in a deep breath. "I'm trying to decide if I'm helping him by playing along, or if it would be better to point out his inconsistencies to him. You know, tell him, 'No, sir, you did not invent the bifocal glasses. They were invented more than a hundred years ago.' He mentioned that a few days ago, and I didn't say a word."

"I know what you mean," John said. "It's like the rocking chair and the heating stove. He thinks he's so clever to come up with these things—"

"Or maybe he's got a copy of Franklin's autobiography and is just clever enough to memorize a lot of things from it. I've been reading that book, and even so, I'm never sure if he's spouting quotations or giving his own observations."

"I've had that feeling too. I wonder if he's seen a doctor since he's been here. I haven't had a chance to speak to Dr. Melvin."

"I have no idea," Alice said. "Mr. Willard has never mentioned any appointments to me."

John sighed. "Well, here's something that might interest you. The marshal left these posters with me."

"Posters?" Alice looked more closely at the sheaf of papers he held.

"More wanted posters. You saw some the other day. Yates said a lot of post offices are beginning to hang them up where the public can see them. The idea is that if a resident sees one of the wanted men, they'll tell the marshal, and he'll know where to look for him."

"But why here?" She took the papers and studied the top one.

"Well, the post office is a place where most people go often. There's a better chance of spreading the word here about who is wanted by the law than there is in the marshal's office. I mean, some people never go to the marshal's office."

"That's true." Alice looked through the posters, amazed at the variety of men wanted for serious crimes, ranging from train robbery to rustling.

"Quite a collection." She stopped cold, staring down at the drawing on the next sheet.

"What is it?" John asked.

"Maybe it's just me, but this man looks something like the one I've seen at Dirk's house twice now." She read the name at the bottom. "Edward Kline. What do you think? He'd be the one who brought him into the post office that first time."

John took the poster and turned it around. "Hmm. I see what you mean. It's not a perfect match, but that could be the artist's fault. There are certain resemblances."

"His nose," Alice said. "It's very distinctive. And if you put a scar on the left side of his chin—"

She broke off as the door swung open.

Chapter 6

John nodded to Frank Drummond, the bank manager. "Morning, Mr. Drummond. Let me get your mail for you."

"Thanks, John." While he waited, Mr. Drummond turned and smiled at Alice. "Hello, Miss Singer. I don't usually pick up the mail myself, but I was walking by on my way home for lunch. I hope I'm not interrupting."

"Not at all," Alice said. "Mr. Goodwin and I were just passing the time. How are things going at the bank?"

"Very well. In fact, we've had quite a few new accounts opened this month."

"I'm glad to hear it," Alice said.

"Yes, some of the new businesses in Wiseman are doing well."

She nodded, wondering about all the poor families who would

receive the Christmas baskets. She supposed Mr. Drummond rarely came into contact with them.

The banker accepted his mail from John with a "Thank you" and nodded to Alice before leaving.

"About that poster," Alice said as soon as he was gone.

"Yes." John checked the clock. "I'll be closing up in about twenty minutes. I usually get my lunch and then start my delivery route. If you could wait that long, we could go over to the marshal's office together."

"You think it is Dirk Willard's friend then?"

"Yes, he does look like the young man who helped Willard get settled." John picked up the poster and scanned it. "At least this man isn't wanted for violent crimes."

"I didn't notice," Alice said. "What has he done?"

"It says here he's a counterfeiter."

They stared at each other, and John's mind clicked through a catalog of things he'd seen at Dirk Willard's house. The deliveries of paper—good-quality paper, better than most people used for writing notes or totting up figures. The printing press.

"That old codger's not printing an almanac," he said.

Alice nodded slowly, her eyes huge and a little fearful. "John, I saw a bottle of green ink there this morning. He's going to print money," she whispered.

"I shouldn't really close the post office again before noon," John said. "I was gone a good half hour this morning."

"I'll step over to the yard goods store and wait for you there."

"All right, and then we'll walk across the square to the jail." An eatery lay just beyond the yard goods store where Alice was headed. Would he dare ask her to join him for lunch at a restaurant?

John decided to wait until they'd told Justin what they'd learned. Alice would be hungry by then. He hoped she would agree to eat with him. "I won't be long," he promised. "Oh, and one of your pa's men came over from the stockyard to get the mail for the business. Guess I should have told you that earlier."

"It's all right. We had other things on our minds," she said gravely.

"Yes."

Daniel Roberts, a local farmer, walked in. "Howdy, John." He tipped his hat. "Miss Singer."

"Hello," Alice said. "If you'll excuse me, I was about to leave."

She hurried out, and John nodded at Mr. Roberts. "How can I help you?"

"Well, you've got to weigh this." Roberts laid a thick envelope on the counter, and John picked it up to put it on the scale.

Somehow, he got through the next twenty minutes. It seemed half the people in town wanted something before he closed for the day. It was actually five past twelve when he finally locked the door and turned toward the yard goods store.

Alice was waiting inside, not browsing the merchandise, just standing there staring out the window, watching for him. When she spotted him, she went straight to the door and met him on the steps.

"All set?" he asked.

"Yes."

"Sorry I was delayed."

"It's all right." He took her arm as they crossed the street, and then they walked through the dead grass on the town square. He wished they were walking together for a less grave purpose. It would be wonderful to take a leisurely stroll with Alice. The day had warmed up enough that he hadn't buttoned his coat, and Alice had removed her mittens and stuck them in her basket.

"May I carry that for you?" John asked.

"Thank you." She surrendered the basket. All too soon they reached the brick building that held Justin's office and the one-cell jail. John reached to open the door, but it was locked. They looked at each other.

"It's the noon hour," Alice said. "He probably went home for lunch."

"We could walk over there. It's not too far." John eyed her, waiting for her decision.

"All right. It's important. I don't think we ought to postpone telling him."

John walked beside her down Maple Street to the corner. He wanted to offer his arm, but that might seem too formal, or too intimate. A lot of people in Texas didn't stand on ceremony or demand perfect etiquette, and usually that was fine with John, but he didn't want to disappoint or annoy Alice. She didn't seem as genteel as Rachel Worth, or as rowdy as the ranch girls who rode into town on horseback and would come into the post office for the mail, all windblown and cheery. Alice was somewhere in between, and he thought she was just right. But he did wish he knew her better. Only one way to fix that.

"I was wondering," he said as they rounded the corner. They had less than a block to go to Justin's house, so he had to speak quickly if he was going to do it.

"Yes?" Alice asked.

"After we see the marshal, would you eat lunch with me? We

could go to that little place between the yard goods and the bakery. I often get my lunch there."

"Well, I. . ." She looked up at him, somber, but suddenly she smiled. "Yes, thank you. I'd like that."

He couldn't stop smiling the rest of the way to the Yateses' house, where they stepped up onto the front porch together and John knocked.

One of Justin's twin sisters came to the door. John thought it was Emma, but it might have been Ella—he was never sure.

"Hello," Alice said with a smile. "We were hoping to catch Marshal Yates here."

"Oh, he's gone," the girl said. She called over her shoulder, "Marta!"

Mrs. Yates came from the kitchen, carrying her baby on her hip. "Well, hello, Miss Singer. Mr. Goodwin."

"What a darling," Alice said, looking at the year-old boy.

"He really is," Marta replied, smoothing her son's hair.

"Luke, isn't it?" Alice couldn't seem to take her eyes off the little fellow.

"Yes," Marta said. "Can I help you folks?"

"They want Justin," the girl said.

Marta's smile skewed. "I'm sorry. He was called over to Trentville an hour or so ago. I doubt he'll be home before suppertime."

"Oh." Alice looked at John.

"We have something we need to tell him," John said. "Could you have him come see me as soon as he gets back?"

"Surely," Marta said.

"Let him eat his supper first," Alice put in.

John nodded. Alice probably knew from her experience with

her father that when a man arrived home after a long day's work, he wanted a meal before another job was thrown at him.

Marta smiled. "Thank you. I'll see that he's fed, but I'll also tell him you have a matter of some importance."

"Thanks a lot," John said.

Alice touched his sleeve as they turned away. "It's all right," she said softly.

They walked down the steps together, and John paused uncertainly. They were closer to her house than the restaurant.

"Still want to get lunch?"

"Yes, please."

Warmth flooded him. Yes, Alice did know when a man wanted his dinner. But she also knew how to make him feel special. When she tucked her hand into the curve of his arm, he thought he might float up the street without ever touching the ground.

Dr. Melvin was eating lunch at the table next to where John and Alice sat down. He nodded and said, "Afternoon, folks."

Alice replied cheerfully but seemed troubled.

"Are you sure I'm not keeping you away from your work too long?"

"I'm sure," John said.

They both ordered the day's special—roast beef with biscuits, gravy, and turnips, and John insisted on paying for both dinners. Alice flushed but gave in and let him. While they waited for their plates, he gazed at her across the table, thinking what a lovely picture she made even though her clothing was simple and of plain material.

"I do wish the marshal was here," he said, "but I suppose it will be all right."

She nodded. "As long as Mr. Willard doesn't know we're suspicious, nothing will happen, right?"

John considered that. "I won't hang up that one poster just yet. I wouldn't want him to come into the post office and see it."

"Good thinking," Alice said. "We'll just wait until Marshal Yates comes back and then let him handle it."

Dr. Melvin set down his coffee cup and pushed back his chair.

"Oh Doc, may I have a moment?" John asked.

"Of course." The doctor stepped closer to them.

"I wondered if you've met Miss Singer's new neighbor, Dirk Willard?"

Dr. Melvin shook his head. "Can't say as I have."

"Oh. We thought he might be a patient of yours," Alice said.

"Does he need medical attention?"

Alice looked at John.

"He's elderly," John said. "We thought perhaps he'd consulted you on some matter or other."

"No, not yet. How long has he been in town?"

"Just a few weeks," Alice said.

"Oh well. If he gets sick, give him my name."

"All right."

As the doctor left, Alice looked questioningly at John.

He shrugged. "I didn't feel we ought to say too much. I mean, we don't *know* he's. . ."

"Right," Alice said.

Their plates came, and they enjoyed the food. The cook here was one of Wiseman's best, in John's opinion. As they finished the main course, the waitress came to ask if they wanted dessert—apple pie today.

"None for me, thanks," Alice said, "but you go ahead, John."

"No, thank you. I'd best start my rounds." He hesitated. "Can I take you home?"

"There's no need," Alice replied. "I'll see myself home. And later I need to take my cookies over to the church for the Christmas baskets. Mrs. Ross said to bring them this evening."

"Might I go with you?" John asked, standing to pull out her chair for her. "I bought the coffee I'm giving. We could go together."

She smiled up at him. "That would be lovely, although it'll be out of your way to go to my house first."

"I don't mind."

They walked out onto Main Street, and she extended her hand. John took it for a moment.

"Thank you for lunch and a pleasant conversation," she said.

"The pleasure's all mine, Alice. I'll see you about six o'clock, if that suits you."

"It's perfect."

She glided away, carrying her basket. John walked toward the post office but turned once to watch her retreating figure. He couldn't describe the feeling Alice Singer gave him. He'd liked other girls before but had never been attracted so strongly. Alice was everything he thought a woman should be. He pulled in a deep breath. Two people were waiting for him to open the post office door, and he greeted them cheerfully.

After hiding her father's Christmas gift at the back of her closet, Alice spent the afternoon writing letters and ironing. She had iced the sugar cookies, and now she set about packing them and the other cookies for the Christmas baskets. Four gingerbread men and a half dozen each of oatmeal and sugar cookies went into every packet. A slight twinge of guilt crept over her as she remembered Mr. Willard's words. Did he think they were doing a disservice to the poor by helping them out with enough food for a good meal or two at Christmas? She couldn't believe that.

Maybe I ought to have made bread, or something more nourishing, she thought, gazing down at one of the whimsical gingerbread boys with raisin eyes and buttons. No, some of those families had young children. The little men ought to put smiles on a few faces, and that was worthwhile.

She wrapped the cookies in brown paper and tied each one neatly with string. She wished she had some bright ribbons to decorate them. Finally, all was ready, and she put the packages into her basket.

When she checked the time, it was after five o'clock and darkness was falling outside. John would have closed the post office and would soon be there to pick her up. She hurried to freshen up. There was no sense wearing anything fancy for their simple errand to the church, but she wanted to look nice anyway. Anticipation of seeing John always seemed to prod her to look and be her best.

She made herself eat a few bites of supper, but she was too excited to sit at the table long. She washed up her dishes and straightened the kitchen, checking the time often. At last she heard footsteps outside. A glance out the kitchen window assured her it was John, and she grabbed the red scarf that matched her mittens as she dashed to the door. Before opening it, she made herself stand still and take two deep breaths.

He knocked, and she pulled the door open.

"Hi." He seemed surprised that she had responded so quickly.

"I—I saw you out the window."

"Oh." He smiled and looked her over. "You look festive."

"Thank you." She still felt a little breathless. "Did you hear anything from the marshal?"

"Not yet."

Alice was a little disappointed. "I've got the cookies all wrapped."

"Can I carry them for you?"

"That would be wonderful."

She stood aside and let him go to the kitchen table, where she had left the laden basket. John added his small bags of coffee, which made the large basket full to overflowing.

He lifted it. "Shall we?"

"I hope that's not as heavy as Mr. Willard's parcels," Alice said.

"No, but it's plenty hefty."

They went out, and before they turned up the street toward the church, she looked at Dirk Willard's house. The curtains were drawn, but a light gleamed softly within.

"He seems to be capable of taking care of himself," she murmured. "I've seen Mr. Lawson's helper deliver goods from the mercantile."

"Yes, I think Mr. Willard is fine," John said. "At least physically."

"I haven't seen him flying the kite lately." Alice glanced up at John. "But we haven't had any electric storms lately either."

"We shouldn't see much lightning over the winter."

"No."

They walked on in silence for a few minutes. Alice hated the way her neighbor cast a shadow over this otherwise joyous time with John.

Candles glowed in the church windows, and a large wreath hung on the door. The Yates twins were just emerging from the church when they arrived, flanked by the Beaumont brothers, Mark and Logan.

"Hello," Emma and Ella called, striding toward them.

"Hello, twins," John said. He greeted the young men and turned to Ella. The only way Alice knew it was Ella, not Emma, was that she was walking with Logan, the older of the Beaumont brothers. It was no secret in Wiseman that Logan, the saddle maker, was courting Ella, and his younger brother, Mark, was sweet on Emma. "I don't guess your brother is home yet."

"Sorry, he's not," Ella replied. "Marta's getting a little nervous for him, so we volunteered to bring stuff for the baskets over and let her wait for him at home."

"That was kind of you," Alice said. "I hope he's there when you get back."

"So do we," Ella said.

"See you Sunday," Emma called as she strolled down the walk on Mark's arm.

Reverend and Mrs. Ross were both in the church. The pastor's wife was directing people who came in with food donations, and she showed Alice and John where to place the cookies and coffee. Alice was happy to see that several other parishioners had been there with their contributions—dry beans, jars of jelly and canned vegetables, loaves of sourdough bread, and several pies.

"Do you think the person who's been giving the poultry for the baskets will do it again this year?" Alice asked.

"We're pretty confident," Mrs. Ross said. "It's become a tradition."

After a short visit with the pastor and his wife, John and Alice left the sanctuary and walked down Church Street once more. Alice tried to think of a way to prolong their time together, but she didn't have the excuse of baking tonight, and she really shouldn't ask a man in when she was alone anyway.

"It's clouding up," John noted.

"I hope we're not in for bad weather." Alice looked up at the dark sky. No moonlight tonight, and she could only make out a few stars at the edge of the cloud bank that seemed to be spreading across the sky from the west.

"It's too warm for snow," John said.

"Mr. Willard thinks it will be a hard winter."

"Oh? How does he know?"

She laughed. "Extra-thick corn husks this year. Things like that."

They reached her side door, and John stood looking down at her. "Thanks for letting me walk with you." She could barely see his face in the darkness, but she caught a gleam from his eyes.

"Thanks for coming and getting me," she said. He wouldn't kiss her again, would he? Not out here where anyone passing by could see them. And what if Mr. Willard was looking out his kitchen window? Sure it was dark, but he'd still be able to see them plain as day from that close.

"Will you go to the Christmas Eve service with me?" John looked a little nervous, and Alice had no desire to draw out his anxiety.

"I'd be happy to."

He smiled. "Terrific."

"Well, good night," she said and turned to open the door.

A moment later she was inside and he was gone. Alice sighed

and leaned against the door panel for a moment. Every time she saw John, even if it was only for a few minutes, she liked him more. What would Pa say when he started coming around to call regularly? A pleasant warmth flooded her as she slowly took off her wraps and lit the lamp.

The evening stretched before her, and she decided to sit in the parlor and read. Franklin's autobiography was so thick, it would give her many more evenings of reading pleasure. It was odd, but the more she read the book, the more she liked Mr. Willard, and the more he seemed to resemble Benjamin Franklin.

She kept the fire going, and the house was warm and cozy—except for the uneasy feeling that touched her now and again. Alice would look up from her book and turn slowly to look all around the room. Twice she went to check that the doors were securely locked.

Another whole day until Pa came home. She forced her attention back to the book and read several more pages. Finally, she began to feel sleepy and reached for her Bible. A log in the fire fell, and she jumped.

She stood and turned to the kitchen. Better to go to bed than to sit here any longer waiting for something to happen. She banked the coals in the cookstove and paused by the window, gazing out toward Mr. Willard's house. The darkness was not as deep as it had been earlier, and she decided the clouds had thinned. Maybe they wouldn't get the rain she'd half expected after all.

Had Marshal Yates returned? So far as she knew, he hadn't come by her house. Had he stopped in to see John? She would go to the post office first thing in the morning, she decided, and ask John if he'd heard anything.

A horse came trotting down Church Street from the direction

of the town square. Alice eased to one side so that she could watch out the window without being seen. It wasn't Marshal Yates. She held her breath as the rider moved steadily past her house. Sure enough, he stopped in front of Mr. Willard's and dismounted.

Alice's pulse sped. Was it Edward Kline, the man on the poster? His hat was pulled low over his brow, and the dim starlight wasn't strong enough to reveal his facial features. He walked up to Mr. Willard's door, and she thought from his profile that he was the man with the scar, but she couldn't be certain.

He knocked and waited a few seconds, until Mr. Willard opened the door and let him in. They gave no hearty greetings, and the door was quickly shut.

Alice frowned. It was nearly half past eight—not horribly late, but still, it was later than most people would go calling. She watched the house, and she thought another lamp was lit and the light inside increased, though the closed curtains kept her from seeing what was going on in there.

If only Marshal Yates were back. She could run around the block to his house in minutes and warn him that the dangerous wanted man was at Dirk Willard's house this very instant. Of course, she'd have to be sure it was the man on the poster. It would be pretty embarrassing if the marshal came to investigate and found she'd made a mistake and Mr. Willard's visitor was somebody else and perfectly innocent.

She hesitated. Maybe Justin Yates had returned home and was having his supper. She wondered if John had walked around to Oak Street to check on his way home. Probably not, since Justin's twin sisters had told them at the church that he wasn't back.

A plan began to form in Alice's mind. If her father was home, she would ask him to step over to Mr. Willard's with her. But Pa wasn't home and wouldn't be for another day.

If she just knew for certain the man was Edward Kline, she could run over to the Yateses' house. And if the marshal still wasn't home, she could go to John's, although that was quite a bit farther away. She really shouldn't go that far alone at night, and if anyone saw her hurrying to a single man's residence at nine o'clock in the evening. . . Perhaps it would be better to go to the Ross house and tell the pastor what was going on. But what could Reverend Ross do?

She sighed and stood there another minute in indecision, and another alternative came to her. The Yates family lived very close to Stephen and Rachel Worth and the Tanner sisters. If the marshal wasn't home, she could call there. Even if no one went to confront the criminals, she was certain the Worths would invite her to stay there tonight. She didn't want to stay here alone if she confirmed that a wanted felon was only yards from her house.

The visitor's horse stood patiently at the hitching post, but if she waited too long, the man would leave. She would never know for certain whether Mr. Willard's caller was the known criminal.

It was her duty to find out. They couldn't let a wanted criminal come and go in Wiseman anytime he pleased, could they? She grabbed her coat.

Chapter 7

John was just about to get ready for bed when he heard a knock. He walked through the kitchen and threw the door open.

"Justin!"

Marshal Yates nodded. "Evening, John. I got home a few minutes ago, and my wife said you were anxious to talk to me."

"She was right. Alice Singer and I discovered something that may be important. Come on in."

John went to the stove and lifted his coffeepot, gauging its weight. He'd banked the fire, but the pot was still hot.

"Coffee?"

"No thanks. What is it?"

"It was those posters you left with me. Did you look at them?"

"I glanced through them before I gave them to you. Did I miss something?"

"Maybe." John sat down at the table and waved Justin into a seat. "Alice is the one who picked up on it, but after she showed me, I had to agree."

"On what?"

"There was one for a counterfeiter named Edward Kline."

Justin nodded slowly. "I seem to recall that one."

"Well, we both think Kline is the man who helped Dirk Willard when he moved into that house over on Church Street. And it seemed to us that the deliveries Willard's been getting are suspicious, especially if he hobnobs with counterfeiters."

"Tell me more." Justin glanced at the stove. "Maybe we'd better have some of that coffee."

John poured him a mugful and set it before him.

"He's had some deliveries so heavy I had to rent a wagon."

"What was in them?"

"I don't know about all of them, but several were paper—good-quality paper. I haven't seen it myself outside the boxes, but Alice has, and she says it's good-quality rag paper. Lots of it. And that's not the clincher."

"Oh?" Justin sipped his coffee.

"This morning guess what came for him?"

Justin shrugged. "I'm sure you're going to tell me."

"A printing press."

"You don't say."

"I do. Not only that, but Alice saw some green ink at his house."

Justin took a deep breath, in and out. His gaze focused somewhere past John, and John kept quiet. After several seconds, Justin looked directly at him. "Do you suppose the old man's gone to bed?"

"He may be up, playing with his new toy."

"Have you been over there tonight?"

John nodded. "I took Alice to the church briefly, around six or half past."

"Everything was quiet then?"

"It was when I took her home. I guess it's been two hours or more since I was there."

"Well, I told Miss Singer I'd check around every night. I expect I'd better mosey along. Feel like a walk?"

"You must be tired, but I admit I'd rest easier if we took a look around her neighborhood." John stood and put on his hat and wool jacket.

Justin rose with a sigh. John was grateful that his friend took him seriously and that he was willing to check into it, even though he'd been working all day.

"I suspect Alice is safely tucked in for the night," he said. "Although her father's not due back until tomorrow afternoon. She may be restless."

"Nervous type?" Justin asked as they left John's house.

"I wouldn't have said so, but this thing with Willard has her a little on edge." John shook his head. "But Alice is a sensible woman. She's probably having sweet dreams right now."

Alice tried not to make a sound as she crept across the yard between her house and Dirk Willard's. The dead grass crinkled beneath her feet. A street away, a dog barked, and she heard a faint shout from somewhere up near the town square, but on this block of Church

Street, all was quiet. A couple of houses had lamps burning inside, but most were dark.

The horse tied in front of Mr. Willard's house stamped a hoof, startling her. She froze halfway to the old man's house and eyed the horse. It shifted and tossed its head but didn't make any loud noises.

Alice took a few more cautious steps and reached the corner of the small rental house. The kitchen window was too high for her to look into. She stayed close to the wall and scurried along the side of the house. A window at the back was dark. That must be Mr. Willard's bedroom. She went on around to the far side of the house, which sat on a corner lot. This side looked out on Oak Street, which was dark and quiet at the moment. But the window that she was sure was set in Mr. Willard's parlor wall emitted a soft glow.

Alice crouched at the corner of the building, measuring with her eye the height of the window. She was pretty sure she would be able to see inside if the curtains weren't drawn tight. She just hoped nobody came along Oak Street and caught her trying to spy on her neighbor.

She looked both ways along the street. Nothing. The horse out front, on the Church Street side, was quiet, and the dog had quit barking. Alice sucked in a deep breath and tiptoed along the wall to the window. She straightened and eyed the curtains inside the glass. Where they met in the middle, there was a significant gap at the bottom. She edged over in front of it and stood on her toes.

She had a view of Dirk's parlor, all right, and two men were inside. They were working the printing press. The visitor was tall, dressed in dark clothes, and he was turned away from her. Alice couldn't be sure she had ever seen him before.

As she watched, the younger man turned partway. His nose was unmistakable. A moment later, he leaned to reach for a tool, and she caught a glimpse of the scar on his chin. Her heart stampeded. It was him, Edward Kline.

Fascinated, she watched as Willard fed sheets of paper into the press, and Kline tightened the part that held the plate with the type. No, it was some kind of design, not text.

Mr. Willard removed the sheet they'd printed and held it up to examine their work. Alice caught her breath. It was a sheet of newly inked money. A dozen bills were lined up neatly on the sheet. They were using plates to produce currency.

Mr. Willard hung the damp sheet of bills on a little clothesline that crossed the parlor while the other man worked at another task—inking the plate, she thought. She supposed they would have to let each sheet dry before they could print the back. Or did the machine print front and back at the same time? Two other sheets already hung on the line, and the sides facing her were blank. The men would probably print several fronts before they changed over to printing the backs.

She'd seen enough. She had to tell someone.

At that moment, as he settled the second clothespin over the edge of the damp sheet of print, Dirk Willard looked toward the window. Despite the small gap in the curtains, Alice felt that his gaze met hers. She gasped and ducked below the windowsill, her chest tightening so that, corset or no corset, she doubted she could draw a deep breath.

But she had to! She pushed to her feet and dashed for the back of the house.

As she ran, Alice planned her route in a flash. If she could make it from the corner of Mr. Willard's house, across the grass between his side yard and her vegetable garden, she could run around her own house and go in the front. They couldn't see where she went if she did that, and she would be safe.

She reached the corner of the house and tore around it, along the back wall and under the dark bedroom window. The open expanse of grass between the two houses would be the most dangerous. If they looked out the kitchen window, they could see her from there.

She pulled up her skirt and pushed her legs harder for a burst of speed across the open ground.

Thump!

Just as she left the shelter of his house wall, she slammed into something hard. Softer than a stone wall, but unyielding. Not something, someone.

She sprawled backward, her arms flailing, and landed on the frigid ground. Alice stared up into the face of the man with the scar. His dark eyes glared at her as she lay there trembling. She tried to speak, but she couldn't.

Dirk Willard came trotting around the back of the house, the way Alice had come.

"You got her!"

"Oh, I got her all right."

"What do we do now?" Willard asked.

"There's only one thing to do." Kline pulled a revolver from his holster.

"No," Willard said. "You can't. A shot would bring the law out faster than a pie-eating contest. And besides, she's got people who care about her. They'll be looking for her soon."

Kline hesitated. "Well, what do you want to do then?"

Willard frowned down at Alice. "Let's get her inside."

He reached solicitously toward her, but Kline grabbed her arms and yanked her to her feet.

"Okay, Miss Nosy, let's go."

Her legs felt boneless as she walked beside him. Only the certainty that he would kill her if she balked kept her moving. Dirk Willard came behind them, around to the front of the house and inside. He looked up and down the street before he closed the door firmly behind them. The warmth of the room smacked Alice, and she felt light-headed.

"I apologize, Miss Singer," Willard said. "You've been nice to me, but this is necessary. And necessity, as you know, never made a good bargain."

"Please—"

Kline poked the gun's muzzle into her side. "Hush, meddling woman."

Willard frowned, his eyes brimming with sadness. "I hoped it wouldn't come to this. But you've got a snooping bent, I'm afraid. All your neighborly visits. . ."

"She figured you were up to something," Kline snapped. "Get some rope."

Alice turned to face the gunman. "I—I was only checking on Mr. Willard. He's an old man, and sometimes he doesn't have his wits about him. I worry about him. Did you know that sometimes he thinks he's Benjamin Franklin?"

Kline shook his head and lowered the pistol a fraction of an inch. "Dirk, I told you that Franklin thing would draw too much attention to you."

"It made people think I'd mellowed." Dirk went out of the room, and she heard him shuffling about in the kitchen.

"You got folks next door?" Kline asked.

Alice felt as though a big hole had opened in her stomach.

"My father. . ."

"Dirk says he's out of town," Kline snarled. "Otherwise we wouldn't be doing this tonight."

Dirk returned carrying a coil of rope and dragging a kitchen chair behind him. Kline glared at him.

"I thought you said her old man was away."

"He is. I understood he wouldn't return until Christmas Eve. That's tomorrow, right? I haven't seen him around all week. Isn't that so, Miss Singer?"

Her breath whooshed out of her. She couldn't lie to his face. She said in a small voice, "He's gone."

"What about Goodwin, the postmaster?" Dirk asked, eyeing her keenly. "He's right friendly with you. He won't come around this late, will he?"

She shook her head helplessly. If only John *was* planning a late visit. But he was too much of a gentleman to even consider such a thing.

"Sit down." Dirk placed the chair in a corner, a few feet from the printing press.

Alice wobbled toward it. What did this mean? She sat down and looked from one man to the other. Kline holstered his gun and took the rope from Dirk.

"Let me do that."

"Don't hurt her," Willard said sternly, and Alice was grateful for that. He seemed at least a little concerned for her comfort, and even for her life.

"You know what this means," Kline growled as he wound the

cord around her arms and the chair back.

"We have to move," Willard said.

"And fast. People will certainly come looking for her in the morning. If the postman's sweet on her, like you say, he'll surely come by. Then the marshal will be after us."

"He'd be hotter after us if we killed her."

Alice shuddered.

"Maybe so, but it would buy us more time if we were sure she couldn't talk."

"No."

Alice looked mournfully at the old gunslinger. So there was some kindness in him. Maybe, as he'd said, he had mellowed in his sunset years, even if he'd deceived people about his supposed delusions. Not once tonight had she heard him speak as if he didn't know what was real and what wasn't—or as if he were Benjamin Franklin. He still had his wits about him, all right.

"Why Franklin?" she asked, frowning at Willard.

He shrugged. "Everyone respects him and thinks of him as a wise but harmless old man. And he had a lot of quirks, so he was easy to imitate."

Alice jumped as Kline raised her skirt several inches.

"How dare you?"

"Just making sure you can't run, lady." He wound the rope about her ankles and tied the knot uncomfortably tight.

"Please," she said. "Let me go. I won't tell anyone what you're doing."

"Sorry," Willard said. He was already throwing tools and stacks of paper into boxes. "I figured it was risky when you noticed the green ink, but I was pretty sure you hadn't seen the printing plates.

We can't take the chance, seeing as how what we're doing is a federal offense."

"No, really," Alice said. "I won't—"

Willard waved a dismissive hand at her. "We'll be miles away before dawn. It may get a little chilly in here, but you'll be fine. If Goodwin doesn't start looking for you until he makes his afternoon deliveries, we ought to be able to put a good amount of distance between us."

"Here." Kline spoke, and Alice jerked her chin up. He held a red bandanna in his hands.

"Oh no. Please don't."

"Got to make sure you can't yell," Kline said.

"I won't."

"Can't you wait until we're ready to leave?" Willard asked with a frown.

"No." Kline clenched his teeth, and the scar on his chin stood out white against his skin. "You don't know when someone might happen by, and she could let loose."

Willard sighed, unpinning the sheets of drying bills. He waved the last one they'd made through the air, as though attempting to dry the ink faster. "All right. But make sure she can breathe. I was in on a heist once where the banker suffocated."

Alice cringed away from Kline, but he wrapped the bandanna around her head.

"Open up."

She pressed her lips firmly together and shook her head, staring at him.

Kline drew back his arm and slapped her.

"Here now!" Willard came over, still holding the sheet of money.

Twenty-dollar bills, Alice saw through the blur of tears, though her cheek stung and her head ached.

"This woman can get us both killed," Kline said. "That or locked up for the rest of our lives."

Willard sighed. "Miss Singer, let him place the gag in your mouth."

"I'm afraid." Tears streamed down her cheeks, and she thought Willard's eyes actually showed sympathy.

Kline, however, had no such feelings. He cursed and wound the cloth around her face again. Alice sobbed, and he worked it between her teeth then tied it tightly. She choked against the foul taste of the fabric. She couldn't stay here like this until tomorrow afternoon. She began to pray in earnest.

"Get that crate over here," Kline told Willard. "We've got to get it packed up."

"Can't leave that behind," Willard agreed. He dragged an empty wooden crate from the back room. Both men strained to lower the machine from the table into the box. It hit bottom with a loud thud. Willard peered at it anxiously, fussing with something attached to the press.

"It'll be all right," Kline said.

"Get the ink while I pack up my clothes and tools," Willard said. "Make sure the bottles are cushioned in straw."

They worked for a few minutes without speaking. Then Kline said, "We'll need a wagon."

Willard grunted.

"Where's the most likely place?" Kline looked at Alice. "Does her father have one?"

"No," Willard said. "At least not here. He runs the stockyard. I don't know if there's one out there or not."

"I'll try the livery," Kline said. "If I can't get one there, I guess I'll have to ride over to the stockyard." He glowered at Alice. "Make sure she stays put."

"I will," Willard said. "I wasn't born yesterday, you know."

Kline clapped his hat on and strode outside. A moment later, the horse's hoofbeats receded up the street, and Alice faintly heard the dog barking again.

She wished the cloth wasn't in her mouth. She and Willard had enjoyed some pleasant conversations. If she could talk to him now, maybe she could help him see reason. She tried to say something around the bandanna, but it only caused her to choke and attempt to cough.

"Easy," Willard said with a glance. "Don't fight it. You're a nice girl, and I don't want to see him hurt you. Because he will, you know, if you don't do as he says."

Alice squeezed her eyes shut. Tears ran down her face and soaked into the bandanna. The man seemed oblivious to her discomfort. She prayed silently for God's mercy and asked him to give Dane McDermott sense enough not to rent a wagon to Kline. But the more she thought about it, the more she was certain Kline wouldn't go to Dane's door. He'd just steal a wagon if he was able to get at one without disturbing anyone.

Willard went into the kitchen and returned a couple of minutes later holding a burlap sack that clanked and chinked as he moved.

"I'll have to leave most of my dishes." He shot her a dark look. "I guess you can have whatever I leave here. Put it all in your hope chest."

Alice sobbed, and that brought on another fit of retching.

"Stay calm," Willard said. "This will be over soon."

She couldn't stop the sobs that clogged her throat, and he came close to her, reached out, and touched her hair gently. "There, now. When nature gave us tears, she gave us leave to weep."

She stared up at him. Franklin, now? He seemed to read her mind and looked away. "I do apologize. Though you are overcurious, you have not been unkind." He walked around behind her and tugged at Kline's knot in the bandanna.

"I don't expect my associate will be back for a few minutes. Let me loosen this a little."

He retied the knot so that the bandanna hung loosely.

"Thank you," Alice managed, although it came out garbled around the cloth.

"You're welcome." He gave her a wry smile. "Do good to your friends to keep them, to your enemies to win them."

She worked at the bandanna with her tongue and was able to push it out so that it drooped wet across her chin. "Are we enemies now, then?"

He sighed and went to a shelf in the corner and lifted down several books. "I didn't wish it to happen this way."

"How then?" she asked. "You thought we could live side by side and talk about books and tea and the founding fathers, and meanwhile you'd print enough money for you and your friends to live on?"

He closed his eyes for a moment. In his hand, he held a large volume, and she recognized it as the same book she'd borrowed from Pastor Ross—*The Autobiography of Benjamin Franklin*. Of course.

"I'll leave you Byron and Tennyson. You'll appreciate them. But I'm keeping Blake and Wordsworth." He laid Franklin's book and a couple of others in one of the boxes.

"You chose this life," she said bitterly. "Franklin said it himself—we choose the thoughts we allow ourselves to think, the passions we allow ourselves to feel, and the actions we allow ourselves to perform. You didn't have to do this, Mr. Willard."

"You're right. I didn't." He grimaced. "Perhaps you are too much of a conscience. It may be time to put that gag back in place."

Alice heard a faint sound outside, and Willard whipped around toward the window.

"What was what?" she asked.

"It wasn't a horse and wagon."

Chapter 8

"All looks quiet here," Justin Yates said, surveying the small house.

"There are lights burning though," John said. "He's still up. Should we knock?"

"I think I'll just take a peek. You wait here."

The marshal melted away into the shadows beside the house. John stood out at the street, watching the door, but after a moment his gaze strayed to the Singer house. The night was dark, and he supposed Alice was sleeping. But still, a lamp glowed behind the kitchen window. Was she still awake? He didn't suppose she would stay up this late or go to bed with a lamp still burning. Maybe she expected her father home late tonight and had left the light for him. Had she heard from him somehow this evening?

Justin came silently across the dead grass. "Something's not right. Willard's in the parlor, and he's talking to somebody, but I can't see who. And there are boxes everywhere, like he's packing up to leave town."

"Which window?" John asked.

"On the left side, the parlor window."

Together they tiptoed back the way Justin had come, to the corner of the house.

"Watch the street," John whispered.

Justin nodded and flattened himself against the house wall, peering out over the quiet neighborhood.

John sidled up to the window frame. Only a small space between the curtains let him see in, but that was good, he thought. The curtains would probably be enough to conceal him. He slowly eased his head over to the gap and immediately spotted Dirk Willard. He stood with a wrench in one hand, waving it and speaking. John caught the word "conscience" and frowned. Was the old duffer talking to himself? Maybe he was memorizing quotations from Franklin, the way John had memorized Bible verses when he was a kid.

Something moved in the corner of the room, and he leaned over a bit to see farther. What he saw was a pair of black women's shoes, tied together at the ankles. Above them was the hem of a green dress.

John jumped back and hurried to Justin's side.

"He's got someone tied up in there. I think it's Alice!"

Justin looked at him blankly for a moment. "Are you sure?"

"I saw her feet and part of her dress. It's a woman anyway. Who else could it be?"

Justin nodded and drew his revolver. "Do you have a weapon?"

"No." John never carried a gun. He'd never had a reason to, since his short stint as a cowpuncher. He'd carried one then against rattlers and varmints. But never in town.

"Right. You go to the back door, and I'll go in the front." The marshal strode determinedly toward Willard's front door.

John hurried around the house to the rear and found a back door. He tried the latch, but it was locked. Unsure of what to do, he ran around the other side of the house to the front, where he found the door wide open in Justin's wake.

"Hands over your head," Justin yelled.

Beyond him, John could see the old man blinking at him and wielding a crescent wrench. Willard hesitated, looking from Justin to John. Slowly he raised his hands high.

"Put the wrench down," Justin said in a more normal tone. "Nice and easy."

Willard lowered his right hand and dropped the wrench on the table beside a book with a thunk.

"Now turn around," Justin said.

Willard complied, and Justin stepped forward to handcuff him. John made a beeline for Alice, who sat in the shadowy corner staring at the marshal and Willard.

"Alice!" John knelt beside her on the board floor. "Are you all right, dearest?" He reached for the grimy bandanna that circled her face.

"Yes. Oh John!" Tears streamed down her cheeks, and she gave him a tremulous smile as he undid the knot. "His partner though. It's Kline, the man with the scar."

"He was here?" John asked, beginning to untie the rope that held her.

"Yes. He went to get a wagon so they can haul away the press and all the other paraphernalia for their printing. And there's money they'd just printed, and— Oh John, he'll be back any minute."

John turned to look at Justin. "You hear that, Marshal?"

"I heard." Justin cocked his head to one side. "I think I hear him coming. Hoofbeats anyway."

John worked the last knot quickly, and Alice shook free of the rope.

"Come on," John said. "Let's get you out of here."

He grabbed her hand and yanked her toward a doorway. Inside it was dark, but it seemed to be Willard's bedroom.

"Keep down and stay quiet," John said. He shut the door and whirled back into the parlor, where Justin had made Willard sit down in the corner where Alice had been. John spotted a hat and a gun belt on top of one of the crates. He clapped the hat onto his head and drew the revolver from its holster. His jacket was dark like Dirk Willard's. He closed the front door and murmured a few words to Justin, who nodded. The marshal hastily tied Willard's feet and positioned himself out of the line of sight, aiming his gun toward the door.

John's heart raced. He could be killed if Kline realized who he was and opened fire. He would be no match for the felon.

Outside he heard the creak of the wagon. The hoofbeats stopped, and there was a moment of near silence. The horse snuffled, and footsteps came up the walk. John looked over at Justin. His friend nodded gravely. John took a deep breath and turned his back to the door. He picked up Willard's wrench and bent over the crate that held the printing press.

Kline didn't bother to knock, but opened the front door and

stepped inside. John kept his back turned and held his breath.

"Hey!"

John turned at the newcomer's voice. Justin stepped out of the corner. "Hands up, Kline!"

The wanted man didn't hesitate but dove out through the doorway. Justin strode to the door and tracked Kline with his gun. He fired once. John hurried to his side.

"Missed him," Justin said. "Come on!"

Justin catapulted onto the porch and down the steps, chasing Kline. The outlaw had hopped over the fence around the Singers' garden, fouling the marshal's aim. Kline was fast escaping through the backyards of the houses along Church Street.

John tore after Justin. The man they pursued swerved into the cemetery, zigzagging among the tombstones. Justin kept after him. John took a straighter line along the edge of the cemetery, heading toward Main Street. The church was just across the street. Would the fleeing man go there, or would he go down the road toward the stockyards? He might even turn right onto Main Street if he got that far and head for the livery to try to steal a mount.

John sucked in shallow breaths of the cold air. Though he walked several miles each day on his mail route, he seldom did much running. Justin's racing form was a blur in the cemetery, and John could just make out a flitting shadow beyond him.

The front of the cemetery was edged with a stone wall along Main Street, with a wrought iron gate in the middle of the wall. John reached the street and veered left, toward the gate, but a dark figure was already halfway across the street and barreling toward the church. John adjusted his direction so he could intercept Kline. His chest ached from the effort. He was relieved to see Justin leap the cemetery wall closer to him than the gate and tear into the street. They had both nearly caught up with the outlaw beside the church steps. John caught sight of a person standing at the top of the steps, watching them.

"Stop that man," he yelled.

The man on the steps jumped down on Kline without hesitation, bringing him to the ground. John piled on too. Kline struggled and kicked, and the barrel of a handgun glinted. John grabbed a wrist and got his knee on it, pinning Kline's arm to the ground. The other fellow punched the outlaw, and Kline lay still, letting the gun slip from his hand.

"Everybody freeze," Justin yelled.

That struck John as funny, since it was so cold outside. He choked back a laugh and rolled off Kline, grabbing the man's revolver before he stood.

"It's okay, Marshal. We got him."

The other man stood too, and Justin squinted at him in the starlight.

"Clint Wiseman, that you?"

"Yeah," Clint said gruffly. "I had some business at the church."

John looked up at the top of the steps, where two lumpy sacks lay.

"You," John said. "You've been bringing the poultry for the Christmas baskets."

"Well. . .yeah. Went hunting today, and I bought a few hens. Don't tell anyone."

"I won't," John promised. A loner like Clint wouldn't want everyone talking about him.

Kline was stirring, and Justin stood over him with his gun

pointed at the outlaw.

"All right, Kline, on your feet. We're just a few yards from the jail."

"Who is he?" Clint asked.

"He's wanted for counterfeiting," John said.

"Wow. Never knew of anyone who actually did that. Here in town?"

"Yeah," John said. "Long story."

"Help me get him over to the jail, and I'll tell it to you," Justin said. "John, you'd better go see if Miss Singer's all right, and stay with Willard until I get there."

Alice! John's heart clenched.

"I sure will." He turned and ran for Dirk Willard's house.

All was quiet in the outer room. Alice crouched in the dark bedroom, her pulse tripping, trying to breathe quietly. Was everyone gone? She'd heard the marshal yell, a gunshot, and then running footsteps, and now nothing. Had Willard and his partner both escaped? She crawled over to the door, where a strip of lamplight showed at the bottom, and listened. She thought she heard rustling.

Sending up a silent prayer, she stood carefully and felt for the door latch. She raised it and pulled the door toward her a couple of inches. Placing her eye to the crack, she could see the room with its crates and boxes ready to load. The printing apparatus still sat in its crate by the table.

A soft thud startled her, and she drew back. Cautiously, she peered out again. Who was out there?

Movement in the corner where she'd been tied drew her eye,

and she stood on tiptoe so she could see over the table, but that didn't help. She went to her knees and looked beneath the table, to the far side of the room.

Dirk Willard lay on his stomach with his hands cuffed together behind his back. He pushed with his bound feet and shoved himself toward the table.

Alice poked the door open a few more inches.

"Mr. Willard?" she whispered loudly.

His head jerked around. "Miss Singer?"

"What happened?" she asked. "Where are they?"

"Dunno."

Alice frowned, trying to put it together. "They must be chasing your friend."

"Untie my feet."

Alice shook her head.

"I helped you," Willard said.

"You did not."

"I certainly did. Ed would have killed you if I hadn't intervened. Don't think he wouldn't have. And if he gets away from the marshal, he'll come right back here and do it."

"Then why should I help you? You'll just go with him and take your fake money and your printing press and start doing this again in some other town."

"I'm an old man, Miss Alice. If they put me in jail now, I won't last long. You've got to help me."

She noticed that he'd switched from calling her Miss Singer to Miss Alice. He inched toward her.

"Help me."

"No." She stepped back.

What if the scar-faced man did elude the marshal and come back here? She could see his horse and wagon waiting outside. Even if he didn't bother to load up the heavy printing press, he might come back here to get the horse so he could get out of Wiseman quickly.

"I'm not helping you!"

She hoisted her skirts and dashed past him and through the doorway.

On the porch, she pulled up short as a man ran toward her up the steps.

"Alice?" he cried.

"Oh John! Thank heaven."

John wrapped her in his embrace. "Are you all right?"

"Yes." She leaned against him, gulping in the cold night air.

"Where's Willard?" John asked.

"Where you left him, or almost. He's trying to get loose. He wanted me to help him."

John squeezed her tight. "Well, the marshal will be here soon to take him over to the jail."

"Did you get the other man?" she gasped.

"Yeah, we got him." John eased her inside and shut the door. He looked down at Willard and shook his head. "You may as well quit trying. You're not getting away with this."

Willard lay back on the floorboards with a sigh and closed his eyes.

"What will happen to my stuff?"

"You mean your printing press and your counterfeit money?" John asked. "I suspect that will all be confiscated as evidence."

"No, my personal things. I meant my books, mostly." Willard

opened his eyes and looked wearily up at Alice. "Miss Singer, I still want you to take whatever you want. The teapot, the books—anything that's useful to you."

Alice didn't know what to say. Did she really want anything that had belonged to the gunfighter? She rubbed her wrists where she'd struggled against the rope.

"And would you do me a favor?" Willard asked.

"What?" she asked, not sure she wanted to do anything for him.

"Take my Franklin autobiography and bring it to me at the jail tomorrow if the marshal will let you. I know they won't let me have much, but you can have the rest of my little library. I have no one else to leave them to, and it would please me to think of you reading my books. Especially Wordsworth."

Alice looked at John. He shrugged.

"All right, Mr. Willard," she said. "And if the marshal will let you have two books, I'll bring you Blake as well."

"Thank you. You're a true lady."

Epilogue

Christmas Eve turned out to be a perfect night. The sky was clear and the stars shone brightly, but the air was unseasonably warm—perfect for strolling to the church together for the children's program and for delivering the Christmas baskets afterward. The schoolchildren all remembered their parts and sang the old carols sweetly. Alice got to hold Rachel Worth's baby while the mother helped her husband keep the pupils on track.

When the program was over, Alice gathered her shawl and handbag. "I do hope Pa's home."

"So do I," John said. "For several reasons."

Alice thought about that. John would feel easier if she wasn't alone tonight, she was sure, and he probably would also be glad to know her father had safely returned. Was there another reason? She thought there might be, and that made her face feel warm.

"He'll be glad to see you," she said.

"I hope so." He squeezed her hand and dropped it before anyone else noticed.

"You folks heading home?" Marshal Yates called as Alice and John walked toward the church door.

"Yes," Alice said. "We're hoping my father has returned from Fort Worth. How's Mr. Willard?" She wouldn't stoop to inquire about Edward Kline.

Justin grinned. "He's fine. Spouting poetry at his fellow prisoner and driving him batty. But the day after tomorrow, two deputy marshals will come from Dallas to collect my prisoners."

"Sad that they have to spend Christmas in jail," Alice said.

John shook his head. "Don't feel sorry for them. They might have killed you."

"Mr. Willard showed mercy," Alice replied. "I can't help feeling a bit of sympathy for him."

"Well, Marta's going to fix them a big Christmas dinner, so they won't have it too rough in the jailhouse," Justin said. Another man came up beside him.

"Hello, Clint," John said.

Alice recognized Clint Wiseman, but she seldom saw him in town. She thought he'd been a bit of a recluse for the last few years.

"We're going to deliver a couple of the baskets together," Justin said.

Alice nodded. "That will be nice."

"It's the first time Clint's ever gone along," the marshal added. "He thought it would be a good opportunity to see how much people appreciate what he's done over the last five years."

Clint frowned at Justin. "Don't you tell them I had anything to do with it."

Justin held up both hands. "Oh, I won't. Don't worry."

"Do they have plenty of folks to make the deliveries?" Alice asked. Stephen and Rachel Worth were heading out with one, sending the baby home with Rachel's aunt Priscilla. The Rosses and several other people were gathered around the corner where the baskets had been assembled.

"I'm pretty sure they do," Justin said. "You two have a nice evening."

"Thank you." Alice walked out with John and down the church steps. As soon as they reached the bottom, he reclaimed her hand. She shot him a warm smile.

Hoofbeats coming from the direction of the road to the stockyards drew her attention.

"Wait, John. Is that—" She stared into the shadows, and a large gray horse jogged toward them. "It's Pa!"

Alice ran toward her father, and he pulled his mount to a halt.

"Well, girl," her father said jovially. "Just getting out of church?"

"It was the Christmas Eve program," Alice said.

"I hoped I wouldn't miss it, but I guess it's later than I thought." Pa dismounted and reached a hand out to John. "How was it?"

"It was great," John said. "The children did very well."

"You must be hungry." Alice eyed her father in the light from the church windows.

"And trail weary," he agreed. "But listen, Alice, I have some news for you."

"What is it?"

"I know how you want to help the ladies—those baskets and all."

Alice nodded. "They're delivering them tonight."

"Well, a man in Fort Worth runs a large emporium with his wife, and she told me she'd like to get some quilts in to display and sell to the city folks."

"Quilts?" Alice blinked at him.

"Well, it might not be something for you to consider," Pa said. "It's just that when she mentioned it, I thought of your sewing circle. Sounded like they'd pay enough to make it worthwhile for some of these ladies who have children and can't work outside their homes."

Alice caught her breath. "Of course! We could invite all the women whose families receive food baskets. The sewing circle could share patterns and help them get the material and do the quilting."

"That's a great idea," John said. "I'm sure several of them would jump at a chance to earn a little money."

Alice looked over her shoulder at the church. "I can't wait to tell Regina and Rachel and Marta and the others. John, would you mind if I ran back inside for a minute?"

He laughed. "Go ahead. I'll wait for you."

"Thank you! And Pa, I kept a plate for you in the warming oven. Go ahead. I'll be there in a few minutes."

Her father sighed in resignation. "You see how it is, John? First it's a minute, and then it's a few minutes. Next it will be half an hour." He shook his head.

"I'm sure Alice will be quick," John said as she left them to dash up the church steps.

She spilled the idea quickly to her friends, and they received it with excitement and lots of questions.

"Let's meet Wednesday afternoon and discuss it," Alice said. "I have to go home now. I'll try to get some more information from Pa, but it sounds to me like a plan that will allow us to help a lot of people."

"Oh yes," Marta said. "Do let's meet here—what time?"

"One o'clock?" Regina suggested.

"Wonderful. Good night!"

"Merry Christmas," the others called after her. Alice hurried out the door and found John waiting, as promised, leaning against the railing at the bottom of the steps.

"Ready?" he asked.

"Yes. And thank you so much for indulging me." She slipped her hand through his arm and walked toward home beside him, thinking of the quilt the sewing circle had made the previous spring and all the lovely patterns the members could offer.

Lamplight poured from the front windows of the house, and Alice's heart leaped. Her father was home, and John was at her side. "You'll come in, won't you?"

"I'd love to," John replied.

When they entered the kitchen, Pa sat at the table with his dirty plate shoved aside. Sitting before him were a mug of coffee and a slice of the apple pie Alice had made that morning.

"Well now. This is a good pie, Daughter." Pa stood and accepted her embrace. "How did you keep while I was away?"

Alice hugged him and pulled away. "*I* kept just fine, but our neighbor didn't fare so well."

"Oh? I noticed his house was dark." Pa nodded at John. "Thanks for seeing my girl home."

"It was a pleasure. Glad you're back, sir."

Her father held Alice with one arm around her waist and looked down at her. "Now, what happened with the gunslinger?"

"Better sit down," Alice said. "It's quite a tale."

"Give me the gist of it," Pa said. "Has he moved away, died, or gone to jail?"

"The last," Alice said.

Pa's eyebrows shot up. "What? I was joking."

"You'd better listen to Alice's story," John said.

"Sit down, both of you." Alice looked over at John. "Coffee?"

"Yes, please."

"Pie?"

"Well. . ."

She laughed. "Of course."

While the men settled in, she got a cup, plate, and fork out for John. Her father had left the pie on the sideboard, and she cut a generous piece.

"When you've heard the tale, there's something unrelated that I'd like to talk to you about," John said softly to Pa, but Alice heard every word.

Her heart raced, and she kept her back turned as she poured the coffee, to give her a moment to collect herself.

"Can't imagine what that might be." Her father sounded the slightest bit sarcastic, and she looked over her shoulder at him. He was forking a bite of pie into his mouth.

She carried John's coffee and pie to him. "Now, Pa, don't be thinking you can read minds."

He held up his cup for more coffee, and she grabbed the pot off the stove.

"It's something other than wanting to keep company with you?" Pa asked.

Alice caught her breath and glanced at John. His cheeks were flushed. He hauled in a deep breath.

"Actually, sir, I'd like to marry her, if she's willing."

Pa looked from his coffee mug to John and then up at Alice. She swallowed hard and began to pour his coffee.

"Thank you," he said when the cup was full. He took a sip then looked at John, who sat there staring at him, waiting for a reply. "Now, John, I don't see what's so unpredictable about that. My daughter makes the best coffee *and* the best pie in town."

Alice let out her breath and turned back to the stove with a smile on her lips.

"Sir?" John sounded as though he might strangle.

"If you're asking my permission. . ."

"I am, sir."

"Fine by me, but it's Alice's decision."

Alice looked back at John. His gaze met hers, and his worried expression melted into a smile.

"Yes, sir."

"And my name is David," Pa said. "You can call me that, or you can call me Singer or Pa—anything but sir."

"Yes—David."

Alice laughed and took down a cup for herself.

"Now about Mr. Willard," her father said. "He's in jail?"

"As we speak," Alice said. She poured coffee for herself and then sat down next to John. "The day after Christmas he'll be taken to Dallas to await trial."

"For gunfighting?" Pa asked.

"No, s— No," John said.

"You remember the packages he was having delivered?" Alice asked. When her father nodded, she said, "Well, they weren't all books and materials for his almanac. Wait until you hear what he was really up to."

Susan Page Davis is the author of more than ninety Christian novels and novellas. Her historical novels have won numerous awards, including the Carol Award, the Will Rogers Medallion for Western Fiction, and the Inspirational Readers' Choice Contest. She has also been a finalist in the More Than Magic Contest and Willa Literary Awards. Reader favorites include the Maine Brides series, the Prairie Dreams series, and the Maine Justice Series. She lives in western Kentucky with her husband. She's the mother of six and grandmother of ten. Visit her website at susanpagedavis.com.

Vickie McDonough is an award-winning author of nearly fifty published books and novellas, with more than 1.5 million copies sold. A bestselling author, Vickie grew up wanting to marry a rancher, but instead she married a computer geek who is scared of horses. She now lives out her dreams penning romance stories about ranchers, cowboys, lawmen, and others living in the Old West. Her novels include *End of the Trail*, winner of the OWFI 2013 Booksellers Best Fiction Novel Award. *Whispers on the Prairie* was a *Romantic Times* Recommended Inspirational Book for July 2013. *Song of the Prairie* won the 2015 Inspirational Readers' Choice Award. *Gabriel's Atonement*, book 1 in the Land Rush Dreams series, placed second in the 2016 Will Rogers Medallion Award. Vickie has recently stepped into independent publishing.

Vickie has been married for more than forty years to Robert. They have four grown sons, one daughter-in-law, and a precocious granddaughter. When she's not writing, Vickie enjoys reading, doing stained glass, watching movies, and traveling. To learn more about Vickie's books or to sign up for her newsletter, visit her website at www.vickiemcdonough.com.